The Christening

Believing himself to be bisexual and too timid to find out by experiment, Miles is tormented by his own nature until he meets Alice and her young son, Rodney. Attracted by both of them, in emotional if not sexual ways, he finds some remedy in hope. Then one night Rodney stays with him and Miles takes the child home in the early hours of the morning. The cab driver believes Miles to have corrupted the boy and in a series of sadistic encounters accuses him of being a pederast. When Alice asks Miles to be godfather to her new baby, the driver threatens exposure. What should Miles do? If he refuses he will lose the intimacy that, for the first time, he has achieved with two people. If he agrees he faces the horror of what the fanatical cab driver will do. In this tender, sensitive and blackly comic first novel Sebastian Shaw, the distinguished Shakespearean actor, explores areas of sexual and emotional encounter that are rarely seen and, unfortunately, too rarely understood.

The Christening

SEBASTIAN SHAW

W. H. Allen · London
A division of Howard & Wyndham Ltd
1975

Printed and bound in Great Britain by Butler & Tanner Ltd, Frome and London, for the publishers, W. H. Allen & Co. Ltd, 44 Hill Street, London W1X 8LB

ISBN 0 491 01823 1

I

Having a baby these days isn't as risky as it used to be, what with all the care and attention and the Health Service and having it in hospital and everything so clean. Alice Remnant took this consoling thought with her to the pre-natal clinic before her third, as she had done before her first and second. Going to the clinic paid off. Anyway you had to do it if you wanted to be sure of a hospital bed.

But this time the visits were a drudgery, because the third was a mistake. At least it wasn't going to be twins. Doctor Fallowfield was reassuring about that after looking at the X-rays. Twins were in Alice's family. Two mistakes for the price of one would have not only been disastrous in themselves, but doubled her already deep resentment. She had always rather liked sex though she never admitted it to anyone else, least of all her husband. George, at first, had been ardent and clumsy. The ardour had slackened over the years; the clumsiness remained. And Alice, who had been brought up to think that sex wasn't respectable, had appeared to suffer his advances with an air of dutiful and patient outrage. On the few occasions she had overheard women talking about it on park seats or under cover of the humming spin-dryers in the laundrette, they always allowed it was something men had to have, and if you didn't let them it was asking for trouble because they'd go off and get it somewhere else. Secretly Alice doubted if George would. Latterly he was disappointingly diffident though she, of course, could do nothing to encourage him except lie on her back and hope. Eight and a half months ago he had pounced on her in her sleep. His special smell of tobacco and mildewed hay mingled deliciously with the scent of the wild roses she had just been given by Clark Gable in the nudist camp and, as she woke, she became for a brief moment uninhibited. His immediate and astonished response warned her how much she was off her guard. It wasn't easy to simulate her usual patient martyrdom, but experience was on her side and she managed fairly successfully to keep her feelings to herself. That these had been strong and deep she couldn't afterwards doubt for it was at least five minutes before she sat bolt upright in the cold darkness.

'You are awful,' she said, 'you never gave me time to put in the . . . to take precautions.' Not martyr-like to call a Dutch cap a Dutch cap. George was on his back sleeping the sleep of the exhausted but she went on talking, loud and indignant.

'So selfish. It's not as if I won't. If you'd only said before we went to bed I'd have known what to do, wouldn't I? As it is, if I've clicked we'll be stuck with the old combination for the rest of our lives and we can whistle for that Mini.'

'Never mind,' Doctor Fallowfield had said. 'It will probably be a genius.'

'I hope not,' Alice replied. 'Between you and me and the gatepost we'd rather have had a Mini.'

She smiled and then was disappointed when Doctor Fallowfield misunderstood her.

'It doesn't have to be a boy to be a genius,' she said severely. 'It may well be a Minnie for all we know.' Alice was too dispirited to explain they were at cross purposes. She was a bit frightened of Doctor Fallowfield with her short bristling hair and clipped speech. Of course it was better to be a woman than a man. But not a woman like her. What chance had she of being pounced on in the night?

And now she had seen Doctor Fallowfield for the last time and she had said everything was fine, and the ginger-haired woman at the desk where you went in had smiled and wished her luck, and it was just a question of waiting.

The children behaved reasonably well. Ethel was seven and Rodney five. Ethel was a vain, mousy little girl. For some unexplained reason Aunt Annie had decided from the start she was a born pop singer. On Saturday evenings, when Aunt Annie always came to tea, she made Ethel stand up in her dark brown velvet with the little bows on the sleeves and down the back and say, 'Now Eth, slay us with it.' And Ethel would nasally sing the latest hot number, her pale little face grimacing indecently, her thin little hands and legs jerking about out of time to the music. Rodney was mousy too but, being a boy, Aunt Annie had no special plans for him. One day he would help George sell sweets and newspapers and tobacco in the shop.

Two days before she was due to go into hospital Alice went with the children to Aunt Annie's room off the Hampstead Road to make final arrangements. It was at the top of a tall narrow house which still, ten years after the war, had huge wooden buttresses to prop it up. The houses on either side had been bombed and it stood, self-consciously detached and forlorn, like a man whose friends had deserted him when he most needed them. The children loved it. Climbing the stairs was always an adventure. They never knew who they were going to meet or what they were going to hear. Pinned to the side of the front door were little cards with instructions—'Knock twice for Madgewick.'—'James. Three rings and a knock. If no answer leave message in milk bottle in basement.'—'Burton. One long followed by three short.' In fact the front door was always open. As they walked through the hall, invariably the door to their left silently opened a crack and they knew they were being watched as they climbed the stairs. On the first landing, more often than not, they'd hear the raised voices of a man and a woman having a row from behind the door to the left; and, if they were particularly lucky, a performance of the Moonlight Sonata from behind the door to the right went with it, an imperfect stop and start rendering which constant practice didn't seem to improve. As if these delights were not enough, half-way up the stairs to the third floor there was a lav door with two frosted glass panels. They'd quite often see an old man with a skull cap going in or coming out. As, for some time, there had been a notice pinned to the door saying 'Out of order' they decided he lived in there and Aunt Annie, when consulted, smiled and said, 'That's about the truth of it' and whispered loudly to Alice, 'Prostrate.' Ethel looked up 'prostrate' in *Pears Encyclopaedia* and it said 'lying at full length face to the ground'. She and Rodney tried it in the lav at home, but it didn't seem to do anything for them and it remained an unsolved mystery. The third-floor landing always had the excitement and suspense of the unpredictable. Occasionally the children caught a glimpse of the glamorous ladies who occupied the two rooms. More often they would see their visitors. They were all men of every size and shape and sometimes colour. But Alice hurried them briskly on to the steep little stairs which led to Aunt Annie's room on the fourth.

To an outsider Aunt Annie's room was a hopeless muddle. There were clothes hanging on hooks behind the door; clothes on the bed and clothes on the chairs; clothes spilling from trunks and bulging out from behind the curtains of a hanging cupboard. Hats too in great profusion; on the mantelpiece, perched on the bed-posts, on the table. 'Clothes,' she used to say, 'they're my passion. And there's method in my madness.' There was. She had been a lady's maid and had even had brief and exciting spells as a theatrical dresser. She used to advertise her employers' cast-off clothing in the *Lady* and get a nice little commission on sales. Now she was drawing the old-age pension she worked only infrequently and to oblige. But she continued to scan the *Lady* advertisements, and by almost every post large parcels of clothes would arrive on appro. Some of these she would wear for a day or so and then return as unsuitable; others she would re-advertise and sell at a modest profit. Her correspondence was enormous and occupied much of her time. She took great pride in it, writing in a long sloping hand and signing herself 'Lady's Maid'. The anonymity gave her a sense of importance and mystery. She had established a good working arrangement with the postman, who considered a cup of tea, a chat and an occasional Mars bar a fair return for toiling up four flights of stairs.

On this hot August afternoon the stairs were almost too much for Alice, and she had to keep pausing for little rests. The children were delighted. It gave them a chance to savour to the full the unique entertainment contributed by each landing.

Aunt Annie received them at the top in an afternoon tea gown of rich blue brocade edged with rather grubby real ermine.

'You look like a duchess,' Alice panted.

'Not bad is it?' said Aunt Annie, slipping a hand into the recesses of her corsage and hitching up the sleeve of her combinations, 'but not a good selling line. I'll be sending it back. You look done up.'

'It's the stairs,' said Alice.

Aunt Annie was affectionately unsympathetic. 'It'll help things on,' she said.

Rodney said, 'If she wasn't so fat she wouldn't get so puffed.'

Ethel giggled. But Aunt Annie was having none of that. 'That's enough of being personal. I might observe that you was both nothing but skin and bones but I wouldn't be so unladylike. There's scones and raspberry jam for tea and she'll soon slim down again once the stork's been.'

The children and Alice munched silently while Aunt Annie poured out, carefully replacing the pot hat trimmed with a feather which was doing temporary duty as a cosy before being returned to its owner as unsuitable.

'When do you think?' she asked, handing Alice her cup.

'Day after tomorrow it should be.'

Aunt Annie spread raspberry jam thickly on the thin bread and considered this.

'Ethel and Rodney was punctual,' Alice said.

'It doesn't signify.' Aunt Annie suddenly shouted, 'Not like that Ethel. Like this. How many more times?' And she picked up her cup, delicately crooking her little finger, and sipped. Ethel gave a passable imitation. Rodney's attempt was less successful; his cup tilted and the hot tea slopped down his white shirt. He started to cry.

'Boys don't cry,' shouted Aunt Annie above his bawls with a patent disregard for the truth. She seized a lady's silk nightie which was lying handy and mopped him.

'I slept in it last night,' she explained, 'so I'll have to wash it anyway before it goes back. I'll be moving in tomorrow, just to be on the safe side like.'

Alice was pleased. If things went well it would be Aunt Annie and not she who would be washing the tea stains out of Rodney's shirt.

'Don't forget about George's bacon,' she said.

There had been trouble about this when Rodney was born. George liked his bacon crisp, and had repeatedly told Aunt Annie so. And every morning he got it flabby. 'I don't ask much,' George had said petulantly while admiring his son at Alice's bedside, 'but I do like my bacon crisp. It's as if she does it on purpose.' He was right. She did. She had ideas about bacon just as she had ideas about everything else, and they were unalterable.

'Bacon is a matter of taste,' she replied equivocally, and Alice knew it was no use arguing. Rodney was still snivelling. He was also fidgeting ominously.

'You want to go somewhere?' said Alice.

'I want to wee. Badly.'

'Say "spend a penny",' said Aunt Annie, 'it's nicer. Mr James is probably in there. Better run down to the one on the ground floor.'

'Supposing that's occupied too?' said Alice primly.

'There's always the street gutter. Tell you what, Eth, I want to talk to your mum. Take him out to the bombed site next door. He can do it there and you can pick me a nice bunch of flowers.'

Ethel took Rodney by the hand and led him out.

'Don't go into the road,' Alice called after them, 'and don't talk to strangers.'

'Now for a bit of peace and quiet,' said Aunt Annie. 'I never can talk with children around.' Alice refrained from pointing out how far from the truth this was. She felt hot and rather dizzy and sick. Also bitterly resentful of the baby inside her which made her so uncomfortably distended and unsightly. She hadn't felt like that about the others. On the contrary, she had been rather proud when her pregnancy became obvious enough to draw solicitous and sometimes speculative glances from men, and to give her the customary little privileges such as going to the head of the queue in the greengrocer's and having other women, especially older ones, give up their seats to her in tubes and buses. But not this time. It was a mistake. And that had given her a bad feeling about it from the start.

Aunt Annie, having got on her hands and knees with a grunt, pulled out a flat trunk from under the bed and was rummaging in it.

'I've got a little surprise for you,' she said, throwing garments out on the floor any old how into a heap. 'Anyone can see you need cheering up. I just thought of it. Belonged to a titled lady . . ."

'I don't need anything.'

'Crêpe-de-Chine bed-jacket with swan's down edgings to

neck and sleeves. Slightly stained under the arms, but I've a way of bleaching that out. You'll look a treat. . . .'

'I don't want it.'

'Yes you do. You've got to snap out of it my girl. Ah, here it is. . . .' She held up the jacket and shook it out daintily. The door opened and Ethel looked round.

'I thought you was picking me flowers,' said Aunt Annie.

'He done it in his knickers. They aren't half wet.'

'Oh my God,' said Alice, 'where is he?'

'In the street. He's crying.'

'You left him out there? You must be daft.'

'He wouldn't come up. He's crying.'

'You go down and fetch him up this instant.' Ethel disappeared.

'Wait till I lay my hands on him,' said Alice.

Aunt Annie chose to be tolerant. 'Always the trouble with boys. Can't hold it like girls. I've got a nice pair of lady's tennis knickers somewhere. He can change into them.' She put down the bed-jacket, pulled out another trunk from under the bed and started rummaging again while she talked. 'She'd no right to leave him on the street though. These men with staring eyes you read about . . . always on the look out . . . they wear macintoshes with belts . . .'

'Oh stop it, Auntie.'

'. . . just waiting to pounce they are . . .'

'Stop it!'

Aunt Annie held up some white shorts. 'They haven't got any flies being lady's. But that won't matter, he can do it through the leg. Now, you try on the jacket.'

Alice put it on, while she was fussed round and lectured and flattered and loved. There was a long mirror propped up against the wall. She stood in front of it while Aunt Annie fetched a hand mirror so that she could turn round and see that the back was as sweetly pretty as the front. She turned back again and stared at herself.

'You vain cat. You're supposed to be looking at the bed-jacket.'

Alice didn't hear. She looked at her reflection. Once she'd had this one she'd make very sure there wasn't another. They took it out of you; spoilt your nice figure. And the work they made, you were never finished. No time to have a bit of fun like in the old days. To have fellows after you. That look they got; hungry, sort of sullen. And you had what they wanted and they had what you wanted, but you never let on. Made your heart quicken and your mouth go dry. And then, just supposing . . .

The door opened. It was Ethel again.

'Well, where is he?'

'He isn't there.'

'What do you mean he isn't there?'

'He's gone.' Ethel's voice was quiet and small and matter of fact.

'Christ,' said Alice, 'I could brain the little sod.' She pushed Ethel roughly out of the way and plunged down the stairs. She dimly heard Ethel start to cry and Aunt Annie saying, 'Come back. I'll go. You oughtn't to tear about in your condition.' But she was far too angry to bother. All her resentment, her frustration, her unfulfilment had been set alight by this spark of irritation and flared suffocatingly, so that her head seemed to be splitting open and her eyes scorched and blinded. She stretched her hands out in front of her, groping widly, and, with a cry, fell heavily down the narrow stairs and hit the landing with a reverberating bump.

She lay, still and limp, on the torn linoleum, her skirt rucked up and showing her naked thighs, both stockings laddered and a broken suspender.

2

George's shop was in a side street near the railway bridge at Chalk Farm. You came on it immediately you turned the corner from the main road into de Vere Terrace and before reaching its two rows of dirty, stucco fronted houses which, with one or two exceptions, almost exactly mirrored each other's dejection.

The exceptions self-consciously signified they had gone up in the world with new paint and front doors in bright primary colours. Two of them had their numbers written out in neat italics. One had a narrow, wrought-iron jardinière on either side of the porch, with three pots of petunias of differing shades in each. Another had a hanging brass bell on an iron bracket. The clapper had been removed after two days had demonstrated its irresistible attraction to every passing child. The rest of the street surveyed these unorthodoxies from behind decent lace curtains with varying degrees of derision, resentment and positive dislike. George took a different view. That kind of frippery went not only with orders for *The Times*, *The Guardian* and *The Observer*, but such extras as *The Spectator*, the *New Statesman*, *The Economist*, *Opera* magazine, *Poetry Review*, *The Listener* and *The Tablet*.

He did the paper rounds himself. Boys nowadays were expensive and unreliable, and besides he rather enjoyed it. 'My exercise' he called it. He would start up the old combination after making Alice a cup of tea and the wholesalers had delivered, bundle the carefully stored papers and periodicals into the side-car and set off. He hated walking so he always left the engine running while he delivered papers to about four adjoining houses, and then drove on to the next four, and so on. The round took him the best part of two hours; he usually got back for breakfast about nine. Alice could hear his progress from the far end of de Vere Terrace, the idling chug chug alternating with the roar of acceleration, and knew precisely when to start frying the bacon so that it reached the state of crispness so dear to him as the engine spluttered to a stop outside the door. Before this she had set off with the children, delivered them at school and was back again all in five minutes. While she was gone she locked the shop door and customers helped themselves to their papers which were arranged on two hanging wire racks either side of the porch after complying with the written request to put the money through the letter-box. With this exception the shop was open from seven in the morning till seven in the evening every day but Thursday, when it shut at one.

George called Thursday his rest day. After a heavy dinner he would go round to the King's Arms till closing time and then sleep it off on his bed. Alice called him with a cup of tea to open the shop from five thirty till seven for the evening paper trade, which wasn't what it used to be but still not to be sneezed at.

After the paper round on fine Sunday mornings they often went to the country or the sea in the combination, Alice and Ethel apparently hermetically sealed into the side-car, and Rodney on the back of the bike clinging tightly to his father in a thick swaddle of clothes, surmounted by an enormous pair of goggles and a peaked cap. George wore macintosh trousers and jacket, a peaked cap and goggles. Alice insisted on these outings as compensation for not getting a summer holiday. They pored over maps on Saturday nights and tried to agree where they should go. George invariably suggested Southend to forestall Alice's more adventurous ideas. By the time she had called him stick-in-the-mud and he had called her scatter-brained the argument had reached only its first phase. It continued, leading them through a succession of accusation, grudging compromise, apparent agreement, uneasy truce, sudden flare up and repeat with variations until they went exhausted to bed and to sleep. When the alarm clock went off in the morning Alice would say, 'Nice of you to say we could go to Burnham Beeches' or 'Just the right day for the sea. Aren't you glad we said Clymping,' and George would be too sleepy to want to argue further so he'd say nothing. And Alice would sing as she cooked the bacon and spread the picnic sandwiches and make tea in the big pot so there was some over to put in the thermos, and away they'd go in the combination. After the shouted argument through the little side-car window about where they'd stop for the picnic they'd finally stop for the picnic and afterwards, while George slept, she and the children went walking in the fields or in the woods or on the sands and she'd take off her shoes to walk through the cool grass in bare feet, or caress the tree trunks, or dance at the sea's edge and lick her hand for the salt taste of it. The children always did as she did, but with the veiled solicitude of adults trying to humour a wayward child. When they returned to George, Ethel loved to tickle his ear with a long grass and he'd wake up swearing. Alice would say, 'Not in front of the children' and he'd say, 'Had a nice walk?' and she'd say, 'Yes. Had a nice sleep?' and he'd say, 'Yes. What about moving on?' and they would pile back into the combination and head for de Vere Terrace and high tea.

'Tea,' said George looking at his watch, 'I could just do with a cup.' Afternoons were a slack time, but after five trade got brisker. The heat was sweltering and he was in his shirt sleeves. The wireless was on in the back room. Never mind about it being Children's Hour, it was company. Alice had said she'd be back at six, and it was now quarter to. Customers came and went but Joe Rumbold, having bought his evening paper and an ounce of Bondman, lingered to talk. He worked in the city—warehouse or something—and lived up the Terrace. Out of loyalty he always bought his *Evening News* from George, having already whetted his appetite for its contents with surreptitious glances over other people's shoulders in the tube.

'Middlesex,' he said, 'are not the side they were.' He paused and read a paragraph while an old lady spent three minutes trying to decide between a crunchie or a chocolate cream. After she had gone out he looked up from the paper and said, 'Not by any means.'

'Not by any means what?' asked George.

'I was saying that Middlesex aren't the side they were.'

'You're right,' said George, and added after a long pause for thought, 'Not by any means.'

'I mean, take their batting . . .' said Joe with his head in the paper as a girl child came in and put three pennies on the counter.

'What's it supposed to be for?' George asked her.

'You may well enquire,' said Joe. 'To make runs you would suppose. But you would be wrong it seems on account they haven't . . .' He stopped abruptly as he caught sight of a paragraph headed 'Judge Quizzes Mr A.'

'Sweets,' said the child, smiling trustfully up at George, 'three penn'orth.'

'They've got a hell of a long tail,' George said, reaching down into one of a row of big glass bottles and bringing out a handful of sweets.

'Who's got a long tail?' Joe was aghast at the straight talk Mr A had got from the bench.

'Middlesex of course,' said George, putting the sweets into a small paper bag, holding it by the corners and twirling it round to close it before handing it to the child.

'Oh Middlesex.' Joe read on, with growing admiration for the polemics British Justice could produce when required. 'What about them?' he added absent mindedly.

'Their long tail.'

'Ah,' said Joe, 'they're not the side they was.' He glanced up from his paper. George was looking at him expectantly. Something else was required. 'Not by any means,' he said.

The child ran out of the shop and when George called after her not to make herself sick with them she turned, put out her tongue and said, 'not by any means' and disappeared up the Terrace.

'Cheeky little sod,' said George good humouredly.

'There's nothing like British Justice,' said Joe.

'What's British Justice got to do with it?'

'That Mr A in the Varley case. The Judge didn't half give him what for.'

'What for?'

'It doesn't exactly say. But you can read between the lines. That Mr A's going to finish up with a full spread in the *News of the World* on Sunday, you mark my words.'

A car drove round the corner from the main road and stopped outside the shop. A policeman got out and, after looking up at the shop sign which read *Newsagent GEORGE REMNANT & SON and Tobacconist*, entered.

Your name Remnant?' he asked.

'Yes,' said George.

'Can I have a word with you?'

'Go ahead.'

'In private.'

George looked at Joe. 'He's my friend,' he said.

'Your wife was visiting a Miss Annie Burton in Fame Street. Right?'

'Her aunt, yes'.

'With two children. A boy and a girl. Right?'

'Our kids, yes. What's happened?'

The policeman referred to his notebook. 'She fell down some stairs,' he said, 'she's been taken to hospital.'

'Is she hurt then?'

'They're not sure. I think . . .' he hesitated for a moment. He was an earnest young policeman who had joined the Force because he wanted to help bring criminals to justice. This kind of thing embarrassed him. 'She was expecting, wasn't she?'

George nodded.

'Well . . . it was coming on like when the ambulance arrived.'

George felt numb. He looked to Joe for support. Joe was his friend. You could count on him.

'If you fall down the stairs,' said Joe staunchly, 'and you're nearly nine months gone, that's what you'd expect, wouldn't you?'

George said, 'I suppose so.'

'If you're a woman,' Joe added gravely.

George felt a little comforted, but only for a moment.

'It's just that she might be hurt . . . broken a leg . . .' he said.

'Or an arm,' said Joe.

'We'll take you to the hospital in a minute,' said the policeman, 'but I'm afraid there's something else.' He looked at his notebook again. 'Miss Burton and the little girl accompanied Mrs Remnant in the ambulance. The boy is reported missing.'

George looked at him, uncomprehending. 'Where is he then?' he asked after a moment.

'That's what we're trying to establish. It seems the available toilets were occupied, so his sister accompanied him to the adjacent bombed site to relieve himself. But before he got there he wetted his pants. His sister left him to report to the mother, and it was then she fell down the stairs. In the subsequent confusion—calling the ambulance and so on—the boy was forgotten. It was only just before the ambulance left they realised he'd disappeared. We searched the immediate neighbourhood with a negative result. We have a full description and you can rest assured everything possible is being done to recover him.'

George looked at Joe again. 'There's always bloody something,' he said. More than ever he needed support and Joe didn't fail him.

'One thing on top of another,' he said.

'You said it, Joe.' George turned to the policeman. 'You see, Alice . . . well, she's my wife and . . .' He stopped.

'I know, mate,' said the policeman.

Joe said, 'They've been married nearly ten years.' He turned to George. 'You go and get your jacket, mate. I'll keep an eye on the shop.'

George looked at him gratefully and went into the back room. He turned off the wireless and slowly put on his jacket, trying to take in what the policeman had said. All right. So life goes on day after day the way you're used to it, the way you like it. And you read about women falling down stairs and breaking their necks and little boys disappearing, and it's good reading. You click your tongue and say, 'what's the world coming to?' And then life plays a dirty trick on you, and it's your wife and your kid. And your brain doesn't do its job. It packs up and leaves you numb and frightened and angry. And the policeman's words are as meaningless as a tune on the brain. 'We searched the immediate neighbourhood with a negative result.' Why talk so pompous? 'Negative result . . . negative result. . . .'

He picked up a scrawled chalk drawing of a house with a path and trees and a yellow spoked sun. Rodney had wanted to finish it before they left, but Alice had packed him off to put on a clean shirt. 'The boy is reported missing. . . .' He put the drawing down and went back to the shop.

Joe was behind the counter and serving Mrs Treasure with twenty Seniors. The policeman was waiting by the door.

'Not interrupting anything, am I?' said Mrs Treasure, scenting drama and looking beakily at the policeman.

'It's Alice,' said George, 'she was taken short like.'

'All right I hope,' said Mrs Treasure, secretly hoping it wasn't.

'Right as rain,' said Joe from behind the counter.

'There's a list of prices by the till.'

'You can trust me.'

'Yes,' said George. At least that was something he could do.

'Ready?' said the policeman.

'Ready.'

The way things come into your head; the history lesson and the funny name, Ethelred the Unready. He often remembered him in moments of stress. He felt like him now.

He got into the police car and it drove off.

3

Miles Madgwick acted on an overpowering impulse. He had been desultorily composing his nine hundred and eighty-first crossword puzzle, surrounded by leaning towers of reference books, and wishing so much that something would happen. Every time he got stuck he went to the window and peered into the street from behind the curtains, hoping. They usually came on Wednesday afternoons; the pregnant mother, the girl and the little boy. He stood for five minutes at a time looking up and down the street and then, with a sigh and a glance at the clock, returned to the crossword.

The editor had written him one of those barbed directives. It had arrived by the morning post, and read: 'Four-letter word the erudition! My readers want thirteen-letter word, "Come in, chaps, without a stain on your character—that'll be fun!" Solution please.'

Miles was an indifferent solver of other people's crosswords and it took him some time to work out that what the editor wanted was 'entertainment'. He was critical of the clue; the equivocal 'without' was objectionable by his own high standards. He also felt wounded and unappreciated. If he could only get more translation work he would send in his resignation. He picked up an old envelope and wrote on the back:

Dear Mr Fison,

I have received and understood your letter. Since to send a contribution of merit to your newspaper is to cast a pearl before a swine, I am happy to inform you that

I am now in a position to tender my resignation, which I do forthwith and with great pleasure.

Yours truly,
Miles Madgwick

As he read it over he considered the effect this would have on the quick tempered Mr Fison. Even if he could afford to resign, and he certainly could not, he knew he would never dare send such a letter. People frightened him at the best of times, but if they were angry and swore at him he trembled and became speechless and his heart thumped alarmingly. All he wanted then was to hide away, away from violence and roughness and the physical pain of fear. He would re-live the experience as he wrote at his table or when he woke in the night, his hands making small, involuntary gestures as if warding off an attacking bee, and sometimes crying out, his thin voice pinched even thinner by the memory.

At such times he retreated further and further into the comfort of the past until he became a child again; recalling in detail a particular period, lingering over its felicities and finding present reassurance in its small tragedies which time had overlaid with a patina of tenderness. His favourite material for this exercise was from the annual summer holidays at Southwold. Now, having retreated rapidly from the explosion of anger with which Mr Fison would certainly have greeted the letter of resignation, had it, by some nightmarish chance, been posted, he was happily sauntering along the beach towards Walberswick. It was his fifth birthday . . . such lovely presents . . . a sparkling sea for the morning bathe . . . he never went further than up to his knees and then lay down and splashed about bravely . . . sticky buns after with one or two currants and still hot with any luck, and that morning they were. Yes, he remembered the wolfish hunger and the first bite, the taste of it mingling with the brine on his lips, and he was shivering uncontrollably like a terrier, and Mary had teased him as usual but that morning he hadn't minded . . . and then lunch back at Mrs Moore's and his favourite pudding which was plum duff with white sauce and brown sugar . . . and then 'what should they do?' his mother had asked . . . and 'oh,' he said, 'to find cornelians, that would be best' . . . and Mary had said 'soppy date' and his mother had said 'not on his birthday, Mary' . . . and they had walked by the sea's edge when the tide was out along a strip of small beach with their eyes on the stones, and dart forward and stoop down to any stone which flashed in the sun and hold it up to the light and almost always it was cloudy and that meant it was a flint, but just occasionally one of them would cry out and the others would come running and it was a cornelian like a Rowntrees clear gum only better, much better . . . and he had wanted to find five because he was five and Mary had found seven to his two and she hadn't called him 'soppy date' but had given him a mean pinch when their mother wasn't looking and he had cried out and . . .

There were voices in the street and he only just got to the window in time to see them coming up the steps and hear the mother say, 'just once more, Rodney, that's all, and you'll get a good hiding', and the girl say 'he's just a big baby isn't he, mum' and the boy say 'I'm not a baby, I'm five' and the mother say 'then don't behave like you was two, I'm warning you, just once more!' and they were through the front door. As they crossed the hall he tiptoed quickly to his door, silently opened it a crack, and, with his heart thumping so loudly he thought they must hear it, watched them climb the first flight of stairs. When they were out of sight he moved silently into the hall and stood listening to their footsteps and the mother's whispered reprimands. He could even hear from far above an indistinct murmur of welcome from the old lady who lived on the top floor. Then silence.

Back in his room, with the door slightly ajar so that he could hear when they came down again, he began what he knew from experience was to be a long vigil. Work now was out of the question; impossible to concentrate knowing they were under the same roof. To help him endure the waiting he played a variant of the one game at which he had really excelled as a child; the one where a tray of twenty-one assorted objects is displayed for one minute, and then you have five minutes to write down as many as you can remember. Slowly, lovingly, he dwelt on every detail of the mother's outward appearance; then the sister's. He saved Rodney to the last, just as he still saved the icing on the Fuller's weekly walnut cake.

Earlier in the year he had bought an exercise book in which

to write about them. It was divided into two parts. Every Wednesday evening, after they'd gone he used to add to the first part fresh details of their personal appearance and accurate records of what he had heard them say or seen them do. Additions to the second part he left till later in the week. The exercise was a delight to him both in anticipation and execution and helped tide over the long wait till their next appearance. It consisted of short, fanciful episodes in which his world and their's fused, and they all met in the resultant paradise. In every episode they remained constant to their appearance and characteristics as recorded in part one. In some he was miraculously Protean, appearing as the loved father and husband, or the jolly understanding uncle, or the family doctor or trusted friend; yet always there were projections of some aspect of himself that at any other time he would not have believed existed. In others they all moved freely about in time, so that Mary and Ethel and Rodney and he were children together either in the present or thirty years ago. These were the most frequent because best loved; and in them Rodney's mother and his own mother were friends or sisters, and Ethel and Mary and he and Rodney were friends or cousins. There was one episode he had never brought himself to write. The thought of it excited him now more than anything, but because he believed it would be grossly misunderstood should it ever be read by someone else, he kept it in his head where it went off, sometimes at inconvenient moments, like an unpredictable alarm clock. It was implicit, though, in every episode; the mystical communion and coming together of each pair, so that his mother was Rodney's mother and Mary was Ethel and he . . . he hardly dare think it even . . . he was Rodney and Rodney was him, the loved and loving child.

He was suddenly alert. He could hear the children's voices. He looked at the clock on the mantelpicee; only ten minutes since they arrived. Most unusual. He tiptoed quickly to the door and opened it an inch. Yes, they were coming down the stairs and in a tearing hurry it seemed. No sign of the mother. Rodney's face was creased with anxiety as they ran past him to the front door. By the time they had opened it he was at his window. At the bottom of the steps Rodney stopped, and Ethel seized his hand and tried to drag him towards the bombed site. 'It's no good,' he wailed. Ethel continued to drag at him. 'Come on,' she kept saying, 'come on.' But Rodney clung to the area railings with his other hand and wouldn't budge. Ethel's eyes were wide with excitement as she surveyed the growing pool at his feet which was beginning to extend a thin monitory finger towards the gutter. There was a pause, while Ethel composed herself and assumed an expression of angelic virtue.

At last she said, 'You dirty little sod. You won't half cop it.'

Rodney wept.

'Well come on,' said Ethel, trying to drag him back to the steps.

But Rodney still clung desperately to the railings.

'Come on, come on,' she kept saying.

Rodney slipped his hand from hers and held on to the railings with that too. Ethel pulled his hair. The wail became a piercing scream.

'I'm going to tell mum.' She walked up the steps, looking over her shoulder to see if he was following. He wasn't. She went back to him, all the pretence gone out of her.

'Are you coming or aren't you?' she asked anxiously.

Rodney hung on to the railings as if they were his only comfort. The screams had given way to a rhythmical sobbing.

'We can't stay here,' said Ethel.

But Rodney had other ideas.

'At your age!' said Ethel, diverted momentarily from her purpose as her eyes followed the serpentine trickle across the pavement. Suddenly she reached a decision. 'If you won't you won't, but when mum comes you'll wish you had,' and she ran up the steps and into the house and her footsteps clattered across the hall and up the stairs.

It was at that moment Miles acted on an overpowering impulse. He was out in the hall, through the front door and down the steps before he realised what he was doing. And there he was, smiling down at Rodney and holding out his hand. And there was Rodney, still gripping the railings, looking up at him and sobbing. For a moment it was touch and go whether he was going to shrink away in fear and shame or respond to this totally unexpected advance. The thought of the beating that was coming so terrified him that he had been frantically searching for some plan at least to postpone it, if not avoid it altogether; if he pretended to be very ill, or if he was on his knees saying 'Our Father', or if his mother suddenly died. . . . And now here was this tall stranger kindly offering his hand. Perhaps this was a way out. He smiled back trustfully, let go of the railings and put a hand into Miles'. It was hot, damp and sticky. To Miles the touch of it produced some unusual phenomena. The sun pulsated like a beating heart, advancing and retreating with each systole and diastole, and the earth responded by behaving like the Big Wheel at Battersea Park, taking him and Rodney over and over with it, and the sun got bigger and bigger and he knew it was going to burst, and just before it did he shut his eyes.

When he opened them again Rodney was still smiling shyly up at him and he was smiling down at Rodney. Without a word he led him into the house, softly closing the front door behind them, and then into the safety of his own room. After locking the door he thought to himself, 'Now what?' Rodney's face was streaked with black smears where he had wiped his eyes with his fists. He had stopped crying and was looking round the room. Every time he caught Miles' eye he smiled and then looked shyly away. So far nothing had been said. Eventually Rodney broke the silence.

'I couldn't help it, honest I couldn't.' He looked as if he was going to cry again.

Miles whispered, 'I know . . . it's all right . . . I know.' Now what? He heard himself saying 'Hadn't you better take them off? You can wrap up in a blanket while they dry.' This was madness. He mustn't let it happen, must do the sensible thing, take him straight upstairs to his mother with suitable explanations. Otherwise no explanations would be suitable. Quite the contrary.

But Rodney was saying 'Yes, take them off,' and in a few moments was standing naked holding out his damp and smelly garments; shirt, shorts, combinations, even his socks were wet. Miles stood speechless looking at this frail child, so tremulous and helpless. He was quite overcome with understanding and pity and love.

Suddenly footsteps down the stairs. Ethel again. He heard her open the front door. There was a pause. Miles and Rodney stood motionless. Then, 'Rodney,' she called, 'Rodney!' And again, louder, her voice less threatening, more anxious, 'Rodney!'

Rodney said, 'It's Eth,' and started to cry softly.

'It's all right,' whispered Miles, 'all right,' and even while he said it he knew it was all wrong. Even now perhaps it wasn't too late. He could call Ethel in; explain in a jolly avuncular way he wasn't going to stand by and see a child with wet pants unattended to. He could hear himself saying it and it not coming out jolly or avuncular, but nervous, stammering, unconvincing. And the ensuing explanations, by now not jolly at all, to the mother; and her incredulity and growing hostility. Impossible to face that.

Ethel's voice was now shrill and frightened. 'If you don't come at once, Rod, I'm going back to mum.' Too late now. Why could he never take his opportunities? Why?

He managed to smile again and put his finger to his lips. Then he took the damp clothes and hung them on the backs of chairs. He took a blanket from his bed and gave it to Rodney. 'It'll be all right,' he whispered. Rodney draped it round his shoulders; it made him look even smaller. The front door banged and he heard Ethel cross the hall and run up the stairs again.

'You'd better lie on the bed,' he said, 'and as soon as they're a bit drier I'll take you home. It'll be all right. You'll see.'

He had intended the child should lie on top of it but he turned the bedclothes back and got right in. He had stopped crying.

'This screen,' Miles said softly, 'was in my nursery. Lots of the fairy-tale people are here. Little Miss Muffett; there's her spider, see? Little Boy Blue who'd gone to sleep under the haystack; and there, look Snow White and the Seven Dwarfs; see them?'

'Yes,' said Rodney.

'And then there are all sorts of birds and animals. I wonder if you know their names. This one for instance, you know what he's called?'

There was silence. Miles turned. Rodney had gone to sleep.

There was a heavy thump from somewhere upstairs followed by a confused murmur of voices and sudden shouts. Doors opened and shut. People were running up and down the stairs.

Miles stood staring at the sleeping child. Slowly he tiptoed to the door to make sure it was locked. He then took two sleeping pills, wrapped himself in the blanket the boy had discarded and lay on top of the bedclothes beside him. He, too, went to sleep.

4

When George arrived at the hospital it was some time before he was allowed to see Alice. The policeman wanted him to call in at the station on the way and see a C.I.D. man, but George said 'I must see her first. Once I know she's all right I'll be able to think straighter.' The policeman tried to argue with him but he was obdurate.

The policeman said, 'But anything can have happened to the kid. They want you quick.'

'I know,' said George stubbornly, 'but first things first. Anything can have happened to Alice.'

So he was dropped at the hospital after promising he would go straight round to the police station as soon as he'd seen Alice. The porter at the entrance gave him a complicated series of directions and he made his way down corridors and up stairs, and eventually saw Aunt Annie and Ethel near the entrance to a ward. Ethel was lazily swinging the cord of a window blind backwards and forwards, and Aunt Annie was seated on the only chair giving an uninterested and inattentive young man a detailed account of the extraordinary events through which she had just lived. Now and again she would break off to reprove Ethel as the blind cord slipped out of her hand and the acorn on the end sharply tapped the window pane. At these moments the young man, who was patently going through the agonising experience of becoming a father for the first time, tried to disengage himself; but she unerringly turned back from Ethel in time to entrammel him again.

It was Ethel who saw George first. In her excitement she let the cord go suddenly and it swung right back and hit the young man on the side of the face.

'Ethel,' said Aunt Annie long-sufferingly, 'where are your manners?'

'Dad's come.'

'That's no reason to knock somebody's eye out with the blind cord. She's having it now George, in there.'

'Is she all right?'

The young man was tactfully tiptoeing up the corridor but Aunt Annie wasn't going to lose her audience so easily.

'I was just saying to this young man . . .' she raised her voice and called after him' . . . 'wasn't I?'

He turned miserably and tiptoed back again. 'You was,' he said, and then addressed George as one fellow sufferer to another, 'My wife's in there too.'

'. . . that to fall down a flight of stairs,' Aunt Annie over-rode him inexorably, 'and bring it on is one thing, and to be told your little boy is missing is quite another. They go about,' she continued darkly, 'in belted macintoshes with staring eyes and if I had my way I'd flog them within an inch of their lives.' She fixed the young man with a militant eye. 'Aren't I right?'

'Are you asking me?' he said, playing for time.

'I am.'

'No.'

'No?' she said, unable to believe her ears.

'I'm against capital punishment.'

'Who's talking about capital punishment?'

'It's not right.'

'I was talking about flogging.'

'That's not right either.'

'I suppose,' said Aunt Annie, 'that it's perfectly all right for men with staring eyes and macintoshes to go about kidnapping defenceless children and strangling them in parks.'

'I never said that.'

'He didn't say that, Auntie,' said George, who was a staunch believer in fair play.

'That's right,' said the young man, encouraged by this unexpected support, 'it's psychosomatic.'

'That's as may be,' said Aunt Annie, for a moment out of her depth and then finding firm ground again, 'but when your kid's strangled in a park you'll think different if you're half a man.'

The young man said, 'What's the use?' and fell silent.

Ethel said, 'Has Rod been strangled? Has he really?'

'Of course not,' said George.

Ethel looked disappointed. The prospect of going back to school and being the girl whose brother had been strangled had been pleasantly occupying her mind.

'We don't know, do we?' said Aunt Annie.

Ethel was encouraged again; she had felt neglected and unimportant; she started to cry.

'Oh, put a sock in it,' said George.

'You can't blame her with people being so unfeeling,' said Aunt Annie loudly and with a meaning look at the young man who was now gazing out of the window and whistling.

A nurse with red hair came out of the ward and approached them.

'You can come in now,' she said to the young man.

'Christ,' he said, 'nothing's happened has it?'

'You've only become a father, that's all.'

'It's all right then?'

'Certainly it's all right. Don't you want to know what you've got?'

'What?'

'A baby girl. Come and see her.'

'Christ!'

The nurse smiled pleasantly at Aunt Annie. 'The young fathers, they're all the same, aren't they?'

'He needs to buck up his ideas,' said Aunt Annie. 'One day he'll learn different.'

At the ward door the nurse turned. 'I don't think you'll have to wait much longer,' she said kindly, and she and the young man went in.

Ethel was now crying quite loudly. George had taken over the young man's place and occupation at the window. He was whistling mournfully.

'It's like being in a morgue,' said Aunt Annie. 'Tell you what Ethel, how about doing *That Sideways Look* for your Auntie?'

'There's no gramophone.'

'You don't need one. Not when you're as good as you are.'

Ethel obliged. She hopped about grotesquely in the middle of the corridor, out of tune and out of time, occasionally stopping to sniff, and feeling someone loved her again. Aunt Annie, who was more than capable of managing two difficult situations at the same time, smiled and nodded at her while carrying on a low and urgent conversation with George.

> '*When you give that sideways look,*' sang Ethel,
> '*Yeh, yeh, oh yeh*
> *I want your number in my book*
> *Baby, yeh, yeh.*
> *I gotta have, by hook or crook,*
> *Yeh, yeh, oh, yeh,*
> *A little bit more than a sideways look,*
> *Baby, yeh, oh yeh!*'

Aunt Annie had just reached the point where Alice had fallen down the stairs. 'You slay me with it, Ethel,' she said without pausing for breath, and she went on with her story to George while Ethel smiled happily and put all she knew, which was really very little, into the next verse.

By the time George had been put in the picture Ethel had worked through most of her repertoire, encouraged constantly by Aunt Annie and the amused glances from passing nurses and medical students. At last the ward door opened and Dr Fallowfield came out with the sister.

'That's enough, Ethel,' said Aunt Annie sharply; and Ethel had to stop in the middle of a pirouette, her arms drooping ungracefully over her head. 'Stand natural can't you or the doctor will think she's got a loony case on her hands.' Ethel was mortified. She pouted and dropped her arms.

The doctor took George on one side. 'She'll be all right,' she said, 'but she's taken quite a beating you know. Very badly bruised, but luckily no bones broken. Mostly shock. She'll have to take things very quietly.'

'How long before she comes out?'

'Depends how she gets on. A week at the very least. Probably longer.'

'You see . . . one of our kids is adrift.'

'I gathered something of the sort.' The doctor glanced at Aunt Annie who was talking to the sister. 'Has he turned up?'

'No. Soon as I've seen her I'm off to the police.'

'Don't tell her, not yet. When he turns up will be time enough.'

'If he turns up. Can I see her now?'

'Only for a moment and by yourself. Sister will take you in.'

Thanks, doctor. . . .'

'By the way, you've got a fine healthy boy. Perfectly all right.'

'Oh yes.' George was curiously uninterested.

Sister took him through the ward down an avenue of mothers and mothers-to-be to a bed surrounded by screens. Alice was lying in it, her face almost the colour of the pillow, her eyes shut, her head bandaged. In a cot beside her was the new-born baby. George went up to her.

'Hello, Alice,' he said.

She opened her eyes and looked up at him.

'Hello.'

'How do you feel?'

'Lousy.'

'Not surprising.'

'Has Auntie moved in?'

'She will.'

'Tell her we need more cornflakes.'

'I will.'

'I was going to get them on the way home. Aren't you going to look at the baby?'

George looked at it. Its head was squashed and it was bright red.

'I suppose its head will come out all right in the wash,' he said.

'They're often like that. I'm glad it's a boy. I want you to give Rod a good hiding. Time he learned.'

'I will.'

'Where was he?'

The sister beckoned him from behind the screen.

'Tell you all about it tomorrow,' he said. 'I got to go now. You have a good sleep.'

Alice smiled faintly. 'Tell her from me you like it crisp.'

'My bacon? Don't worry, I will.'

She sighed and shut her eyes again.

Out in the corridor George dealt as briefly as he could with Aunt Annie's innumerable and searching questions and arranged that she and Ethel should go back to her room and collect her things so that she could move over to de Vere Terrace right away. They walked down the stairs and along the corridors together, Ethel following demurely, gaily humming snatches of *When you give that sideways look*. The porter at the entrance looked out of his box and said, 'less noise please.' She stopped and, after he had turned away, continued through the revolving doors, came round full circle, put out her tongue at him and went out again. She felt altogether happier.

George parted from them at the end of the street and went to the police station. As he walked he tried to imagine why anyone should want to kidnap Rodney. 'Kids,' he thought, 'what can anyone see in them . . . that way? And as for killing the poor little sods, well . . . it's beyond me. Psychosomatic that young man said. Give it a fancy name and it's all right of course.' A picture of Rodney lying in a pool of blood kept coming into his mind. Perhaps Aunt Annie was right. If some dirty sod had got hold of Rodney nothing was too bad for him, nothing; flogging, hanging, the lot. By the time he arrived at the station he was far from his usual impassive self. He was angry and vengeful.

'No news for you I'm afraid, Mr Remnant,' the C.I.D. man said. 'We've got a fairly detailed description of the boy. I wonder if you could add to it?' He offered George a cigarette while he read it through.

'Seems all right,' George said.

The detective gave him a light. 'No relations or friends he might have run to?'

'He wouldn't do that.'

'Kids do funny things when they want to avoid a larruping.'

'It wouldn't be like him.'

The detective smiled wearily. He hid a yawn and wished to God he wasn't so overworked and that people would be more helpful.

'I don't mean to be unsympathetic,' he went on, 'but if I told you the number of good working hours we waste chasing after lost kids it would make your hair stand on end. And it's your money and mine.'

George was indignant. 'What if he's been got hold of by some dirty bastard?' he said. 'What if he's been killed? Lying in a pool of blood somewhere? Assaulted or something?'

'Steady on, mate. Can't rule that out I'm afraid, but what I mean is that most times, thank God, they come trotting home as simple as kiss your arse. Met a pal and spent an hour or so on the swings in Regent's Park, or playing 'last across' or 'ring and run' or what have you.'

'Not Rod.'

The detective looked at him keenly. 'You should know,' he said. 'All right then. If he should come in give us a ring at once. Otherwise . . . well, I want you to know the whole bloody force has got his description and the search is on. And when I say on, I mean on.'

'If it's one of those,' said George, 'I'll wring his neck, so help me. That kind ought to be wiped off the face of the earth.'

'Too right. But I'm still hoping he'll come in. By the way, how's the wife?'

'All right. It was a boy.'

'Does she know the kid's still missing?'

'The doctor said not to tell her.'

'The doctor's got sense. We'll keep in touch. Thanks for coming in. Try not to worry. So long.'

'So long,' said George.

He walked home, zigzagging through a maze of small streets. It was a stifling evening and he sweated as he walked. His anger had left him. He felt weary and oppressed and sorry for himself. The people he met were ordinary people doing ordinary things; wheeling prams, taking dogs for walks, laughing as they came out of pubs. Only two hours ago he had been one of them. Now he felt like a stranger. It might have been New York or Paris or Brussels or somewhere, not London.

5

Going to sleep was like entering a safe shelter, deep underground and double locked. People had knocked on the door. There had been voices; loud, demanding voices. He had been aware of them and had ignored them because he was safe, and they had gone away. His brief consciousness that he was going to sleep merged into timeless unconsciousness and he moved in and out of his dreams helplessly and unwillingly. They were seldom pleasant, often horrific. Just before he woke Mr Fison had given him a kitten. 'Though it's desirable,' he said, 'it's not the sort of thing to be seen about with. Take my advice. Dispose of it.' So he filled a pail and put the kitten into it. It swam around happily. 'Thank you,' it mewed, 'thank you.' Miles said, 'This hurts me more than it hurts you.' He pushed it down to the bottom of the pail and held it there. It didn't struggle. A string of bubbles rose to the surface. 'Thank you,' they said, 'thank you.' He woke unhappily. Rodney was stirring and whimpering in his sleep.

Miles briefly switched on the light over his bed and looked at his watch. It was two fifty-two. He was cold, hungry and frightened. He mustn't move or he would wake Rodney. He knew he must decide what to do and, worse than that, having decided, he must do it. He lay motionless in the dark, but though he was now wide awake it was difficult to concentrate. Long practice in composing crossword puzzles had given him a facility for providing solutions to seemingly intractable problems. There must be an answer to this one, he thought. There's always an answer. But every time he set about finding it, unwanted thoughts drifted into his brain as inconsequentially as the dreams. 'I must ask you to accompany me to the station,' the contemptuous, holier-than-thou voice. 'Miles Standish Madgwick (that ridiculous second name, how did they know it?), you are charged with . . .' With what, for God's sake? With being a paederast? Was he a paederast? 'But I don't even *like* children.' 'Don't you? What about this one?' Well, what about him? Rodney had stopped whimpering and was breathing lightly and rhythmically. Miles listened. Extraordinary that people should want to assault children and then murder them. Inconceivable. And yet quite often they did, and sometimes got away with it. He supposed that when the assault was over there was always this terrible problem, what to do with the child? If it went free, ten to one it would blab. And then there'd be no escaping the nightmare police courts and the long degradation of prison. He had read that sexual offenders against children were not only despised by warders and prisoners alike, but were sometimes beaten up.

He sat up suddenly, groped under the pillow and found a miniature teddy bear. He clutched it tightly and stared into the dark. He was now so frightened he couldn't think straight. The teddy bear had been a last resort in the greatest distresses of his life. 'Now,' he whispered, 'now of all times you mustn't fail me.' He thought how ridiculous he must look, a grown man, sitting up in bed and clutching a teddy bear. And yet really he was being sensible because it was a reminder of the sanity and safety of his childhood; the sort of safety he associated with set teas in hotel lounges and croquet in the vicarage garden. He groped cautiously around the bedside and found a tin of sweet biscuits. After eating two he felt better. There is always an answer. Methodically he set to work to find it. The law would consider he had abducted Rodney and probably assaulted him. Very well, he would outwit the law. He stared into the dark with the unseeing stare of intense concentration.

Half an hour later he put the teddy bear gratefully back under the pillow. Then he got up and dressed. He dare not draw back the curtains and he thought putting on the light might wake Rodney. It was important not to, not yet. He found his things with the assurance of a blind man, used the pot, rinsed his face in the portable hand basin and put on his overcoat. He bent over the bed. Rodney was still sleeping. He switched on the bed lamp. Very gently, in hardly more than a whisper, he began to talk.

'Rodney. Rodney, you are still asleep, but you can hear me. You can hear what I am saying and you will answer me.'

He repeated this several times, over and over. Rodney stirred and turned on his back.

At last Miles said, 'You can hear me, can't you? Say you can hear me.'

Rodney's lips moved as if trying to speak.

'Say yes distinctly. Say yes.'

'Yes.'

'Very well. When you wake you will see me for the first time. Do you understand? You have never seen me before. This is the first time you have seen me. The first time. You won't be frightened; you will like me, and you will tell me what happened. You will remember wetting your pants on the doorstep and your sister going to fetch your mother and how frightened you were. You wanted to run away and hide, anywhere, because you were afraid of being beaten. You ran into this room and hid under the bedclothes and eventually went to sleep. To escape being beaten. Because you were frightened.'

Miles patiently went through the story, point by point, three times. His reading had been professional and voluminous and he had an amazingly retentive memory. He recalled one book on hypnotism had stressed that children were not good subjects, since they lacked the necessary concentration. Idiots and people of a low I.Q. were the same.

'Now,' he said, accurately remembering the formula recommended in the book, 'I am going to count three and when I say "three" you will wake up. Do you understand?'

'Yes,' murmured Rodney.

In spite of his new determination Miles hesitated and with difficulty fought down another attack of jitters.

At last he said, 'Now, Rodney, I am going to count. One . . . two . . . THREE!'

After a moment of suspense Rodney opened his eyes with a snap and slowly smiled.

'Good gracious me,' said Miles, 'my dear child, what are you doing in my bed?' This sounded altogether too much like the

Three Bears talking to Goldilocks, so he quickly continued, 'It's all right. You're quite safe. Tell me how you got here.'

Rodney looked puzzled and fidgeted in the bed. 'I want to wee,' he said.

Miles had already seen with his own eyes that to deny Rodney's bladder immediate relief was to court disaster, so he indicated the pot under the bed.

'It isn't half full,' said Rodney, using it noisily.

Miles was feeling Rodney's garments. They were still damp but much less so. 'You can put them on now,' he said, holding them out.

Rodney jumped back into the bed and pulled the bedclothes up under his chin.

'It isn't morning yet.'

'You can tell me how you got here first. Then you must dress because I'm going to take you home.'

Rodney's face puckered. 'Mum'll give me a hiding.'

'Have a biscuit,' Miles said hastily. He dropped the garments in a little heap and proffered the tin.

'They've got animals on,' said Rodney, seizing three and beginning to eat them ravenously.

'Now,' said Miles, 'tell me how you got here.'

'Mustn't speak with my mouth full.' He eyed a bottle of milk on the washstand. 'I'm thirsty.' He went red in the face and started to choke. 'Crumb,' he spluttered, 'gone down the wrong way.'

'You mustn't make so much noise.'

'I can't help it.' He choked and coughed noisily.

Miles hastily poured some milk into a cup. After a gulp the choking gradually ceased. Rodney's eyes were streaming.

'I'm not crying. It's the choking.' He wiped his eyes with the sheet and then blew his nose on it. Miles' offer of a handkerchief was too late by several seconds.

'Now you really must tell me. How did you get here?'

'I wet my pants.'

'Where did you?'

'Out there in the street. Ethel went to fetch mum.'

'And you didn't want to see her?'

'No.'

'Why not?'

'I'd have got a hiding.'

'So what did you do?'

'I cried.'

'Yes. And then?'

Rodney noisily gulped down the rest of the milk. He gave a contented sigh and politely used the sheet again to wipe his mouth. And again Miles was too late with the proffered handkerchief.

'I come in here.'

'Why?'

'I didn't want a hiding.'

'You were frightened and you wanted to hide?'

'Yes.'

'So you took off your clothes . . .'

'Yes. To dry them like.'

'. . . and got into bed and went to sleep?'

'Yes.'

This was splendid. Everything going beautifully to plan.

'You see, I was out late. Since I got back I've been working. I often work late. I noticed it was about three and decided I really must turn in. I came round the screen and was amazed to find there was someone in the bed. You!'

Rodney sat up in the bed, round-eyed and smiling oddly.

'What about my clothes?' he said.

'What about them?'

'Didn't you see them? They was hanging on the chairs.'

Miles' heart seemed to miss a beat. He hadn't thought of that.

'They'd slipped to the floor,' he said, and added rather lamely, 'When you're working you don't notice things much.'

Rodney looked at him unwinkingly, still with that odd little smile. He was annoyed with himself. It would have been so easy to have convinced Rodney while under hypnosis that he had bundled his clothes under the bed. He was also annoyed with him for being so sharp. He should have been much too drowsy to think up such awkward questions.

'Now,' he said softly, 'you mustn't be frightened.'

'I'm not.'

This was puzzling. He ought to be

'What's your name?'

'Rodney Winston Remnant. I'm five.'

'A very nice name too. Well Rodney you must tell me where you live.'

'What for?'

'So that I can take you home.'

'I'm all right here.'

'Oh yes, of course you are. Perfectly safe. But your mother will be wondering where you are; she'll be worrying about you.'

'Can I have another biscuit?'

'If you're good and when you're dressed.'

'Biscuit first.'

'Very well.'

Rodney ate the biscuit thoughtfully. His eyes kept wandering to the screen. He swallowed the last mouthful, sighed contentedly and smiled again at Miles.

'Good old Snow White,' he said.

There was a long silence. Miles stared back at him blankly.

'Snow White?'

'Snow White. You know. You said she was on the screen.'

'I never said anything about Snow White.'

There was another silence. Rodney suddenly got out of bed and started to dress. He drew on his shorts with distaste.

'You never dried them proper,' he said accusingly.

Miles fought hard not to panic again.

'Don't be silly,' he said with an attempt at brusqueness, 'I didn't know you were here.' But he couldn't keep a slight quaver out of his voice.

Rodney stopped tucking his shirt in and looked up. He was smiling again.

'I shan't take you home if you're going to say things like that. Stop smiling. There's nothing to smile at.'

Rodney went on dressing.

'Mustn't tell fibs, must I?' he said self-righteously.

'No, you must not.'

What sort of a nightmare was this, where truth was lying and lying was truth? Yet it was his one hope and he must go on with it. At this moment he could understand all too well why children got murdered.

When Rodney was dressed Miles said, 'You must promise me that you'll tell your parents what really happened. No made-up stories, no bringing me into them.'

'They'll beat me.'

'I'll promise to see they won't.'

Rodney smiled charmingly.

'Honour bright?'

'Honour bright.'

'All right. I'll tell them what really happened. What you said.'

'No, what you said.'

'What I said.' He smiled again. 'If they beat me it'll be different, won't it?'

'They won't. I've promised.'

Miles was appalled. This was blackmail, and though put across so charmingly the threat was there, stark and inescapable. He stared at this frail child, the picture of purity and innocence, already corrupt. Perhaps after all it would have been better to tell the truth with all its consequences. But too late now. He was in it up to the neck.

Rodney was smiling again. 'I like you all right,' he said, and he put his arms round Miles' neck and gave him a soft, wet kiss full on the lips.

Miles was touched. For a moment he closed his eyes. He hadn't been wrong after all. This was the Rodney of his imagination. Here were the warmth, the affection, the innocence with which he had so longed to identify himself. When Rodney released him he absent-mindedly felt for his handkerchief and wiped his lips. Even the smell of stale urine was somehow part of this unexpected revelation.

'I know I can trust you,' he said.

'Yes,' said Rodney. It was obvious he hadn't understood.

'Now I want you to wait here while I get a taxi.'

'I've never been in a taxi.' He was suddenly excited. 'You mustn't half be rich.'

'You must promise to stay here and be as quiet as a mouse. I'll give you a picture book to look at.'

Rodney settled down with the precious Hieronymus Bosch.

Miles had to walk through to Euston before he found a taxi. He told the driver to wait on the corner for fear of waking the other tenants. He was taking no risks. He opened the front door silently and tiptoed to his room. He had taken the precaution of locking Rodney in. He was fascinated by the book.

'Look,' he said, pointing delightedly, 'That one's sticking a fork up that one's arsehole.'

He looked up shyly and charmingly. For a moment Miles had the impression the shyness and charm were consciously assumed. But almost in the same moment he remembered that spontaneous kiss of affection, and the impression was gone.

'Can I have it?'

His Hieronymus Bosch. He remembered that wonderful day, in Spalding of all places, when he had found it on a stall in the market. It was like finding gold.

'Well . . .' he began doubtfully.

'I promise I'll say what you told me. I want it.'

'We'll see,' said Miles. 'Now come on. The taxi's waiting. Very quiet. Tiptoes.'

They stole out of the house and down the street to the waiting taxi, Rodney still clutching Hieronymus Bosch. Miles was terrified. He knew the police would have been alerted. Even if they hadn't been it seemed to him that bundling a small child into a waiting taxi at three-thirty a.m. would take a lot of explaining. The taxi driver was massively indifferent. They got in and shut the door.

'Posh,' said Rodney, sinking back on the seat so that his legs stuck out.

The driver slid back the communicating glass panel and without looking round said, 'I'm not psychic.'

In his nervous state Miles didn't immediately get the point.

'Oh, aren't you?' he said, trying to appear interested.

'Or telepathic,' continued the driver. 'No doubt you've got some idea where you want to go, but the message has passed me by.'

'What's the address?' Miles hastily whispered.

'De Vere Terrace,' said Rodney, investigating the exciting possibilities of the two tip-up seats facing him.

'What number?'

Rodney pulled down one of the tip-up seats and sat on it. 'Three,' he said, and stood up suddenly so that the seat snapped back into place with a thump.

'Three de Vere Terrace,' Miles said to the driver's back.

'Very nice too,' it said, 'but we aren't out of the wood yet. The trouble with de Vere Terraces is there are three of the buggers.

To be precise, one in Kensington, one in Finsbury and one in Chalk Farm. It'd be helpful to know which of the perishers you have in mind.'

'Which?' whispered Miles.

Rodney was now busy pulling down each tip-up seat in turn and releasing them in rapid tattoo.

'Stop doing that and tell me which.'

'Which what?' said Rodney.

'Don't mind my cab will you?' said the driver. 'Its sole purpose is to give pleasure to the children.' Though he hadn't apparently moved a muscle his back now appeared uncompromisingly hostile.

'If you don't sit down beside me quietly you'll have to get out and walk,' said Miles desperately. 'That's better. Now, which de Vere Terrace do you live in?'

'Three. Three de Vere Terrace.'

'Is it in Kensington?'

Rodney looked blank.

'Or Finsbury?'

'I don't know.'

'You must know.'

'I don't.'

The driver's back was looking more relaxed and sympathetic. 'Or Chalk Farm?' he asked kindly.

'Yes,' said Rodney. 'Near the bridge'

'I know the bastard,' said the driver and the taxi began to move. Rodney stood up and looked first out of one window and then the other. As the taxi swung round the corner into the Hampstead Road he lost his balance and lurched back on top of Miles. Miles clutched him to stop his falling on the floor. Rodney gave him another wet kiss. 'I like you,' he said.

The driver was talkative. He seemed to look on every London street as a personal enemy lying in wait for him, ready to spring some fresh and unpleasant surprise.

'The Hampstead Road,' he was saying, 'I've always hated the bugger. See what I mean,' he continued as he pulled up sharply at a pedestrian crossing while an old lady aggressively asserted her rights, 'you'd go through any self-respecting road like a dose of salts at this time of night, but oh no, not the Hampstead.'

Miles didn't know whether he was expected to join in the conversation. He made polite noises and tried to brace himself for the ordeal ahead. Rodney was still in his arms and already going to sleep. 'I like you,' he had said. So appealing. So trustful. But trustworthy? That remained to be seen. They were now in the Camden Town High Street.

'Camden Town,' the driver was saying as he pulled up at the first set of traffic lights which turned against him the moment they saw him, 'I never could do with it. If it isn't the lights it's the buses, and if it isn't the buses it's the lorries. As for the amateurs,' he said scathingly as a sports car drew up beside him, 'the sooner they're banned in London the better.'

The lights turned green and as they moved forward the sports car accelerated noisily, swung across the taxi's bows and turned left up a side street.

'See what I mean,' said the driver, 'that's Camden Town all over.'

After stopping at each set of lights to the driver's increasing and outspoken disgust, they were bowling along the Chalk Farm Road.

'Lost child?' said the driver unexpectedly.

Miles wasn't listening. He was trying to work out how best to begin the explanations ahead.

'I was saying,' the driver repeated, raising his voice, 'lost child?'

Miles started. 'Yes,' he said, 'I'm taking him home.'

'I wondered.'

There was a pause. If only he would continue with a few crisp comments on the Chalk Farm Road. But no.

'What happened?'

Oh really. Bad enough to try to explain to the parents, but to this bonehead . . .

'It's a long story.'

'Is it now?'

'He found his way into my room.'

'How?'

It wasn't so much the question. It was the way he said it; and that uncompromising back. 'I should have refused to answer,' he thought.

'How?' he repeated.

'That's what I said, how? I mean, kids wandering into people's rooms and not coming out till three-thirty in the bloody morning. Bit fishy, isn't it?'

'I don't know what you mean. If you're suggesting . . .'

'I'm not suggesting anything. I asked a civil question and I'd like a civil answer. Unless of course,' he continued darkly, 'you've got something to hide.'

'Is it likely I'd be taking him home if I had?'

'Ah, but then we've only got your word for that.'

'He told you himself it was Chalk Farm.'

The driver considered this.

'It could be,' he said, 'you'd put him up to it.'

There was silence as they turned up the bridge just before Chalk Farm station. If this was a sample of the difficulties ahead, Miles knew it would need the tenacity and persuasiveness of a super salesman to see this thing through. And he was no super salesman. He wished that he'd brought the teddy bear for luck and comfort; something to hold on to, something he believed in. He always slipped it into his jacket pocket for important occasions. How idiotic to be without it now.

The driver said, 'I never go across this bridge without there's something. As for Regent's Park Road . . .' His voice trailed away, leaving a string of unpleasant question marks behind it. As the road appeared unobstructed, Miles guiltily took the unspoken strictures to himself. They turned into de Vere Terrace and stopped outside the shop.

Rodney woke up and said, 'Have we got there?'

'Yes,' said Miles.

'You won't let me get a hiding?'

'I promised.'

'Yes. I know what I got to say.'

'You're going to tell the truth.'

'Yes,' said Rodney, looking up and smiling knowingly.

That was it then. They were conspirators. Only Miles had everything to lose and his fellow conspirator was a child of five and quite unpredictable. He gripped Rodney's arm suddenly and savagely.

'If you don't say it right I'll . . . I'll . . .' He stopped himself just in time. He realised with horror he was going to say 'I'll kill you.'

'You're hurting me,' said Rodney, beginning to cry.

The near side door opened sharply. The driver was looking in. He had a moon face with little pig eyes which were as hostile as his back.

'So what's going on?'

'Nothing.'

'He's crying isn't he? You made him cry.'

'He's frightened of getting a whipping.'

'That'd be all right only it so happens I heard what you said.'

'How much do I owe you?'

'There's other things to settle besides the fare.'

Miles helped Rodney out. He looked up at the windows above the shop. A light had been switched on. As the three moved over to the door beside the shop, the lighted window opened and Aunt Annie looked out.

'Is it Rodney?' she called. 'Are you all right, Rodney?'

For answer Rodney gave a loud wail.

'I can hear you are,' said Aunt Annie, 'as long as they cry you know they're alive. Just a minute while I wake his dad.'

She disappeared and they heard the window shut above them.

6

They waited in the doorway for what seemed ten minutes. The driver was ominously silent. Rodney alternated snivels and sniffs.

'You see,' said Miles, 'it is his home.'

'Even so . . .' said the driver, obstinately standing his ground.

Eventually the door opened and there was George in trousers and shirt and Aunt Annie in a fetching negligee of pink watered silk trimmed with swansdown and Ethel in the background on the lowest stair in a smocked nightdress with little puffed sleeves.

Come in,' said George and he led the way to the sitting room at the back of the shop. When they were all assembled he looked at Miles and said, 'You're a detective I suppose?'

'He's not,' said the driver.

'Oh,' said George, 'then who is he?'

Miles cleared his throat nervously. 'I should prefer to have this conversation in private.' He looked meaningly at the driver.

'To be fair,' said George, also looking at the driver, 'I don't quite see where you come in, mate.'

The driver's little eyes became even smaller. 'Some people,' he said, 'have eyes in their heads. And noses they can smell a rat with.'

Ethel giggled.

'Stop that, Ethel,' said Aunt Annie, 'it's rude to giggle.'

'I'll stay on the touch-line like if you don't mind,' said the driver.

'Ah . . . on the touch-line,' echoed George uncertainly.

There was a silence. No one knew how to begin. They were all looking at Miles. He knew what he ought to do. Show the driver up for the silly, interfering ass he was. Take the situation in hand with ease and assurance. Make light of it.

At last he said with an attempt at jocularity, 'The trouble with smelling a rat is that it can easily turn out to be a harmless little mouse.'

'I hate mice,' said Ethel, 'worse than rats I do.'

'Ah,' said the driver, 'exactly so.'

This was an unfortunate start.

'Look,' said Miles, exasperated, 'this man has got it into his head that I . . .' He faltered; if only he could keep the shake out of his voice.

'Go on,' said the driver sarcastically, 'we're all ears.'

'As well as eyes and noses?' said Miles. But he didn't get the laugh he was hoping for.

'Don't be so bloody funny,' said the driver. 'If you know what I've got into my head it's because you've got a guilty conscience.'

George said mildly, 'I don't understand. What's it all about?'

Suddenly Aunt Annie exploded. 'Men!' she said. 'It's always the same. Round and round for hours and hours and never get to the point. It'd try the patience of a saint. It's the middle of the night and we all want to get back to our beds.' She turned to Miles. 'You're the man on the ground floor, aren't you? Why can't you say what happened and be done with it? Where was he?'

'I found him in my room.'

'How did he get there?'

'I've no idea. I came in late and worked till three o'clock. I often work late. My bed's behind a screen. I found Rodney in it. He was asleep.'

'How did you get there, Rodney?'

Rodney looked at Miles slyly.

'Don't know,' he said.

'Oh yes you do,' said Aunt Annie, 'you come out with it good and sharp.'

'Before he does,' said Miles hastily, 'I think I ought to say that I gave him my word he wouldn't get into trouble when I brought him back. He was afraid he'd be beaten.'

He glanced quickly at Rodney and then at the driver who was watching him suspiciously.

'He'll get what he deserves,' said George.

'No, really,' said Miles, 'he's been very frightened and I'm sure you'll agree that's punishment enough. I gave him my solemn promise if he was good and let me bring him home you'd forgive him.'

'Took a lot on yourself, didn't you?' said the driver. He turned to George and said, 'See what I mean? Fishy.'

But Aunt Annie intervened. 'First it's rats and now it's fish. You want to have your nose seen to. The gentleman's been kind enough to bring him back. If he hasn't treated him right we'll soon know from Rodney.'

They all looked at Rodney, who shifted uncomfortably and fingered his crutch.

'Leave yourself alone and speak up like a little man.'

Rodney looked up. When Aunt Annie spoke like that there was no way out. He folded his hands in front of him and, staring straight at Miles, repeated with astonishing accuracy what he had been told to say. To Miles it sounded unnaturally glib, but it seemed to satisfy Aunt Annie. If Miles had had staring eyes and worn a macintosh it would have been different.

'Well, that's that,' she said. 'Now say thank you to the gentleman. I'm sure he's been kindness itself.'

'Thank you,' said Rodney, 'you've been kindness itself.'

'Huh!' snorted the driver derisively.

'Huh yourself!' retorted Aunt Annie. 'That clever nose of yours has played you false. Before you poke it into other people's business in future, go and get your adenoids done.'

But the driver wasn't going to be put down so easily.

'There's nothing wrong with my nose, and right now it's getting a strong whiff of old age and second childhood.'

'Steady on,' said George, 'no need to get heated.'

'Well,' said the driver, 'it makes me sick, so it does, to see decent people being made a monkey of. . . . The kid's been put up to it; anyone with half an eye could tell that the way he said it. Like a lesson. And I'll tell you something else.' He turned to Miles. 'You was threatening him, wasn't you? When I opened the cab door. And just to refresh your memory I'll tell you what you was saying. You was saying, "If you don't tell it right I'll

. . ." and then you saw me and stopped. Aren't I right, son? And he'd got you by the arm, hadn't he?'

'Yes,' said Rodney.

'And you was crying?'

'Yes.'

The driver turned to Aunt Annie. 'Now what about my adenoids?' His big face was as impassive as ever, but his eyes were glittering unpleasantly.

Aunt Annie opened her mouth to reply but, to his own astonishment, was forestalled by Miles, who was speaking with a cold, biting anger.

'I think,' he said, addressing Aunt Annie, 'that this interfering idiot is trying to accuse me of sexually assaulting the child. You are witness to what he has said. It is of course the worst kind of criminal slander.' He felt for his notebook and pencil, but realised he had left them in his room. He turned to George. 'I wonder if I could have a piece of paper and a pencil?'

'Of course, mate.'

There was silence as George searched for them and couldn't find them.

'There's a box of Royal Sovereigns in the shop,' Ethel reminded him.

'We don't get much call for pencils these days,' said George apologetically, disappearing into the shop.

The silence continued uncomfortably until he returned with a new pencil and a sheet of paper.

'I took it off the top of a Basildon Bond pad. It's a good line, and no one will know.'

Miles thanked him and then turned to the driver who was standing massively defiant. 'Now, I'll have your name and address.'

'You won't, you know.'

'Very well,' said Miles, reading it off his licence tab and writing it down, 'I have your number.'

'I've often wondered why they had to wear those things,' said Aunt Annie, 'now we know.'

'You can't scare me,' said the driver.

'I'm not trying to. I'm just telling you. By implication you have made a serious charge against me. Either you withdraw it unconditionally and apologise . . .'

'Huh!' said the driver, and just stopped himself spitting on the carpet as he caught Aunt Annie's scandalised eye.

'Or,' continued Miles, 'you'll be hearing from my solicitor.'

'So what?'

'You've got a new baby brother,' Ethel said to Rodney, badly missing the limelight and determined to get it. The surprise interpolation into adult conversation had served her well in the past and she wasn't disappointed this time.

'I don't want one,' said Rodney.

'You're wicked. But for you mum wouldn't of fallen down them stairs and be in hospital. She might die. Oh Auntie, I don't want her to die. She's my mum.'

Ethel burst into tears and made a dramatic dive for Aunt Annie's lap and the comfort of her bosom.

'Now look what you've done,' Aunt Annie said to the driver rather unreasonably, 'butting into people's homes in the middle of the night without a by your leave.' She had to shout to make herself heard above Ethel's bawling. 'She's not going to die,' she yelled, pulling down Ethel's nightdress which was immodestly hitched above the knee.

'I don't like that man,' sobbed Ethel.

'Which one, my little duck?'

Miles and the driver shifted uncomfortably as they realised that in these few seconds Ethel had been accepted as their judge.

'Which one? Tell Auntie.'

She disengaged herself momentarily from Aunt Annie's breasts and pointed at the driver.

'Him,' she said with a sudden icy calm. 'I don't like his eyes. They frighten me.'

Having delivered herself of this she returned to the shelter of the breasts, bawling louder than ever.

'There you are,' shouted Aunt Annie fiercely, 'out of the lips of a little child. They always know what's bad for them, and your sort of eyes is as bad as staring ones. I knew it the instant you came in. You better make yourself scarce because George is going off this minute for the police, aren't you George?'

George looked surprised and embarrassed and murmured something about fair play and everyone having the right to their opinions but Aunt Annie didn't hear him. She was in full spate again, Ethel was howling in her bosom, and Rodney had begun to cry too, for no particular reason except that it seemed the right thing to do. The noise was deafening. Miles stood irresolutely. For a brief moment he thought he had the situation in hand but now it was far beyond him. Anyway, there wasn't a hope of being heard. At last Aunt Annie had to pause for breath and the driver got the chance he was waiting for.

'It's all right,' he said, 'I'm going.'

'It's deeds we want, not words,' panted Aunt Annie, 'isn't it, George?'

'I suppose so . . . yes . . .' said George unhappily, hoping the deeds would be peaceful ones.

'I've said nothing, have I? Nothing at all,' the driver went on glaring at Miles, 'except I was suspicious. You've got nothing on me, mate, and you know it. As for your solicitor,' he imitated Miles' posh voice, 'you can tell him from me he can stuff it up.'

Miles could only hear bits of this above the din, but he got the gist of it. He shrank back involuntarily as the driver strode over to him and hissed into his ear menacingly, 'You haven't seen the last of me you sod, not by a long chalk.'

Miles said, 'I don't know how much was on the clock but here's ten shillings.'

'I wouldn't demean myself,' said the driver, taking the note, crumpling it up into a little ball and throwing it so that it rolled under the table. He walked out quickly and they heard the front door slam.

'Good riddance,' commented Aunt Annie.

Ethel and Rodney had stopped crying as suddenly as they had begun. They dived noiselessly under the table from either side and met head on as they scrabbled for the note. After a fierce but wordless struggle, Ethel emerged with it. With a self-conscious little simper she proffered it to Miles.

'Wouldn't you like to keep it?' he said.

Ethel was quite certain she would, but politely said she mustn't take money from strangers.

'I'm not exactly a stranger,' said Miles, 'I've known this lady by sight for some time, and I've seen you before when you came to the house.'

Ethel turned dutifully to Aunt Annie who looked at George.

He said, 'I don't see why not.'

Ethel did a little pirouette during which she cleverly managed to put out her tongue at Rodney without anyone else seeing her.

'I don't care,' he said staunchly, 'he give me a book.'

'Liar!'

He looked at Miles with his charming little smile. 'You did, didn't you?'

'All right then, where is it?' Ethel said.

Rodney's face puckered. 'I don't know.'

'You see,' said Ethel, laughing happily.

For a moment Miles was speechless as he realised it had been left in the taxi. The thought of those hulking, insensitive hands pawing his book sickened him. He could hear the gross comments, the obscene chuckles.

'Excuse me,' he said, and rushed to the front door, but the taxi had gone.

When he returned to the sitting room Aunt Annie said, 'I'm sure it's very kind of you to have looked after Rodney and brought him back. George wants to thank you, don't you George?'

'Yes,' said George, 'very kind.'

'And never mind about the book. Ethel's going to give Rodney half the ten shillings, aren't you, Eth?'

'No,' said Ethel sulkily.

'You're going to give it to him like the good generous little soul you are. And Rodney would rather have the money than the book any old day, wouldn't you Rod?'

'No,' said Rodney.

'So you see,' Aunt Annie continued, brushing aside this puny opposition, 'it's all settled.'

'The book was rather valuable,' said Miles.

Rodney was smiling at him again. 'It's got pictures. I want it. You said if I spoke the truth . . . what you said . . .'

Miles cut in hastily. 'I explained he must tell you exactly what happened.'

Rodney had never looked so angelic. 'And I done it, didn't I?'

'I'll do my best to get the book back. Now I must go.'

On his way to the door Rodney intercepted him and put his arms up to be kissed. Miles gave him an embarrassed little peck.

'Can I come and see you some more?'

Miles said that was up to Aunt Annie and his parents. For himself he'd be delighted.

'I should think he's seen enough of you to last him his natural. What do you think George?'

'We'll see what Alice says. You walking back to Frame Street?'

'Yes,' said Miles.

'I'll stroll up as far as the 'phone kiosk with you. I got to talk to the police. They're still looking for him.'

'If the taxi driver had his way they'd be looking for me too.' Miles was pleased with this. Just the right note of light irony.

George guffawed. 'Very good,' he said, 'oh very good.'

Ethel came between them. She shyly picked up the hem of her nightdress and fiddled with it as she smiled up ingratiatingly.

'Can I come and see you too?'

'Hark at miss,' rapped Aunt Annie. 'Not backward in coming forward is she? We're wearing out nighties long Ethel; stay with the fashion and spare the gentleman's blushes.'

Ethel let the hem drop and ostentatiously smoothed out the creases by stroking them with the palms of her hands.

'What I mean is,' continued Aunt Annie, 'there's nothing like waiting to be asked.'

'I hope you'll all come and see me.' Miles felt exhausted and longed for the safety of his own room. 'And now I'm sure you'll be wanting to get the children to bed.'

Aunt Annie, however, seemed disposed to make a night of it.

'Oh, they'll be all right,' she said, 'you can see they're enjoying themselves; and anyway nowadays children get too much attention and fuss. All these child clinics, they fill you up with a load of rubbish and fancy talk like, "Let them have their own way or they'll get turned in on themselves." I ask you! "Seen and not heard." That's what I was told when I was a little girl. One wrong word and you got your jacket dusted for you. And look at me. I never got turned in on myself, did I?'

Miles looked at her and had to agree.

'They'll sleep it out in the morning. Commonsense, that's what I believe in, same with bringing up children as everything else. Talking of which,' she added, with a logic only apparent to herself, 'how would you like a nice cup of tea?'

Miles excused himself.

'No trouble. I'll be making one for me and George. And a nice glass of warm Ribena for the children. How about that?'

'No really, thank you.'

At last he got out of the room accompanied by George. Just before they shut the front door he heard Ethel asking what about chocolate biscuits with the Ribena, and Aunt Annie saying no and Ethel saying yes and Aunt Annie saying Ethel could always twist her round her little finger, so she supposed so, just one. Ethel was embarking on some hard bargaining for two when the door shut and they were out in the street.

George grunted, 'So much for commonsense.'

The street was preternaturally quiet and Miles instinctively trod lightly and wished George would do the same. Neither spoke until just before they reached the 'phone kiosk when George said, 'It's a funny old world, isn't it?'

Miles took this to be a rhetorical question, but to be on the safe side he said 'Yes.'

'I mean,' continued George after a pause, 'whatever you do someone's going to think the worst. Take that cab driver, I'm not going to say he was wrong.'

They had stopped walking and were facing each other.

'But surely,' said Miles, 'you can't believe that I . . .' He stopped awkwardly.

'I mean,' George explained, 'in saying what was on his mind. You've got to be fair, haven't you? Play the game and all that. Mind you, I expect he was wrong. But he thought he was right. You could see that, couldn't you? Otherwise why say it? Not that I took to him. Oh no. Rubbed me up the wrong way he did.'

'It was a quite unwarranted insinuation.'

'Oh yes. Quite unwarranted as you might say. Still, he wouldn't have said it if he hadn't believed it, would he?'

'But he'd nothing to go on. Nothing at all.'

George's expression was earnest and righteous. 'Oh, nothing of course. Still, you've got to be fair, haven't you? Same as I want to be fair to you. Well . . . thank you for bringing him back. You did the right thing I'm sure. Good night.'

He went into the kiosk and Miles walked back through the empty streets wondering what he was saying to the police.

7

When they brought in the baby for its feed Alice presented it with her left breast and pushed the nipple gently against its lips. Neither she nor the baby were particularly interested. The red-haired nurse watched her make three shots at getting him to suck and then said, 'We've got ways of making babies do what they don't want to, my lad,' and leaned over and pinched his nose. After a moment of asphyxia he opened his mouth to breathe and Alice popped the nipple in. The nurse let go of his nose. He shut his eyes and started to suck discriminately, like a member of the wine committee trying out the suspect claret.

The nurse said, 'Men are all the same. Don't know what's good for them till a woman points it out. Is he getting it all right?'

'Seems to be.'

'Ten minutes each side then. Got your watch?'

'Yes.'

'Then I can leave you to it. Thank God for an experienced mother.'

She hurried away to fetch yet another baby to yet another mother. Alice sat propped against the pillows and had a think while the baby sucked her. She rather enjoyed it. For the first time since it was born she felt properly maternal. It was a nuisance but she couldn't help loving it. And what a funny sort of way to arrive. Still, good had come of it so it only went to show, because she'd decided this man was coming to see her. Aunt Annie had given her the long of it, George had given a shorter, authorised version, there had been some irrelevant but none the less riveting details from Ethel and she had closely questioned Rodney. He had been evasive about details but stuck resolutely and, in a curious way, defiantly to his story, almost as if he expected it not to be believed. And he finished almost every sentence with 'he said I can go and see him, can I mum?'

So she had thought up an exciting plan. This Mr Madgwick should come and visit her in the hospital. Alone. She didn't want George or Aunt Annie or the children there. If there had been anything wrong that night she would know.

'How?' said George.

'Instinct. Maternal instinct.'

He knew from experience it was no good trying to argue against that.

'I suppose it's all right. But remember, when I told the police sergeant how Rod had turned up he said he didn't like the sound of it.'

'I don't like the sound of church bells, but you can't say they're not respectable.'

He grudgingly agreed.

'Well then, unless I see him we shan't ever know.'

George was puzzled. 'The police said there was nothing to go on even if something did happen.'

'So what?'

'Then why do you want to see him? I don't see the point.'

But she had it all worked out. 'You're losing your grip, George. If I decide there was any funny business you can go and tip off the police.'

'I don't see the point of that either.'

She tried to keep the impatience out of her voice. 'If he'd done it once he'd do it again. They could keep an eye on him, couldn't they? It'd be a public duty, only fair to other kids.'

'Ah, fair.' George was on firm, familiar ground. 'Yes, I see that, Alice.'

So Alice, her burning curiosity to meet this strange man now likely to be gratified under the guise of public duty, had written a little note.

Dear Sir,

I would like to see you and say thank you for bringing my little boy back. I am in Varley Maternity Ward,

Gower Hospital, handy for you as round the corner. Visiting hours 2.30 to 4.30. Can you come Wednesday? Trusting you won't take offence me writing.

Yours truly,
(Signed) Mrs Remnant

George had taken it to Frame Street the same evening and slipped it noiselessly through the letter-box. He had left the combination round the corner. The last thing he wanted was a meeting with explanations; he hadn't made up his mind if Miles was on the level and Miles would sense this and they wouldn't know what to say to each other. Much better to leave it to Alice.

The baby had gone to sleep after five minutes' rather half-hearted work on the second nipple and Alice lay back on the pillows, drowsy and content. The baby gave a charming smile when the nurse came to fetch him and belched milkily.

'He needs changing, nurse.'

'They always do.'

'Rather you than me.'

Alice closed her eyes. This man, this Mr Madgwick; he might, just might, turn out to be Mr R. The future opened like a flower in the warmth of her imagination. Because such things did happen; you read about them in magazines. The chance meeting, the casual chat about this and that and him not able to keep his eyes off her and she pretending not to notice, ever so nonchalant as she glanced occasionally up at him from beneath drooping eyelids; and the moment when she reached over to the bedside table to offer him one of Aunt Annie's grapes and her bed jacket slipped revealingly off one shoulder and she knew he hadn't missed the sight of her milk white bosom but of course nothing was said; and when they parted he had pressed her hand and the touch of him had made her shiver and he said 'are you cold?' and she said 'no, someone walking over my grave' and he had suddenly put her hand to his lips like a foreigner in a film and said 'we must meet again' and she had said 'yes, I hope so'; and then she was in the nudist camp and said 'don't be silly Alice it's a dream, but all the same I hope it goes on' and it did, and there he was giving her a red rose and he was a bit like Clark Gable.

On Wednesday she couldn't keep it to herself and confided to the red-haired nurse she had a man coming to see her. The nurse cottoned on at once and said, 'Oh, a man? You must look your best,' and lent her a pale pink lipstick called *Interesting* and told her to put on some light foundation because she was looking so much better and if she wanted to get anywhere she'd have to play for sympathy. 'The bandage can help,' she said and she rearranged it so that it looked as much as possible like the close fitting turban the model was wearing on the cover of an old *Vogue*, and Alice was pleased when she said 'You look fit to kill, absolutely fabulous,' and helped her into the bed jacket with swansdown trimmings. Aunt Annie had been true to her word and got the stains out from under the arms but it exuded a lingering and unattractive smell of chemicals so the nurse went off and got some scent called *Get You* and dabbed some behind Alice's ears and between her breasts. It didn't altogether do the trick; the chemical obstinately predominated.

By two-thirty Alice felt nervous. The excitement had gone and her head was beginning to throb again. She almost hoped he wouldn't come. She recalled Aunt Annie's description, 'Quite nice looking but not what I call a real man.' That didn't sound like Mr R.

The visiting hour invasion had begun punctually on time. There was a noisy group round Mrs Starey on her left and a young clergyman talking in earnest whispers to Mrs Yates on her right whose first baby hadn't yet arrived. Most of the mothers had their babies on display, but Alice and the nurse had decided she would make a more telling impression on her own. Babies effectively stole the limelight.

Alice lay listening to the snatches of baby talk and the rise and fall of family gossip and firmly resisting the kindly attempts of Mrs Starey's relatives to draw her into their conversation.

'Hubby not coming today?'

'Not today.'

'Work I suppose?'

'Yes, work.'

'Your Aunt's usually here before now.'

'She's not coming today.'

'Oh. All on your tiny own?'

They were bursting with curiosity. They could go on bursting. She pretended to be unaware of the speculative glances that bombarded her from all over the ward. But she couldn't resist a quick look up at each new arrival. By three thirty she made up her mind he wasn't coming. She felt lonely and longed for the comfort of Aunt Annie. She had been inclined to side with her about the cab driver but now his insinuations blended unpleasantly with the smell of chemicals from the dainty bed-jacket. And then the way this man had threatened Rodney in the taxi.

'Usually,' George had said, 'there's no smoke without fire. You can't get away from it, Alice.' And this afternoon she couldn't. There had been some funny business, no doubt of it. Disgusting. Poor little Rodney; he'd been scared into saying what he'd been told.

She caught the nurse's eye and beckoned her over.

'This bed-jacket stinks,' she said, 'I'd sooner have had the stains.'

The nurse helped her out of it and into the old pink woolly.

'He's probably got delayed,' she whispered.

'I'd like my baby.'

'It's only quarter to four.'

'Never mind. I'd like him.'

The nurse brought him and the Starey family clustered round and said he was a proper boy, you could see that, and Alice wasn't too pleased because that meant they thought it was ugly which it certainly was, but they'd no call to draw attention to it. Then it smiled and the Stareys said, 'Look, it's smiling,' and instead of belching it was sick over the old pink woolly. The nurse mopped it up and as the Stareys tactfully moved away Alice saw a youngish man standing at the bottom of her bed. He was tall with a slight stoop, had mousy hair receding at the temples, a kindly, nervous expression and wasn't all that bad to look at. He gave what was intended to be a reassuring, easy smile, but the corners of his mouth trembled and the smile was switched off abruptly. He was carrying a bunch of red roses.

'Mrs Remnant?' His face puckered with what appeared to be an intense solicitude.

There was silence in the ward. The Stareys gave up all pretence and frankly gawped. Even the young clergyman stopped whispering to Mrs Yates. Everyone was watching. Like it was the telly, Alice thought, the nosy cats.

The nurse said, 'Here's a chair,' and took the roses. She thrust them under Alice's nose. 'They're lovely, aren't they dear? I'll put them in water.' With her back to Miles she winked broadly at Alice before she carried them off.

Haughtily and putting on a posh accent, Alice turned to the Stareys.

'Do go on with your conversation. I'd so hate to disturb you.'

But it took more than that to put the Stareys out of countenance. Not only did they continue gawping but Mrs Starey's old mother had the nerve to smile toothily at Miles and say, 'Good afternoon. Warm enough for you?'

Alice cut in before Miles could reply. 'Anyone can see it's too warm for you, Grannie, the sweat's running down your nose.'

This had the desired effect.

'There's no call to be personal, I'm sure,' said the old lady. The Stareys turned in on themselves and muttered indignantly.

Miles sat on the chair. There was a pause. Alice was looking at him. He glanced quickly at her and looked away again. Then he told the ceiling his name was Miles Madgwick.

'I like his voice,' Alice thought, 'musical and quite the gentleman.' 'My name,' she said, 'is Mrs Remnant.'

'Yes, I knew that. The sister pointed you out.'

'I hope you didn't think it pre . . . presumptuous me asking you to call.'

'It was very kind.'

She noticed his eyes were greyish green.

'It was about Rodney.'

He coloured slightly and gazed at the ceiling again.

'Yes?'

'I wanted to say thank you.'

'It was nothing.' He glanced fleetingly at the baby and then at her. 'He's a nice child.'

'He's just been sick.'

'I meant Rodney.'

'Oh, him. He's all right when he tells the truth which isn't as often as he should.'

The slightly awkward silence which followed was broken by the nurse returning with the roses in a vase.

'Sorry to interrupt,' she said, 'I thought you'd like them right away. The smell goes off so quick.'

Alice held out her spare hand for them.

'You'd better let me have baby,' said the nurse, picking him up and laying him over her shoulder, 'he's quite damp enough without having the vase spilt over him. Anyway two's company,' she added, winking at Alice from behind the baby's head, 'so us two will make ourselves scarce.'

She put up her other hand to steady the baby's head which was wobbling alarmingly and bore him off.

Alice sniffed at the roses.

He said, 'They're so fragile, aren't they?'

'They smell of the country.'

'I meant babies.'

'Oh,' Alice laughed. 'They smell too. Farmyards more likely.'

'Do you like the country?'

She looked at him now without embarrassment, plain curious. This wasn't small talk. He wanted to know.

'Yes,' she said, 'and the sea. I love the sea.'

He smiled. A real smile this time, attractive all right. 'I was partly brought up by the sea. Southwold. Ever been there?'

'No. Clymping's about as far as we can manage Sundays. Know it?'

'No.'

'You'd love it.'

'Yes, I would.'

He said this with such conviction and so abruptly she thought it must have some special association for him.

'You've heard of it then?'

'No, I haven't.'

'Then how do you know you'd love it?'

For a moment he didn't answer. Then he got up and said, 'Would you like me to put the flowers on your table?'

'I don't mind.'

He took them from her and stood uncertainly. 'I think perhaps I ought to get along.'

'You don't have to go till four-thirty.'

'I'm afraid I must. An appointment.'

'Oh, go on. You can manage another five minutes.'

He hesitated. The entire Starey contingent, silent and unabashed, waited for his reply.

'Trouble with this place,' said Alice loudly, 'you might as well try to have a private talk on the telly.'

All the Stareys except one became ostentatiously engaged in conversation. Only Mrs Starey's mother remained silent and motionless, her eyes fixed on them.

He put the flowers on the table and sat down again.

'Five minutes,' he said, looking at his watch.

'Bring your chair in a bit closer.' As he did so she turned witheringly to Mrs Starey's mother. 'You wouldn't care to join us I suppose?' She went on in a whisper, 'I don't want her to hear this. I'm not good at saying things but I wanted to see you because . . . well, you know some funny things have been said. That cab driver . . .'

Miles shifted uncomfortably.

'I hope you'll believe me . . .' he began.

But she interrupted him. 'Well, that's the thing. If there's one thing I believe in it's the truth; and fair play, that too. You mustn't mind me. I'm a regular Mrs Blunt I expect. But I want to ask you a straight question and I want a straight answer.' She looked searchingly at him, almost anxiously. 'Was there or was there not any funny business with Rod? You know what I mean.'

He looked directly into her eyes and said no.

'I believe you. I had to know you see. I hope you don't mind me asking.'

'Of course not.'

They were both so absorbed in their search for mutual trust they hadn't noticed Mrs Starey's mother had moved across and was standing over them in rapt attention.

'Was you wanting something?' said Alice.

'I understood you asked me to join you.'

Alice was bitingly sarcastic. 'I didn't want you to miss anything.'

'Then you ought to speak up. I'm a bit hard of hearing.'

'I bet she heard every word,' Alice whispered.

'You're wrong. There was one thing I missed. What was it you asked him?'

Alice winked at Miles. 'I asked him whether he believes in Jesus Christ.'

'He said no.'

'I believe him.'

The old lady looked shocked. She fumbled in her bag and produced a tract which she handed to Miles. He glanced at it and saw it began, 'Whosoever will be saved . . . THIS MEANS YOU!'

'I'll be praying for you, though, by the look of you, I'd say I'd be wasting my time.'

'I'm an agnostic.'

'I thought as much. Tell 'em a mile off I can. If I had my way I'd lump 'em all together with the commies and shoot 'em down with machine guns I would.'

'You're working yourself up,' said Alice.

'It's enough to.'

'Your daughter's beckoning.'

The old lady called across to Mrs Starey, 'I'm doing the Lord's work, Effie.'

'You can do it just as well over here,' said Mrs Starey.

'What did you say, dear?'

'You can do it just as well over here.'

The old lady turned back to Miles. 'There's sin everywhere, even in the family circle. Charity begins at home.'

'Must you go?' said Alice.

'Before I do, I take back what I said about shooting them with machine guns. It wasn't right.'

'Who, the agnostics?'

'And the commies. Too good for them. They ought to be blown to bits with one of them atom bombs.' She glared at Miles. 'You'll think the same when you've read that tract.'

She smiled her toothy smile at Alice, asked her to remember her in her prayers and returned to the Starey family circle.

Alice giggled and whispered the old lady was a bit touched but she meant well. Miles whispered back she had a funny way of showing it. They both laughed. Grannie Starey had been an unexpected catalyst. Alice liked this man. He was shy and awkward, but something about him appealed to her. They talked easily. In the end he stayed till four-thirty. She told him the children wanted to see him again. He said that would be nice and if she liked the sea there were day excursions to Hastings or Brighton and might he take them all? She knew she would like that very much and would certainly accept, but it wouldn't be right without going through the ritual of asking George. He politely included George and was relieved when she said he had to mind the shop weekdays. He was even more relieved when she said it would have to be after the new baby was weaned so she could leave it with Aunt Annie. He had taken it for granted she was also included, but Alice explained that now the old girl was settled in London nothing would induce her to leave it.

At four twenty-five she surreptitiously loosened the ribbon which tied the old woolly bed-jacket and leaned across to the table.

'I was nearly forgetting to offer you one of these grapes Aunt Annie brought me.'

She handed him the plate with quite a flourish but the wool disappointingly clung to her shoulder and refused to slip down revealingly. Still, the bed jacket parted satisfactorily enough, she thought, because he looked away quickly and said, 'No thanks, really' in the direction of Grannie Starey who caught his eye and said, 'Speak up, I can't hear.'

He smiled rather foolishly, shook his head and pointed to the grapes.

'Very kind, I'm sure,' she said, 'I'm partial to them.'

She got to her feet with surprising agility, made for the grapes which Alice was still holding out, snatched a sizeable bunch and popped them one after the other into her mouth. Alice withdrew the plate to the safety of the table on the far side of the bed. As she did so the bed jacket really did slide off her shoulder and Grannie Starey was dreadfully shocked.

Having dexterously isolated the pips in her mouth she spat them out into a puffy hand, smacked her lips and said, 'You ought to be more careful, dear. Let me do it up for you.' She leaned forward, stopped suddenly and looked hastily round for somewhere to put the pips. 'Hold these for a moment,' she said to Miles with such urgency that he put out his hand to receive them. Just as quickly he withdrew it and the glutinous little ball of pips hit the floor with a soft smack.

'Now look at the mess you've made,' she said.

Alice had hastily rearranged the bed jacket and tied the ribbons.

'I've done it,' she said as the old lady turned back to her.

'He'd better clean up that mess before the authorities see it.

That's commies all over. Ask for a helping hand and they take it away. As for you dear,' she continued, leaning right over Alice to the grapes on the far side of the bed and snatching two more, 'remember what Saint Paul said about modesty, and that don't mean showing everything you got. Next time your Aunt gets grapes, tell her to taste them first. This lot's sour.'

She rejoined the family group, leaving Miles staring like a hypnotised rabbit at the small snake of pips on the floor. Alice signalled the nurse who cheerfully cleaned up the mess, saying it was all in the day's work and you had to have a strong stomach in her job or you couldn't do it.

When they parted Alice and Miles shook hands and it was arranged she would look in on him as soon as she was out of hospital and well enough to resume the routine visits to Aunt Annie. She said it was nice of him to come. He said it had been a pleasure. She agreed it had. As he walked to the door she kept hoping he would turn and wave or smile. But he was quickly hidden from her by the Stareys who walked out backwards as if from a Royal presence, waving and smiling at the waving and smiling Mrs Starey.

After the visitors had all left, the ward hummed with the interchange of freshly acquired family gossip, but Alice lay silently back against the pillows. She was smiling contentedly.

8

Driving a taxi in London night in and night out is perhaps not so hard on the nerves as driving it by day, but it has its own special irritations and frustrations and they were telling on Albert Shoesmith. 'My husband,' Mrs Shoesmith used to say, 'don't ask me what he's like. I never see him.' This was an exaggeration. She saw him in the early morning and gave him his dinner. She saw him during the day if she happened to go into the bedroom where he was asleep. And she saw him when she gave him his breakfast before he set off for work at night. But seeing him gave her no pleasure. They rarely spoke to each other and when they did it was only to communicate such basic facts as today was Friday and what about him handing over the housekeeping, or why did she give him fish on Wednesdays when she knew he liked steak Wednesdays? all right, the steak looked tough, but he'd rather have tough steak Wednesdays than tender steak Thursdays. The slightest deviation from his fixed habits had always irritated him but lately drove him into the kind of rage which, in the old days, was a rarity. Daisy Shoesmith had a short way with him when this happened. As a good wife it could be held against her, as it is sometimes held against modern medicine, that she was more interested in treating symptoms than causes. But then she disliked him intensely.

The moment he started, she would rush from the room and lock the door on the outside. As she was slim and agile, his lumbering attempts to forestall her invariably failed. He would shout at her through the door for about five minutes and threaten to bash it in and give her what for. Usually he would then quieten down and go on with his meal. But she knew he was not to be trusted. She would put on her hat and coat and go down into the street. 'Bert,' she would cry in a thin, piercing voice, 'Ber . . . ert!' He would open the window and let down a string to which she tied the key and, as he pulled it up, she hurried down the street to the safety of her friend, Mrs Combermere.

Mr Combermere was an all-in wrestler who had once been a boxer and everyone knew he could make mincemeat of Bert.

'Just let me hear of the bastard knocking you about,' he said, flexing his enormous muscles. 'Just let me hear of it!'

And Minnie Combermere always added, 'He means it, Daisy, so don't hesitate to call on him.'

Daisy hadn't the slightest intention of hesitating. She longed for the day. But so far it hadn't come. If it was the morning she would do the shopping and then tiptoe nervously into the house and peep round the bedroom door. He was always asleep. If it was at night he would have gone off to work by the time she got back.

Bert had many shortcomings but he didn't lack tenacity. He had a simple mind and it fastened on simple ideas like a bulldog's bite. There was no shifting it, Daisy knew that. 'Obstinate,' she said. 'He'd argue black was white if it suited him and he'd go to the bloody stake for it.'

Minnie Combermere's wide open blue eyes opened even wider. 'It could be a virtue,' she said, 'if his ideas wasn't so cock-eyed. Have a choc mint, Dais. Cheer you up. They do wonders for me."

Reg's enormous face and cauliflower ears appeared above the evening paper. 'Wonders is the word,' he said, 'talk about Two Ton Tess.'

Minnie's first chin tucked itself into her others and the whole of her wobbled. This meant she was laughing. No sound came out.

'He's jealous. He only just tops fifteen stone. . . .'

Daisy took a choc mint and ate it thoughtfully while Minnie disposed of four.

'People with blue eyes, we never know when we've had enough.'

Daisy knew perfectly well she'd had enough of Bert. She'd

known it all those years ago when they were courting. But he'd got his hooks into her and there was no shaking him off. There'd been another boy she'd fancied but Bert had frightened him away. 'If I catch that bugger nosing round again,' he'd said, 'I'll half kill him.' He had caught him and he had half killed him. There was a nasty little court case, assault and battery. 'If he don't give her a wide berth,' he told the magistrate, 'I'll bloody do it again and make a better job of it.' He got a month for the assault and an extra two for contempt. The boy never came near her after he left hospital. She went to meet Bert at the gates of Wormwood Scrubs because he'd written he would carve her up if she didn't. He told her he was set on marrying her and she'd better agree because he'd go to any lengths, any, if she refused.

Oddly enough she wasn't frightened of him. Her friends told her marriage would be disastrous. They begged her to be firm. But she knew he would never give up, and the thought of standing out against him for the rest of her life daunted her so much she thought it would be less harassing to make the best of him. She told herself everyone had a good side and she would discover his. There must be something to be said for a man who would go to any lengths for a woman.

So they married, and Bert drove her back from the Chapel with a glove over the meter flag and they went straight to bed. She was a virgin and he was rough and she decided it wasn't all it was cracked up to be and said so. She gave him breakfast and, after he'd gone off to work, she went round to Minnie Combermere and said she was never going to bed with him again. Minnie said no man would stand for that, least of all Bert. But Daisy said she meant every word of it and Minnie would see. Minnie started talking about conjugal rights but Daisy said if Bert didn't like it he knew what to do.

The next morning she gave him his dinner when he got back from work. She'd gone to considerable trouble to provide exactly what he'd asked for and serve it daintily and rather hoped for a word of appreciation. He ate it without speaking, but not silently, while she sat watching him and telling him how she planned to spend the day. But when she began outlining the little improvements and alterations which would make the flat more comfortable and easier to run, he put down his knife and fork and said, 'No changes. I don't want no changes.'

She started to argue but he put up a grimy hand. 'And I don't want no argument. What's been good enough for me is good enough for you. Get that straight and you'll do.'

This effectively put a stop to further conversation. She gave him the suet pudding and golden syrup. When he'd eaten it he sat back in his chair and yawned enormously, stretching his arms and legs.

'Well,' he said, 'shut eye. What about it?'

'What about what?'

'Shut eye.'

'You must be tired.'

'Not too tired for a good old I'm-in-luck.'

'You're disgusting.'

'That's right.'

'I'm not doing it no more.'

'We'll see about that.'

'You can't make me.'

'We'll bloody see.'

He got to his feet and walked towards her. She wanted to run away, out of the room, down the stairs into the street and down to Minnie Combermere's. He raised his fist but she stood still.

'You do that just once and I'll tell Reg. He'll make mincemeat of you.'

He stopped, his fist still raised, his little eyes as expressionless as pebbles. She sensed her advantage and pressed it.

'You know what I'll do if you try and make me? Laugh! Laugh my head off, giving out you was the big strong man and all the time . . . why, even my little brother when he was thirteen had . . .'

He suddenly put his raised hand over his mouth as if he himself were about to say something unmentionable and must be stopped at all costs. They stood staring at each other. She knew she mustn't move.

At last he whispered, 'If you ever tell Minnie, or anyone else for that matter, I'll bloody murder you."

She knew he would. She forced herself to smile.

'They've got bigger things to talk about.'

He opened his mouth to say something but no words came.

Then he slowly turned and went to bed. Five minutes later she heard him snoring.

She didn't sleep with him again. On the rare occasions when he was ill or took a night off she made herself a bed on the sitting room sofa. He never mentioned conjugal rights. She was there for as long as she wanted to stay. In many ways it suited her. Apart from giving him his dinner in the mornings and breakfast at night, she could spend the days as she pleased. She had friends, went shopping, went to the cinema, went to Bingo, did the football pools and was house proud. She altered and improved the flat so gradually he didn't notice. Sometimes she gave tea parties. Some of her acquaintances thought it an ideal marriage.

But, since Sunday, things had been difficult; there was something on his mind, all the signs pointed to it. He spoke even less than usual, his temper was constantly foul, and she had to lock him in two evenings running. On Wednesday, when she tiptoed into his room to fetch his underclothes for the wash, she caught a glimpse of him sitting up in bed looking at a book. It was the first time she had ever seen him awake during the day. She was so surprised she drew back and shut the door again. When she re-entered a moment later he was pretending to be asleep. There was no sign of the book. After he left for work she ransacked the bedroom and when she took his sheets off the bed and put her own on ready for the night, she had the mattress off. She went through all his drawers, looked in the suitcases and even poked an umbrella up the chimney. It wasn't there. She concluded he must have taken it with him: he hadn't been carrying it, she was watching for that. He must have had it under his old leather overcoat. What was he up to? He never read books, only the paper. The same went for her. There was hardly a book in the place and certainly not as sizeable. She finished up the meat pie and then wished she hadn't; it gave her indigestion.

She slept badly and got up very early. She was determined not to miss his return. The sausages made such a noise frying, she kept running to the hall to listen for him coming up the stairs. The fourth time she ran out, the front door opened in her face and gave her a nasty bang on the forehead. She put her hand to it and said, 'Ow! you ought to be more careful.'

'If you will get in the way . . . What was you doing there anyway?'

'I suppose I can walk about my own hall.'

'And I suppose I can bloody open my own front door.'

He wasn't carrying the book. She was dying to know whether it was under his coat.

'Aren't you going to take your coat off?'

He went into the bedroom without answering and slammed the door. When his dinner was ready she walked stealthily up to the door and listened. There was no sound from inside. She opened the door very suddenly. He was sitting on the side of the bed, the book open in front of him. She had time to see there were pictures in it before he drew the turned sheet over it.

'Dinner,' she said.

He ate it without speaking. Ordinarily the sight and sound of him eating would have driven her from the room. This morning she bore it in the hope she might get an inkling of what was going on. He glowered at her.

'What are you hanging about for?'

'I suppose I can take the weight off my feet if I feel like it.'

'I don't like being watched.'

'Something on your mind?'

She gave him the rice pudding and he ate it without answering. He put the last spoonful in his mouth and went to the bedroom, swallowing it noisily. At the door he hesitated. Then he turned and gave her a long, searching look, sucking his teeth and flushing out fugitive grains of rice with his tongue.

She couldn't help saying, 'If you've got something on your mind, why don't you come out with it?'

'Who says I've got something on my mind?'

'Telling somebody, it helps sometimes.' She tried to sound sympathetic and understanding, but she couldn't conceal the curiosity.

'Women!' he said with blistering contempt, and disappeared into the bedroom.

She started to clear the table. After a minute or so he reappeared in vest and trousers carrying the book.

'Sincc you're so nosy, get an eyeful of that.'

'Where'd you get it?'

He threw the book at her. She tried to catch it but it fell

heavily to the floor, open and face downwards, so that the leaves splayed out and were squashed under its own weight.

He laughed shortly.

'You can't even bloody catch.'

He went back into the bedroom and shut the door.

She knelt down and turned the book over. It was nearly all pictures. She smoothed out the creased pages and looked at them one by one. She must have spent half an hour on the floor there. Then she spoke aloud.

'He must be mad,' she said, 'he must be mad.'

She meant Bert. By implication she also meant Hieronymus Bosch. Later she tiptoed into the bedroom and put the book on the dressing table. He didn't wake up.

9

Aunt Annie and George weren't getting on too well while Alice was in hospital. The question of crisp or flabby bacon had become a minor issue, though it cropped up every morning with irritating persistence. She had a habit of altering meal times to suit herself and forgetting to tell him. If he was late he'd find the table cleared and Aunt Annie washing up reproachfully and suggesting he boil himself a couple of eggs, she had to go over to Frame Street, there were three parcels to be sent off to customers that wouldn't wait.

She was far too indulgent with Ethel who was tiresome enough at the best of times but was now behaving like a miniature prima donna; and she constantly reproached Rodney for having caused his mother's accident and the ensuing embarrassment to that nice gentleman who had brought him home. George thought she wasn't being fair. Tick him off once and be done with it, but to go on and on . . . not fair. In addition she always went to Frame Street at the most inconvenient times, taking the children with her and often keeping them up late at night. That wasn't fair either. Spoilt his evenings which he liked to spend in his armchair, dozing and waking and dozing again. And then they'd come trooping in, chattering, wanting chocolate, glasses of milk and his attention. Unfair. He was not one for having words but he believed strongly he should be master in his own house. Aunt Annie on the contrary believed she should be mistress wherever she was and, moreover, was one for having words if anyone questioned her belief. So George was circumspect. To her face he was polite enough, protesting mildly when he had a more than ordinary pressing grievance, and afterwards passing on the full extent of his indignation to Joe Rumbold when he came in for his evening paper. Then he'd feel better. He gave Joe the impression that Aunt Annie quailed at his lightest word and, under the lash of his tongue, was fast becoming a model of obedient womanhood. Joe listened admiringly and said things like 'you did right George' and 'she had that coming to her' and 'I'd have said the same'.

Unfortunately Ethel overheard one of these conversations from behind the half-open shop door and recounted it in detail to Aunt Annie who had just returned from the hospital. It was the day after Miles' visit. Alice had given her a full account of it together with her considered opinion that he was 'nice' and, in spite of his looks, was a real man, having tested him out with the revealing bed-jacket. Aunt Annie laughed and said she was a fast piece and knew a thing or two about men. George of course didn't. He had allowed himself to be influenced by that cab driver. Anyone with half an eye could see he was a mischief maker and out for no good.

All this put Aunt Annie in her sunniest mood. To have had her own judgement so resoundingly confirmed was, of course, what she had expected. But, better still, it was one in the eye for George. When Grannie Starey, in answer to polite enquiry, replied her indigestion was something chronic, she beamed indulgently and said, 'You ought to go easy on the grapes, Grannie,' and to Mrs Yates, whose baby still hadn't arrived and who was to have an induction, she exuded confidence and encouragement with a little story of a friend of hers whose refusal to be inducted had resulted in appalling complications followed by a particularly painful death.

Just before she left, Doctor Fallowfield had come into the ward and asked for a private talk with Alice. Aunt Annie went through the motions of withdrawing out of earshot but, to her annoyance, Alice didn't immediately call her back and explain to the doctor she had no secrets from her aunt. She stood a few paces away from the bed, straining her ears to catch what was being said and trying to look as if she wasn't. The Stareys chose that moment to deafen her with their goodbyes to Mrs Starey. She was infuriatingly aware of Grannie Starey drawing their attention to her predicament and the giggles that followed. The leaving bell rang, but she stood her ground until a nurse politely reminded her she was expected to go. She broke into the whispered conversation, gave Alice a cold little kiss and walked out of the ward in a rage.

Alice had said, 'I'll tell you all about it tomorrow, Auntie,' but she thought she already knew. She had, in approaching the bed, overheard one revealing word.

By the time she reached de Vere Terrace she had decided on action. But when Ethel sidled up to her and said, 'I do love you, Auntie,' she sensed at once this was a prelude to something else she wasn't going to like. Ethel went about her story with considerable artistry, dwelling lovingly on the high spots and scurrying over the dull, linking patches with a throw-away technique worthy of Aunt Annie herself.

At the end of it Aunt Annie kissed her and said thoughtfully, 'I expect you did right to tell me.'

But when Ethel, cashing in on this, said what about a Mars bar, she hadn't at all reckoned on the fury Aunt Annie suddenly let loose.

'Get to bed this instant, you prying little cat.'

'But I haven't had any supper, Auntie.'

'Supper! You dare talk to me about supper after what you just told me.'

'But you said . . .'

'Never mind what I said. You get to bed and think yourself lucky you can still sit on your bottom with any comfort.'

At this moment, Rodney came into the room and, seeing Ethel for once getting the rough side of Aunt Annie's tongue which he had come to think was kept exclusively for him, made the mistake of smirking.

Aunt Annie rounded on him. 'I saw you smirk. A nice pair! Betraying your father who loves you and slaves for you for the sake of a Mars bar.'

Ethel was already in tears and Rodney followed suit.

'But I never said nothing,' he snivelled.

'It's not what you say, it's what you think.'

'I never thought nothing.'

'Then it's time you did. It's time you learned not to go spying on your mum and dad and telling tales out of school.'

'But I never . . .'

'All right, you never. But you would if you could, and don't tell me different.'

Ethel had edged out of the room. It was nice to think Rodney was bearing the brunt of this totally unexpected onslaught. Knowing her Aunt Annie she still had hopes of a Mars bar.

Rodney had no such thoughts. He was bewildered and rather frightened.

'I never done nothing,' he cried.

'Never done nothing! Who was it wet his pants like a baby and caused his loving mother a nasty fall which might have been the death of her? And your poor little baby brother she was carrying?'

Rodney stopped crying.

'You said the stork give it her in the hospital.'

But consistency was never Aunt Annie's strong suit.

'That doesn't signify,' she said, 'you'd have done in the stork too and well you know it, if it hadn't happened to have wings. Now get off to bed before I . . .'

She raised her hand threateningly and a very puzzled Rodney scuttled from the room.

Left to herself, she began to pace up and down, muttering to herself, breathing noisily and punctuating these activities with short sardonic laughs. Occasionally she stood still and uttered one word. The sound of it immediately set her pacing again; the muttering, the breathing and the sardonic laughs increasing in tempo and intensity until she judged she had reached the necessary emotional pitch to annihilate George. At this point, in the middle of her pacing, she suddenly changed direction, opened the door leading to the shop and charged.

George was leaning over the counter, resting on his elbows and talking to Joe, who was in a similar position the other side of it about a yard further down. She drew up short inside the door and snorted. The two men raised their heads momentarily and then continued their conversation.

'Mind you,' Joe was saying, 'you got to keep a pipe clean.'

'That's right,' said George.

'I always say there's a difference between being a wet smoker and a dry smoker.'

Aunt Annie snorted again.

'A big difference,' said George. 'You got a cold, Auntie?'

'I mean,' continued Joe, 'take me for instance. You wouldn't exactly call me a dry smoker.'

'No, I wouldn't.'

'But if you was to call me a wet smoker you'd be wrong again.'

'Something between the two.'

'Something between the two. I don't have to be a fussy pipe cleaner but I have to be a regular pipe cleaner. There's a difference'.

'I see that.' George glanced up apprehensively. 'Something wrong, Auntie?'

This was her moment. She took a deep breath and let fly.

'Snakes in the grass,' she began, 'that's what you are.'

George, sensing at once this was the opening range finder in what promised to be a prolonged and one-sided encounter, whispered hastily to Joe that he'd better make himself scarce. After the brave victories he'd recounted, it wouldn't do to be seen taking the pounding that undoubtedly was coming to him. But she was quick to forestall him.

'No you don't,' she said with such intensity that Joe stopped instantly in his tracks. At the same moment Mrs Treasure came into the shop for twenty Seniors and stood just inside the door like a sentinel, hardly able to believe her luck in being a witness to such drama and spectacle.

'If you try and leave the shop, Mr Rumbold,' continued Aunt Annie with brilliant opportunism, 'it'll be over Mrs Treasure's dead body.'

'They shall not pass,' said Mrs Treasure, aptly snatching the quotation out of the air and presenting it as a little thing of her own.

'I appreciate that Mrs Treasure and I shan't forget it. Loyalty to your friends and relations is something you'd think you could count on. But there's snakes in the grass that bites the hand that feeds them and don't know the meaning of gratitude when their loving wife's Aunt moves in to look after them, and where would they be if she hadn't I should like to know? But they take no account of that. Oh no, they go off behind her back and tell another snake wicked falsehoods about her, and what does the other snake do but go and encourage them so they make out they're little Hitlers whose lightest word is law and think all women, especially their loving wife's Aunt, was put into the world to minister to their every whim, kiss their arse, just like that.'

She paused for breath. George hastily asked Mrs Treasure if it was twenty Seniors and Mrs Treasure just had time to say yes it was, but there wasn't any hurry when Aunt Annie resumed.

'Look at him,' she said, addressing Mrs Treasure and indicating George, 'two-faced, that's what he is. Two-faced and sly! And all these years I trusted him.'

Joe managed to get a word in. 'You can always trust George. He's my friend.'

'I wonder,' said Aunt Annie, turning on him witheringly, 'that you have the bounce to open your mouth Mr Rumbold, after encouraging him to say such things about me. His evil genius, that's what you are, plotting and planning behind my back and undermining my rightful authority. As for trusting him, he give me a kiss last night before going to bed. He never does that. "Oh, ho," I thought, "the kiss of betrayal. Judas Iscariot in person!" And wasn't I right?'

It was bad enough, George felt, to lose face in front of Joe, but to lose face in front of Mrs Treasure was too much.

He said with as much dignity as he could muster, 'If you don't mind Auntie, we'll continue this discussion elsewhere and in private.'

'Hoity-toity! Hark at Mister-me-gentleman! "We'll continue this discussion elsewhere." High and mighty we've become all of a sudden, haven't we? As if butter wouldn't melt in our mouths.'

It was at this moment that Mrs Treasure made a mistake. Up to now, except when called on, she had remained a silent and delighted spectator. But now her enthusiasm spilled over, like a little boy rushing on to the football pitch from behind the barrier and giving the scorer of the wonder goal a quick slap on the back before being chased off again.

'Sly and two-faced is what he is Miss Burton, you're ever so right. I've had my suspicions this many a day he monkeys with the confectionery.' She looked to Aunt Annie for approval.

She didn't get it. All right for Aunt Annie to give George a public ticking off. But Mrs Treasure . . . who did she think she was?

'Did I understand you to say,' she asked ominously, 'that George is dishonest?'

'Well, for instance,' said Mrs Treasure, still quite unaware of the retribution she was about to bring on herself, 'them bulls' eyes I had from him the other week. . . . '

'What about them?'

'They could have been short weight, Miss Burton.'

'Short weight?'

'Definitely.'

'How may I ask, do you know?'

'Because I weighed them when I got home.'

'You wouldn't, by any chance, have eaten some on the way?'

'One or two maybe, but it didn't ought to have made that difference.'

Aunt Annie was quivering with indignation.

'George,' she said, 'give this . . . lady . . . what she come for. You don't want to keep her waiting.'

'There's no hurry,' said Mrs Treasure.

'Oh, isn't there? You ought to think again, Mrs Treasure. You might sully yourself in such company. If I was you I'd shake the dust off of your sandals while the going's good or some of it might stick. But before you hand Mrs Treasure the Seniors, George, you better count them in case you nicked one and there's only nineteen.'

Mrs Treasure began to feel discomforted.

'There's no call for that,' she protested.

'Oh yes there is,' insisted Aunt Annie, 'you might find one missing when you get back. And of course you couldn't be expected to remember whether you'd smoked it on the way or it's George up to his tricks again.'

George had opened the packet and displayed it under Mrs Treasure's nose. Joe couldn't keep silent any longer.

'What you said about George is flat libel and punishable with the full rigours of the law. George is my friend and doesn't know the meaning of dishonest, and unless there's a public apology I shall institute proceedings.'

'You haven't a hope, Mr Rumbold,' Aunt Annie's voice shook with the effort of sublimating uncontrollable rage into biting sarcasm, 'not against cast iron evidence like what Mrs Treasure's got. What's George's honesty all these years and vouched for by thousands of loyal and satisfied customers against Mrs Treasure's perishing bulls' eyes being short when she gets home after gorging herself on the way?'

Mrs Treasure at last realised she had put her foot in it. She took the Seniors from George, paid for them, and then opened the shop door, prepared to run for it if necessary.

'I only said I had my suspicions,' she said.

'Other people have suspicions.' Aunt Annie was poised for the *coup de grâce*. 'And my suspicions tell me that you, Mrs Treasure, are a low-down, sneaking, mischief-making old cow with a nose for scandal and a tongue for gossip that's the envy of every other old cow in the district. Of course,' she added, vocally underlining every word, 'I might or might not be wrong.'

There was a tense pause, during which George went quietly over to Mrs Treasure at the door. She was about to answer back in kind but changed her mind, uncertain of his intentions.

He said, 'You done wrong saying what you said. You better go now. If you come back I shall take it as an apology. If not, you know what to expect.'

The mildness, yet firmness of this deflated her. She had been steeling herself against physical assault at least.

She smiled nervously. 'It's always possible, I suppose, even the most honest of us can make mistakes.'

'Not me. Not with weighing bulls' eyes.'

'I said I might be wrong.'

'You are wrong.'

'See you tomorrow then.'

'There are plenty of other shops,' said Aunt Annie.

'This one's convenient.' She started to go and then, unable to resist it, turned to George and said, 'It's not you I object to. It's your Aunt. She's no lady.'

'Thank God for that,' replied Aunt Annie, overhearing this as was intended, 'for if you're an example of one I'm a bloody duchess.'

'You better go,' said George hastily. And Mrs Treasure went.

George returned to the counter and settled down on his elbows again. Aunt Annie stood still, somewhat breathless after the fray.

Joe said, 'You handled that just right, George. But then I always said you was good in a crisis.'

George said, 'I'm sorry if I upset you, Auntie. I expect I been a bit short-tempered like.'

Joe endorsed this. 'It's worry, Miss Burton. We all get like that sometimes.'

'And if I blow off steam to Joe sometimes, well, no harm intended, Auntie, none in the world.'

Aunt Annie remained silent.

'Come on, Miss Burton,' said Joe, 'he's proffered you the olive branch. What about it?'

She was still silent. George went to one of the glass jars and took off the stopper.

'Have a bulls' eye?' he said.

'I couldn't touch it. It would choke me.'

'Don't tell me there's something else wrong?'

'I'll say there is.'

'Well, out with it.'

'I don't know how to tell you, George. I don't indeed. It's put me into such a flaming temper I haven't known myself since. As if it wasn't bad enough for you to go telling tales behind my back with that Ethel such a prying little cat, and that Treasure saying you give short weight, and Mr Rumbold encouraging you, and all the time it's going over and over in my brain he's abnormal.'

'Abnormal? Joe?' said George.

'What me?' said Joe.

'No. What I overheard the doctor whispering to Alice this afternoon. I heard it distinctly. Abnormal.'

'What's abnormal?'

'Alice's baby of course. And your's too come to think of it George. It made my blood boil, like it was a freak or something.'

'What did she mean?'

'As if Alice and you could have brought a freak into the world. The shame of it! I could have wrung that doctor's neck.'

'But what sort of abnormal?'

'I never took to her. Like a man dressed as a woman she is. How should I know what sort of abnormal? They didn't deign to tell me.'

George didn't speak for a moment. He looked to Joe for support. He got it.

Then he said, 'I'm going up to the hospital, and you better have a lie down, Auntie, after all this to do.'

Aunt Annie was exhausted now and looked it.

'I think I will,' she said, 'I've got a head fit to split.'

'Take a couple of aspirin,' said Joe, 'and I'll bring you a cup of tea.'

'You're very kind, Mr Rumbold. I've always said so,' said Aunt Annie with her usual disregard for accuracy.

When she'd gone George turned to Joe.

'Will you look after the shop while I'm gone?'

'Goes without saying, George.'

'Abnormal. What next I wonder?'

'Might mean anything.'

'That's what I'm afraid of.'

George put on his jacket and fetched his hat from the living room. On his way back through the shop he said, 'If it isn't one thing it's another.'

'You're right,' said Joe.

'I'm off now.'

'It may not be as bad as you think.'

'It might be worse.'

'Mustn't look on the dark side.'

'It's the only side I can see.'

'Every cloud's got a silver lining.'

'This one's an exception.'

Joe shook his head reprovingly. 'I said every cloud. Have I ever let you down George?'

'No, never. I'll give you that.'

'That's something.'

'That's something, yes.'

'So long then.'

'So long.'

George felt a little better as he stepped out into the street and made for the hospital. Good old Joe.

10

The composition of crossword puzzles is something of an art. So, according to the addicts, is the solving of them. But to some readers the chequered square in a corner of their newspaper is a waste of space; perhaps because they consider finding the answer is a knack, a puerile exercise in out-smarting Mr Clever unworthy of their attention, perhaps because each day it is a rankling reminder of their lack of erudition and mental sprightliness.

Fortunately for Miles, the number of brains daily competing with his in this exciting pastime remained fairly constant. He knew as well as Mr Fison that a falling off would mean the sack. The job was poorly paid, but there were many would-be composers waiting to pounce as Mr Fison constantly reminded him. It suited him well. He found it congenial, even rather amusing, and it paid his rent and kept him in food. He had no money of his own, but his translations from the French added a little to his earnings.

When he was thirteen he had spent two years with a family in Geneva; being bullied by the athletic son of his own age, despised by the elder daughter and mercilessly teased by the younger. On the rare occasions when he tried to speak, his accent was atrocious. And because of his accent he spoke as little as possible. The jolly papa called him *Le grand silencieux.* The conscientious mama wrote quarterly reports to his mother in Clapham assuring her it gave them much pleasure and amusement to have him with them, such a *good* boy, no trouble at all, and so delightfully, typically *English.* Reading these letters she felt marvellously proud, not detecting their veiled irony.

He arrived back in England precociously accomplished in the reading and, especially, in the writing of French; also in other and more esoteric pursuits he had at first unwillingly, but later enthusiastically learned from the Swiss boy in the bedroom they shared. He was, not unnaturally, proud of his French; even the Swiss boy had grudgingly congratulated him. Nothing was ever said between them about the other accomplishment, not even in bed.

He was deeply religious at this time and was quite certain he had unforgivably sinned against the Holy Ghost. He used to kneel down and pray, not for himself for he was already lost, but for his mentor; hoping this act might mitigate to some slight extent the appalling punishments that were chalked up for him in the next world. The object of his prayers remained unaltered by them. Time after time when Miles had proof of this he would guiltily welcome his failure, reflecting that since he must already have earned the maximum retribution he might as well be hung for a sheep as a lamb. But afterwards the remorse would return worse than ever and he would go through torments of fright and despair.

His return coincided with the summer holiday at Southwold, but for once its charms failed to work. He went for lonely, desperate walks by the sea and envied the gulls their innocence. His sister had a schoolfriend to stay. He scarcely noticed her. He yearned for Geneva which he had hated so much while he was there; or rather, no, not for Geneva, they could keep that, Rue de Mont Blanc, lake, watches, perfect French accents in smug Swiss voices, all of it; if he could have one more silent, guilty night with his dislikable companion who had bullied him so remorselessly.

And then one day Mary had sprained her ankle and was made to keep it up and his mother had to stay in to look after her and suggested he and the friend shouldn't waste the lovely afternoon indoors, and what about walking across the common to Walberswick and taking a boat up the river? They both reluctantly agreed. After an almost completely silent walk he managed to get a boat and said, 'Shall I row?'

'You might as well,' she replied.

She sat in the stern facing him. He didn't look at her. He disliked rowing because he did it badly.

After about half an hour she said, 'I'll have a go if you like.'

He was glad to let her. They changed places and the boat rocked dangerously. For a moment she clung to him and nearly had him overboard.

'Sorry,' she said.

He was only aware of the touch of her after he sat in the stern and she began to row, which she did well. He forced himself to look at her. It was the first time he had consciously wanted to look at a girl. He started modestly at her feet; then, after a quick glance at her face to see she wasn't watching, surveyed her bare legs. She was wearing shorts and he became fascinated by the rhythmic movement of her thighs inside them, the slight flexion at the knees as her arms reached forward and the smooth tension of all the muscles as she braced her feet against the stretcher and leaned back on the resistance of the water. He found himself framing urgent sentences.

'Would you mind awfully if I touched your legs just between the knee and your shorts?'

'I hope you won't be offended if I actually feel the way those muscles work?'

'I've never wanted to touch anything quite so much as your legs. Only for a moment. May I?'

He was suddenly conscious that she was looking at him.

He heard himself say, 'Would you mind awfully if I . . .' He stopped.

She was looking embarrassed and puzzled.

'Yes?' she asked. 'Would I mind awfully if you what?'

He couldn't go on.

Then she laughed. 'Oh,' she said, 'if you want to go behind a bush why not say so? I'll land you.'

It seemed the best way out of their mutual embarrassment. The next day she left. He never saw her again. Mary decided she didn't like her.

From then on he couldn't make up his mind whether he'd rather be in Geneva or in the boat with Mary's friend. As it was, he went to the Grammar school in Clapham and then on to University College in Gower Street. But he failed his degree because, when it came to the viva, his nerve failed him and he could only stammer apologetically in his atrocious accent that though he really knew exactly what he wanted to say, for some inexplicable reason he couldn't say it. His failure seemed to break his mother's heart. She had staked everything on his brains and he was to reward her with a brilliant career. When she died, there was no money left and no brilliant career. Mary was in the north training to be a nurse. That took care of her. He was faced with the daunting prospect of having to take care of himself.

Answering newspaper advertisements brought in a few replies all suggesting interviews. With the fiasco of the viva still fresh in his mind he attended them. He could hear himself being ineffective, apologetic and nervous, and the brave attempts at confidence going off like dud cartridges. So, though he wasn't in the least surprised, he became increasingly alarmed that he was still without a job three weeks after his mother's funeral. Grief at her death was intensified by guilt. He was convinced he was responsible for it as surely as if he had murdered her. Murder by ineffectiveness, by the lost cause, by the unredeemed promise; he might just as well have strangled her. In spending such disproportionate time trying to resolve his own physical needs and mental conflict he had been inexcusably selfish. And all to no purpose. He was as far away as ever from a solution and came to think of himself as a lost soul. He haunted bridges, made elaborate preparations for turning on the gas, counted aspirin tablets. But suicide needs its own particular courage and at six o'clock one cold November morning he found he lacked that too. In despair he lay across his bed and cried. His hands kept beating the pillow as if it were he, and he a disciplinarian hurting himself more than he hurt the pillow. His cries had subsided into moans, long drawn-out, soft, high-pitched.

He rolled over and found he was lying across *The Times* in which he had been job hunting the day before. It was lying on its face, and upside down in front of his eyes was the crossword puzzle. He went on moaning as he looked at it. Then he pulled the top of the paper from under him and turned it the right way up. He read the clues through mechanically and without reference to their meaning until he realised he had solved one. He leaned over to the chair across which his jacket was lying, took a pencil from it and filled in the word. Shortly after he filled in two more. The moans became spasmodic, but continued at increasingly longer intervals. When he got stuck he turned to his despair almost as if it were an old friend, but each time was drawn back to the puzzle to try a fresh approach to a recalcitrant clue. Once he got up to consult the dictionary. In two hours the puzzle was finished. Then he made himself some tea and ate a bowl of cornflakes and milk, wandering back to the bed at intervals to admire the fulfilled puzzle and once smiling, in spite of himself, at the ingenuity of thirteen across.

After breakfast he drew a chequered square on a sheet of paper, made a geometrical pattern of black squares within it, filled in the crosswords and spent a fascinating morning inventing clues for them. Then, encouraged to boldness by the result, he sent it with a short covering note to one of the more serious weeklies. After an anxious ten days the reply came back. It enclosed a cheque for a guinea and the suggestion that he might care to send a few more.

At last he had achieved something for himself. Encouraged by this, he wrote a good letter in French to an advertiser in *The Times* Personal column, resulting, without interview, in some commercial translating from time to time. By 1939 he was contributing regular crosswords to a daily, a weekly and a monthly and doing translations for several business firms. All this work didn't bring in much money, but then he didn't need much. He had found the room in Frame Street which was cheap and, except for himself, he had no other responsibilities.

Some time before the war, the director of one of the firms for which he translated wrote to him with a surprising suggestion. He had met a friend at the B.B.C. who had asked him if he knew of any first-class translators. If war broke out they would need to increase their staff. Would Miles like him to put his name forward? He replied that he would, as long as he never had to broadcast or go within a hundred yards of a studio.

At the outbreak he was immediately posted to Wales. He kept on the room in Frame Street in case he should be moved back. Several times he was, and was so frightened of the air raids he always sheltered in the tubes at nights and was a great help to the aged and infirm.

After the war he got the sack from the B.B.C., not because he was incompetent but because they were cutting down staff and, of those under review, he made the poorest impression, having neither the courage or inclination for the occasional get-together with his colleagues at the local. He was glad to get back to the old life where all communications, except those of his choice, were through the post. He had gone on composing crosswords during the war and, if anything, had increased his standing with the papers he had contributed to, as well as achieving occasional commissions from new ones.

The evening after his visit to the hospital he was sitting at his work table in Frame Street and trying to decide whether he should clue the word 'restrain' as 'Stop the deluge prayed Noah' or 'The thing with carriages is put on the brake' or 'Forcibly repress backward skills, putting them in harness'. But he found it hard to concentrate. Again and again he had gone over each detail of the meeting with Alice. He was doing it now. It had been an ordeal which he had come through so much better than he had a right to expect. And it hadn't been an end in itself; it was a beginning also. That was what was so exciting. Previously, when trying to justify his way of life which he constantly did, he always told himself that he lived in his phantasies and they transcended reality. But what if phantasy and reality merged and became one? No need for justification when such fulfilment beckoned.

He put the crossword aside and took out his precious exercise book. Now he had learned the family's name he had given it a title, *Remnants of my Past, Present and Future,* and spent some time inscribing it on the cover in bold, Roman capitals, executed meticulously in Indian ink. He handled the book as his mother had taught him to handle the Bible when he was a child, tenderly and respectfully. He went carefully through the first, the factual part, stopping from time to time to savour again some incident which had given him particular pleasure, and adding one or two freshly remembered details to the long description of his visit to the hospital, which he had written immediately on his return. When he reached the second part he read it more closely and with a different kind of pleasure. If things went well all the roles in which he had cast himself, the loved and loving husband, the jolly uncle, the doctor, the trusted friend, could be realised. More—he hardly dare contemplate the possibility, it excited him so much—the fusion and mystical communion, the final coming together, so that his mother was Alice and Mary was Ethel and he, he was Rodney and Rodney . . .

He frowned and looked up from the book. Was that what he wanted? Was it? To love Alice as he had loved his mother? As Rodney loved her? Sometimes yes, but not always. That was what was so confusing. In hospital for instance, when she had leaned over to put the grapes on the table and her bed-jacket slipped off her shoulders and the curve of her breast under the thin nightdress didn't droop but seemed to thrust upwards and outwards, and he wanted so much to touch and he knew she was aware of this and was pleased while they laughed together over Grannie Starey and the grapes. He sighed. How much easier life was for people who knew what they wanted. As he thought of Alice's breast now it was just as desirable but not for the same reason. It was desirable because it had suckled Rodney and was, perhaps at this very moment, suckling the new baby. He went to the window and stared moodily out. He must get this thing sorted out once and for all. It was ridiculous at his age to live in a continuing and adolescent ambivalence; to be still heterosexually a virgin, not even to have put himself to the test. God knows, he thought, as he watched a taxi draw up at the door, he had plenty of opportunity on the third floor where the two tarts did such a flourishing trade. Once he had talked to them; they were very polite. Why didn't he come up and have a drink occasionally, a bit of a lark? They worked separately or together and they betted they could show him a few things he didn't know. If only they realised how right they were! He knew nothing. He had tried to smile, to appear grateful and unembarrassed. He was neither. At that time his mind had been going back deliciously to the delights of being bullied in Geneva, not by a woman.

Odd that no one had got out of the taxi; perhaps it was waiting for one of the clients upstairs. He saw the driver was looking directly at him and was about to move back into the room when he realised who it was. His heart seemed to turn a rapid somersault; he felt sick, not only with fear but with a strange excitement. He went behind the patchwork screen and sat on the bed. He must have waited at least a minute before he heard the two knocks on the front door. It never occurred to him not to answer. The driver had on a huge leather overcoat in spite of the warm evening and his peaked cap gave him an official air.

'I'd like a word with you.'

'Yes?'

'Inside if you don't mind.'

He pushed past Miles and walked through the hall and into the room as if he owned it. Miles followed. The driver sat in the working chair in front of the table, took off his greasy cap, put it on the precious exercise book and wiped his forehead with the palm of his hand.

'If you'll excuse me . . .' Miles moved forward anxiously to recover the diary.

'I won't,' said the driver.

'You've put your cap on my book.'

'So what?'

'I'd rather you didn't.'

'Oh, would you? I wonder why.' He picked up his cap with one hand and the diary with the other.

As he touched it Miles cried out, 'No, no you mustn't . . . you mustn't,' and ran forward but the driver, in spite of his bulk, moved with surprising speed and put the table between them. Then, in a mock posh accent, he read the title out loud, '*Remnants of my Past, Present and Future.*'

'If you open it,' cried Miles, 'I'll . . . I'll . . .'

'Kill me? Like what you was going to do to that poor kid in my cab the other night. Listen, mate. I know what you are; that's why I come here. You give yourself away everything you do and every word you say. That book you left in the cab . . .'

'You don't mean to say you've still got it?'

'I've got it all right.'

'Oh . . . Oh, I see . . .'

Miles sat in his chair and regarded the driver on the other side of the table. He told himself he was panicking unnecessarily. The man was a brute of course, but at least he was honest. He'd come to return the Hieronymus Bosch.

'Where is it then?'

'What?'

'My book. I went to the Lost Property. They hadn't got it. It didn't occur to me you would be kind enough to bring it back yourself.'

The driver laughed shortly. He walked over to the window, opened it at the bottom, spat out of it with accuracy and venom, closed it and turned.

'That book,' he said, picking his words deliberately, 'that book is a funny old book. Very funny.'

Best to be conciliatory. 'In some ways I suppose it is. It's also one of my most treasured possessions.'

'Is that so? Well, mate, I've given that book a bit of my time, quite a bit, and I come to the conclusion whoever done them pictures was up the pole.'

No use arguing, not with this man. 'Of course, they're not everyone's taste. But I'll be very glad to have them back.'

But the driver wasn't to be diverted from his line of thought. 'Some of them pictures is nothing short of disgusting.'

He leaned right over Miles so that their faces were only a few inches apart, forcing him to turn sideways in the chair to avoid the unbearable stench of his breath.

'I'll tell you what I think, mate. I think anyone says he likes them pictures is up the pole and disgusting himself.'

As he spoke he rolled the exercise book into a hard little baton and hit Miles sharply across the cheek with it.

'Look at me you dirty bastard.'

Miles put his hand to his face protectively. It stung like hell. He forced himself to turn back in the chair and tried to speak with dignity, but his voice was trembling and high-pitched with fear.

'How dare you! How dare you invade my room and ... Give me back my exercise book at once.' He held out his hand for it.

'You asked for it,' said the driver, and hit him viciously across the palm with it. Miles withdrew his hand with a sharp little cry. He started to get to his feet saying 'Unless you give me that book and leave at once I shall go for the police,' but the driver roughly pushed him back into his chair. It tilted and fell on its back, taking him with it. His head hit the floor with a bump. He lay there feeling stunned and helpless. The driver picked up the chair and sat on it.

'Don't make me laugh saying you'll go for the police,' he said, 'because I'll probably be there before you. And don't make me laugh thinking I come here to give you back your book. I come here because you and me's going to have a little talk. I know what you are, see? I can tell your sort a mile off. There isn't a kid in the district's safe from you. Not unless you got someone to keep an eye on you like. Well, that's what you bloody got. Me!'

He emphasised the 'Me' by leaning back in the chair and stretching out his foot so that it prodded Miles painfully in the stomach. He didn't cry out or protest. He lay there wondering what on earth to do. Useless to try to rush from the room; this brute was so much stronger than him. And even if he did get out he could hardly go to the police while the driver had the exercise book. It wasn't so much that it contained details of his feelings towards Alice and Ethel and Rodney, though God knows these could be misunderstood and misinterpreted to a frightening and dangerous degree; it contained himself, naked and vulnerable. He thought he would die if anyone else read it. He must get it back. Somehow he must.

He sat up, rubbing his head and thinking how foolish he must look; he on the floor and this loathsome man sitting in his chair and holding the exercise book as if it were a symbol of power, which indeed it was only he didn't know it.

'If you will go now,' he said, 'I will overlook this monstrous intrusion, but on the strict understanding that you give me your word you won't . . .' He hesitated. He was going to say 'molest me further' but, overwrought as he was, he rejected it as far too ridiculous a cliché for such outrageous circumstances.

But the driver interrupted. 'I know what you was going to say. You was going to say, "as long as I don't come back". You could have saved your breath, mate. Anyone could see you was scared stiff. Why? Because you're guilty. But not any more. Not from now on. You got me to reckon with, that's why.'

He kept gesticulating and hitting the table with the exercise book as he spoke.

Miles was unable to stop himself crying out, 'Please, please! You're hurting my book. You're a brute, a brute . . .' and realised immediately he couldn't have made a worse mistake.

The driver gave him a crafty sort of look. Then he deliberately unrolled the book, opened it and flipped through the pages without attempting to read it. Once or twice he wet his middle finger on his tongue and pushed the pages across from their corners so that they curved up and creased. Once the book slipped and was suspended by a single page which tore. Miles watched in silent horror.

The driver was saying, 'Set a lot of store by this book, don't you, mate? Enough of it, isn't there? Going to take me quite a while to wade through this lot.'

All coherent thought had deserted Miles. One question kept running through his head, 'What can I do? Oh God, what can I do to stop this happening? What can I do? What?'

He didn't realise he was mouthing the words until the driver replied. 'You can't do nothing. No, I'm a liar. One thing you can do; lay off the kids. If it wasn't for you being such a low-down crawling bastard I might feel sorry for you. But you bloody are, so I'm bloody not.'

Miles said, 'Look, I swear you've got this wrong. I've never hurt a child in my life. I swear it on my solemn word. That exercise book is private. It contains a great deal of material which couldn't make sense to anyone else but me. Please give it back to me. Can't you understand that a person's private papers are . . . are . . . sacred? You must have a spark of human feeling and decency. I'm appealing to that in you. Please . . .'

In his distress he was kneeling in front of the driver; his voice had risen to a falsetto of anxiety and his hands made small grotesque snatches at the air.

The driver looked steadily at him. He was smiling slightly and his little eyes were screwed up appraisingly. Once he licked his lips, the tongue flickering delicately round the corners of his big mouth. At last he spoke.

'Everything you say gives me more appetite. Just everything. I'm not much of a reader. Waste of time I call it. But this I'm looking forward to.'

He put on his cap, stood up, undid the top button of his overcoat and crammed the exercise book deep into an inner pocket.

As he did up the button again he said, 'For the moment what's in this book's between you and me. For the moment, see? When I've had a bit of a read of it I'll be back and then . . . well, we'll see about what's next.'

'I shall go and see my solicitors,' stammered Miles, 'they'll force you to . . .'

'Go on, go. But you can't prove nothing, you cringing bastard, and you bloody know it. You asked me to drop round and see you. You asked me to read this crap. You asked my opinion. That's my story and I'm sticking to it. You prove it different.'

He walked to the door and turned. The sun had gone down and the room was getting dark. From where Miles knelt, crouched back on his heels, the doorway seemed to be dwarfed by the bulk of the man. He expected him to have to stoop to go through. His mind was empty; beyond feeling, beyond caring. He saw what he saw out of focus, as if he were looking past it at something in the distance. He heard the voice without understanding.

'And just in case you get ideas mate, dirty ideas, I don't have to go into details, do I?—remember I got ways of knowing, same as I had ways of knowing where you live. I don't claim I got the all-seeing eye, but it don't miss much, least of all you from this moment on. And I'll see you get what's coming to you if I have to do it myself. Christ, you make me sick!'

He spat savagely on the floor and went out. In a moment the front door slammed, the taxi started up, crashed its gears angrily and drove off.

11

Doctor Fallowfield had warned Alice she'd have to stay in hospital at least a week and probably ten days; partly because she had suffered severe abrasions and shock from the fall downstairs and needed complete rest under supervision, partly because the baby appeared to be abnormal.

'Not physically you understand,' she had said to Alice, 'he's a healthy specimen, though a bit light weight. Mentally.'

Alice's face fell.

'You don't mean to say he's going to be one of them idiots, doctor?'

'Good God no, quite the contrary. We've been watching him closely. Have you noticed his eyes?'

'Blue like mine.'

'I don't mean their colour, dear girl. I mean their expression.'

'What about it?'

'Extraordinary. They seem to be noticing things. Follow you around. Well, I mean, you get that in a baby of about three months but after—what it it?—five days . . . most abnormal. Nothing to worry about. Quite the contrary. You've probably got a genius on your hands.'

Alice remembered Doctor Fallowfield threatening her with a genius before the birth. She hadn't liked the idea then. She didn't like it now. The doctor went on to say they wanted to watch the baby carefully because it might well prove important to the study of childhood development. She was enthusiastic. She wasn't going to indulge in peeps into the future but she didn't rule out the possibility that, just as nature produced the occasional throw-back—the mongols and morons of this world—

this child might be a sort of throw-forward, a preview so to speak of every infant's development in the unforeseeable future.

'So you see, dear girl, you and your baby might become pretty important people.'

'I don't want to become an important person.'

'Whether you want to or not, you've possibly made a unique contribution to science. Of course it's early days yet and we may be wrong. But I don't think so. I'll come and see you again at the end of the week. Don't look so worried, dear girl.'

Alice felt worried and said so.

'I don't know what my husband will say,' she added, 'he's ever so quiet and retiring and he wouldn't want to be mixed up with all that carry on.'

'He'll be very proud if he's any sense.'

'Not George. He's got sense all right but he's obstinate.'

'Obstinacy won't change the baby for him. I'll have a word with him.' The doctor moved on to Mrs Starey.

Alice had of course been aware of Aunt Annie hovering in the background and then momentarily cutting into the conversation to say goodbye, but she hadn't realised her exclusion had given offence or that she had overheard anything. So she was surprised when, later in the evening, she was told George was demanding to see her. It was against the rules of course but, being her husband, the sister was prepared to give him ten minutes if Alice wanted it. Most unusual for George to ask to break rules, he was always such a stickler. Must be something up.

She had been thinking a great deal about the prospect of having a genius in the family. Bad enough to have had the brat at all; as if she hadn't enough to do looking after the other two. Now they were beginning to do things for themselves, she'd got to start all over again with nappies and feeding and all the rest of the palaver of being a good mum. And for a genius, thank you very much. All very well for Doctor Fallowfield to talk about scientific study but geniuses, Alice supposed, wet their pants and had to be fed and clothed and looked after same as anyone else. And all this just as she had met Mr Madgwick and he had been so nice and suggested, quite off his own bat, a trip to the sea. And if one trip to the sea she didn't see why there shouldn't be others.

Her imagination got to work. They would walk along the beach till they were away from the town and find a cove where the cliffs curved down almost to the level of the shore. And they'd find a sheltered spot on the short grass behind some bushes, out of the wind and in the sun. After she'd sent the children down to the shore with spades and pails, she and Mr Madgwick would talk easily for a while of this and that and then a silence, and she wasn't looking at him but she knew he was looking at her and after a bit he said, 'I've picked a flower for you. May I give it you?' and she said, 'Please do.' So he came and sat beside her and said 'Here it is', and he was breathing rather quickly and said, 'I've got something else I'd like to give you and it's this', and he suddenly took her in his arms and crushed her tremulous mouth to his and kept whispering, 'I want you I want you I want you' and . . .

Not much chance of that now. Not with her being at the beck and call of doctors and scientists and interviewed on the telly and articles in the papers. A fine thing to happen just when you'd had the chance of a—what did they call it?—an intrigue, yes that was it, an intrigue, and what you needed for that were time and secrecy. Not a bloody hope of either.

George came into the ward, sheepishly conscious he was a lone male among women, but nevertheless anxiously determined.

He drew up a chair and whispered to Alice, 'What's all this about abnormal?'

Alice told him. She kept her voice down because everyone in the ward was trying to listen and she had made up her mind they shouldn't.

When she'd finished she added that she supposed Aunt Annie had overheard a few words and got it all wrong, and George said yes and told her about the row in the shop.

Alice laughed. 'Good old Auntie,' she said.

'Mind you,' whispered George, 'I don't blame her. I'd have thought the same.'

'About it being a freak?'

'Yes.'

'Well it is, isn't it?'

George considered this. 'What about having a look at him?'

Alice signalled the red-haired nurse who said she'd have to ask the sister.

While she was gone Alice said, 'If the doctor's right it's going to mean nothing but trouble. I told you at the time, didn't I? You ought to have warned me before instead of pouncing on me like that in the middle of the night. Like an animal you were.'

Her voice had risen and George, nervously looking round, caught Mrs Starey's eye. She was leaning right out of the bed, pretending to look for something in the bed-table drawer and he knew she must have heard. She quickly looked away.

'Put a sock in it,' he whispered, indicating Mrs Starey with a jerk of his head. He was dreadfully embarrassed.

'Takes two to do the trick,' he added reproachfully.

'I was half asleep.'

Alice knew she was being unfair but she didn't mind. The nurse brought the baby and gave it to her. She took it as if she had never seen it before.

'Got to treat him with respect now, haven't we?' said the nurse knowingly.

'I don't want this to get around the ward. Nothing's certain yet. That's what the doctor said.'

'We've had our orders, strict secrecy.' The nurse smiled. 'But isn't it thrilling?'

'I'm not so sure.'

'Sister says you can have him for five minutes.'

When the nurse had gone, Alice whispered, 'Now let's see what's so special about him.'

George leaned forward and they both peered at him. He was lying in Alice's arms and staring at the ceiling. George advanced a stubby finger, touched his cheek and said, 'Goo-goo.'

The baby looked at him dispassionately.

'Goo-goo,' said George and prodded his cheek again.

The baby yawned a miniature yawn and looked commiseratingly up at Alice.

'I don't see nothing special about that,' said George.

Alice laughed. 'What did you expect?'

'I thought he might say "goo-goo" back, or smile or something.'

'Don't be so daft. You don't want him to think he's got an idiot for his dad.'

The baby now transferred his gaze to George again. It was an unwinking and exploratory gaze and it made George feel uncomfortable. He was, after all, supposed to be the inspector, not the inspected. He tried to stare back. The baby's eyes were large and blue and slightly protuberant like Alice's and, like hers, seemed full of brooding wonder. He could hear her laughing.

'What's funny,' he asked, not shifting his eyes.

'You are. Having a staring match with a baby.'

At this it gave George a break and transferred its stare to Alice, so saving him just in time from the shame of having to lower his eyes and admit defeat.

'What shall we call you?' said Alice, looking down at it.

'I've been thinking about that. I've been thinking of Gordon.'

'Whatever for?'

'It was my granddad's second name. You know, after that General.'

'What General?'

'He got bumped off by the fuzzy-wuzzies. It's quite a nice name. I've known several Gordons. All quite nice and . . .'

Alice caught his sleeve.

'Look, George, look at him."

'What about him?'

'Don't you see? Looking backwards and forwards between us as we speak. Just like he understands. You say something.'

At first George couldn't think of anything. Then he began rather self-consciously, 'As I was saying, Alice, Gordon is quite a nice name, it's . . .' and then stopped.

The baby's eyes rolled sideways and looked at him.

'I hate it,' said Alice.

Its eyes rolled back and looked up into hers.

'See what I mean?' she said excitedly.

'Yes, I do.'

'I was thinking of Miles.' She spoke casually. She knew there was going to be opposition.

'No.'

The concentrated effort of shifting his gaze from parent to parent was telling on the baby. His eyelids began to droop.

'Come closer.'

Alice gave a warning jerk of the head in the direction of Mrs Starey, who was leaning over the bed-table drawer again and now not even pretending to look for anything. George moved his chair as near to the bed head as it would go and Alice leaned over to him so that their faces almost touched.

'It's Mr Madgwick's name,' she whispered.

'That's why I don't like it.'

'I want him to be a godfather.'

'You're up the pole.'

'He's a scholar.'

'What's that got to do with it?'

'His nibs is going to be a genius. Right?'

'Right.'

'I'm not clever, George. No more are you. But Mr Madgwick is. And if Mr Madgwick's his godfather he's going to take an interest in him, isn't he?'

'That's what I'm afraid of. If that taximan's right . . .'

'He's not right.'

It was always the same. She had things so beautifully worked out in her mind. When she explained them to Aunt Annie they sounded logical and inevitable. Not so with George because she knew he expected her ideas to be cockeyed. The baby's eyelids flickered and then opened. He looked up at her and gave her a reassuring little smile. It might have been wind but she felt comforted.

'See that smile. He likes his name. Aunt Annie's going to like it too. So are you, George.'

'No.'

'You'll get used to it.'

'I still like Gordon.'

Alice thought for a moment. Inspiration wasn't long in coming. 'Gordon can be his second name. Miles Gordon. Not bad, eh?'

The nurse came back.

'Time's up,' she said, looking at George, 'both for you and baby I'm afraid.'

George said, 'I don't know what Aunt Annie will think of all this.'

'She'll be glad to know we didn't produce one of them idiots.'

'We'd hardly do that, would we, Alice?'

'People do.'

'Not us. Not you and me.' He looked at her affectionately.

Sensing the moment she said, 'I'm glad you agree about Miles.'

He didn't answer. Just hinted at a shrug of the shoulders and left. At the door he turned and waved. She blew him a kiss. He smiled and went out. The nurse was looking at her quizzically.

'I'm very fond of him,' Alice said, 'he's the salt of the earth.'

'Anyone could see that.'

But Alice was living in a golden future. It was a brilliant idea to make Mr Madgwick his godfather. He wouldn't refuse, she knew that, not when he understood about the baby being a genius and them needing someone around with a posh brain to give clever answers to clever questions and advise him about schooling and lead him—yes, that was it—lead him in the way a genius ought to go. Even George would see the sense of that. 'Mr Madgwick, our boy's godfather, such a clever brain and a real gentleman. With a genius on our hands we'd have been lost without him.' She could hear herself saying it, enjoying the envy of the friends and neighbours and having a quiet laugh because none of them knew there was so much more to it than just that. Oh, it was heaven sent, this infant of hers! 'George, I must just slip round to Frame Street and have a word with Mr Madgwick about little Miles' algebra.' As simple as that. Her mind darted from one possibility to another. Mr Madgwick was shy and reserved, but that didn't always signify; smouldering fires and all that. Fanned by the gusty breezes of her own desires they would leap into tongues of flame and consume her, consume her utterly . . .

'Are you all right, dear?'

It was Mrs Starey. She was sitting on the side of her bed facing Alice, and getting into her dressing gown.

'Of course, Mrs Starey. Why shouldn't I be?'

'Such a funny look on your face you had, and breathing funny. I thought you was having a fit or something.'

'I'm all right.'

Mrs Starey felt under the bed with her foot and produced a pair of mules decorated with mauve feathers. Her feet chased them around and finally found the way into them. Alice wondered if they'd been chosen to match her varicose veins.

'I'm off down the passage to make myself comfy, dear. But if there's anything I can do . . .'

'Nothing. Honest.'

Mrs Starey's face was glistening with the effort of cloaking her burning curiosity with a mantle of motherly concern.

'Something wrong with baby, isn't there?'

Alice didn't reply.

'I know what it is to have trouble. Lost my second, a dear little girl. It was me or her and they chose me, not being R. C.s if you know what I mean.'

Alice said 'What a shame' and then realised how double-edged she'd been.

'Trouble,' went on Mrs Starey, 'trouble, it comes to all of us some of the time and to some of us all the time. And now my latest, Doctor Fallowfield says he's got to have a little operation . . . you know . . . well, I mean, it's not as if it's serious but . . . well, it's not as if we're Jews.'

Alice smiled. 'It's nothing. We had to have Rodney done. You should have heard our Aunt Annie. "Why can't they leave people alone?" she said. "No sooner do they come into the world than the surgeons are waiting to snip, and if they're not snipping one thing it's another." '

'Just what my hubby said.' Mrs Starey was warming to this promising subject. 'But mum pointed out they done Jesus Christ, "and what's good enough for our Lord," she says, "is good enough for us." She's ever so religious of course, but if you think of it like that it makes you feel better about it.'

She came over and sat on Alice's bed, put a hot hand on hers and gave it a little squeeze.

'We all got to help each other in this world. We only pass through it once, dear. And if I can help you bear your cross, whatever it may be, just say the word. Because you can trust me. I can see you're in trouble and I know from experience it will make you feel a whole lot better to share it with another.'

She sat head slightly on one side, her tongue just showing between her teeth, the picture of the trustworthy confidante. So much so that Alice was tempted to tell her everything.

But she said, 'There's nothing exactly wrong, Mrs Starey. It's ever so kind of you to want to help me, but it's one of those things you can only do for yourself, like going to the toilet if you know what I mean.'

Mrs Starey's frustrated curiosity almost choked her. She got up, pulled her dressing gown modestly round her already modest nightdress and said untruthfully, 'I'm the last to want to poke my nose into other people's business.'

'I know that,' Alice replied, equally untruthfully.

'Of course,' went on Mrs Starey, admiring the mauve plumes on her mules, 'that's the risk you run when you offer a helping hand.'

'What is?'

'Getting it slapped. By the way, I know you won't mind me mentioning it, Mrs Remnant—even your best friend isn't supposed to tell you—but I'm sure you'll take it as a kindness. I always take Chloritabs for my bad breath. And you'd do well to do the same. And now I really must . . .'

She started to go. Alice couldn't resist it.

'Chloritabs,' she called after her, '—I'm sure you'll take it as a kindness—don't do the trick.'

She watched with satisfaction the mauve mules put to flight and snuggled down in bed to live her own life in her own private world.

12

Immediately the cab driver left with *Remnants of my Past, Present and Future* Miles took four sleeping pills and lay on his bed. Two usually worked well, but he wanted to be quite sure of his escape from such hideous reality. For a long time he didn't sleep. The driver's visit went through and through his brain, out of sequence, distorted, nightmarish and vivid. It was as if those horrors were happening to someone else and he desperately wished they wouldn't obtrude on his bruised and exhausted brain. Without opening his eyes he found the miniature teddy bear under the pillow, but for once it brought no comfort.

Short, disconnected moments of the interview progressed like an endless and crazily edited band of film which he was forced to witness against his will. After an hour of this torture he opened his eyes. It was dark. And vividly out of the darkness the non-stop film went on. He tried turning on the light. It continued in a dazzle that hurt his eyes. He quickly turned it off again. Then he got up in the darkness and, with the assurance of a blind man, wandered slowly about the room touching familiar objects and trying to bring his brain to consider them, to visualise them. The philosophical concept of Subjective Realism for instance; was the typewriter really there or just an idea in his brain? Or the little pile of shillings he prudently kept on the mantelpiece for the gas meter? Or his mother's photograph in the leather frame? He had tried this successfully in the past when he wanted to escape from obsessive thought. No good. The horror went on relentlessly and simultaneously so that consecutive thought of any kind was impossible and he soon gave up the attempt.

He moved about the room in swift little darts, pressing his fists against his eyes in the hope of blotting out what his brain forced him to see and continually retreating from his continual failure to do so. He must have collapsed on the floor from utter exhaustion.

He woke next morning, cramped, stiff and cold, wondering how on earth he had got there. When the enormity of what had happened returned to him he took two more sleeping pills, crawled into bed and slept till late in the evening. On re-awakening he got out of bed and went mechanically through his customary routine of getting up. After washing and shaving, he picked up the slop pail to take it down the hall to the lavatory. First he looked out of the window. All clear. As he approached the door he gave way to an unreasoning flurry of panic when he remembered he had forgotten to lock it after the driver had left. He stood irresolutely for at least a minute before he could bring himself to go into the hall. Then he stepped out and tiptoed to the lavatory. The house was unusually quiet. Before he came out he waited for the noise from the filling cistern to stop so that he could hear if anyone was in the hall or coming down the stairs. When he judged it was safe, he tiptoed back to his room. As he reached it the front door suddenly opened and he couldn't stifle a gasp of fear. It was one of the tarts from above with a customer.

'Something wrong, dear?'

He couldn't trust himself to answer. He shook his head, bolted into the room and locked the door. He made tea and got himself a meal. He even managed to eat it. All the time he was successfully making an effort not to think. But whenever the front door opened and shut he stopped whatever he was doing and listened to the ensuing footsteps in the hall, afraid they should stop outside his door. Once he heard a taxi draw up outside. He crept to the window and peered out from behind the curtain. Even then he managed not to let himself think. He endured what seemed like an endless hiatus of meaningless fear. The fare got out, not the driver: another customer for upstairs.

He would have to let himself think sooner or later. But not yet. He couldn't even admit to himself yet that what had happened had happened. He succeeded in existing from moment to moment in the small and tangible world of his own things and his personal routines.

He composed a more than ordinarily clever set of clues for the current crossword, only once having to refer to Brewer's *Dictionary of Phrase and Fable* where he found, as he had expected, that Hebron was one of the six Cities of Refuge under Mosaic Law. He put the completed puzzle in an envelope, addressed it to Mr Fison and stamped it. All the time he was aware that the monster of realisation was waiting behind the flimsy barrier he had set up. It must break through soon. But still not yet. He turned on the wireless and recognised with nostalgic joy Brahms conjuring order out of chaos in the last movement of the third symphony and resolving it finally into a mystery of peace and assurance. He felt the peace and assurance as always, but second-hand, as he had momentarily felt the laughing delight of some children playing hop-scotch when he was on his way to his mother's funeral.

As he turned off the wireless he wondered what he should do next to keep his brain busy. He dare not indulge in his customary phantasies for they would bring the monster of reality rampaging into the open. He felt like a man with only an umbrella between him and a man-eating tiger. Desperately he arranged twenty-one objects on a tray, memorised them for one minute by the clock, covered the tray and was beginning to write them down when there was a sharp tap on the door.

He glanced at the clock. Ten-fifteen. He sat motionless, hoping whoever it was would go away. But the tap was repeated, sharper and more insistent. He walked noiselessly to the door and pressed his ear against it, hoping to catch some slight sound which might identify the visitor.

Involuntarily he called out, 'Who is it?'

And a child's voice replied, 'It's me.'

He opened the door at once. It was Ethel smiling up at him and wriggling with what experience had taught her to suppose was irresistible charm.

'My Aunt Annie wants to see you,' she said.

Without a word he followed her up the stairs. On the top flight she turned to him and said, 'This is where mum fell down. We thought she was dead but she wasn't.' She looked tragically down at the landing. 'But she might have been.' He thought he detected a fleeting pang of disappointment. She sat astride the banister rail, slid down it, giggling pleasurably, and arrived on the newel with a satisfying bump, jumped off it and ran past him up the stairs calling out, 'Auntie, Auntie, I found him!'

He followed her into the room. Aunt Annie was seated at a trestle table surrounded by garments festooning from every hook, picture rail and ledge. She was re-winding a spool on the sewing machine. Rodney was watching over her shoulder, quite fascinated by the precision with which the little pendulum arm fed the cotton backwards and forwards along the crescive cylinder. Aunt Annie didn't look up but turned the handle at increased speed so that, to Rodney's eyes, her hand became a circular pink ambience miraculously imparting energy and frenzied power. The machine whirred and rattled and buzzed and gave out rhythmical squeaks of protest.

'Don't breathe down my neck, Rodney,' Aunt Annie shouted above the din, 'it makes me feel nervous.'

Rodney's fascination was too much for him. He put out a finger and tried to touch the spool. Aunt Annie's hand materialised out of the pink ambience, gave him a sharp slap, and returned to it so swiftly that the machine continued without a pause. Rodney sprang back with a yelp and trod heavily on Miles' toe. He was about to cry, but changed his mind and smiled his wistful smile instead, putting his hand trustfully into Miles'. Not to be outdone, Ethel seized his other hand and smiled competitively.

The machine suddenly stopped. Aunt Annie rose from the table and surveyed the group with amusement.

'What are you playing at? Statues? Sometimes I wish they was, Mr Madgwick. Pretty to look at, no trouble except flicking over with a duster and silent as tombstones. Sit down.' She picked up an afternoon tea-gown and revealed a chair. 'Ethel, you put the kettle on. You'd like a cup of tea, Mr Madgwick.'

As this was a statement of fact and not a question Miles hardly liked to refuse, though a cup of tea was the last thing he wanted. He sat down and Rodney immediately climbed on his knee.

'Cupboard love,' said Aunt Annie, 'he's after something.'

Rodney smiled and hunched his shoulders appealingly.

'That old book. What you promised.'

'Books,' said Aunt Annie, 'isn't on the agenda.'

Ethel returned with a full kettle and lit the gas ring under it. She immediately noticed Rodney had taken advantage of her absence to achieve Miles' lap. She knew exactly how to show her displeasure. She stood quite still and pouted. Aunt Annie removed a great heap of frilly nightwear from another armchair, sat in it and beckoned her.

'Come and sit on your old Auntie's knee like the little love you are.'

For answer Ethel turned her back and sauntered impertinently to the window, humming a little tune.

'She's put about,' said Aunt Annie indulgently, 'you can always tell with her. What's got into you, my pet?'

'Nothing.' Ethel was sulking with just the right mixture of hurt and indignation.

'Oh yes there is. Can't deceive your Auntie.'

Ethel sniffed ominously.

'Tears isn't on the agenda neither.'

'I want to sit on his knee too.'

Rodney said quickly, 'I found him first. He's mine,' and gave Miles a hug.

'I hate you,' said Ethel, 'I wish you'd been done in by one of them macintoshes and staring eyes. I wish . . .'

But Aunt Annie cut this short.

'That's no way to talk about your own flesh and blood. Tell Rod you're sorry.'

'I'm not.'

'Oh yes you are. She's too proud to say so, Mr Madgwick, but she is.'

Having settled this to no one's satisfaction but her own, Aunt Annie set about re-establishing good relations by suggesting to Rodney he should give up his seat to a little lady like a little gentleman, but Rodney clung fiercely to Miles and said he wasn't going to. Miles, who was re-discovering the ferocious cut and thrust of childhood, suddenly placed his knees wide apart, sat Rodney firmly on one and offered the other to Ethel. She accepted it haughtily and the two children sat glowering at each other. Miles put an arm round each and drew them to him so that their heads rested against his shoulders.

'Good children,' he said, 'good children.'

'That they're not,' said Aunt Annie briskly, 'and they'd better look to their laurels because their little noses are going to be out of joint if they don't look sharp.'

She got up as the kettle started whistling softly and snatched it off the gas ring.

'Whistling kettles,' she said, 'are a great comfort, but you never want to let them whistle; partly because they waste the gas and partly because the postman's uncle claimed it was a whistling kettle that perforated his ear drum.'

She made the tea while she talked and collected two cups and saucers into which she put spoonfuls of sherbet. These she filled with water and handed to the children who drank them greedily.

'You'd think they was shipwrecked mariners with water water everywhere and never a drop to drink the way they go at it. But not a thank you between them.'

'Thank you,' said Ethel.

'Thank you,' said Rodney.

'I should hope so.'

She poured out the tea and handed a cup to Miles, proffering him the milk bottle and a bag of sugar cubes.

'Thank you,' said Miles hastily, and then added, 'I think it would be safer if the children were off my lap while I drink it.'

Ethel at once got up and dragged the protesting Rodney off his other knee. Then she went behind the chair, leaned over it and loudly whispered in Miles' ear so that it tickled unbearably, 'I'll tell you a secret. You're going to be my little baby brother's godfather.'

Aunt Annie pretended to be furious.

'Who asked you to let the cat out of the bag? Takes a lot on herself I must say.'

But Ethel eluded her grasp and went laughing and skipping round the room, singing over and over again in her tuneless little voice, 'My baby brother's a genius, a genius, a genius; my baby brother's a genius, a geni . . .'

Aunt Annie grabbed her as she passed and gave her a sharp

smack across the cheek and Ethel stopped singing and didn't even cry she was so surprised by the sudden sting of it.

'You'll be wondering what this is all about, Mr Madgwick,' said Aunt Annie, 'and indeed, I don't know how to set about telling you.'

She knew perfectly well and set about telling him at length and with a wealth of detail, much of it quite irrelevant. But Miles could have listened indefinitely. As a story-teller she was a spell-binder; the asides, the digressions, the impersonations, the embellishments, the critical footnotes were consummately marshalled to give spice and variety without seriously detracting from the narrative flow. Even Ethel, who was given to cheeky interpolations on such occasions, was very nearly reduced to silence, for Aunt Annie was in such tremendous form that she never paused for breath, having mastered the knack of speaking during inhalation. Twice Ethel tried to interrupt. She was a mouse defying a steamroller, and was squashed flat without anyone even noticing.

Suddenly Miles realised she had stopped. The three of them were looking at him like three question marks which were there for formality's sake only. They took it for granted he would say yes.

He said, 'I wonder if I could have another cup of tea?'

'As many as you like, Mr Madgwick, and much more besides. Eth, show Mr Madgwick what a good little tea pourer you are. It's the least you can do when he's been so kind.'

'There's just one thing,' said Miles, as Ethel demurely advanced with the tea-pot, 'you see, I'm an agnostic.'

Aunt Annie was now busy fitting the spool of cotton into the shuttle and the shuttle into the machine. She turned the wheel slowly so that the needle descended and caught up the protruding end of cotton. Miles and the children watched her in silence. She gave a small grunt of satisfaction and turned again to Miles.

'You don't have to let on to the vicar.'

'What's an agnostic?' Ethel asked.

'Ask no questions and you'll be told no lies, Ethel.'

Having placed the edge of a pinned skirt hem under the machine and clamped down the lever, she rapidly turned the handle. The noise was deafening.

Miles said, 'I'm afraid it's not as easy as that,' but might as well have spared his breath.

Ethel nudged him. 'She didn't hear you. You'll have to shout.'

Rodney plucked at Aunt Annie's sleeve. She looked up for a second and he pointed to Miles.

'Was you wanting to say something?' she bawled. 'You'll have to shout, Mr Madgwick. Can't stop now.'

And the pink ambience of her revolving hand imparted a renewed frenzy to the machine as her other hand guided the moving hem to receive its line of tiny stitches.

'An agnostic can't be a godfather,' yelled Miles.

'I knew you wouldn't say no,' she replied at the top of her voice and whirling the handle still faster.

'I am saying no,'

'That's very kind. My niece will be ever so grateful.'

He decided to wait for the machine to stop, but Aunt Annie had other ideas.

'What do you think they're going to call him?'

Miles waited to hear.

'What do you think they're going to call him?'

He shouted, 'I don't know.'

'Miles.'

'What?'

'Miles. After his godfather.'

'After who?'

'After you, Mr Madgwick.'

He drank his tea while Aunt Annie continued her hemming. It seemed further talk was out of order till the job was done. To be godfather to the new baby? Well, why not? His own godfathers had taken their responsibilities lightly enough; a silver spoon with his initials on it from one and a Post Office Savings book with a first payment of ten pounds from the other. One had gone to Australia and had never been heard of again; the other had once visited his mother when Miles had measles. He was allowed to look down from the bedroom window and failed to catch the half-crown his godfather threw up to him. 'Butterfingers!' He remembered the good-humoured contemptuous voice as the coin rolled down the sloping tiles over the French windows below, and stuck in the gutter. 'Butterfingers! When you're better you can get a ladder and find it.'

He did, but the half-crown had gone. He suspected his sister had taken it but she indignantly denied it. The mystery was never solved. Only his godmother, Miss Verney, an old school friend of his mother's, was concerned with his spiritual upbringing. Her christening present was an illustrated Bible with a set of brightly coloured maps at the end. Miss Verney—he called her Aunt Vera—was reproachful when he put *Chums Annual* on top of it.

'The Holy Book,' she said, 'must always be on top.'

'Yes, Auntie Vera.'

'Never be disrespectful to the Holy Book.'

'No, Auntie Vera.'

Even now he felt uncomfortable if he saw a Bible under a pile of books, and rather sheepishly transferred it to the top.

The machine was still rattling and banging and squeaking away like mad. Yes. He would say yes. To have the chance to teach a little child not to grow up as he had done; to take his chances, to be aggressive and masculine, to be proud and scornful and selfish, and glory shamelessly and exultantly in his sex, matching mental with physical prowess; above all not to be frightened, to tell the Mr Fisons of this world where they got off, to walk into rooms as if he owned them, to give inadequate tips and have them gratefully accepted, not to approach the boss like a guilty schoolboy about to be caned by the headmaster, to give a cheery good-day to passing policemen instead of wondering which law he had broken, to cut people down to size and remain massively larger than life himself; then, oh then, God help the bosses, the bureaucrats, the headmasters, the head-tossing women and girls, the insolent waiters and railway porters, the cab drivers . . .

The machine stopped.

He heard Aunt Annie saying, 'Well begun is half done, but it's time you children was in bed,' and the whining, ritual protests from the children and Aunt Annie taking no notice of them but saying to him, 'You won't think me rude but it's getting late and I got my niece coming home from hospital next week, any day it might be, and so much to do I shan't know which way to turn,' and him saying he had to go anyway, his work, and thank you again for the tea and Rodney kissing him on one cheek and Ethel on the other and getting out of the room somehow and down the stairs back to his own room.

It wasn't safe any more.

13

Daisy Shoesmith had of course discussed the Hieronymus Bosch book with Minnie Combermere the very day Bert had flung it at her.

'He's up to something, Minnie, I know he is. Something funny, too; and when I say funny, I mean funny peculiar.'

'Have another piece of the gâteau,' said Minnie, 'it'll calm you down, and another cup of tea. What sort of pictures?'

'I mustn't. Got to get back. Feed the brute.'

'Breakfast is a lovely meal, no matter what time of day.'

'Like a nightmare they are. I'd have brought the book along, but if he found out . . . well, you know Bert.'

Minnie collected the crumbs of her third piece of chocolate cake by pressing down on them with the end of her forefinger and popping it into her mouth.

'I got an idea that Bert of yours is going to finish up in the loony-bin.'

'Not Bert. Too crafty by a long chalk. I've got him for keeps all right.'

She went into the hall for her coat and Minnie followed her, wrapping a large slice of chocolate cake in a piece of grease-proof paper.

'It'll sustain you. Never meet trouble with an empty stomach. That's what I always say.'

'You're the kindest person I know and what I'd do without you . . . well, I don't have to say it. Love to Reg and tell him good luck for the fight tonight.'

'Win or lose,' said Minnie proudly, 'don't make no difference to Reg. He's always good value whatever.'

As Daisy strolled back up the street she thought gratefully of Reg. An insurance, that's what he was; good value all right. When Bert was at his worst, a casual reference to Reg was usually enough to get him off the boil. Maybe Minnie was right. Perhaps he did have a screw loose. She frowned and pursed her lips. Not loose enough to have him put away, worse luck. Her curiosity was still nagging her. Who'd he got the book from? And why? And what was he going to do with it? Something. No doubt of that. But he would come to it with the slowness of one of those giant tortoises at the zoo making for a bit of lettuce. All day he'd cogitate and still he hadn't made up his mind.

She cooked his breakfast and when she called him he was awake. She noticed the book had disappeared again. He came to the table in the vest he had slept in and a pair of crumpled pyjama trousers. He was unwashed and unshaven; his eyes were puffy with sleep. He ate his breakfast in the usual noisy silence. After he'd finished and was on his last cup of tea she said, 'I've got a little treat for you.'

He just looked at her.

'Gâteau. It's lovely.'

'Where'd you get it?'

'Never mind.'

He resented her friendship with the Combermeres. He took it and ate it greedily, washing it down with the remains of the tea.

Suddenly he said, 'What do you make of it?'

'The book?'

'What do you think I meant, the fucking weather?'

'It's sort of . . . funny.'

He laughed shortly. 'The understatement of the year.'

'Where'd you get it?'

No sooner had she spoken than she realised her mistake. He hated being asked questions; shut him up like a clam. She could have kicked herself. After he went to the bathroom she put the radio on and washed up. Later in the evening when she went to change the sheets, there was no sign of the book.

During the next few days she could tell it was on his mind. Once or twice he stopped eating and looked up at her as if he was about to speak, then changed his mind. About a week later when he came in from work, she noticed how unusually affable he was. This time she didn't ask questions. He made some obscene references to the traffic in the city and gave her a pretty little account of how he had diddled an old lady into letting him keep the change from a pound when the fare was only nine and six.

'Easy meat. I could tell she was nervous of me. And she's not the only one.'

'People can't get away with things, not with you, Bert.'

'Right.'

He went on eating with grudging appreciation.

'Not bad. If you always cooked as good I wouldn't have to complain, would I?'

She pretended not to mind. 'I try, really I do, Bert.'

He gave a non-committal grunt. When he had finished eating he stretched and yawned. Then he pulled a rolled-up exercise book from his trouser pocket. She watched, fascinated, and managed with difficulty not to appear too curious.

'Remember that book?'

As if she could have forgotten it!

'Now I got this.'

He unrolled it and, as he flipped through the pages, she saw it was torn and crumpled.

'I'm going to have a read of this before I go off.'

'There's plenty of it.'

'No hurry. A bit at a time, in instalments like.'

He took it into the bedroom. Daisy's frustration was at bursting point. After a moment he put his head round the door; his shirt was half over his head, his arms raised in the sleeves above him.

'Do you know what I expect to find in that book?'

She shook her head.

'Filth! Some people have a sense of duty. I'm like that. And when I've finished it . . . '

He paused while he drew the shirt over his head.

'Yes?' She couldn't help it.

'. . . I'll have got the dirty bastard like that, see?'

He stretched out his hand and closed it tight. She looked at his face. It never changed expression much, not even when he was angry, so it was difficult to tell. But his little eyes were bright. He wasn't angry. He was pleased.

He didn't say anything that evening when she gave him breakfast, except to complain that she'd overcooked the bacon. After he'd left she re-made the bed for herself and didn't even bother to look for the exercise book; she knew he would have taken it with him. Then she almost ran down the street to tell Minnie and Reg. He had fallen all wrong in the ring the night before and twisted his ankle.

'He was fighting one of his buddies,' Minnie explained. 'Reg got the first fall all right and then Jack got mad at him and started throwing him around.'

'You don't get hurt if you fall right,' said Reg, who was lying on the sofa nursing the damaged ankle.

'It's the know-how, isn't it Reg?'

'Right, Min. But this time I fell wrong, see?' He waved his huge foot at Daisy. Minnie had prescribed a cold compress, which made it look even bigger.

'And then the dirty bastard sees what Reg has done and starts twisting his ankle.'

Reg smiled ruefully. 'I'd have done the same.'

'He had to submit.'

'I don't often, but this was different.'

Daisy almost forgot her mission for a moment she was so concerned. If Bert got to hear . . . well, goodbye to the hold she had over him. A protector with a sprained ankle; fat lot of good that was. 'What happened?' she asked anxiously.

'It was the last round, see? And that Jack—he's not called "Fowler" Jack for nothing—goes straight for the ankle again, doesn't he, Reg?'

'Right, Min. I'd have done the same, mind you. But as he was diving for it I hopped aside on the other leg and got him in a head chancery.'

'It was the one chance,' Minnie cried, re-living it. Daisy looked puzzled. 'Like this!' Minnie dashed at her, put a fat arm round her neck, bent her forward and then tried to interlock the fingers of both hands so that Daisy's head was pressed into her side.

'Ouch! You're hurting," gasped Daisy.

Minnie let her go. Reg told her she'd better calm down, and look at Daisy's hair. Daisy told them it didn't matter; she was having a perm tomorrow and go on, what happened?

'It was as good a head chancery as ever I done,' said Reg. 'He tried every trick in the book to get out, grape-vine, head mare, cross-buttock, the lot.'

'He even tried to kick Reg's bad ankle, the dirty son of a bitch.'

'Right, Min. Well, he had to, didn't he?'

'The crowd was roaring for Reg. They knew once he let go he'd had it.'

Reg explained that head chanceries, once laid on proper, were for keeps, and this was as good a one as ever he'd done. No hint of vanity; just stating a fact.

Minnie subsided breathily into a chair which creaked ominously. 'You ought to have heard that crowd; they raised the bloody roof. And you ought to have seen that Jack arguing with the ref, making out it wasn't fair. The way he got booed!'

'Luck,' said Reg modestly, 'You don't often get a chancery on just right like that. It was as good a one as ever I done.'

'How long before it gets better?'

'Couple of days at the most. Think nothing of it.'

Daisy felt reassured. Minnie made tea and Daisy told them about the exercise book. Minnie said she didn't like the sound of it and Daisy said neither did she, and what did Minnie think Bert was up to. She said ask her another but she wouldn't be surprised at anything, not with Bert, and Daisy had better watch him. Daisy agreed, but explained all over again that once Bert got an idea into his head he'd never let go, like it was Reg's head chancery only more so.

Then they started speculating. Minnie thought he might be going to blackmail some poor fellow but Daisy wouldn't have that; what about him saying he knew where his duty lay and all that pi crap? And if it was blackmail he'd hardly have told her even that much, would he? One thing she was sure of; he'd got it in for some poor sod, she could tell by his look. Minnie asked what sort of look and Daisy thought for a moment and then she said it was like he was enjoying himself in a cruel sort of way. Minnie said mark her words he wasn't all there sometimes and she'd be afraid of him if she were Daisy. But Daisy replied, as she always did, that you get used to anything, even Bert.

Then they turned to Reg, who had been listening impassively, and asked him what he thought. He'd seen this coming and had his answer ready.

'I don't think nothing,' he said truthfully, 'but I got my uses,' and he held up an enormous fist.

Daisy felt comforted and went home with a couple of milk flakes Minnie slipped into her hand at the door and had them with a Guinness before going to bed.

The next afternoon, when she came back from the hairdresser's, she was amazed to find Bert already up and seated at the table with the exercise book in front of him. He took no notice of her; he was reading avidly. She went to the kitchen and hurriedly began to get things ready to cook his breakfast.

He called out from the other room, 'I'll eat later.'

She went to the door; he was still reading, his huge bulk hunched over the table. He kept on turning back a page and reading it again as if its meaning had eluded him.

She said, 'It's five twenty-five.'

He read to the end of the page and, without looking up, said, 'I'm not working tonight.'

'Aren't you well?'

She thought he wasn't going to answer. She stood in the doorway uncertainly. This was unprecedented; unless he was ill he always had his meal punctually at six and was away by seven to catch the theatre trade.

'Shall I go round and tell Oliphant?'

'No.'

'He'll wonder.'

'He can stuff it.'

Jim Oliphant had a garage up a nearby mews and owned a small fleet of taxis. Bert had been one of his drivers for some years and, though surly and a prize grumbler, had the merit of being reliable. Daisy hesitated. The *Daily Mirror* was on the table. She moved slowly towards it and, as she leaned forward to pick it up, she took a quick look at the exercise book from behind Bert's shoulder. Such small, neat writing; she only managed to read one sentence, something about a starfish. *Ethel*—it looked like Ethel—*Rodney's taken my starfish and I can't . . .*

'Get out of my fucking hair.' Bert didn't raise his voice, but she recognised the menace of it.

'If you don't mind,' she said icily, picking up the *Mirror*, 'I'm going to have a read of the paper.'

She sat down and skimmed the headlines but couldn't settle down to it; her attention was on Bert. She thought she knew him pretty well; knew his moods, his likes, his dislikes and what he would do in any given situation. But this was something different. He had been given the situation. She hadn't. He remained massively immovable except when he turned a page backwards or forwards. Half an hour later, not taking his eyes off the book, he groped in his pocket for a cigarette and said: 'If you read the bloody paper instead of turning the pages back and forth like thunder claps, I might be able to hear myself think.'

She put the paper down and tiptoed ostentatiously to the kitchen. She could have saved herself the trouble; he didn't look up. She made herself some tea, then opened the window and gazed unseeingly at the street below, leaning her elbows on the sill, her cup between both hands, sipping. And she thought: 'I'm going to find out. If it kills me I'm going to.'

14

The double line of elms threw long shadows across the Broad Walk in Regent's Park and on to the sunburnt playing field that flanked it. Londoners had come out to find space and air. There didn't seem to be either. The sun had shone majestically all day out of a hot blue and was starting its descent, the blue imperceptibly transformed into a dome of burnished brass, containing and reflecting the heat of the day. Only the squirrels and the pigeons seemed unaffected, comfortably insulated inside their fur and their feathers. Less fortunate human beings in summer dresses, in open-necked shirts and slacks, sauntered slowly in a tangled and two way procession, with prams and push-chairs, with babies in arms, with babies taking their first steps in reins, with toddlers by the hand and older children within call, with dogs straining at their leads to near throttling point at the sight of a squirrel snatching a nut from outstretched fingers and darting up an elm bole and along the black branches to disappear into the cover of wilting leaves.

On the exhausted stretches of grass either side of the Walk, those who didn't wish to process were engaged in an assortment of seemingly incompatible activities: youths playing football, playing cricket; lonely middle-aged men in shorts running doggedly and wiping the sweat from their eyes as they side-stepped a football, or a couple who had reached the moment beyond which they couldn't go without offending public decency; small knots of teenagers playing cards, whispering smut and raucously laughing at it; a pair of dogs copulating to the envy of three other dogs, the admiration of four small boys and an old man in an astrakhan hat and to the embarrassment of a maiden lady who owned one of them but was anxious not to appear to do so; people comfortably asleep on the uncomfortable ground; people reading, surreptitiously playing forbidden radios; children playing touch, playing rounders, playing Grandmother's Footsteps or rolling over each other with a sweaty enjoyment which they were not yet supposed to appreciate. All pervasive in the still air, the stench of humanity mingled incongruously with the insistent jollity of a distant brass band.

Miles, from the end of a crowded seat half way up the Walk, observed, listened, breathed the stale air, smelt the smell, sweated and for once was relieved to be amongst so many people. He felt safe and anonymous. His brain had been at full stretch trying to decide how to retrive the exercise book without calling in the police. He had considered every type of murder and decided poison was the only way.

'At least you will let me make you a cup of tea? Sugar I suppose? Two lumps?' Easy enough; but what then? He couldn't possibly touch that huge corpse, let alone dispose of it. Threaten him with a gun? He could hear the driver's taunts: 'Don't make me laugh. You haven't got the guts and well you know it.'

And well he knew it. But somehow, somehow he must get it back, otherwise . . . otherwise . . . what? Already that hulking brute knew more about him than anyone else in the world, had been fingering his most secret self and turning what was beautiful and precious into a shameful and shaming guilt.

'I must,' he thought, 'must get it back,' and then realised he had said it aloud.

'They say,' said an old lady sitting beside him and looking up for a moment from her knitting, 'talking to oneself is a sign of approaching old age. Lost something, dear?'

'Oh, no.' Then, after a pause, 'Well, yes I have. A book as a matter of fact.'

'It could be worse.'

'No.'

'I beg your pardon?'

'It couldn't be worse.'

'I've dropped a stitch.'

'I'm sorry.'

'Why couldn't it be worse?' She cast off a couple of stitches, picked up the dropped one with practised fingers and then looked up at him over her spectacles. 'Go on, why?'

It was like telling himself. 'Because if I don't get it back I shall probably end up in gaol.'

'Oh dear, oh dear!' She returned to her knitting. After a long silence she said, 'Have you done something bad?'

'I don't think so. Other people might.'

'Oh!' She nodded her head gravely over the knitting. 'Other people. Yes. Oh dear!'

He got up. 'Excuse me, please.'

She didn't answer; her knitting became more important. As he moved away he heard her say to a youth sitting next to her with his arms round a girl, 'Did you hear that?' He heard them giggle and the old lady saying 'Oh dear!' as she went on with her knitting.

But it wasn't pity, he thought, as he made his way necessarily slowly through the crowded Walk and headed for Queen Mary's Gardens and the roses, it wasn't pity he would get. He would get the contempt, the loathing and the savage retribution reserved for the guilty by the self-righteous. He could smell the roses as he approached the tall iron gates. To be punished for one's secret thoughts, that would be unspeakably unfair. He was walking aimlessly and found himself by one of the beds of small species roses, his favourites. How many men, how many women for that matter, could come spotlessly through such an inquisition? None of course. He was standing in front of a *Blanc Double de Coubert* and took one of the roses carefully between two fingers and bent over it to smell. Fragile, yes; but its smell was strong and sweet. Even that delicate flower had guts. And yet he . . .

'Why, it's Mr Madgwick. Fancy seeing you.'

He looked up, startled, the rose still between his fingers. It was one of the tarts from upstairs, the dark vivacious one.

'Sweets to the sweet, eh?'

He let go of the rose and stood up.

'I'm fond of roses too.'

'Are you?' He couldn't think of anything else to say.

'Well, but it's the smell isn't it? Christ, it's hot.'

She was standing feet slightly apart and balancing expertly on absurdly high-heeled shoes. Come to think of it her whole appearance was an outrageous caricature of a well-dressed woman. Taken separately, each item might just have passed muster. But together, the short skirt, slit and tight, the low-cut lace blouse, the tailored black jacket with high pointed shoulders, the bangles, the costume jewellery and the little pill-box hat proclaimed her for what she was. Miles thought she might just as well have hung a label round her neck with 'I am a tart' written on it.

'I've had to put two faces on already today,' she said, taking a mirror from her heart-shaped handbag and powdering her face with careful little dabs. 'The stuff's supposed to be rain-proof and sun-proof and kiss-proof but it's bloody well not sweat-proof.'

Miles laughed politely.

'Which way are you walking then?'

He thought quickly; the last thing he wanted was conversation. He looked at his watch. 'As a matter of fact I must dash home.'

'Well, isn't that nice, dear? We can go together.'

She tucked her arm inside his and they set off. He was acutely conscious of the knowing stares and smiles, envious from the men, hostile from their wives. Another pick-up. He had to walk slowly as she teetered along beside him.

'I expect you're wondering what brings me to the Park this time of day.'

'Not at all,' said Miles, who had been.

'Well you see it's Sunday, dear.'

'You mean because . . .' Miles tried to phrase it delicately, 'because Sunday in the Park is suitable for . . . for business.'

She laughed; a husky amusement. 'You make me laugh,' she said.

'Do I?'

'You're funny. The way you put things. Toffee-nosed way of speaking, ever so genteel. "Sunday in the Park is not suitable for business." ' She was taking him off. 'Weekdays you might be lucky. But Sundays, not on your Nellie, old boy.'

'I'm afraid I don't follow.'

She laughed up at him again. 'There you go. "I'm afraid I don't follow." I shall wet my knickers in a minute.' Then in her normal voice which was cockney with an accent; was it French?

Belgian perhaps? 'Don't mind me. Can't help seeing the funny side; gets me into trouble sometimes. No, what I mean is Sundays in the Park they've all got their wives and sweethearts tagging along, haven't they?'

'I hadn't thought of that. I see the logic of that.'

His interest was overcoming his embarrassment. They were back in the Broad Walk now. The sun had set some time ago; not in red splendour but in a yellow brilliance to the last, leaving a copper sky behind it. Slowly this gave way to violet, with a few green and yellow streaks in the west. The crowds had thinned but were still considerable and the two way procession had accelerated. The keepers' whistles shrilled mournfully as the Londoners made for home.

She was saying, 'No, what I mean is Sundays is my day off.'

He tried to cover his surprise. It hadn't occurred to him that tarts had days off.

'I never work Sundays. Never have. And do you know why? Go on, ask me.'

'Very well, why?'

'I'm a Catholic, that's why.' She said it as simply as a child.

Well, thought Miles, how utterly incongruous. Little pictures flashed through his mind. Saying her prayers after a hard night's work? 'Please, Jesus, bring me plenty of customers tomorrow.' In the confessional? 'I know I'm bad, Father. I'm a miserable sinner, but so was Mary Magdalene. Jesus saved her. Pray gentle Jesus save me. But not yet, Father. Not till my figure's gone and they don't go for me any more. Not till I retire, Father.' They had reached the turning to Albert Gate and the keepers were blowing their whistles more shrilly and shouting, 'All out! All out!'

'Change down,' she said, 'what's the hurry?'

He slackened speed. 'We don't want to get locked in do we?'

'I wouldn't mind. Would you mind?'

'Well, I would rather. I mean, what on earth should we do?'

She grinned up at him professionally. 'You tell me, darling.' They passed the keeper at the gate. He looked at them, sharply inquisitive. But this time he didn't feel guilty or embarrassed, though he knew what an incongruous pair they were, he and this exotic creature on his arm, saying surprising things as if they were commonplace, exuding too sweet perfume, tap-

tapping the pavements as her rapid steps kept pace with his slow ones, her talk, her laughter, her appearance, her gait, her gestures, her make-up, all flamboyant, all too much. And he, just the reverse; quietly spoken, reserved, goodish clothes but unpressed, his scholar's stoop and untidy walk, his pale face, his glasses temporarily mended with sticky tape, all mousy, all too little. He began to feel a slight but suffusing return of confidence; enough anyway to see this walk home through. Odd, he thought, that the only other woman he'd had on his arm was his mother. They had crossed Albany Street and were walking east by the railway wall towards Mornington Crescent.

She was smiling at him mischievously. 'What do you do, darling?'

'Do?'

'Yes do. You know what I mean.'

'I'm a writer.'

She laughed again. 'I know that. I don't mean for work. I mean for play. Girls? You got a nice girl?'

He saw where this was leading. 'Not at the moment,' he said, and then went on hastily, 'I'm fond of music.'

'So am I, darling.'

'Really?'

'Oh yes. Classical, mind you. I like classical.'

How unexpected! He warmed to her.

'Opera,' she continued, 'I could listen all day. I got a client who must have Wagner for background or he can't do it. Götterdämmerung, the bit at the end where they all burn up.'

He wondered whether Wagner would have approved up in Valhalla and decided perhaps he would.

'Lucky you happen to have the record.'

'Don't be daft, darling, he brings it with him. Do you have it?'

'Flagstad. Furtwangler conducting.'

She squeezed his arm. 'You must bring it with you, darling.'

How to parry this? He thought quickly. 'But you don't work on Sundays.'

'No, but I can have friends, can't I?'

They walked on in silence, turned into the Hampstead Road and made for Frame Street. Why not? he thought. Ridiculous a man of his age had never gone with a woman. He was a free agent. Nothing wrong about it; a perfectly natural function. The girl in the boat. Her legs. Alice's breast. Well, and this woman. He looked at her and she smiled back.

'I'm nice, aren't I, darling?'

Automatically he said yes, but he was disappointed; not even a hint of sexual desire did he feel. Only the desire for sexual desire. They were passing a pub.

'Aren't you going to give me a drink? Christ, I've got a thirst!'

He took her into the crowded saloon bar. Over their drinks he said: 'How's your friend?'

'Lola? On holiday, the lucky bitch.'

This was intriguing. What sort of a holiday did a tart have? She supplied the information without being asked.

'Her people live in Bruges. Goes over twice a year. She's the eldest of six. They're crazy about her.'

'Do they know? I mean about . . . what she does over here?'

'Do you mind? They're religious, darling; they'd go up the wall. They think she's a masseuse.' She laughed. 'Well, she is in a way, isn't she? We both are.'

'What's your name?'

'Elsa. I hate it.' She passed him her empty glass and he took it to the bar for another double gin. When he returned she was talking to a portly, middle-aged man with a brick red face and wisps of oiled hair brushed forward from the back of his head in an unsuccessful attempt to cover his baldness.

'Anyone could tell,' she was saying, 'you're the virile type.'

He laughed and shifted his gaze from her legs to her face. 'What makes you think that?'

'Experience, darling. Tell at a glance.'

He looked back at her legs. 'I could show you a thing or two.'

'I can hardly wait, darling.'

'Well, but . . .' He eyed Miles suspiciously, not quite so sure of himself.

Miles gave her the gin and sat beside her. She leaned right over to the fat man and spoke into his ear: 'He's my hubby. Jealous as a tom-cat. He'd kill you if he thought . . .'

But the fat man, his face a degree redder, had risen with surprising agility, swallowed his drink in one and was making for the door. She laughed and called out after him, 'Shit scared and flaccid, darling!' which immediately drew all eyes to her. She waved her glass and smiled widely. 'If you'll pardon my French.'

Miles rose nervously and said he really must be getting along. She put her hand on his arm.

'Give us a chance to finish my drink. You see, that's me; I'm choosey. There aren't many I wouldn't go with, fat slobs and all. But not that fat slob. I took against him.'

She opened her mouth wide, tilted her head back and poured the cold gin and tonic slowly down. He watched her throat move as she swallowed. She sighed and put the glass on the table.

'Lola says I'm crazy. What does it matter, she says, money's the same wherever it comes from.'

'I'm rather glad you're choosey.'

'Only about once in several hundred. I'm no amateur, thank Christ. Hope you enjoyed being my hubby.'

'I was honoured.'

She raised her empty glass in mock salute. 'Such a gentleman.'

When they reached Frame Street it was quite dark. They could see up between the separate glares of the street lamps into the night sky. She squeezed his arm and he stopped.

'You can't help wondering.' He felt her shiver as she said it. 'You're lucky. You've got your religion.'

'You've got to believe in something.'

'I don't.'

'Atheist?'

'Agnostic.'

She thought for a moment and then shook her head. 'Oh no. You've got to believe in something.'

He became increasingly nervous as they approached the front door, because he had no idea what was going to happen. As he opened it he felt the sweat trickling down his chest. His hand was trembling as he put it out politely to shake hers.

'Well . . . that was nice. Thank you.'

'What for?'

'For your company.'

In the harsh light under the cracked flying saucer shade he saw her laugh again. She was always laughing. She took his hand and moved towards him so that he was touching her breast.

'Good night.' He made a quick little peck at her and his lips landed on top of her hat.

'But you're going to play me the record. You promised.'

He tried to pull himself away but she held on to his hand.

'I've got some work to finish.'

'Give yourself a break.'

'You don't work on Sundays but some of us have to.' But he knew he was going to agree. He felt excited and rather breathless.

'Because I like you.' She was still laughing but he sensed that somehow she was intrigued.

'Hold on a second while I find it.'

He unlocked the door, switched on the light and searched for the record while she stood on the threshold watching him. He couldn't find it. Not anywhere.

'I don't know when I last played it. Ages ago. It's here somewhere.'

She still didn't speak. He kept looking up at her with little smiles of apology, gestures of frustration. He had been right through the records and was starting again.

'Stupid, isn't it?' It always annoyed him to mislay something; he prided himself he was methodical. And the delay was undermining his precarious hold on his new-won confidence.

At last he looked up, defeated and puzzled. 'It's not here. It really isn't.'

'So what?' She hunched her shoulders.

'I don't want to lose it. I value it.'

'It'll turn up.'

There was a pause while he looked at her uncertainly. She lit a cigarette and inhaled it lazily and deeply. Then she said, 'Come on, darling,' turned and walked slowly up the stairs. All the doubts, the fears, the inhibitions crowded in on him. But the excitement and, above all, the curiosity prevailed. He followed her obediently and in silence, praying they wouldn't meet anybody. Not a sign or sound of life on the first floor. As they mounted the second flight, the loo door half-way up suddenly opened and old Mr James came out adjusting his skull cap with one hand and his flies with the other. Elsa ran past him and disappeared inside, locking the door behind her.

'How very opportune,' said Mr James, he descended stair

by stair with the aid of the banister, 'I sometimes feel that my frequent but extremely necessary visits to the W.C. are an inconvenience to others. The great thing in life is to strike a nice balance between consideration for others and obligation to one's own needs. Don't you agree, Mr Madgwick?' He stopped and twisted round to gaze at Miles with watery, yellowish eyes.

Miles agreed.

Mr James took another step down and stopped once more. 'My daughter is always on at me to have the operation.' He looked up at Miles again. 'I don't have to go into details, do I?'

'No,' said Miles hastily.

'Unfortunately my doctor is of another opinion. My heart you know . . . at my age . . . dangerous, Mr Madgwick.'

Miles nodded sympathetically. 'How is your daughter?'

'A saint, Mr Madgwick, if ever there was one. On the one hand her piano and a glittering career on the concert platform; on the other, her father, sick and alone. She never hesitated, Mr Madgwick.' He turned round and started to pull himself back up the stairs. 'She chose to look after her . . . father.' He was panting now with the effort.

'Can I help you?' Miles moved towards him.

'No, no. It's not that. It's just that . . . I hope . . .' He was looking anxiously at the loo door.

At that moment the chain was pulled, the cistern flushed and Elsa came out.

'How opportune,' said Mr James, as he fumbled past her and disappeared inside.

Elsa smiled indulgently as they went on up the stairs. 'Poor old Mr James.' She unlocked her door and ushered Miles in. 'But it isn't prostate, it's incontinence. You have to be sorry for him. He's got pride you know.'

Miles was looking round her room. It was a fair reflection of its owner. The prevailing colours were pink and grey; pink walls, a grey divan, two armchairs with pink cushions, a grey kidney-shaped dressing table decorated with pink bows and behind a grey screen, which was painted with a trellis and climbing pink roses, he caught sight of a gas cooker and a wash-stand with basin and ewer. Against the pink walls flared the hot yellows of two Van Gogh reproductions. All flamboyant; too much. And not all that clean, he thought.

She had kicked her shoes off and was sitting at the dressing table taking off her pill-box hat, patting her hair, doing running repairs to her face.

She said, 'The records are over there by the player.'

He sorted through the heaps on the floor: Tchaikovski and Frank Sinatra, Sibelius and Donovan, Anna Russell, Vera Lynn, Mozart and plenty more; no Brahms. He put on Beethoven's eighth.

'That's nice,' she said, getting up and twirling, with her arms outstretched, towards the divan. When she was near it she gave a little jump and landed on her back among the cushions. 'Sit down, darling.'

He made for a chair.

'No, by me.'

He sat on the edge of the divan beside her.

'Nice,' she said, 'that's nice.'

But he was conscious not so much of her but of the divan. Like one of those inanimate pieces of history, the Great Bed of Ware, the Book of Kells, Ann Hathaway's cottage, the Roman wall at Housesteads, the execution block at the Tower, it set his imagination racing outwards, exploring beyond the known into a coloured world of speculation. Ridiculous, but it did. The divan was history all right, and recent history; the orgasms of human beings. Three or four or five—or even six, was it?—every night of the week except Sundays: somewhere between eighteen and thirty-six a week. Give a fortnight's holiday and say twelve weeks, at a generous allowance, for her periods and incidental sickness; that would make six hundred and eighty-four minimum and twelve hundred and fifty-eight maximum per year. He looked down at the divan with awe and noticed the spots and stains on the grey cover between all those pink cushions.

Elsa's hands were clasped behind her neck and she was looking up at the ceiling. She seemed to be listening to the music.

'Lola and I won't be here in the Autumn.'

So she wasn't listening. It was Beethoven as background.

'Are you going back to Belgium?'

'Don't be daft, darling. We're going up in the world. Albemarle Street for Lola, St James' for me. And maids of course. Very plush. We're in the money. Because we're good, see?'

He was staring at her. She thought he was fascinated. He was; but not in that way.

'The real money,' she went on, with Beethoven in his sunniest mood backing her up, underlining a statement here, delicately laughing there, syncopating mischievously, politely pausing—'you next' he seemed to suggest—astonishing with false endings and surprise beginnings, 'the *real* money is with the kinks. You'd be surprised, darling, really surprised. You've got to be an actress, got to have a wardrobe; hospital nurse, children's nurse, governess, schoolgirl—I've got a lovely wig with pigtails—Gestapo and—get this—a schoolboy. I make a lovely boy. Show you one day, darling.'

His face was like the boy Drake's in that picture, listening to the old sea-farer as he tells him that truth is stranger than phantasy.

'Do you enjoy . . . that . . . sort of thing?'

She looked up at him from the pillows, wide-eyed, impatient. 'It's my job darling. I'm not on the receiving end. They pay for the kicks; we supply them. We're good. I told you.'

As if to change the subject, Beethoven was now poised for the slow movement. She kicked her legs right over Miles' head, swung herself round, got up and switched off the player. The slow movement died the death with a descending glissando groan. She poured a couple of gins, mixed them with sweet Votrix and sat herself beside him, handing him his glass.

'I like you . . . something about you, I don't know. You don't seem to want . . . anything. You're not kinky, are you?'

'I don't think so.' There was doubt in his voice. Perhaps he was?

'Or queer or something?'

'I don't think so.'

'Well, whatever you are, I like you darling, see? Elsa likes you.'

For a moment he thought he was going to cry. He turned away, took another sip, cleared his throat, recovered. Then he was talking; trying to tell her about himself, but with difficulty, haltingly, correcting himself, primly clutching at euphemisms, not looking at her, awkward pauses while he searched for a word, couldn't find it, went into a paraphrase, half-way through remembering it, using it, some touches of humour, able to laugh at himself, but really to cover his embarrassment, doggedly continuing while fighting down a growing diffidence, knowing even while he was talking there were some things he couldn't tell her so that she wouldn't have the whole picture, not the whole of him, no he couldn't, not his book, not the precious book, because that was sacred and secret, only it wasn't any longer, but somehow it must be. . . somehow. . . yes, but how?

'Go on, darling.'

He hadn't realised he had stopped.

'I must be boring you.'

'How old are you?'

'Twenty-seven.'

'You look older.'

'I know.'

'But you don't act like you're older.'

'I know I don't.'

'You need a woman, darling.' She said it like a doctor prescribing a cough mixture. 'Because I tell you what. You're one of them mother's boys. Everything you tell me.'

'You could be right.' He thought of his mother for a moment, the grave sweet smile, her innate dignity and goodness, her love. He realised he was uneasy discussing her with this woman, this prostitute, disloyal somehow. He suppressed a little surge of resentment. 'I don't know what I want, that's the trouble.'

She put her hand into his lap and gently opened his clenched fist, smoothed the palm, stroked his fingers.

'We'll see darling, won't we? We'll see what you want.' She was opening his flies. Her hand slipped inside and was exploring. He was trembling, but throttled his first impulse to resist.

'Relax, relax,' she kept on saying. Then: 'You're all right. Not bad at all, darling. Good, I'd say. You work.'

Miles gasped. Not so much because of what she was achieving which was considerable, but because he was astonished to find these preliminaries, far from initiating him into an esoteric mystery which he had always contemplated with awe and apprehension, were, in the event, pleasantly familiar. But the familiarity was short lived.

She got up, moved over to the dressing table and started to

undress with the studied exhibitionism of a stripper. He was profoundly embarrassed.

'Look at me, darling. You're supposed to look at me.'

She'd got as far as a little black suspender belt. He stood up and surveyed her with what he hoped would look like an expert eye. But she had turned her back and was admiring herself in the mirror.

'I'm nice. Aren't I nice, Mr Madgwick, darling?' Her hands moved over her breasts.

'Very nice.' He hoped his voice didn't sound as shaky to her as it did to him.

Now she was looking at his reflection. 'What are you waiting for? Do you want me to undress you or what?'

He took his clothes off as if he was preparing for a medical check-up. She swung round and looked him up and down. Then she beckoned him to follow her behind the screen, poured some water into the basin, added a few drops of Dettol.

'I know you're clean, darling but even so . . . Here, I'll do it for you.' And she proceeded to wash and dry him clinically and dispassionately.

'I'm afraid . . .' he began, and stopped.

'What are you afraid of, darling?'

'It's just that . . . well, I'm not awfully sure that . . . well, that I'm going to be able to . . .'

She laughed. 'Don't worry, darling. I've never had a failure yet.' She was washing herself now. 'And don't worry about hygiene. I'm very hygienic, very. I have to be.'

He went back to the divan, sat down and waited. He had stopped panicking, no longer felt shy or surprised or excited. He was about to take part in an act for which he could conjure no desire, no enthusiasm. His brain was automatically receiving, and presumably storing, the images and sensa as they arrived; but it made no comment, not even when she came round the screen, the palms of her hands glistening with oil, and gently laid him out on the divan like a patient on the operating table. No anticipation, no arousal, no quickening of the senses. Nothing. When her hands started ministering to him it flashed through his mind that perhaps he was going to be her first failure. But even as the thought arrived it was obliterated by the urgent and insistent messages from below that she hadn't boasted in vain. Judging her moment, and without ceasing her ministrations, she lay beside him and encouraged him with small shifts and movements of her body to lie on top of her and then guided him to penetration. And as he moved purposefully and rhythmically towards detumescence, thrusting for it, retreating from it, dreading it, demanding it, his heart syncopating wildly with the accelerando of his breathing and the crescendo of coitus, he suddenly remembered exactly what he had done with the Wagner record. And now he was gasping and laughing at the same time and he saw her look puzzled and heard her say 'What is it?' and he shook his head as he reached the point of no return and 'yes' he was saying, the words spurting out as involuntarily as his semen, 'yes, yes, yes, yes, yes . . . .'

Later, after further ablutions behind the screen and while he was dressing, she said, 'You were laughing. Why?'

'The Götterdämmerung record! I remembered, the old sleeve had torn. I put it in with the Meistersinger overture. Months ago it was. I'll get it.'

She had put on a short and fussy little bed-jacket and was drawing on a pair of lacey French knickers over the black stockings and suspender belt.

'No hurry,' she said. 'I feel yawny. I feel sleepy.' She lay back again on the divan and closed her eyes. 'We'll sleep a little, and then some food, eh?'

'I won't be long.' He ran down the stairs. He felt elated. He had done it, had a woman. Never mind it was a cold-blooded affair, a set of reactions to physical stimuli; he had gone through with it, hadn't made a fool of himself, hadn't been a failure, had even derived some pleasure from it. 'Das ist kein Mann', Siegfried had sung discovering Brunnhilde stretched out on the rock. 'It nearly always gets a laugh in the opera house,' he thought, 'but there's the unsung corollary. Now, at this instant, he realises for the first time that he is. So do I, so do I?' And, as he reached the bottom of the stairs, he was pom-pom-pomming Siegfried's hunting horn motif.

He took out his key and then remembered he'd forgotten to lock the door and while he was reproaching himself for his carelessness he opened it, still singing, and there was the cab driver seated at his table, the exercise book open in front of him.

15

When Miles was holding the rose between his fingers in Queen Mary's gardens, Alice was holding little Miles in her arms and smiling at him. She couldn't help smiling at him. Such a plain little object he was, and looking into her eyes unwinkingly, with a bland curiosity which she found irresistibly comical and incongruous in a new born baby. As she smiled down at him, the corners of his mouth began to twitch and move apart, his eyes never leaving hers and his lips formed a small half-moon, answering smile. In her delight and surprise she kissed him and shifted him over to her breast and he got to work on it with enthusiasm.

While she suckled him, she decided she wasn't going to cooperate with Doctor Fallowfield who was showing every sign of poking her nose into her affairs, not only now but in the years to come. That child psychologist she had brought to watch mother and baby together, she didn't like him; no, not at all; the way he talked down to her when she didn't understand his long words, talked down to her as if she was a child herself; and all that high-falutin' stuff about the responsibility she had to others and to science and to the future. He was a mean-looking man, she thought, with eyes like gimlets which kept boring into everything around him as if they were afraid they might miss something; but never for long, always shifting they were. Yes, he was shifty and she didn't fancy the thought of regular visits from him, because that's what he had suggested. 'Yes,' he had said, 'because, my dear Mrs Remnant, I take it you'll have no objection . . .'—he hadn't even waited for her to say yes or no—'and I'll arrange my visits to suit you, of course, twice a week preferably, and your co-operation in noting down and reporting his day to day behaviour patterns will, of course, be invaluable.' Twice a week! Once a week would be one too many. She hadn't said no. She hadn't said anything, not even when he said 'That's all settled then.' The cheek of it! Who did he think he was?

Her indignation was making her restless. The nipple had slipped out of the baby's mouth and he was indignant too and making little coughs and cries of protest.

'I suppose,' she thought, 'they'd like me to tell them about that smile he give me. "A smile at one week old. Very significant, Mrs Remnant." But they can whistle for it.' She moved him over to her other breast and his jaws worked happily again. Because, if he was going to be a genius, what sort of a life would it be for him, with every lightest word taken down and reported, and perhaps a book written about him? Wouldn't it give any child a swollen head and make him impossible in the home? Let him grow up like ordinary and if he really was a genius he'd make his own way, not with a lot of mean, nosey parkers interfering, but with the friendly advice of a man of her own choosing who'd lead him by the hand—yes, that was how she saw them, hand in hand—through all his boyhood problems and tell him what scholarships to win and books to read and worlds to conquer. And that friend would have a very special interest in him, not only because he was his godfather, but also because he was the man his mother had chosen and he would do anything for that mother, anything she cared to ask, because he worshipped the ground she trod on, because he loved her; because, after the christening, he'd be the one who'd be looking in twice a week; and of course George would be busy in the shop and Ethel and Rod at school and . . . oh, it wouldn't happen all of a sudden but gradually, a smile here, a touch there, and then the trip to the sea and both of them talking as if nothing was going to happen, only they knew it was; and then it did and from then on he was her slave. . . .

The nurse had come to collect the baby.

'A couple of sleeping beauties.'

'I wasn't asleep.'

'You were giving a pretty good imitation.' She hoisted him on to her shoulder. He stirred and gave a milky little belch and she patted him on the small of the back.

Alice said, 'I was thinking.'

'Some people have the time.'

'No, but seriously . . . you won't mind me asking but . . . what do you think you're here for?'

'To look after mothers and babies.' She was mopping up the dribble from the baby's chin.

Alice smiled. She went on earnestly, 'I mean what we're put in the world for. Don't you often wonder?'

The nurse looked wary. 'I'm not religious or any of that stuff, if that's what you mean.'

'Well,' said Alice, relieved, 'I sort of guessed you weren't. That's why I asked. Secretly, I'm not either, though of course we had the children christened and all that. Everybody does, don't they? But life, most of it, it's so . . .'

'Bloody dull?'

'That's it. And boring. Sometimes I feel I could, well . . . break out like. Most people would say it's wicked to think such things. I mean they'd say, "You've got a good home, a good husband, children, the telly, and you've been promised a washing machine. What more do you want?" '

'Well, what more do you want?'

The sister appeared at the other end of the ward.

Alice said, 'I shall get you into trouble, talking.'

The nurse bent over her and whispered, 'You've got yourself to think of. I'm the most important person in my life same as you are in yours. Chance is a funny thing. When it comes it's sort of . . .'

Sister was approaching. 'Nurse, are you going to be all day with that mother?'

'. . . meant. Coming sister.' She hurried away with the baby.

Alice got out of bed and put on her dressing gown. On her way to the lav she stopped at a corridor window and looked down at the street. The traffic was light and there were few pedestrians. A man was waiting at the corner looking anxiously about him. A girl hurried out of one of the office buildings opposite, saw him, crossed the road, stood still, gazed at him, savouring the moment as it were, then walked slowly into his outstretched arms. There was a certainty about it. More than a promise.

'Nurse was right,' Alice mused, 'these things . . . you can't get away from it . . . they're meant.'

She was longing to get home.

16

For once Miles wasn't frightened. He stopped in the doorway, expecting the driver to look up, but he went on reading. He closed the door, locked it on the inside and put the key in his pocket. The driver took no notice. 'All right,' thought Miles, 'if it's a question of who's going to speak first he'll find he's met his match.' And he drew a chair up to the table and sat looking at him, seeing him as if for the first time. And really, Miles decided, he wasn't appetising; fat and white and gently perspiring, his eyes almost disappearing in the creases round them as he bent over the book, a cigarette hanging limp and wet from his lips, the grey arc of ash long overdue for the ashtray. Miles resisted the impulse to proffer one; fascinated, he waited for it to drop; the cigarette had burned down well over half way before it did; all over the exercise book which was already crumpled and dog-eared, spotted and stained. The driver swore softly and brushed it off with the damp palm of his hand so that it smeared across the page, glancing quickly up at Miles as he did so and then returning to the book.

Miles, with difficulty, restrained his mounting anger. He had no idea what he was going to do, but for the moment it was sufficient he should win this opening round by keeping his mouth shut. Apart from the driver's inhalations and exhalations of breath either side of the soggy cigarette butt and an occasional car passing, the silence seemed absolute. After about five minutes, the driver looked up again. For a brief moment they were staring at each other. Then he looked away, spat on the floor and went on reading. 'Good,' thought Miles, 'he's getting rattled.' Several minutes more went by. And then the driver, his eyes still on the exercise book, said:

'Lost our tongue, have we?'

Miles didn't reply. His brain was racing. His first, however small, victory over the man. He was beginning to see his way. God knows what would come of it. But yes, now or never. He thought of Elsa, two floors above, perhaps wondering why he was so long bringing the record; perhaps asleep. He hoped she wouldn't come looking for him.

'I thought,' said the driver, his eyes still on the book, 'it was time you and I had another get-together, during the course of which I might give you a few observations of my own on your nasty little mind as expressed in this.' He held the book up and looked at Miles again.

Miles still said nothing. He got up and started across the room, but the driver was up in a flash barring his way.

'And where are we off to in such a tearing hurry?'

'I was going to make some tea.'

The driver considered this. He said, 'And why not? Go ahead, do.' But he still stood in front of him.

Miles side-stepped and walked past him, but the driver swung round and caught him by the hair.

'Tea, okay, but don't count on the sympathy.' He twisted the hair hard. Miles was clenching his teeth in an effort not to cry out. 'And I don't like locked doors.'

'I'll unlock it in a minute.'

'Now!' He gave an extra twist.

'Yes,' said Miles.

After he'd unlocked it and while he was filling the kettle, the driver said, 'Keys, they're useful things. But they get lost sometimes. You got a spare, I suppose?'

Miles lit the gas ring under the kettle. He found this waiting game terribly difficult and it was affecting his breathing. 'I must keep calm,' he thought, 'must.'

'Deaf as well as tongue-tied. I said, you got a spare, I suppose?'

He nodded. He didn't trust himself to speak.

'I'll have this one, then.'

The kettle was already beginning to sing. He pointed to it and took the tea-pot and two cups from a shelf.

'Because it'll be nice to know I can drop in as the fancy takes me.' The driver got up, took the key from the lock and put it in his pocket.

Miles warmed the pot and put in the tea.

'Strong. I like it strong.'

Miles put in two more teaspoonfuls.

'Like I like everything else strong and that goes for my feelings. I got strong feelings.'

The kettle boiled and Miles filled the pot.

'And when I get them there's no stopping them. They tell me what I got to do, and I got to do it. They tell me what I got to do about you.'

Milk, sugar, tea-pot, mugs on the tray. Bring it over to the table. Put it down. Stand facing him.

'Because, perusing this load of shit,' he held up the exercise book, 'which has cost me many hours of my valuable time—no, don't pour it yet, let it draw, all the time in the world we've got—I begin to feel sorry for you. Does that surprise you? It surprises me.'

How soon will it be possible? The waiting is unbearable. But inescapable.

'Because everything I read in this tells me I'm right. Not in so many words. Oh no. Too smart for that, we are. All dressed up in fancy language. But it's there all right, if you know what you're looking for. Which I do. So I come to a decision. You need care. That's where I come in.'

Perhaps now. Simple to pour tea into a mug. Best things in life, simple and . . .

'Not yet. I said let it draw.'

More agony of waiting.

'I said I felt sorry for you. Christ knows why, seeing what a rotten bastard you are.' He paused. His eyes were glittering and he was smiling. He cleared his throat, was about to spit, changed his mind and continued like a schoolmaster savouring the words of the punishing sentence.

'I think to myself, here's this rotten bastard could do with a helping hand. Because if he goes on the way he is, one of these days he's going to finish up behind bars. And the inmates of H.M. prisons don't feel too kindly towards nasty little child molesters. I don't hide the fact I was an inmate myself for a short while—oh, I was innocent all right but the judge and me didn't see eye to eye on a little matter of principle—and I seen one of your sort roughed up. The result wasn't pretty. No, what I say is, if there's to be a beating up it ought to be done according to the rules. Me, I'm all in favour of corporal punishment. Look at it this way. Every time those nasty thoughts come into your head, it's going to cost you a beating. See what I mean?'

Long silence. So that was it. The way chance brings two people together and what an incongruous pair! Nothing in common, nothing whatever, until this; until now. Sadism in the guise of the righteous watch-dog guarding public morality. Any action however bizarre, however immoral, however vicious is justifiable by perversely following one set of principles to the exclusion of others. Like the Inquisition, like Stalinism, the Nazis, those guards in the concentration camps. Duty moving pleasurably to cruelty, and cruelty to lust. Not long now. Not long.

'Silence, I take it, means consent. And since there's no time like the present, we'll start now.' He stood up. 'While the tea's drawing.'

The suddenness of this switch in tactics was shocking. And revolting. This man, this hideous animal, was planning to use him in order to get some perverted sexual satisfaction. Half of him rejected it as unthinkable. The other half, he realised with a strange and fascinated horror, was pulling at him to submit; the conditioning all those years ago in Geneva, the bullying and the resulting guilty pleasure; something he had missed without realising it. And here was this chance to renew it. The temptation was momentarily overpowering. If it wasn't for the exercise book . . .

'Strip off.' The driver had produced a thin cane from down the leg of his trousers, and was swishing at the air with it.

'All right,' said Miles, 'but I'm going to have a cup of tea first.' And he poured the tea into one of the mugs.

'Tea after,' said the driver, raising the cane and bringing it down none too lightly across Miles' cheek.

'Now,' said Miles. And he threw the scalding contents of the mug straight into those piggy eyes.

Utterly surprised, he roared out a string of obscenities with the pain of it and covered his face with his hands. Miles snatched the exercise book from the table and bolted from the room, slamming the door in the pursuing driver's face. He rushed up the stairs and waited, panting, on the landing. He heard the driver's footsteps start up the stairs and was preparing to take refuge with Elsa; but the footsteps stopped and returned to his room. After about five minutes, he heard the front door slam. He waited several minutes more before venturing downstairs. He cautiously opened his door. On the table was a note. It read, *What happened makes no difference. Lucky I got the key. Expect me when you see me.*

He found his spare key. Locking the stable door . . . He couldn't help smiling ruefully as he turned the key in the lock before taking the record up to Elsa. She must have gone to sleep or she would have heard him on the landing. Must have.

17

When Daisy got back from Minnie Combermere's that night she was amazed to find Bert in bed. He was sitting propped up uncomfortably against the bed-head and wearing dark glasses.

'To what,' she asked, 'am I indebted for this delightful surprise?'

She couldn't tell whether he was staring at her, or whether he was asleep behind the spectacles. His face was seldom expressive, but she could usually judge his mood from his eyes. Now she couldn't, and that was disturbing.

She said, 'Sorry to interrupt your siesta, but you're sleeping in my bed linen.'

The bed lamp was behind him from where she stood and in its shadow the glasses looked like unfilled eye sockets. She wished he'd say something, or move. For a moment she wondered if he was dead. She moved hopefully towards him with a vague idea of listening for his heart beats. She put out her hand.

Suddenly he said, 'I got trouble with my eyes.'

She couldn't keep back a little gasp. If only he'd behave like ordinary.

'Why couldn't you say so before? What sort of trouble?'

'The hospital said I got to rest them. I got these drops.'

He was so bloody secretive. She said, 'Some punch up, I suppose.'

He ignored this. 'I could do with a beer and less talk.'

While she was getting it she thought back over the evening with Minnie. 'We've talked and talked about what Bert's up to—because up to something he is, no doubt of that—and we keep saying we got to find out; but we don't do anything.' Minnie was on the violet-flavoured chocolate creams. 'I get these penchants,' she said, 'and when I get them, nothing else will do.'

'You'd think she'd got a bun in the oven, the way she carries on,' said Reg.

Minnie's chins shook convulsively. 'It wouldn't be Reg's fault if I hadn't. He's quite a considerable baker, is Reg.' Then she said rather sadly, 'But he can't make buns in this oven. We found that out long ago.' She popped another chocolate cream between her lips and sucked it reflectively. 'It doesn't deter him. Look at him, Dais, he's blushing.'

Daisy looked at him and he was. And Minnie's chins were wobbling again.

'So what are we going to do?' she said, suddenly becoming all serious and business-like.

And they sat in silence for quite a while trying to think of something. And then, to everyone's surprise, including his own, it was Reg who came out with a stunning idea.

'It's these private dicks.'

'What are you talking about, Reg?'

'What I say. Like on the telly. Follow him up. See where he goes.'

Minnie said Reg had hidden depths of genius which didn't often come to the surface; but when they did—wow! But Daisy said wouldn't it be rather costly, she wasn't made of money and Minnie talked to her like a Dutch aunt and said anybody could see Daisy was making herself ill with worry on account Bert might be bringing a whole load of trouble on himself and she, having the misfortune to be married to him, would probably have to bear the brunt of it and that was part of it; but the other part was she'd simply got to satisfy her curiosity which was making her even more ill than the worry, wasn't that right? And what was money compared to your health? Hadn't she better think about it? And Daisy said perhaps she'd better.

She walked home slowly and thoughtfully and by the time she arrived she'd decided there'd be no harm in going down to the post office in the morning and leafing through the yellow pages of the directory to see if there was a detective agency anywhere handy.

And now, she thought, with this business of Bert's eyes on top of everything else, she was thankful she'd at last come to a decision and was going to do something about it. Minnie was right. She was making herself ill with curiosity. She took the can of beer into the bedroom. But Bert was already asleep, slumped sideways, the spectacles still on and breathing heavily. She left the beer by his bed and spent the night on the sofa.

The next morning she gave him his supper in the bedroom and left him to it. The only thing he said was to ask her to go down to the garage with a message that he'd not be working that night, but expect him tomorrow.

After doing this, she went in to the post office and there, sure enough, were a couple of pages of detective agencies in the yellow book. What did they all find to do, she wondered. And what sort of people were they, willing to spend their lives snooping round, nosing into other people's business? Some of them stated they employed only ex-policemen and C.I.D. officers. To make it seem more respectable she supposed. They all seemed much of a muchness, so she chose the nearest which was called *Undercover Ltd.* After a threepenny bus ride, during which she had deflating qualms about the whole project, she arrived at a door, inconspicuously sandwiched between a pet shop and a furniture store on Lavender Hill. She learned from a painted board in the passageway that *Undercover Ltd.* was on the third floor. Rather breathless from climbing the stairs, she paused in front of a door with frosted glass panes and a sign saying, '*Undercover Ltd.* Please ring.'

While she was trying to convince herself all over again that she was doing the right thing, and feeling small and nervous, she heard someone coming up the stairs behind her and suddenly was quite certain it was going to be Bert. Just like him to have got up and followed her to see what she was up to. And she got quite panicky. But of course it wasn't Bert; it was a large man in a bowler hat and a macintosh. He glanced at her and then stood beside her in front of the door. He looked like an ex-policeman and Daisy made up her mind he was one of the detectives, and felt more nervous than ever. He began to hum and Daisy supposed he was being tactful and wanted to put her at her ease.

'It's about my husband. It's rather private,' she said, looking meaningly at the door. Surely he didn't expect her to be interviewed on the landing?

'Haven't you rung the bell?'

'No.'

'Oh, I thought you had.'

'I was about to when you arrived.'

'Oh. Shall I ring it?'

'I shouldn't have thought you'd have to.'

The large man looked surprised and said, 'We'll be here all day unless one of us rings it.'

Daisy said, 'I'd have thought you'd have had a key, working here.'

'I don't work here.'

'Oh, I thought . . .' Her voice disappeared into an embarrassed silence as he rang the bell.

The door was opened almost immediately by a lady of uncertain age with a grumpy face. She asked the man if he had an appointment.

'Yes,' he said, 'the name is . . .' He stopped and looked suspiciously at Daisy, then fished an envelope out of his pocket and showed it to the lady who looked a little brighter and said 'Oh' and beckoned him inside. She re-appeared shortly after and, with a jerk of her head, invited Daisy in.

Inside was a small vestibule, with doors leading off and a desk with a miniature switchboard. The lady sat at the desk and said, 'I don't believe you have an appointment. Is there anyone in particular you wish to see?'

'Well,' said Daisy, 'who can I see?'

'It depends.' The lady was now looking not only grumpy, but unhelpful.

'On what?'

'On what you've come about.'

'It's private.'

'If I don't know what it's about I can't tell you who you should see, can I?'

Daisy was furious. Who did she think she was, sitting there and treating her like dirt? She said sharply, 'I haven't come here to be treated like . . .'

But the switchboard buzzed and the lady said, 'Just a minute,' slipped on a pair of headphones, plugged in, and said sweetly into the mouthpiece, 'Yes, Mr Moffatt?' and then, after a pause, 'Yes, Mr Moffatt.' She took off the headphones and unplugged. 'Excuse me,' she said to Daisy, 'I'll be back in a minute. Perhaps you'd like to look at *Woman's Own.*' She pointed to a pile of old magazines on a table by the wall and a couple of upright chairs. 'Do sit down,' and she disappeared through one of the doors with an unmistakable air of having got the better of somebody.

'Cheeky bitch,' murmured Daisy, whose indignation was rapidly overcoming her nervousness. Nothing would now induce her to sit down, let alone look at *Woman's Own.* She stood in front of the desk and lit a cigarette. She would like to have paced up and down, but there wasn't room. She was considering several annihilating things she could say to the lady on her return, when one of the doors opened and a small man with a sharp nose and glasses looked out. He looked surprised to see her and said, 'Are you waiting to see somebody?'

'Yes,' she said, her nervousness at once returning.

'Which of us?'

'You tell me.'

'Have you seen the receptionist?'

'She went in there.' She pointed to Mr Moffatt's door.

'Perhaps I can help you. What's it about?'

'It's private.'

'Of course. I've got a few minutes. Come in.'

As she followed him, the receptionist came out of Mr Moffatt's room and looked even grumpier as she saw how well Daisy had managed without her. This was a nice little morale booster.

The small man sat her down in front of his desk and went quite out of his way to be nice to her. A bit too far perhaps, she thought; she wasn't used to being buttered up except by Minnie. He started by telling her his name was Dash, ex-inspector, which she thought rather funny, but of course she didn't smile. Then he asked her name and address and, when she hesitated, he assured her that it would be as safe with him as with The Bank of England, which she thought was fair enough, so she gave it to him. He sat back in his chair, pushed his spectacles up on to his forehead, closed his eyes and said, 'Now, tell me all about it.'

Daisy was just about to, when her natural caution came to her rescue just in time and she asked if it was going to cost her a lot of money; because if it was, not being made of it, she couldn't afford it.

Mr Dash sat forward, pulled his glasses down on to his nose again, extracted a printed scale of charges from a drawer and handed it to her. 'I think you will find them reasonable, madam. You will readily understand why they have to vary from case to case according to time, amount of work involved, distance and necessary expenses. When you have told me your little problem, we shall be able to be more specific.' And he leaned back again as before with his eyes closed, his spectacles up on his forehead and just a hint of a sympathetic smile under his neat moustache.

Daisy started rather tentatively, but she quickly got into her stride and gave a good account of herself. Occasionally Mr Dash nodded and, once or twice, he put his spectacles back on his nose to look at her quite sharply and ask a question. When she had finished, he put the tips of his fingers together in front of his nose and considered. Then he said: 'I take it you're afraid he may be engaged in some form of blackmail?'

'I never know what he's up to, he's so secretive. He's never been like this before and I'm worried sick.'

Mr Dash nodded sympathetically. 'I think I can say we should be justified in taking your case.'

'But he mustn't ever know I put you on to him,' said Daisy. 'Talk about the balloon going up.'

Mr Dash looked pained. 'We are very experienced, madam.'

'You'd better be.' And she told him about Bert going to jail for assault and Mr Dash looked serious and made a note on his pad.

Then they discussed terms and he said of course she would understand there were rather special problems in following a cab at night once the traffic quietened down and the streets were empty. But he dared say they would manage. And the first thing to find out was if Bert was paying regular visits to some address, because from what she had told him this seemed likely and she agreed it was. Then they arranged *Undercover* would tail Bert for three nights. She reckoned she could just about afford this, but that would be her limit and if they hadn't news for her by then she'd have to skip it. Mr Dash said it was just as she liked and they must hope for the best and he was sure she wouldn't mind paying something on account as this was usual and, as it were, in earnest of good faith and they'd better have a photo of Bert. She told him the only photo existing was one of them both coming out of the registry office which was on the mantelpiece and she'd bring it and the money the next morning.

When she got home, Bert was in the sitting room. He said he couldn't sleep because his eyes hurt and where the fuck had she been all that time.

'If you can't go and see your friends . . .' she said—it was second nature, that sort of evasion—'and . . .'—attack being always the best defence—'I'll thank you not to use that word in my presence. How many more times do I have to tell you?'

'I'll say what I fucking like.'

Daisy couldn't resist it. She got to the door. 'Seeing Mother Nature's been unkind to you Bert—you won't mind me mentioning such a tiny thing—I'd have thought you'd keep that word, if you must say it, for those who don't know.'

She was out of the door with the key and had locked it as he started hammering it with his fists and shouting. After the customary routine of sending the key up on the string, she went round to Minnie's place, calling at the post office on the way to cash ten pounds of savings and filling in the forms to draw more in time to foot the *Undercover Ltd* bill. Minnie was agog.

'I'm proud of you, Dais. You was never one to let the grass grow under your feet.'

They had a game of cards, Beggar-my-neighbour to please Reg, and while they played Daisy told them in the smallest detail about her visit to *Undercover* and what Mr Dash had said and how she was going to take the photo from the mantelpiece and tell Bert she'd broken the glass and was having it repaired. Minnie made approving noises like a mother hen and they talked so much that Reg won easily, which pleased them as much as it did him.

18

Miles had been round to a little shop in the Hampstead Road which had a giant Yale key suspended above it and a notice underneath saying 'Keys Cut While U Wait.' The shopkeeper was unhelpful. He said that cutting keys was one thing and changing locks different altogether. It wasn't so much a question of could the lock be changed, of course it could. The question was when.

'Well,' said Miles patiently, 'when?'

The shopkeeper said Miles would be surprised if he knew the number of locks in the neighbourhood waiting to be changed. People lose their keys; they get nervous, specially at night, specially women. His uncle did his best. He couldn't do more than that, could he? He was rising seventy-nine, his bronchitis was chronic and he couldn't be expected to be as quick as when he was hale and hearty.

Miles said he wanted it done immediately. It was urgent.

The shopkeeper looked despairingly at the ceiling, from which hung a variety of kettles, saucepans, lavatory brushes, feather dusters, balls of string, clothes-horses, brooms, asbestos mats and fish slices. The shop smelt strongly, but not unpleasantly, of camphor balls and paraffin.

'That's what they all say. Immediate. Urgent. Ever heard of a waiting list? If you care to give me your name and address, I'll put you on it. If not, not.'

Miles told him and asked when he could expect his turn to come.

'Any time over the next three weeks. All depends on my uncle. Don't forget he has to come over from Clapham and at his age.'

The room was unsafe and vulnerable that night in spite of the chair wedged under the door handle. Sleep was fitful and frightening until the early hours. He woke by a series of progressions through layers of consciousness to an awareness that someone was gently, but persistently, trying to open the door.

He got out of bed and stood watching it advance an inch forward till the handle knocked against the top of the chair and moved it a fraction further into the room. Then it retreated and advanced again, pushing the chair in still further. He was still drugged with sleep and he stood stupidly watching, quite unable to say anything. At last, when the door was sufficiently open, the head of a very old man in a bowler hat looked round and surveyed him balefully.

'I knocked like it said twice, three times.'

'I'm afraid I was asleep.'

'You'd think twice, three times, would be enough for anybody, but no.'

Miles removed the chair and opened the door. 'I'm afraid I sleep very heavily.'

The old man was neatly dressed in a dark suit and wore button boots with frayed cloth tops. He carried a small Gladstone bag and looked for all the world like an unsuccessful G.P. who should have retired twenty or thirty years back.

'I met a stout party, female, going out, said you lived in here. I don't make journeys for the fun of it, not at my age and with my bronchitis. No reply to my knock on this door, twice, three times; so I tried the handle and . . .'

The old man was overcome with a wheezing cough which claimed his whole attention for a good two minutes, during which Miles made attempts to persuade him to sit down, offer a drink of water and even pat him in the small of the back; but they were ignored. He got alarmingly redder and redder in the face, his eyes popping and streaming, a handkerchief to his mouth, his body racked with the coughing. When it stopped, he stood there for at least a minute, regaining his breath and wiping his mouth.

Then he continued as if nothing had happened, '. . . . there was this chair and knowing you must be there—chairs not being able to use their legs and me getting no response—I come in expecting the worst, but I'm happy to see you alive and well.'

He was already inspecting the lock. 'The work of a moment,' he said and, opening his bag and producing tools and a new lock, he knelt down rather shakily and got to work.

Miles watched the dexterous old hands moving with the absolute assurance of all those years of experience and was surprised when they stopped for a moment.

'I'm very religious.'

'Are you?'

'Yes. I believe in the Holy Spirit. You haven't got a drop, have you?'

'I've got a little brandy. I keep it for emergencies.'

The old man started another coughing fit and Miles fetched the brandy flask with his father's initials on it and poured a little into a tumbler. The eyes looked at it gratefully, but the hands were too involved in the coughing to take it until the fit was over.

Then he said, 'I'm an emergency,' took the glass, swallowed the brandy, wiped his mouth and went back to work, but this time not in silence.

'Every year for the last twenty or so they said to me I won't get through the winter. You'll be carried off, they said. I'd welcome it, I said. I'd sooner live in the spirit. But every Spring I've come through. And I got to live in hopes the next winter will do the trick.' He had removed the lock and was trying the new one for size.

Miles said, 'What makes you so sure that you'll go on living in the spirit?'

The old man now had a small mallet in one hand and a chisel in the other. He thought for a moment. 'I answer your question by asking you another,' he said. 'What do you mean by spirit?'

'The dictionary gives a variety of definitions. The one that comes immediately to my mind is "a disembodied soul".'

The old man started to chisel round the existing mortise, delicately tapping with the mallet. 'The one that comes immediately to my mind is whisky, brandy and the like. You lead a good life. Result? You go to heaven. What's heaven? The best you can think of; like whisky, like brandy. I look forward to it, young man.'

Miles wasn't sure if he was expected to take this seriously. Then he laughed. 'You've got a lot of courage.'

The old man paused to put down the mallet and devote both hands to the chisel. A thin sliver of wood curled down from the top of the mortise like a spring. He pressed the cutting edge into the corner and the sliver fell to the floor.

'Courage,' he said, 'what's that? I'll tell you, young man. You get medals for it, a nice thank you letter from the King and Queen maybe and your picture in the papers. I've had all of that; oh, very fine, top of the world, one of the brave, one of the few. But the reverse side of that medal you wear so bravely, what do you find? Fear. Be so kind as to pass me that lock.'

Miles handed it to him and watched him press it into place. It fitted exactly. He picked up a screwdriver and methodically fitted each screw and drove it home.

'We spend most of our lives pretending we're not frightened. We act brave, we act don't care, we act funny and flippant, angry and bossy, meek and mild, religious or atheist, we drink ourselves silly; but in our hearts we're shit scared, if you'll pardon the expression. And you're no exception, young man. Well, there's your new lock done and one bit of fear the less.'

He slowly got to his feet and immediately started another coughing fit. Miles helped him to a chair. When the coughing was over, he lay back exhausted and put out a hand for the glass. Miles hastily replenished it.

'You're very kind,' he whispered, 'very kind.'

After he had gone, Miles felt strangely comforted. Strangely, because what the old man had said was bleak and depressing in the extreme. And yet, if it were true, if the brotherhood of man really meant the brotherhood of fear, all the people who scared him, yes, even the most arrogant like Mr Fison, the bullies like the Swiss boy and the cab driver weren't as he had always supposed, a different species of human being from himself. At least he and they had this one thing in common, and it was inescapable. He was grateful to the old man for bringing it home to him so clearly. He had known it and used it in his thinking as one knows and uses a word without considering its etymology. Now he thought he really understood it.

He worked through the afternoon and then decided to go to the first house of *Mayerling* which, as he understood it, drove home the old man's words as surely as he had driven home the screws in the lock. When he got back, he found a note pushed under his door. It read, 'Changing locks don't change anything.'

He boiled a couple of eggs and made some toast and tea and, while he had his meal, he propped up the note in front of him and tried to work out why the common factor of fear made bullies of some people and victims of others. Was it something in him, some negative quality, that attracted the positive aggression in the driver? And was this persecution to become a way of life that supplied a necessary satisfaction to them both? Why else had he allowed it to continue? He had only to go to the police. Even if there had been anything incriminating in his precious notebook—and there wasn't except possibly by implication—it was now safely under lock and key in his desk. The driver wouldn't have a leg to stand on. And yet . . . supposing he had taken a copy? Some of it, taken out of context, might lay him open to most unpleasant suspicions and accusations, perhaps to some sort of police surveillance. That would be unthinkable. No, he would have to tackle the driver himself; his brain against the driver's brawn, one manifestation of fear against another. And there he was again, back with his own brand of fear, his timidity, his ineffectiveness. Because when you are frightened, you can't think straight and so your mental strength dwindles to a weakness as vulnerable as your physical inferiority. And you're wide open.

Ridiculous, he thought, to be back in the same old world of indecision and perpetual self-consciousness, where every passing laugh is a snide jab, every simple remark is loaded. Well, there was Elsa. At least she knew he wasn't entirely lacking in manhood. After he'd thrown the tea in the driver's face and recovered the exercise book, after he'd heard the front door slam, he went down and collected the record and took it up for her. He tapped on the door. No reply. So, feeling rather proud and pleased with himself, he had walked in. She was asleep, sprawled across the settee, her arms above her head, the negligee parted showing everything she'd got and he had felt a surge of lust; well, nothing wrong with that, everything right in fact. And yet something, even in that moment of delighted realisation, some innate shyness, over concern about what somebody else might think, had stopped him. He had left the record by her side and tiptoed out. Stupid! He ought to have had her again, there and then. She'd have loved to be woken up like that, fiercely, masterfully. Instead, he had gone back to his room and imagined it all, masturbating elaborately. Well, he wouldn't make the same mistake this time.

He went up the stairs, having carefully locked the door behind him and pocketed the key. Miss James was practising, the young married couple in the room opposite were silent or out. For once, the loo half-way up the second flight was empty, the door ajar. He went in. That schoolmaster who had recounted to Form VI at his prep school what the Duke of Wellington or someone had said, 'Always take the opportunity when it presents itself. The future is unpredictable and may be inconvenient.' He remembered Giles Major putting up his hand and saying, 'May I take the opportunity now please sir?' and the laugh it got. And the still louder laugh and Giles' discomfiture when the master replied, 'Alas, Giles, the moment is inconvenient.' And how he wriggled and held himself for the rest of the lesson, and some of them followed his frantic rush to the loos when the bell rang and watched him take it out as he ran—the biggest in the school by common consent—and leave a trail of pee down the corridor. How he had admired him! Most of them wouldn't have dared even if they'd thought of it. And his thoughts moved on to Rodney, clutching the railings outside his window, doing it in his knickers. And he felt again the compassion and love which made him want to be part of Rodney's life, to re-live his own adolescence in his and to seek a love for himself through his love for a child.

And now, being godfather to the baby, it was all happening just as he wanted it and if he played his cards right he . . . He was aware his penis was becoming tumescent. For what? Not Elsa as he had planned, but for the promise of his own adolescent phantasies renewed in Rodney. And if this were so, then the cab driver was right; he was a paederast. He deserved the whippings, must suffer them. Welcome them? Yes—the tumescence continued relentlessly—welcome them. A masochist, too, who had found his sadist. He whispered, 'Oh God, Elsa, help me. You said I was all right, and I was. You helped me prove it. I'm a man and I want to behave like one, not like an adolescent.' And, as if in answer, detumescence obligingly set in and he buttoned up and couldn't help smiling to himself at the irony of it.

He pulled the chain and, as he came out, old Mr James was heaving himself up the stairs and saying, 'Very timely, Mr Madgwick. Always take the opportunity, as Dr Johnson is reported to have said.'

'I thought it was the Duke of Wellington.'

'I hardly think so. Possibly Charles the Second. It could conceivably have been Alfred Lord Tennyson, he had an apt way with words. Excuse me, won't you?'

Miles went on up the stairs with a new and rather desperate determination and stopped opposite Elsa's door. As he was about to knock, he heard the opening bars of Brunnhilde's immolation from inside and, as the music drove forward irresistibly, he tried to guess whether Elsa was playing it for herself or for her Wagnerian fixated customer. The record sounded worn and scratched like his own. But then, if she was to be believed, the customer was a regular and played his record on each and every occasion, so God knows, that too must be the worse for wear. After a full minute and a half of indecision, he knocked loudly. He had expected the music to stop, but it went majestically on. Perhaps she hadn't heard. Blast the woman, he must see her, this was desperately important. He didn't care any more whether he was interrupting or not. He knocked again, louder. He heard the key turn and the door opened a crack. Through it she whispered, 'Get the hell out of here. I'm busy.'

'I must see you.'

The door opened a little wider and her tousled head and a bare shoulder appeared.

'Oh, it's you darling. Too bad. I'm busy all evening.'

'It's important.'

'I could manage tomorrow.'

'It won't wait.'

'That's what they all say, darling. Sorry.'

The door closed. The key turned. The Wagner continued; and there he was, on the landing, alone, and wanting to scream with frustration. Only, of course, he didn't. He went down to his room, went to bed and fell asleep reading *Remnants of my Past, Present and Future.*

19

Alice had looked forward so much to getting home that the reality was something of an anti-climax. Aunt Annie had prepared a welcoming tea while Ethel kept the shop. But she wasn't to be trusted not to help herself to the confectionery, so Aunt Annie had to keep interrupting the preparations and make forays into the shop to see what she was up to.

Ethel was hurt. 'You put me on my honour,' she whined.

'Some people's honour is different from others. You're acting up altogether too innocent for my liking.'

Rodney, sensing trouble, put his head round the door.

'It's him,' said Ethel, pointing.

'Don't point. It's rude.'

'It's Rod.'

'What is?'

'Coming in here when your back's turned and asking me for toffee crisps.'

Rodney was outraged. 'Ooh, I never.'

Aunt Annie was in no mood for argument. She cuffed them both and, as they started to bawl, a cab drew up at the door and there was Alice carrying the new baby and George with her suitcase paying off the driver. Alice walked into the shop to a crescendo of howling from Ethel and Rodney and a tirade from Aunt Annie.

'What's it all in aid of?' she shouted, trying to make herself heard.

They crowded round her, the children complaining through their tears that they'd been hit, Aunt Annie justifying herself at the top of her voice. This cacophony understandably frightened the baby; it cried too.

Alice, indignant at such a non-welcome, lost her temper. 'Shut up,' she yelled, 'shut up, shut up!'

George came in, but didn't notice Mrs Treasure had followed him. She stood behind him, savouring the drama and the spectacle. In the middle of a particularly telling sentence Aunt Annie noticed her and, breaking off, gave vent to such a portentous 'Sh . . . sh . . . sh . . .' that suddenly they were all silent. Except the baby; its cry sounded small and lonely in such a hostile world. It was looking directly at Mrs Treasure, who shifted slightly under its gaze and said: 'Poor little thing. And real tears, too. You can hardly blame it, can you?'

Though this was addressed to the room in general, Aunt Annie took it to herself and took it hard. 'If you ask me, Mrs Treasure,' she said, 'babies cry because they don't like something. I notice it was as good as gold till you came in.'

Mrs Treasure was nettled. 'I never asked you nothing, let alone making free with personal remarks. I come into the shop like ordinary for my Seniors. I might be forgiven for thinking I'd strayed into the parrot house at the zoo.'

She should have known better.

'You must feel quite at home then, Mrs Treasure. George, sell her her Seniors, and don't forget to count them. Come on, Alice.' And Aunt Annie marched into the back living room followed by Alice and the children, leaving George to pacify Mrs Treasure.

The welcoming tea was an unqualified failure. To begin with, Alice realised she had over-estimated her strength; she felt drained and rather faint. She gave the baby to Aunt Annie to hold and had to sit down. Aunt Annie told her she looked like a ghost and sent Ethel for the Sal Volatile. George, having disposed of Mrs Treasure, carried the suitcase upstairs and met Ethel coming out of the bathroom.

'I can't find it,' she said.

'What?'

'The Sal Vol . . . what's its name.'

'I don't know what you're talking about.'

'For mum. What Auntie sent me for.'

'Oh! It's in the bathroom cupboard.'

'It's not.'

From downstairs Aunt Annie shouted, 'Are you going to be all day, Eth?'

'I can't find it, Auntie.'

'It's in the bathroom cupboard.'

'It's not.'

George emerged from the bathroom and confirmed this. Aunt Annie dumped the baby on the sofa, instructing Rodney to see it didn't fall off but otherwise not to touch it, gave Alice a little pat and a word of encouragement and then heaved herself up the stairs, brushed past George and Ethel who were standing helplessly on the landing and disappeared into the bathroom, muttering: 'Some people don't know what their eyes are for.'

'It's not there,' said George.

'We both looked,' said Ethel.

Aunt Annie was angrily rattling about among the bottles and ointments. After a short while she emerged from the bathroom breathing heavily, descended the stairs without a word, went through to the kitchen and straight to the shelf over the sink.

'I would have thought,' she said, reproachfully taking the Sal Volatile bottle from the shelf and mixing Alice a stiff dose in a tea-cup, 'I would have thought one of you would have reminded me.'

'What of?' said George, timidly.

'When I got upset the other night about the baby being abnormal. Anyone in their senses would have known I had to have a pick-me-up.' She took the cup into Alice and stood over her while she drank it.

George said, 'You must have got it yourself after I left.'

'Of course I got it myself—drink it down, Alice, it'll put heart into you—if you don't do things for yourself in this house nobody else will. I can't be expected to remember everything. I'm not the all-s eing eye.'

'Don't get yourself worked up, Auntie.'

'I am worked up.'

'Then you'd better have a dose yourself.'

Aunt Annie was red in the face and her breathing alarmingly stertorous. 'I climbed them stairs too fast,' she said, and sat down rather suddenly. Alice got up. 'Don't you get it, Alice,' Aunt Annie managed to whisper.

'Keep quiet, Auntie, I'm all right.' Alice took the tea-cup into the kitchen and mixed another dose. She still felt weak and swimmy and her legs felt cotton-woolly and her head ached. The Sal Volatile had helped though; she was conscious of it inside her, a spot of comfort in the middle of a cold despondency. She was sorry for Aunt Annie, who had gone to so much trouble with the tea and the cake in the middle of the table with 'welcome' on it and a little gnome holding a Union Jack. And all to no purpose, because she couldn't eat anything and knew she must get to bed or she would flop out. And she felt guilty about this, though God knows she didn't need to. She took a gulp of the Sal Volatile and then wearily took the cup in to Aunt Annie, helped her drink it down and arranged her on the sofa.

Then she said, 'Help me up the stairs, George. I got to go to bed. When I'm in you can bring me up the baby.'

She had to pause and rest twice going up the stairs and stood, supported by George, listening to the subdued snivelling of the children.

'I've disappointed them, George. But it's not my fault.'

'You couldn't help it.' George felt exhausted and would have liked to sink back in his chair with the evening paper and doze off. But what with Aunt Annie recumbent downstairs and Alice flopping out, he thought it was scarcely the moment.

Later, when she was tucked up in bed with the baby and listening to the desultory murmuring from the tea-party downstairs, Alice began to feel drowsy. But she didn't drop off to sleep immediately because she was worried about Aunt Annie.

'I'm worried about your great Aunt Annie,' she said to the baby. 'Never had a day's illness, not to my knowledge, and now she goes and gets these turns. She can be a bloody pain sometimes, but she's all I got, excepting you and your brother and sister, and I wouldn't like anything to happen to her. Because, being that lot older, she makes me feel . . . well . . . safe. I suppose like I make you feel safe. If you're as clever as that lot up at the hospital say you are, you'll know what I'm getting at.'

The baby looked rather knowing, his face puckered slightly and went red. He farted surprisingly loudly and then smiled as his eyes closed and he went to sleep.

But Alice went on talking to him. 'I make no mention of your godfather. He doesn't make me feel safe, not by a long chalk. But after the christening, when things get sorted out a bit, there's just a chance he could make me feel safer than anyone.'

Then she closed her eyes and started planning the christening. And her brain went racing away with her as it always did and she wasn't a bit surprised to find it was that cab driver who was the parson and was asking Mr Madgwick, 'Who gives this child away?' and Mr Madgwick said, 'I do' and the baby said quite distinctly, 'Not on your life' and disappeared down the plug-hole and Aunt Annie was saying, 'Now look what you've done.' And Alice said, 'What?'

'Gone off to sleep and I've gone and woke you up.'

Alice rubbed her eyes and yawned. 'Feeling better then? You didn't ought to have climbed them stairs again.'

Aunt Annie said she had to say cheery-bye, hadn't she? before getting back to Frame Street. They asked each other if they were sure they'd be all right and they both said they would be. Then Aunt Annie sat on the bed and Alice told her what she planned for the christening and apologised all over again for spoiling the tea-party and by the time they'd finished with that and discussed Ethel's pertness and Rodney's artfulness and George's stubbornness and Mrs Treasure's poking her nose into other people's affairs it was quite late. George got a cab for Aunt Annie and sent the protesting children to bed.

Later, he crawled in beside Alice. The baby was still asleep. She pretended to be. Then, soon after George started snoring, she was.

She took it easy during the first few days at home because she had to. She kept Ethel away from school to help her with fetching and carrying and shopping and washing up, and wrote a note for Rodney to give to the teacher:

> My little girl, Ethel, is suffering from a severe cold in the head. I am keeping her home for a few days on account she might infect the other boys and girls. Hoping this is all right with you, I remain,
>
> Yours truly,
> (Signed) Mrs Remnant

You had to be careful with teachers. If you told the truth you could be in trouble with the authorities. Rodney was delighted to be an instrument of this little deception, but, with sure motherly instinct, was warned not to overplay it.

'If asked, just say she's got a bad cold. Anything else, you don't know, see?'

Rodney twinkled. 'Not half I don't.'

'That's a good boy.'

Then there was the visit to the vicar to fix up the christening at St Mary's. Alice put on her best for this and took the baby. She worked it out the vicar would want to give it the once over before agreeing to baptise it. She left the pram inside the gate and carried the baby up the grand steps and rang the bell. The vicar answered the door himself, which surprised her; she had been bracing herself not to be intimidated by some chit of a maid in cap and apron.

He was tall and wore a cassock which made him look even taller; his hair was dark and brushed back either side of a centre parting; it looked and smelt as if he used Brylcreem. The top part of his face, high forehead, dark eyes behind horn-rimmed spectacles, belonged to a scholar; the lower part contradicted this; pendulous nose, full lips, fleshy jowls, these could be the outward and visible signs of an inward and sensual disgrace.

'Who are you? What do you want?' He spoke very quickly and abruptly.

'It's my baby. I want to have him christened.'

'Well, I can't do it now. I'm very busy.'

'I wanted to fix up a time.'

'After evensong one Sunday. I'm baptising two next Sunday. Enough is enough. How about the one after?'

'Yes, thank you.'

He was looking at her keenly. 'By the way, I take it you're one of my parishioners. Why don't I know you?'

The way he shot questions at you as if you were a kid in school! 'I'm not quite sure.'

'Come in.' He led the way into his study, shouting, 'Shut the door, will you?'

She gave the door a kick behind her and it slammed shut. He was already sitting at his desk when she entered the room.

'Shut the door,' he said.

She kicked that one shut too. 'It's a bit awkward with baby.'

'Think, think! You must know.' He didn't ask her to sit down.

'The curate called about three years ago. I gave him a cup of tea.'

'I haven't seen you in church, have I?'

'We came when Rodney was christened. That was the old vicar.'

'How old is Rodney?'

'Five.'

'So you haven't been to church for five years. Why?'

She began to feel resentful under this catechism and he hadn't even noticed the baby, let alone admired it. She sat herself down on the edge of a hard chair facing him and said, rather defiantly: 'Well for one thing it's the incense. It gets up my nose.'

'We hope it gets up God's nose. We think he likes it, but if you don't like it, there are plenty of other churches that agree with you. But you don't go to them, do you?'

She admitted she didn't. The vicar put the palm of his hand against the back of his head and scratched the top of his scalp with the tips of his fingers. Then he stood up, went behind her and put his hands on her shoulders. He asked if there were other children besides Rodney.

'Ethel. She's nearly eight.' She wished he'd take his hands off her. She didn't like to move away, but she was afraid for her clothes; hair cream was greasy stuff.

'The trouble is, my dear,' he was saying, 'that you come to God to christen you and marry you and bury you; the rest of your life you hardly give him a thought. How would you like it if someone you love just made use of you once or twice because it suited him and otherwise avoided you?'

She supposed she'd better say something. She certainly hadn't bargained for being preached at. Why couldn't he just give her the time of the christening and let her go? She opened her mouth to say she wouldn't like it, but before she could speak, he went on: 'You wouldn't like it, would you?'

She shook her head.

'There's no need to cry.'

'I'm not crying.' But of all the stupid things, she was and, when he moved round in front of her, she turned her head away and fumbled in her bag for a handkerchief. 'I've got a bit of a cold.' She blew her nose.

'So have I,' he said, and blew his. Suddenly he laughed. A loud, barking sort of laugh which startled her.

She said, 'What's so funny?'

'You are my dear. And I am. And all the rest of the inhabitants of this extraordinary world. I should think God must be in stitches when he's not in tears.'

She felt quite shocked. All right for ordinary people to talk about God in that light-hearted sort of way, but a vicar . . . that wasn't what you expected.

'Bring your family and the godparents to evensong on Sunday week. Six o'clock. Christening immediately after. Off you go. Bless you. And shut the door.'

He went back to his desk and started to write. He didn't look up again, so she found her own way out and, wheeling the baby home, thought how odd he had never even noticed it. He was funny all right. She couldn't make up her mind whether she liked him or hated him.

'Like no one else you ever met,' she told George. 'So rude. But there's something about him.'

'There must be,' said George, 'he's got ten children.'

She wrote a note to Mr Madgwick to tell him the date, time and place of the christening and how pleased and honoured she was that he had agreed to be godfather, and perhaps he would care to come to tea the day after tomorrow to give his godson the proper once over. Ethel was getting the tea things together in the kitchen, so she gave it to Rodney to post. He had just come back from school. 'Down to the pillar box and straight back,' he was told.

George came in from the shop, where business was slack. He pottered about and fidgeted while Alice, remembering she should also have written to the red-haired nurse who had agreed to be the godmother, sat down at the table with pen poised over the Basildon Bond and realised she had no idea what her name was. After some thought, during which she twice told George how could she be expected to concentrate with him pacing up and down like a caged elephant, she wrote:

> I'm mad. I just realised I never asked your name. Please tell my husband who will bring this. The vicar says we got to have the christening Sunday week at six at St Mary's

where I told you. He got ten children. Imagine! Hope you can manage.

She folded the letter and asked George what was the matter—he was so restless—and was there something on his mind? He said there was, so she told him to come out with it.

'Well,' he said, 'it's the christening.'

'What about it?' She was on the defensive immediately. 'For God's sake stop fingering the ornaments.'

He moved to the window and appeared to be seeking inspiration from the back yard. At last he said, 'I am the father.'

'I should hope so. I'm not the Virgin Mary or something.'

'I got a right to be consulted. You get all this fixed up and I'm not consulted. I mean this Mr Madgwick and this nurse.'

'You were consulted.'

'Only after you made up your mind. There's got to be two godfathers. Who's the other I ask myself? Prince Philip I suppose, or General de bloody Gaulle!'

Alice said, 'You've no call to say you wasn't consulted because you was. You agreed. As for the other godfather, I was thinking of that cousin of Aunt Annie's, you know . . . Art Jobson. What do you think of that?'

George frowned.

'I'm consulting you, George. What's wrong with Art?'

'He's an undertaker.'

'He's very respectable.'

'No son of mine's going to have a godfather who's an undertaker.'

Alice knew perfectly well what was coming and had only suggested Art Jobson so that she could give way gracefully.

She sighed and said, 'Oh well,' and then smiled resignedly and asked if George had anyone in mind.

He prowled round the room again, pretending to rack his brains, suddenly stopped and said, 'I know.'

'Who?'

'Joe.'

Alice said what an extraordinary idea and was told it was no more extraordinary than Mr Madgwick, and if George had agreed to him it was only fair she should agree to Joe. So she gave way not quite as gracefully as she had planned, but he was delighted and, as a result, was quite pleasant about taking the note up to the hospital to the red-headed nurse. They were laughing at how ridiculous it was not to know her name when Alice remembered it must have been at least ten minutes ago she had sent Rodney to the post and he hadn't come back.

'The little perisher,' she said.

'I'll go after him.' George went through the shop and out into the street. He was astonished to see a cab draw up at the door and Rodney getting out of it.

'Enjoy the ride?' the driver asked.

'Not half.' Rodney was grinning delightedly as he slammed the cab door shut.

'What's all this about?' asked George, recognising the driver immediately in spite of his dark glasses.

'He gave me a lift, Dad.' Rodney was dancing with excitement.

The driver called out, 'Dropped a fare this side of the bridge. Saw your kid at the pillar box. You want to be careful letting him out on his own. He's had a basinful already. Him and me's been having a little chat. You must be up the pole asking that bugger to be godfather.'

The taxi was pinking loudly as it idled. Alice had come to the door and Rodney ran to her. She pushed him roughly inside the shop and her voice was sharp with indignation as she called out: 'You mind your business and we'll mind ours.'

The driver turned his dark glasses in her direction for a moment and said, 'A fine mother you are, I don't think.' Then he got into gear and, with a roar of acceleration, the cab moved off. But it hadn't gone more than a few yards when it stopped and his head appeared out of the window.

'You're not having that bastard for no godfather. I'll see to that if it's the last thing I do.' And he drove on up the road.

Alice and George watched the cab till it turned the corner. They walked back through the shop and into the sitting room in silence. Rodney had disappeared upstairs and Ethel was laying the tea.

There was a long, awkward pause. George was fiddling with the tea things. Then he cleared his throat and said, 'It might be better after all if you asked Art Jobson instead of this Madgwick.

It's not as if we know much about him, Alice. I mean . . . we don't want trouble, do we?'

He looked anxiously at her, wanting her to agree and knowing she wasn't going to. The way her lips set into that tight little line, always a bad sign.

She said, 'I'm surprised at you, George, letting that man talk to me like that.'

'I didn't exactly have the chance to stop him, did I?' So unfair to take it out on him.

'You could have said something. Told him off. You just stood there.'

This was too much. He'd played along with her over this godfather business because, after all, she'd been through a bad time in hospital. Women got funny ideas at such times; best to humour them. Since she was better he'd been screwing himself up to have it out with her, but somehow the moment never seemed right. Now it had been forced on him with a vengeance.

Ethel had finished laying the table and was leaning against the lintel, pushing the door with her foot so that it kept bouncing back off the door stop. Maddening at any time, but unbearable at this moment.

'For Christ's sake leave that door alone,' he shouted angrily. 'What do you think it is, a bloody yo-yo or something?'

Ethel stopped kicking the door and looked astonished. She was used to being shouted at by Mum and Aunt Annie, never by Dad. She began to snivel.

But he was shouting again. 'None of that, my girl. You bloody stop it or you'll get a sight more than you bargained for.'

Ethel bawled and cringed back into the kitchen as he advanced on her.

Alice's voice cut in, ominously controlled and prim. 'Leave her alone, George.'

'I know what I'm doing.'

'I said leave her alone.'

'Don't you bloody tell me what to do.'

'If you touch that child, I'll never speak to you again.'

But he was already chasing Ethel round the table. She suddenly disappeared underneath. He caught her as she was crawling out the other side and picked her up. She was looking up at him, panting and frightened. Then, deliberately, he smacked her face; not very hard, but hard enough to sting. She screamed as she struggled out of his grasp and ran to Alice.

Alice sat on a chair and took her in her arms. Ethel went on sobbing for several minutes. At intervals she stopped and said, 'He hurt me, Mum, he hurt me,' and then started sobbing again. Alice kept stroking her hair and patting her.

George stood watching them. He wasn't angry any more. He said, 'I'm sorry. These kids are getting too big for their boots. Somebody's got to teach them. Well, haven't they?'

Ethel stopped crying to hear what Alice would say. But she didn't say anything.

'What I was going to say,' he went on, 'before all this started is there's no smoke without fire.'

Alice told Ethel to go and put the kettle on and Ethel made a great show of going round the other side of the table to avoid him.

'Be reasonable, Alice. I don't say this Madgwick is a wrong-un. But we don't know, do we? That cab driver's got a point of view. We got to be fair all round.'

Alice got up. She looked pale and purposeful and made for the kitchen.

'Just a minute, Alice. I haven't finished. What I ask myself is why that driver goes to all this carry-on if there isn't something he . . .'

But she'd shut the kitchen door behind her. He sat down with the *Evening News* and looked at the latest scores without taking them in. He felt aggrieved, nervous, angry, guilty, defiant and genuinely worried.

After a minute the door opened again and Ethel came through, her expression martyred but maintaining a fine Christian charity. 'Mum says she'll be speaking to Rod after tea. I'm to bring you out yours. We're having ours in the kitchen.'

He went to the door. Alice was at the stove making the tea.

'What's all this?' he said.

She didn't turn round.

'Ethel.'

'Yes, Mum?'

'Tell your father I'm not speaking to him like I said.'

Ethel pretended to look embarrassed, but was enjoying herself immensely.

'Go on. Do what I say.'

'Mum says she's not speaking to you like she said.'

'I won't be wanting tea, Alice.' He wanted sympathy. He wanted advice. He wanted Joe. He should be back from work. He went to find him.

20

Daisy received the following report from *Undercover Ltd*, also the wedding photograph. They were delivered at Minnie Combermere's by arrangement.

> Our man followed your husband's cab from garage at 18.00 hours as arranged. Fare picked up at Waterloo Station. Paid off by pillar box south of Chalk Farm bridge. Accosted small boy posting letter. Conversed with him for seven minutes, after which boy got into cab which drove down de Vere Terrace to stationer and tobacconist—Remnant. Boy got out. Mr Shoesmith called out to man and woman who came out of shop. Proprietor and wife(?). Did not hear first part of conversation, but final words were: 'You're not having that bastard for no godfather. I'll see to that if it's the last thing I do.' Followed cab, which drove to No. 23 Frame Street. Mr Shoesmith entered house after giving two knocks and getting no reply. After ten minutes he came out and drove his cab to rank at Euston Station. At this point appeared to become suspicious and our man drove off, bearing in mind your desire for extreme caution. Returned to Frame Street and noted card by front door 'Madgwick—2 knocks.' We trust this information is satisfactory. We do not feel we can help further in this matter in view of your husband's apparent suspicions he was being followed. We enclose our account and shall be glad of settlement in due course.
>
> (Signed) A. B. Dash
> Director. *Undercover Ltd*

21

Miles woke up with the postman's knock. Someone from the basement, he never knew who, always sorted the letters. After a pause, three appeared under his door. He called out thank you to whoever it was and, as usual, there was no reply, only retreating footsteps. He went through the customary routine of getting up and only when he had made his coffee did he feel capable of dealing with his mail.

'If you expect the worst you can only be surprised by the best.' That's what the old lady in the Southwold sweet shop used to say. The sing-song of her Suffolk accent saying it had stayed with him through the years, especially when he was about to open his mail. He always slit the top of the envelopes with a small ivory paper-knife which had belonged to his mother. It was she who had taught him to do this. 'Tidy habits breed tidy minds.' Come to think of it, his whole life had been guided by a collection of aphoristic clichés. But 'If you expect the worst' etc had served him well. Now, for instance, as he read the first letter, which was from his landlady's solicitors saying his share of the rates was going up. No surprise there. And again, with the second from Mr Fison, sharply critical of a clue which had an offensive double entendre which had never occurred to him. Still no surprise. And a triumphant vindication with the third, because it surprised him most marvellously with the best.

An invitation from Rodney's mother to go to tea the next day. The jolly uncle, the family friend, 'This is Mr Madgwick—Miles to us, Uncle Miles to the kids—one of the family.' 'Uncle Miles is taking us to Hastings'—'Mum, know what this is? Miles says it's a cornelian'—'Say Uncle Miles'—'Uncle Miles'

—'Get that wet bathing slip off, Rodney. Uncle Miles will dry you. Ethel and I will dry behind that rock'—sticky buns with currants; possible, all of it now, more than possible, probable; the almost unbearably sweet nostalgia of it!

He spent most of the day adding a further chapter to Part II of *Remnants* and went for a rapid walk round Regent's Park. He didn't try to see Elsa.

22

Alice had got it all worked out. Greetings; just the two of them and the children. The baby was asleep upstairs. First they went to have a peep at him, then a bit of a sit down, talking about the weather and so on, with cups of tea and thin bread and butter the way he'd be used to, and after: 'I was wondering if you'd care to take a little stroll on Primrose Hill seeing what a lovely afternoon it is? My hubby has to mind the shop. We can talk about the christening; I could show you the church if you don't know it. Can't put two sentences together with the children interrupting. Ethel will keep an eye on baby. No, you can't come too; you'll do as you're told. Mr Madgwick and I got to talk in private. Rod, tell your father I'll be back in about an hour.'

An odd request, Miles noted, since they went out through the shop and she could perfectly well have told him herself.

She walked slowly as they zigzagged through to Regent's Park Road. She told him the time of the christening and about her visit to the vicar and Miles laughed and said he sounded quite a character and she said yes, she hadn't thought of him like that, people were sometimes, weren't they? But you didn't expect a clergyman to be one, and Miles said oh yes you did, the Church was famous for its characters, what about the Red Dean at Canterbury and what about the gloomy Dean at St Paul's and the rector of Stiffkey who finished up by being eaten by a lion after spending quite a time of it as a side-show in a barrel? Alice said it was a shame and it was awful to laugh, but you couldn't help it, could you?

When they reached the Hill she said she didn't think she

could manage the climb, so they decided to walk round it. He asked her if it reminded her of anything, the smooth, steep curve of it, and of course it did, a woman's breast, only she couldn't possibly say so, so she said no it didn't, what did it remind him of? One of those little hills in the background landscape of a Fra Angelico, he said, but of course the trees were wrong, they ought to be cypresses, and wasn't it an extraordinary geological freak for it to have been thrown up just like that in such splendid isolation and it was a great place for duels in the eighteenth century.

Alice asked would he mind if she took his arm, she wasn't feeling all that strong yet, she was sure he'd understand. He was apologetic. He should have remembered and hadn't he better take her back? Not just yet. She'd like to sit down and rest for a few minutes. He took off his jacket and spread it out for her. She said he shouldn't have bothered, the ground was as dry as a bone but she sat on it just the same and he lay on the grass beside her.

They were silent for quite a while. He was on his back, his hands clasped behind his head, looking up into the sky. She sat sideways, her legs drawn up under her, resting on one arm and pulling at the grasses with her other hand. She was staring at him with undisguised admiration. She'd been right. Of course she had. The thing Aunt Annie had always said about her, 'You know where you are with Alice. If she wants something she goes straight for it.' He raised his head and their eyes met briefly before she looked down at the fine lace of the flowering grass in her hand.

'That Angelico, was he a painter?'

'He was indeed. He was a monk. Italian. Fourteen hundreds I think.'

'All those years ago. I'd like to see his painting.'

'You can. National Gallery.'

'I'm not speaking to my hubby.'

He sat up quite startled, uncertain what he should say. 'Aren't you?' seemed safe enough.

'No, you probably noticed.'

'I did as a matter of fact.'

'Never mind why. I thought I'd better mention it. Like I told you, Mrs Blunt in person.'

He lay back again and looked up at her, feeling faintly embarrassed. She had a long stalk of grass dangling from her mouth.

He said, 'Even the best of marriages have their ups and downs.'

'Mine isn't the best of marriages.'

'I'm sorry.' He was, too. George didn't feature at all in *Remnants* and, even now he'd met him in the flesh, he remained a fairly shadowy figure. But since he existed, he didn't want him pushing his way into the foreground and disrupting the idyllic family life of his imagination.

As she talked, she had to clench her teeth on the grass to keep it in her mouth so that the flowering end waved about and her speech came out distorted and slurred.

'I wouldn't want to be a man. What they miss! All the same, they get the best of it when it comes to a dud marriage. They can go off. Be free. Find someone else.'

She took the grass out of her mouth and held it up to examine the result of her chewing. It was mashed and soggy. She made a little face and threw it away. He noted how restless she was. She started to pick daisies, moving around on her hands and knees.

'I thought you were supposed to be resting.'

'I'm all right. Can't sit still for long, never could.'

He picked the few daisies within his reach and handed them to her as she returned on all fours to his jacket. She took them without acknowledgment, adding them to her own and seemed to become absorbed in making a daisy chain.

Suddenly she said, 'You must think I'm funny talking to you like this. I mean I hardly know you, do I?'

'Easier to talk to strangers, they say. There was an old boy came to fix my lock yesterday. Very forthcoming.'

'Well, I can talk to you easy enough.' She was looking right at him. No looking away now. Her fingers went on making the daisy chain automatically as if she was knitting. 'You don't seem like a stranger. What makes people click, I wonder?'

The invitation was blatant. She was breathing quickly, her full breasts moving excitedly under her satin blouse, her lips parted, her eyes laughing.

'Look,' she said, 'I'm going to crown you,' She leaned over and arranged the unfinished daisy chain round his head.

He knew what she was on about. Of course he knew. And he knew what he ought to be doing; feeling hot and horny and rolling her over in the grass and getting themselves worked up to an almost unbearable sexual excitement. Walking over Primrose Hill at any hour of the day or night would often provide demonstrations of what was expected. He liked the touch of her, her bare arm on his as he put his hands up to help arrange the daisy chain, and the way she stopped him, saying not to touch it, it looks fine as it is. And he was pleased she accidentally knocked his spectacles off so that he could laugh with her as she placed them on his nose again. They were laughing in each other's faces. But he stopped before she did, because he knew she was going to kiss him and he wished she'd wait until that man, who was walking unnecessarily close and was staring at them, had passed. But she didn't. She kissed him there and then and full on the lips. He could see out of the corner of his eye that the man had stopped and was pretending to do up his shoelace in order to get a better view.

She was affecting contrition. That was part of the game too. 'Oooh! I shouldn't have done that, should I?'

He would have liked to have stopped her mouth with the sort of kiss that hurt, because he knew that was what she wanted and, if they'd been in a room alone together, he'd have had a shot at it, not wholly self-conscious because there'd have been a part of him really wanting it too. But not here and now, not in public with a voyeur in attendance. He took her hand and kissed the back of it. She looked astonished and as momentarily ill at ease as he had been a few seconds before.

'Nobody ever done that to me before.'

She sounded almost shocked. He could see the voyeur walking away. Frustration everywhere!

He said, 'It's continental.'

'But you're English.'

'I spent some time in Switzerland.'

'I never been abroad.'

Somewhat safer ground telling her about Switzerland. She was genuinely interested. Asked searching questions, her forehead puckered appealingly in an effort not only to understand, but anticipate his explanations. 'Easy to talk to strangers.' He was telling her an awful lot. A censored version of course, but sufficiently revealing about his shyness and his loneliness.

'So you never married? I had you a young widower or something of the sort. Or crossed in love, that sort of thing.'

'No such luck, I'm afraid.'

'You never fell for anybody then?'

Careful now, This could be dangerous. He smiled enigmatically. 'I wouldn't say that.'

'What would you say?'

'I would say it depends what you mean by "fell for". Fallen in love with no. Attracted by, yes of course.'

She was looking directly at him again. 'That goes for me too. Here, let me take that off. You look a right Charlie.'

She leaned over to take the daisy chain, overbalanced and fell against him. He put his arm round her to check her fall; and there she was, the weight of her, her warmth and softness, her hot woman smell and to his surprise, but not to hers, he bent down to her upturned face and kissed her between her parted lips. He heard himself whisper, 'attracted by, yes of course'. And even as he did so, he was thinking his performance was only partly genuine. Because all the time at the back of his mind somewhere, beating excitedly like a pulse, was the qualifying recognition that this was Rodney's mother, the mouth that had kissed him, the arms that had comforted him, the breasts he had sucked. Desirable, yes, but not altogether in her own right.

She sat up suddenly and looked about with the wariness of a sparrow. 'What would people think? We ought to be careful.'

So already there was a conspiracy; a shared secret, a bond between them. And an implicit assumption it would continue.

She was on her feet and handing him his jacket. 'We'll go on round. I hate going the same way back.'

Too hot to wear the jacket. He carried it over his shoulder, one finger through the collar tape. This time she put her arm through his without asking permission, as if by right. She was telling him about her aspirations for the baby and how she hoped he would help and advise; she wasn't going to have those toffee-nosed doctors interfering. You'd think it was them who'd arranged for it to be born a genius.

They came off the Hill through Elsworthy Terrace and

turned right so that she could show him the vicarage and the church. She walked slower and slower as they approached de Vere Terrace. Before they reached the corner she gave his bare arm a farewell squeeze against her side so that it touched her breast and, for a moment, he desired her directly and without complication. They stopped outside the shop and she thanked him for taking her out and he said it had been a pleasure and he would look forward to seeing her at the christening.

'Before then I should hope. Wouldn't you?' She whispered it as they shook hands.

Even if he'd wanted to, he couldn't really say no, not when it was put like that and accompanied by such a knowing hand squeeze. So he said yes, of course.

She went into the shop and he saw George come to the door and say something to her. But she ignored him. As he turned to go, George said: 'Could I have a word with you, Mr Madgwick?'

'Of course.'

They stood on the pavement and, in a low voice, with glances towards the shop, George explained what a difficult position he was in. Miles had probably noticed he and Alice weren't speaking; only a little tiff of course, he would appreciate women were apt to be a bit funny after childbirth. He hoped he wouldn't be accused of speaking out of turn if her asked what were Miles' own feelings about this godfather question. Did he not perhaps think in view of the cab driver's insinuations—not that George believed them, not for a moment; still, they left a nasty taste in the mouth, Miles must see that—did he not think it might be to everyone's benefit if he gave up the idea? Whatever George and his family felt, whatever Miles felt, it had to be admitted the driver was convinced he had some sort of right on his side, otherwise why go to so much trouble? There'd be no slur on Miles if he agreed to withdraw. George and his family would consider it an honour for him to visit. But not, please *not* as the baby's godfather. That would be trying to turn a casual acquaintance into a lifelong friend in the twinkling of an eye and Miles knew as well as anyone else that was asking the impossible. Would he please think it over?

George was sweating with the effort to put into effect the tactics Joe had advised. A man to man talk was what was needed, Joe had said, no hard feelings either side. 'Make "reasonable" your watchword and he won't fail to respond. If he were a woman I'd advise different, because reasonable and woman don't go together.'

George had been impressed but said what about Alice? She wasn't speaking to him as it was and this would be the last straw. Joe said ha-ha, this was where they'd kill two birds with one stone and George said stop looking mysterious and out with it.

'Well,' said Joe, 'we've agreed the real reason she's not speaking is not because you slapped the kid—anyone might have done that and no blame attached—but because you crossed her over this Madgwick being godfather. Yes?'

'Ye . . . s. So all the more reason why she'll go up the wall when she finds I've talked him out of it.'

'She won't find out.'

'She bloody well will.'

'Not if you get him on your side. Explain.'

'Explain what?'

'That he talked to you about it.'

'But he didn't.'

'I know he didn't. But you and he *pretend* he did. He said he'd rather not be godfather, only he hasn't the heart to say so to Alice, so would you break it to her.'

George looked at Joe almost with reverence. This indeed was genius.

'And when you tell her, you act up you're sorry about it because you knew she'd set her heart on it and, though it went against the grain, for her sake you tried to persuade him different, but he wasn't having any.'

So far so good. George's face was screwed up with anxiety and a desire to get what he wanted without hurting Miles' feelings. Joe had been insistent about this. 'You got to win him over,' he had said. It all sounded marvellously plausible and when Miles said, 'It puts me in rather a difficult position. But of course I want to do the right thing,' he took courage and said the right thing was not to come between a husband and wife, Miles must see that and, further than that, it would help no end if he might say it was Miles' own decision and he had asked him to tell Alice as he hadn't the heart to say so himself.

Miles looked worried and was silent for quite a while, so

much so that George got impatient and said could he take it it was all settled. In fact Miles was in an agony of indecision.

'If you don't mind, I'd like to think it over.'

'Ah, but we're short of time.'

'Day after tomorrow?' Miles knew he wouldn't be any nearer a decision by then, but took comfort from the thought that anything might happen in the meantime—earthquake, sudden death, cosmic cataclysm—and then he wouldn't have to make it at all.

George said, 'Okay. I'd better come round to your place about eight a.m. She mustn't see us together. I'm very obliged to you, Mr Madgwick. No hard feelings I hope?'

'You couldn't make it a bit later?' Eight o'clock in the morning was bad enough anyway. But to have it looming as a deadline for an important decision, and one he had no wish to make, gave it a kind of Doomsday horror.

'It's the paper round,' said George, 'the only time I can be away from the place without her asking questions.'

Miles was clutching at straws. 'But if she's not speaking to you?'

'She'll get the kids to ask them.'

'All right,' said Miles, 'eight o'clock.'

23

Daisy and Minnie had discussed the implications of the *Undercover* report till they were quite dizzy and drawing the wildest conclusions from it. At one stage Minnie thought Bert was mixed up with an international spy ring; just the sort, she said, to sell his country's secrets to the enemy. Daisy, while agreeing he'd not think twice about being a traitor, said how did Minnie account for the 'godfather at the christening' reference, and Minnie said that was an easy one, it was a code and probably meant meet me at Wapping Old Stairs at midnight. Later, after Daisy had thought this all a bit far-fetched, Minnie said well then she bet sex was at the bottom of it, with Daisy denying him his conjugal rights and all. Bert was probably leading a double life and was bigamously married to a woman in Frame Street, who had this child by him and he was being bloody minded about who should be godfather. Daisy thought that was more likely than Minnie's spy theory, but how to find out? Reg, who had appeared to be dozing, startled them by making a practical suggestion.

'You've got these two addresses. A bit of private detective work's the answer.'

Daisy reminded him *Undercover* weren't willing to carry on, even if she could afford it, which she couldn't.

'I meant a bit of do it yourself.'

There was quite a long silence while they thought about it. Minnie had time to unwrap a Fry's chocolate cream bar and share it with Daisy before either of them was ready to give an opinion.

'They really make the world a better place,' said Minnie thoughtfully.

Reg was dozing again. Daisy still had a section of cream bar left. She popped it into her mouth and, without giving any indication of her own views, asked Minnie what she thought. Minnie pursed her lips, weighing up the pros and cons.

Finally she said, 'If you decide yes, would you have the nerve to go through with it, Dais? I mean, supposing you met him at one of those places?'

'He'd murder me.' Daisy was speaking the truth as far as she knew it. 'All the same, I'm going to do it.'

Minnie's admiration overflowed physically as she heaved herself out of her chair, crossed over to Daisy, gave her a smacking kiss and then waltzed round the room with astonishing lightness and agility.

'You're a great girl,' she said as she subsided into her chair again, 'I celebrate you'.' She was out of breath and her bulk was enormous but her eyes were dancing like a child's. 'All the same and just in case, you'd better have Reg go along with you.'

At the sound of his name, Reg woke up and asked what it was all about. They told him it was what he'd thought up and he ought to set up as an ideas man, he'd make his fortune. After much discussion they arranged to try their luck at the de Vere Terrace newsagent the following morning, after Daisy had seen Bert safely in bed for the day.

There had been a bit of an argument about how to get over to Chalk Farm. In the end they settled for a bus to Charing Cross and then the Hampstead tube. Daisy found Reg's size and physique attracted a lot of attention and she quickly realised he wasn't the ideal companion to go snooping with. She tried to explain this to him without hurting his feelings. He understood perfectly.

'Just holler if you want me. I'll be strolling up and down outside, inconspicuous like.'

The idea of the gigantic Reg being inconspicuous struck her as funny, but she tried not to smile and said there was no one she'd rather have with her.

They came out of Chalk Farm station, famous for the shortest tube stairs in London, as Reg explained.

'I don't care how many stairs,' she said. 'There are always too many for me, so we're taking the lift. And that's the shortest *lift* in London.'

They were laughing about it as they crossed Adelaide Road

and walked over the railway bridge. But when they came to the pillar box on the corner of de Vere Terrace, they fell silent as Daisy remembered this was where the *Undercover* report had said Bert had stopped and given a lift to the little boy. And, as they walked towards Remnant's shop she felt quite fluttery and was glad Reg was with her, conspicuous or not. He whispered good luck to her at the door and then strolled on, looking bigger than ever and extremely self-conscious.

Daisy hadn't prepared anything to say; she had decided to play it by ear. There were two other customers, which gave her the chance to look round. The man behind the counter, presumably Mr Remnant, seemed friendly and affable when it came to her turn. She asked for ten Player's cork tipped and, while he was getting the change from a pound and in order to play for time, she asked if he had a copy of the *Nursing Times*. To her surprise, he said he thought he might have an odd one, so she hastily said not to bother, she thought she'd like a copy of *Mothers and Babies*, she might get an idea for a christening present and her heart seemed to miss a beat when he said they'd got a christening in his family, quite a coincidence. She asked if it was one of his and he said yes, the newest arrival. She was asking him what other children he had and he was saying an older girl and boy, when she noticed he kept looking over her shoulder at the shop window behind her and finally he said: 'Excuse me changing the subject, but there's a kind of walking giant with a cauliflower ear keeps passing by and stopping to stare through my shop window. You didn't notice him in the street, did you?'

Daisy looked round and there was Reg with his nose flattened against the window pane and giving her a reassuring wink.

'There,' said George, 'he's winking at you.'

'I never saw him before in my life,' said Daisy, feeling furious with Reg and just as she was getting on so well.

George came out from behind the counter and went to the shop door. 'Were you wanting anything?' he asked.

The giant turned in a startled sort of way, shook his head and strolled on up the street.

'Bit touched, I should say,' said George, coming back into the shop. 'Outgrew his strength in early youth or something. Was there anything else?'

Daisy thought she ought to have one more try, so she said, 'I think I'll take a packet of envelopes.' While George was getting them, she said, 'We've had quite a time of it choosing the godparents. You'd never believe it could cause such hard feelings.'

This obviously touched a chord. 'Don't talk to me about it,' said George. 'The carry-on we've had!'

'Oh, really?' Daisy tried to appear only politely interested.

'Yes, we've had quite a rift in the lute, as you might say. You see, my wife wanted . . .' He stopped, and Daisy's heart sank as she realised he was looking over her shoulder again. 'There he is again. If you ask me, he's behaving in a highly suspicious manner. I wonder if I shouldn't call the police.'

'You leave him to me.' She strode out and whispered to Reg, 'You do nothing but draw attention to yourself.'

Reg looked dreadfully hurt. 'I had to keep an eye on you, hadn't I?'

'That doesn't mean winking with it for all to behold. Meet me at the tube.' Reg retreated, shamefaced, as she went back into the shop.

'You saw him off good and proper,' said George admiringly.

'He wasn't winking at me. He explained it's a nervous twitch.' She was proud of this improvisation, which at the same time cleared poor Reg's reputation for respectability and herself of being even the innocent object of illicit desire. 'Your christening soon?' she asked casually.

'Sunday week.'

'Local of course?'

'St Mary's. We don't hold with the incense but it's convenient.'

Daisy said goodbye and thank you and, by the time she rejoined Reg at Chalk Farm station, she was so delighted with her prowess as a private detective she hadn't the heart to be cross with him.

'I'm not cut out for the job,' he said ruefully, 'being me, like.'

When she told him she wouldn't have had the nerve to go through with it without him, he blushed with pleasure and, while they were waiting for the train, he got a bar of chocolate out of a slot machine and presented it to her. When she thanked him, he said it was second nature, he was always doing it for Minnie.

In the train, between Chalk Farm and Mornington Crescent, she explained to him the most difficult part was still to come. Comparatively easy to get into conversation with a shopkeeper; but to knock on someone's door you never met before and convince them you were the person you were pretending to be would be quite something and she was feeling a bit worked up and nervous. The question was, if she needed a bit of strong arm help, how to keep in touch with Reg without his being seen?

As they walked up the Hampstead Road looking for Frame Street, she was still trying to solve this problem. She had already hit on what seemed to her a clever and plausible reason for getting this Mr Madgwick to the front door.

At the Frame Street turning, she stopped and said, 'The best I can think of is this. If I haven't come out within quarter of an hour, you come to the door and give two knocks. I'll have said I got a friend got business in the Hampstead Road and is calling for me.'

Reg looked every inch dependable. 'And if you don't come out then, you can rely on me to bust my way in, Dais.'

She couldn't help smiling. 'Let's hope that won't be necessary. You stay on the corner till fifteen minutes. I'll probably be out before.'

As soon as she'd knocked loudly on the door twice, she felt panicky. She was certain the story she'd prepared would be seen through immediately for the pack of lies it was; and she was on the point of throwing in her hand and making a run for it when the door was suddenly opened by a tall man, with mousy hair and spectacles, who looked at her in silent enquiry. She took a deep breath. 'This is it,' she thought, 'now or never, Dais.'

'I'm ever so sorry to trouble you,' she said, 'I wasn't quite sure who to ask so, seeing your name, I took a chance and knocked twice. You see, I was born and bred in this house. But I haven't been back for all of thirty years. I got a friend has some business in the Hampstead Road, so I said to him, "While you're in there, I can't resist going round to my birth place in Frame Street just for old times' sake, just to have a look, like." Well of course, seeing it after all those years, the memories came flooding back and I thought I'd just got to have a peep inside. I'm sure you must think I'm a bit cracked, but would you mind if I had a teeny-weeny look?'

She paused to get her breath back and hardly dared look at him in case he hadn't believed her. But he was opening the door and looking very friendly and nice. So in she went into the hall and clapped her hands and said there they were, the same old stairs, but oh dear, the place wanted re-papering and a lick of paint. Then she saw his door ajar and said she was sure he wouldn't mind and darted in. And there, on the table, she recognised the exercise book Bert had been glued to. She'd only had half a glance at it before Mr Madgwick had picked it up in a protective sort of way and locked it up in his desk. While this was going on, she was telling him how well she remembered the room from the old days, and that was the very window her old grannie used to sit at behind the lace curtains and watch the traffic go by. She noticed, once the exercise book was safely locked away, he seemed to relax and look quite friendly again.

'You can't be too careful,' she said, as he pocketed the key, 'I mean, if you don't want to lose things, lock them up. That's what I always say.'

All this time, Mr Madgwick (presumably this was he) hadn't said a word. Daisy was racking her brains how to get him talking.

'For instance,' she went on rather desperately, 'I'm very fond of painting. I had a lovely book on one of my favourite painters pinched the other day.' She was on the right track all right. She could see he was interested. 'I lent it to a friend—"never lend books" is something else I always say, but she was an exception—and she was reading it in the train, put it down while she went down the corridor and when she came back . . . vanished!'

'What was the book?' He spoke quietly with a posh accent and he sounded quite casual, but he wanted to know all right.

'My friends think I'm up the pole liking that stuff. His name's Bosch, if that's how it's pronounced, and of course they say his painting's bosh too.'

She'd rung the bell good and proper. He gave a little swallow and said, 'What an extraordinary coincidence.'

'Come again.'

'I lost a book of paintings by Bosch.'

'In a train?'

'In a cab.'

'Ah!' All she needed to know. Now for it! 'Look. I got to talk to you. Everything I said up till now is lies and just an excuse to get in here.'

He looked startled, then said, 'I don't understand. What . . .'

'I know who's got your book. It's my husband's cab you left it in. He showed it to me, that writing you just locked up in your desk. I see him reading it.'

He swallowed once or twice, started to say something and stopped, stood quite still, myopic and incredulous. At last he said, 'You'd better sit down.'

'I think I'd better.' She took the chair he offered. 'He'd kill me if he knew I'd come here. He's up to something, Mr Madgwick, and I'm worried sick. I come to you because I think you know what it is. He's dangerous and violent and I'm sometimes afraid he's going off his head. I've risked a lot coming to you like this. The reason I done it is because I've a feeling in my bones what he's up to is wrong and I got to try and put it right.'

She looked anxiously at him. Even now she might have got him wrong. That gentlemanly manner might be a cover. He and Bert might be ganging up on some third party and she might get the brush-off and pay for it when Bert got to know.

He took off his spectacles, put his hand to his eyes as if they hurt, put back the spectacles, sat down at the table opposite her and looked at her for a long time before he spoke. She returned his stare defiantly.

'Did you read any of it?' He spoke quite sharply.

'I saw the picture book.'

'Not the other?'

'Never got a chance.'

'I see.' He was silent again. She felt she'd better say something. Anything.

'I thought we might be able to help each other. If I done wrong, I'm sorry.'

But he still seemed to be tongue-tied. He had picked up a pencil and was doodling on the writing pad in front of him.

'Well,' she said, getting up, 'I seem to have put my foot in it. I'd better shove off.'

Quite suddenly he was talking; not looking at her, still doodling, each sentence starting tentatively and gaining momentum, as if in spite of himself.

'It's true there's been something going on between your husband and me. It was good of you to come here and I appreciate it. I want you to know that. So it makes it all the more difficult to say this.' He was bending over the table and becoming more and more engrossed in the doodling. 'You see, it's something we've got to try and settle between us, him and me. I can't expect you to understand because I can't tell you any details. Any more than he can. Perhaps one day . . .'

The words faded out. He looked acutely embarrassed. Even Daisy, who was not all that sensitive to other people's feelings, pitied him. 'He seemed so . . . I don't know . . . not with it; not able to cope and yet he'd got to,' she explained to Minnie when she and Reg got back. And she told how she had asked him to send an S.O.S. to Reg if things got too much for him and, just as he'd asked who Reg was, there were two enormous knocks on the front door and, while she was quickly putting him in the picture before going to open it, they heard Reg storming into the hall and yelling 'Daisy!' at the top of his voice. So she'd called out, 'I'm in here,' and Reg came busting in with the light of battle in his eye and had poor, weedy Mr Madgwick in a terrible great head lock before she could stop him. She only just managed to prevent him delivering the father and mother of a forearm smash, which would undoubtedly have sent him to kingdom come.

'He always takes things so literal,' said Minnie, 'but you can't help laughing.' And her chins shook and she had to put down her tea-cup for fear she'd spill it over the lace table cloth. Reg took this in good part and said, 'We all make mistakes,' and Min said, 'yes, but this was what you'd call O.S.', and when Reg asked what O.S. meant, Min and Daisy laughed all the more. And then Daisy went very serious indeed and said there wasn't much doubt in her mind Bert was blackmailing Mr Madgwick, and that's why he wasn't for giving details, because he was ashamed of something and perhaps feared the law. Min agreed and said it all fitted in, so what was Daisy going to do now?

Daisy said she'd have to think. But one thing was certain. If

Bert had said he'd stop Mr Madgwick being godfather at the christening if it was the last thing he did, he bloody well meant it. And maybe Reg had better be at the christening, just in case.

Reg smiled slowly and widely. 'I always enjoy a good christening,' he said.

When Daisy got home, she found Bert already up and raging for his breakfast. She got it ready in her own good time and took no notice when he kept shouting at her to hurry.

'If you'd told me you wanted it early I'd have come home sooner,' she said.

He ate it and left without another word. While she washed up, she went over the events of the day and decided she supposed she was sorry for Mr Madgwick in a way, but she was raging mad with him just the same because, after all she'd been through, her curiosity still wasn't satisfied and it was killing her.

24

After Daisy and Reg had left, Miles sat for some time thinking how dream-like his life was becoming. The kind of dream you wanted to fight your way out of and yet the harder you fought, the faster you became entrammelled, as more and more bizarre and unlikely events crowded in on you. He'd been so constantly interrupted he was finding it difficult to get his work done. Old Mr James had been down twice in three days on some trumped-up excuse—could Miles spare a cupful of milk, another time a spoonful of mustard—but really for companionable chat, which meant discussing the vagaries of his bladder. Sympathetic as he was, Miles found this as embarrassing as trying to get rid of the old man. Elsa had tapped on his door the previous night. She thought he'd like to know she'd had a cancellation. He made some excuse—work he had to finish—nice of her to have thought of him. He heard her laughing to herself as she went up the stairs and saying, 'Funny! He's so funny!' He didn't feel funny, only self-conscious. And yet he couldn't have gone with her, not following an afternoon of such marvellous promise; when the worlds of phantasy and reality had momentarily coincided, or rather overlapped, so that his identification with Rodney had sexually attracted him to Alice, because without her there would have been no Rodney and without Rodney no self-love; when the heady equation 'if X = Y and A attracts X, then A attracts Y' could be written down Q.E.D.

He had met Aunt Annie on her way out when he got back from de Vere Terrace. She addressed him now almost with a proprietary air, as one in the process of becoming one of the family. But his pleasure in this recognition faded quickly when she tried to follow him into his room as she questioned him in close detail about his visit to Alice. He wondered what she would have said if he'd told her the truth. That it so often wounded was, he supposed, as good an excuse as any for not telling it. He stood in the doorway so that she would have had to push him aside to enter, which she would dearly have liked to have done. Curiosity to see inside was fighting a losing battle with decorum as she stood in front of him, plying him with questions.

Finally she said, 'I'm going round to see Alice now and, of course, I'll hear all about it from her.'

'Then why did she have to ask me?' he thought, after she'd gone.

He woke at about seven, feeling vaguely apprehensive, and remembered George was calling at eight, by which time he'd have to make up his mind. He had hoped, when he'd slept on it, he'd wake with the decision miraculously ready made. No such luck! He lay, his body quite still, but his mind in a turmoil and must have dropped off to sleep again.

The two loud knocks he was dreading startled him awake. He slipped on a pair of trousers and his dressing gown and went to the front door, and there was George, goggles up on his forehead, in peaked cap and old macintosh, astride the combination; the engine still pop-popping and then, just as it seemed to be dying out, accelerating to a roar, above which he was yelling something. He yelled it three times before Miles understood him to be saying, 'Well?'

He said, 'I don't think I can do it.'

'What you say?'

'I don't think I can do it.'

George was so downcast by this that he forgot to accelerate and the engine died on him.

'I'd like to explain. But it's difficult out here. Can't you come in for a minute?'

'Not really,' George shouted and then, realising he no longer had the engine to compete with, he continued in a conspiratorial whisper, 'By the time I get back and deliver down our own street I'll be ten minutes over time as it is and she'll be getting worried about the bacon.'

'The bacon?'

'I like it crisp but not burnt. Also, I don't want Aunt Annie to see me. Are you sure?'

Miles tried to sound objective and reasonable. 'I hate to be the cause of friction between you and your wife. But, as I see it, that's what I'm going to be whichever way I decide. I was grateful to her for her belief in me, which I hoped you'd share. I particularly value her asking me to be your child's godfather, which I see as a token of that belief. She was saying yesterday she hoped I'd help and advise with its education. I believe I'm right for the job. To give it up because of the scandalous insinuations of an ignorant cab driver would, it seems to me, be as good as admitting he was right. Do you see that?'

George pushed back the peaked cap and scratched his head. Miles couldn't help feeling sorry for him, he looked so worried.

'Put like that, Mr Madgwick, I do. And yet . . .' He stood up on the kick starter and bounced lightly up and down on it two or three times in preparation for the final sharp and powerful down-thrust, which caused the engine to backfire loudly and then die out again after several despairing wheezes. A second attempt was more successful and the engine roared jubilantly till he throttled back to idling speed. The noise gave him courage, as if it blanketed and protected his private thoughts even when he voiced them. The more private the thought the more throttle he gave the engine, so that Miles didn't hear it all and had to fill in the gaps as best he could.

The gist of it seemed to be that he and his friend, Joe Rumbold, had been considering ways and means to heal the breach (the acceleration here was deafening) and, that though it wasn't a thing you'd mention, he did in fact love Alice with a deep devotion. You heard about husbands and wives not speaking; you didn't expect it to happen to you. And yet she hadn't spoken to him for three days and that was something that couldn't be allowed to continue. As his friend Joe had said, if ever a marriage was made in heaven George's was, and yet look at it now! If Miles couldn't help in one way, and they had taken that into account, Joe had suggested he might help in another. No man wanted to admit to another he wasn't able to manage his wife, but Joe had thought things were serious enough to suggest Miles might ease them by asking for a bit of a get together about the new baby's education—just the three of them, Alice, Miles and him—and then she'd be bloody shamed into talking to him. What about it? Would Miles think it over? Soon please, because time was short. And he hoped to Christ there wasn't going to be trouble from that cab driver, who had shown every sign that there was.

At this he got into gear, accelerated and set off down Frame Street with a roar. In the ensuing silence Miles felt he'd been heartless and that perhaps, after all, he'd made the wrong decision. He'd been courageous enough a few minutes before, but the fact of the matter was he was worried sick by what the driver intended. And although Rodney, in himself, was a pitiable enough little object, it was the idea of him and his own identification with him that made him sexually exciting; to that extent the driver was on to something. He was in a fix all right and was now quite certain he should have gone along with George's request. Infuriating so often to see clearly what you should have done when it was too late.

He tried to work during the morning, but his frustration and inadequacy hung over him and he made small progress. He kept going back to the extraordinary visit of the cab driver's wife. He hadn't liked her from the start, but her story was plausible enough for him to give her the benefit of the doubt. When she owned up who she was and showed such concern for her husband, he didn't altogether believe it was the real reason for her visit. He sensed there was a pretty cool brain behind the worried look and the engaging manner. What she had said increased his apprehension of what the man might do, so he would like to have felt he was no longer on his own. But this would mean long explanations and only half truths, because he knew he could never trust her with the reality. She would judge and condemn as harshly as her husband, but more equivocally. She had a thin, bitchy little face; might have been quite pretty once. But dissatisfaction was showing through.

And then, early in the afternoon and when he had given up all pretence of working, Alice arrived. She was at pains to make it clear she had really come to show Aunt Annie how much better and stronger she was but suddenly, at the thought of those stairs which she hadn't seen since the accident, she had come over dizzy and could she sit down for a few minutes. He said hadn't he better get Aunt Annie down, but she said no, it wasn't necessary and this was the first chance to see his room and what a lot of books and that patchwork screen and such beautiful old furniture and the photo on the mantel, she could see it must be his mother, and the one of the little boy at the seaside, just about Rodney's age, was that really Miles? And the room was spotless, not dusty as she'd expected and did he do it himself? Well, it wasn't half bad for a man and the bed made up neatly which, come to think of it, was where he'd found Rodney asleep in the middle of the night. Once you'd seen the lay-out it was easy to understand how Miles wouldn't have noticed him behind the screen like that. So then she was talking about the cab driver and what a nasty piece of work he was and Miles thought the time had come to tell her about the bullying and blackmail. She said that was ridiculous, he'd nothing to go on and Miles had to say of course not, and indeed he'd only told her because he'd had a visit from the man's wife that morning and she'd warned him she thought her husband had a screw loose somewhere and might do anything, so they ought to take his threats very seriously. Alice said what was she like, this wife, and Miles gave an unfavourable report which she seemed to be considering fairly happily when she suddenly said, 'What threats?'

'That he'd stop me being godfather if it was the last thing he did.'

'But you weren't there when he said it.'

She was looking at him accusingly. He realised he had put his foot in it.

'George has been talking. I could kill that man sometimes. Interfering like that. . . .'

Interfering? He was, after all, the child's father.

'He's very worried. Doesn't want there to be a scene at the christening.'

'So I bet I know what he does. He gets at you. "Please say you won't be the godfather. Then everything in the garden's lovely and there won't be no trouble." He'd sell his soul, that one, rather than stand up for himself, let alone me.'

Poor George! She'd got it in for him and no mistake. Even telling the truth is a matter of presentation, so here goes: 'It wasn't quite like that. He accepts we should all stick to our guns about my being godfather. What he's anxious to arrange is some sort of get together between you and him and me to discuss the child's upbringing and education. If you don't mind my saying so, he's feeling very left out of it.'

She got up and went over to the screen. 'Look,' she said, 'Snow White and the Seven Dwarfs. And there's Little Boy Blue. Who did it?'

'I had it in my nursery.' He stood behind her.

'Oh . . . "in my nursery". Very posh.' She was laughing at him over her shoulder. Then, still examining the screen, she said, 'He brought it on himself. I said I'm not speaking to him. I meant it.'

But after further promptings she agreed that, as the father, George had every right to have some say in what happened to his son, but if she agreed to a discussion, they should both talk to Miles and not to each other.

She was sitting on the bed now so that she could examine the back of the screen, looking up and smiling at him from time to time as she discovered new nursery rhyme characters.

'It was done by my mother when she was a little girl. It took several years. She used to cut out old picture books and Christmas cards.'

She undid her head scarf and shook out her hair. Then found a comb, got up, went to the mirror over the wash basin and sorted out the tangles. 'My hair's a disgrace. I'm going in to have a perm tomorrow; the waves will be nice and soft by Sunday week. Is your mother dead?'

'Yes.'

'So's mine. She never made no screens when she was a kid. No time. Eldest of seven she was; Aunt Annie was the youngest. Mum spent her childhood looking after them. When she got them off her hands, she married my dad and began looking after all of us instead. She didn't have much of a life, come to think of it.' She gave a little squeak as the comb stuck in a tangle and pulled her hair.

He was sitting at the table now, half amused, half responding to this flamboyant, yet completely unselfconscious sexual display. She was pulling her mouth into strange shapes as she applied the lipstick and speaking through her teeth which unintentionally gave what she said an added, almost bitter determination.

'Women get trapped. Like my mum. Nearly all of them sooner or later. But not me. No thank you.'

She turned from the mirror, moving her lips against each other to spread the lipstick and then smiled at him, her teeth very white and even against the crimson lips. It was an attractive smile.

'Do you blame me?'

'Of course not.'

'No of course about it. Most people would.'

'I don't.'

She crossed the room and stood over him, still smiling.

'You kissed me on the Hill.'

So this was it. This was the prelude to the love play he'd read about and always shrunk from for fear of ultimate incompetence. Which was why he had found Elsa's professionalism unalarming, even reassuring. No danger there of involvement, no teasing games; no misunderstandings, reconciliations. Straight uncomplicated sex. Now there was no fear of incompetence, no fear of anything, because he was far too absorbed in the ritual of the game, the built-in response to the small mental nudges and hints, encouraging their physical counterparts.

Things were happening, and happening fast. Somehow they had moved to the bed, were sitting side by side on the edge of it. And then were lying across it uncomfortably, because their feet were still on the floor and he was half on top of her and they were kissing and their tongues moved compulsively into each other's mouths and he was fumbling unsuccessfully to open her blouse and was overcome with excitement when she helped him and before he knew what he was doing he had wriggled down and was sucking her breast and, as he felt the warmth of her milk in his mouth, he experienced a complete feeling of identification with Rodney, which excited him almost to the point of orgasm. Instinctively, his hand moved to pull up her skirt. She didn't resist. She lay with her eyes closed, her eyebrows contracted, smiling. His hand was now moving up between her thighs, which were bare above her stocking tops, warm and slightly moist. But as it continued up through the wide leg of her French knickers and began a somewhat diffident exploration, she suddenly sat up and said: 'You didn't ought to do that, did you?'

He looked up at her, a tiny trickle of milk on his chin from the nipple, which had been jerked from his lips.

'Taking the milk out of my baby's mouth!' She giggled nervously.

He put his hands round her neck to pull her down again, but she resisted, trying to unclasp them, trying to take the urgency out of him and only succeeding in fomenting it as they struggled, she giggling, he desperate; she playing the age-old, teasing game, he with a stubborn, animal solemnity as he realised the point of no return had not been reached by him, as he had supposed, and was not going to be reached by her, not if she could help it. And of course she could.

'Not yet,' she whispered. 'One of these days. But not yet.'

He said, 'Now. It must be now.' And wanted to add, 'While I can.'

It seemed to him unlikely he would ever feel towards her as he felt now; just that combination of circumstances, time, place, opportunity had made him incontinently randy.

'You've got that look in your eye,' she said, 'you're naughty. I mean, just supposing . . .' She giggled again.

'Supposing what?' He could hear the frustration and anger in his own voice.

'You mustn't be angry. I mean, when I let you we got to take precautions, haven't we? Your godson was a mistake. We don't want no more, do we?'

It hadn't occurred to her he might have a French letter to produce at the last moment. Which, of course, he hadn't. Hadn't even thought about it. But she was right. He sat up, all the steam gone out of him.

'What's the matter?' She was replacing her breast in its bra and buttoning her blouse, pausing and looking at him solicitously.

Everything was the matter. She'd made a fool of him, had led him on with no intention of fulfilment, cock-teasing in fact. More than that, the unique opportunity to resolve his sexual duality, which a few moments before had been there for the taking, she had made impossible and, in retrospect, unattractive. What was the matter indeed?

'Nothing,' he said.

'There is. I can tell. You ought to see yourself. You're cross with me.'

'No.'

She leaned to him and put her cheek against his. 'After the christening. There'll be all the time in the world then. Not long to wait, only tomorrow week. We got to be patient. I want it too. Like crazy. But somehow it wouldn't be right, not till after the christening. Now I'd better get up them stairs and see if Aunt Annie's alive and kicking. Can you come Thursday for tea? That's early closing and George can give his whole mind to things.'

After she'd gone, he lay back on his bed and travelled nostalgically back in time, which had obliterated the griefs and in preserving the happinesses, had enhanced them.

25

George shut up shop at one o'clock the following Thursday with some apprehension. It had been a reasonably lucrative morning, but he got small satisfaction from it. He was far too busy trying to remember Joe's advice as to how he should play his part in the afternoon's meeting with Mr Madgwick and Alice.

'She'll start,' said Joe, 'by addressing all her remarks to this Madgwick. What you got to do is to trap her into saying something to you without realising she's done it. Once she's done that, she's done it. She can't go back on it, like.'

'You don't know Alice if you say that, mate,' George had said. 'She can go back on anything, Alice can.'

This had caused Joe quite a bit of thought. He took a swig of beer, wiped his mouth with the back of his hand and asked the barman if it was hot enough for him. The barman said too bloody hot and Joe said wait till the cold weather came and he'd think back to this evening and realise he hadn't known what was good for him.

Then he turned back to George. 'What's done is done and can't be undone.'

'That's as maybe, but she don't have to do it again just because.'

'Ah, but if you can trap her once, you can trap her twice.'

'All very well to say trap her. Just tell me how.'

There was a long pause while Joe considered this. 'The element of surprise,' he said at last, 'like for instance you say "Look at that mouse!" sudden and startled like.'

'Be practical. The chances of a mouse at the right moment are small.'

'There won't be a mouse.'

'But you said . . .'

Joe held up his left hand for silence; produced a matchbox from his trouser pocket, extracted a match, struck it, lit his pipe, all with his right hand, lowered the left and continued, 'There won't be a mouse because there won't be one. You will have told a white lie. She will respond like any member of the fair sex, with an "ooh" or an "ow". You will then say quite casual, "Did you see it?" or something of the sort and, before she's time to think what she's about, she will say "no" or quite possibly "yes". '

'Not Alice.'

'I know a thing or two about women.'

He said this with such conviction, George looked at him with renewed faith. When Joe had made this bold assertion on a previous occasion, he had questioned it. What should a bachelor like Joe know about women? To which Joe had replied it was a gift. Most, like George, hadn't got it. A few, like Joe, had.

After a pause for thought, George said he thought a mouse was going too far. What about a wasp?'

'Not bad,' said Joe, 'the only thing being a wasp buzzes and a mouse doesn't. If you want my advice, you'll stick to the mouse. It's safer.'

It all seemed so plausible and possible the way Joe put it. 'The strain of it all has told on you. . . .'

'No need for you to tell me that.'

'Try not to interrupt, George. I have to follow through my ideas without interruption or I'm apt to lose them. You complain about the strain. You complain constantly . . .'

George couldn't help breaking in. 'That's not like me. I never complain. I'm not that sort.'

'Just this once you've got to be.'

'I couldn't.'

'Oh yes, you could. You got to act it.'

'I can't act.'

Joe looked at him. A look of surprise and disappointment. 'Do you want your loving wife back in your arms where she belongs, or don't you?'

'Put like that, yes I do.'

'Well then, where were we? The strain of the past few days . . . you've been feeling it. It's brought on them dizzy spells. The ones you've been complaining about. Suddenly you have to sit down. You are breathless and your hand goes up to loosen your collar. You are about to slide off your chair into a senseless heap on the floor. You ask for a quick nip of something. Brandy, whisky, anything.'

'I thought he was coming to tea.'

'He is coming to tea.'

'Well then, what's the use of asking for brandy or whisky when the pubs are closed?'

Joe put up his left hand and once more re-lit his pipe with the other. Then he spoke again, slowly and with abundant patience. 'If you happen to be feeling faint, you don't wait for the pubs to open. Well, do you?'

'I suppose not.'

'I should think not. So you ask for brandy or whisky regardless. She sees you are on the point of collapse which rouses all her womanly instincts. She'll no longer talk to you through this Madgwick. She'll talk to you direct. Full of compassion, I dare say. Loving.'

By the time Miles arrived at the shop and put his head round the door and asked if it was convenient to come in, George had worked himself into such a state of nerves he felt he really might come over faint or see mice that weren't there.

He went to the inside door and called out, 'Alice, here's Mr Madgwick.'

She came out and was all smiles, though she took no notice of George beyond a slight toss of the head as she led Miles into the back parlour. George followed, his heart beating much faster than it had a right to.

After a few polite exchanges, Alice went out to get the tea. 'I never cut the thin bread and butter till the last moment so it's real fresh, Mr Madgwick.'

There was an awkward silence after she left. They could hear her humming cheerfully in the kitchen.

One of us is enjoying themselves and that's Alice, George thought, thin bread and butter indeed! And the way she said it, as if she did it every day. Why does she have to put on airs?

But he didn't say any of this to Miles. What he did say was, 'You feeling all right, Mr Madgwick?'

'Yes.'

'I wish I could say the same. I think I'm suffering from strain.'

Alice came bustling in with a tray of the best china and set it for three on the table with what seemed to George an excess of fuss and clatter.

'Ethel's looking after his nibs and she and Rod's having theirs in the kitchen so we can talk.'

Rodney sidled round the open door.

'What do you want, nosy parker?'

'I want to see him.'

George said, 'Say Mr Madgwick.'

Rodney looked at Alice who said, 'Say Uncle Miles.'

'Uncle Miles. I want to see him.'

He went to Miles, who shook him solemnly by the hand and said, 'How do you do, Rodney?'

Rodney looked up with his endearing smile. 'You never gave me that book like you said.'

'It was stolen by the cab driver. Don't you remember?'

'I want it.'

George said, 'You can't have it if the gentleman hasn't got it.'

'He promised.'

'When I get it back from the driver,' said Miles.

Rodney stopped smiling. 'He said you could whistle for it.'

Miles sat down. Extraordinary how the child was still trying to blackmail him. Was the book really so important to him? He felt nervous and puzzled.

George said, 'Was that when he give you the ride back from the pillar box last Tuesday, son?'

Rodney nodded and, turning to Miles, he went on with growing confidence, 'He said what happened that night wasn't what you said.'

'And what did you say to that?' George persisted.

Rodney was wearing his most angelic expression. Suddenly, with a stabbing horror, Miles knew he was going to spill the beans. 'I hope you told him the truth,' he managed to say.

But Alice was getting impatient. No amount of threats,

cajoling, teasing, ridiculing or persuading had induced Rodney to reveal what the driver had said to him or what he had said to the driver up till this moment. In any event, she had already written it off as being of no consequence and had no intention of letting Rodney divert them from the purpose of the tea party.

'You go back to your tea, Mister Smartie Pants,' she said. 'You'd think that precious book was the be-all and end-all.'

Rodney looked discouraged and was making for the door when George stopped him.

'Hold on, Alice,' he said, 'we ought to know what happened in that cab. And if he wants to tell us . . .'

Rodney stopped and said, 'I want to tell Uncle Miles.'

'We ought to let him,' George went on. 'If he won't tell us, let him tell Mr Madgwick.'

Alice was furious. She said, 'He'll tell me another time.' She was studiously talking to Miles.

'I won't,' said Rodney, 'I'll tell Uncle Miles.' He was smiling lovingly at him. 'That driver's going to give me that book if I tell him what really happened. He's going to bring it and give us another ride in his cab.'

Alice said, 'He's got another think coming. He knows the truth. He was told it that night, even though it wasn't his business. If he brings the book back, he'll leave it with me for Mr Madgwick and no conditions.'

'I think that's right.' Miles was thankful the danger was over, at any rate for the moment. 'And then I'll give it to Rodney. Just as I promised you, Rodney.' The thought of that hulking bully bribing Rodney with the book to tell him 'what really happened' disturbed him dreadfully. He must warn Alice on no account to let him go out alone.

She was still indignant. 'That child would say anything to get what he wanted. They're all the same. Sell their souls, they would.'

'I want another ride in his cab.' Rodney was snivelling.

Miles said, 'He's a bad man. If you want a cab ride I'll take you in another one.'

Rodney stopped snivelling. 'And I can have the book?'

'Yes.'

'You promise?'

'As soon as I get it back.' Those clear, trusting eyes looking up at him.

'Say "thank you, Uncle Miles". '

'Thank you, Uncle Miles.' Was there just a suspicion of a wink in the left clear, trustful eye; a reaffirmation of the bond between them, the bond of a shared deception? Rodney sidled out, smiling his enigmatic smile.

'Now,' said Alice, 'perhaps we can get on with things.' And she followed Rodney out to make the tea, as the whistling kettle insisted she should.

George offered Miles a cigarette.

'Thank you, I don't smoke.'

They sat in silence until Alice returned. As soon as tea was poured and the bread and butter passed round, she said, 'Unfortunately, as I think you know Mr Madgwick, me and Mr Remnant have had a difference of opinion, which makes it impossible for me to speak to him direct so, if you don't mind, we will both address our remarks to you. Seeing as I have given birth to a wonder child—potted meat or strawberry jam, Mr Madgwick?—it's important he has a bringing up to match. Nobody's going to poke their prying noses in unasked, like that doctor who thinks the kid was born specially so he can make experiments and write a book about him. He's going to be brought up like ordinary and undisturbed. But he's going to have—more bread and butter, Mr Madgwick? Help yourself, do, and pass some to Mr Remnant—the lucky little sod's going to have a godfather who'll answer his clever questions the way they ought to be answered and when he wants them answered and who'll be a guide to him in every way. Ask Mr Remnant and he'll tell you the same.'

Miles, who couldn't help feeling rather embarrassed, glanced at George, who shifted in his chair, nodded and cleared his throat as if to say something.

But Alice forestalled him. 'Whatever our differences, if one has the right to discuss the kid's future, so has the other. That's why we're here.'

'That's fair enough, Alice.' George managed to interpolate.

She bridled. 'Please ask Mr Remnant to address his remarks to you, Mr Madgwick.'

Miles began to wish he hadn't agreed to come. The role of go-between was proving more awkward and bizarre than even he had expected. He turned to George and was about to go through the formality of passing on Alice's request, when he noticed he had gone red in the face and was staring anxiously at the far corner of the room.

'Is anything the matter?' Miles asked.

George swallowed twice and then, in a strangled sort of whisper, said, 'Alice, look at that mouse.'

Alice was standing on her chair in one swift movement. 'Where?' she screamed.

'I think it went under the table, right by your chair.'

'Oh, my God! Well don't just sit there. Do something.'

Miles was scared of mice and would like to have stood on his chair too, but this would hardly have been compatible with his role of dependable counsellor, so he cautiously raised the edge of the cloth and peered under the table, having already lifted his feet well above floor level.

The door opened and Ethel and Rodney appeared, hearing the raised voices and determined not to miss what promised to be a new and exciting widening in the already exciting breach between their parents.

'What is it, mum?' Ethel asked hopefully. 'Has he struck you same like he struck me?'

'It's a mouse,' said George, 'under the table.'

Ethel gave a piercing scream and, with a bound, joined Alice on the chair, clinging to her so that she swayed dangerously and then sat down heavily on the thin bread and butter plate, which broke under her with a loud crack as Ethel fell on top of her. Alice rolled her off on to her own little plate of bread and butter and jam, which also broke, and, in trying to save herself, Ethel knocked Alice's cup of tea over the dainty, clean table-cloth and on to the floor. It, too, broke.

There was silence for a moment. Then Alice sat up, her behind still in the thin bread and butter, her feet still on the chair. She pulled Ethel up beside her. 'Now look what you've done,' she said, and she smacked her face as hard as she could. Ethel was too amazed to react in any way for quite some moments. By the time she had decided to yell her head off, it was too late. Alice had got in first. She sat there, her face in her hands, rocking backwards and forwards and sobbing bitterly. Within a few seconds, her tea party had been ruined; she had smacked Ethel harder than George had smacked her, she had made a fool of herself in front of Mr Madgwick, she had broken the best bread and butter plate, her dainty tea-cloth was stained with tea, one of the best cups was in pieces on the floor and heaven knows what had happened to the backside of her afternoon tea dress.

'It's all your fault,' she shouted angrily at George.

George, whose respect for Joe as a strategist was now euphoric decided to ward off recrimininations by trying the second ploy. He said, 'I'm feeling a bit faint, Alice.'

But she didn't hear because, by this time Ethel had found her voice and was bawling in her ear. He got up and went round the table and said quite loudly in her other ear, 'I'm feeling a bit faint.' He remembered to gasp and clutch at his throat.

She stood up, bits of bread and butter and jam falling from the back of her dress. 'Stop that noise this instant, Ethel,' she said.

Ethel, still sobbing, jumped down from the table to avoid further retribution, a piece of thin bread and butter and jam clinging tenaciously to her behind. Rodney, always the opportunist, snatched it from her dress and began to eat it. Ethel forgot to sob. She wasn't going to allow that. 'It's mine,' she said, and tried to snatch it back.

'Did you hear what I said?' George insisted.

'No.'

'I'm feeling rather faint.'

'I'm not surprised. So am I.'

'I think I'm going to pass out. It's the strain . . .'

'I wish you would.'

'I mean it.'

For answer, Alice took a piece of sticky bread and jam and threw it so that it landed smack in his face.

'Take that then and much fucking good may it do you.' She rushed from the room.

'I wonder where I went wrong with that. I must ask Joe,' George thought, as he removed the sticky mess from his cheek.

The children, now silent and awed by such a fascinating

spectacle, were chewing and swallowing the last of the bread and jam they had fought for. Miles had sat, helpless and speechless through it all. At last he said, because he thought the silence was going on too long, 'I didn't see the mouse.'

'Ah!' said George non-committally. He was tempted to take Miles into his confidence but not, of course, in front of the children. Later. Because he was beginning to feel quite a man again.

'She spoke to me,' he said, and he didn't try to conceal the pride in his voice.

Ethel, having finished the half piece of bread and jam she had wrested from Rodney, saw her opportunity. Her face puckered. She stretched out her thin little arms towards her father and ran to him, crying loudly, 'She hit me, Dad. Oh, Dad, it hurt, so it did.'

This sudden change of allegiance caught George unawares and he didn't quite know what to do. He said, 'I expect you deserved it, Eth.'

Ethel edged him to a chair, climbed on to his lap and reached up her tear-stained face to his. 'She hadn't no call to hit me harder than you done.'

Rodney said, 'I don't expect Dad will speak to Mum now, do you, Eth?' He then climbed up on to Miles' lap and whispered as he snuggled against him, 'Fancy you hanging up my wet pants.'

Miles whispered back, 'They were in a heap on the floor when I discovered you. That's when I hung them up. You know that, don't you?'

Rodney smiled and kissed him and whispered, 'You're going to take me a cab ride.' He didn't say any more for the moment.

Miles said he thought perhaps he ought to go, but George wouldn't have it. He said Alice would never forgive him. They still had to talk about the baby's education. Miles said surely she wouldn't want to after what had just happened, but George said, 'Mark my words, she'll come round to it.'

Up in the bathroom, Alice was having a struggle with herself while sponging off the remains of the butter and jam. She was furious with herself, with Ethel, with George, with Rodney and even with Miles. 'Just sitting there,' she said, dabbing viciously at the dress with the corner of a wet towel. 'You'd think he'd do something. But no. Men! They're all the same. Take all, give nothing.' She felt like flinging the dress out of the window and herself on to the bed. She felt like kicking and screaming. She wished she'd had the strength to smack Ethel's face twice as hard. She felt she'd never be able to face Mr Madgwick again. How could he feel passionate towards someone who'd been made such a fool of? She sat on the edge of the bed with her fists pressed against her eyes, trying to keep the tears back. Because, somehow, she'd got to have the guts to go downstairs again and carry on as if nothing out of the ordinary had happened and she was damned if she was going to do it with a give-away, tear-stained face. She went back to the bathroom and splashed her face with cold water, hung up the dress to dry, went back to the bedroom, put some new lips on, changed into a skirt and frilly blouse and then surveyed herself in the mirror.

'You look all right, Alice,' she said to her reflection. 'And, all right, so you did talk to George when you swore you never would. But then we haven't had a mouse since George put down that poison, three years ago it must have been. I can't bear them, they run so quick. Anyway, I wouldn't have kept it up, not talking to him. Only did it to teach him a lesson. I like this blouse. Like the way it's low cut. I bet Miles will like it too. I bet he'll wish he could slip his hand down and feel my milky breasts. I think he's mad about them, the way he sucked them. He's right, of course. They're lovely. If I were a man, I'd be after them. Not only them. There's other things. I'd be after that too.'

Downstairs, George had persuaded Ethel to start clearing up the mess. 'You want to get back in your Mum's good books, don't you?'

Ethel pouted. 'No! She's cruel. She hit me. You didn't ought to speak to her, Dad.'

'Well,' said George, choosing his words carefully, 'if your Mum and I wasn't speaking, I couldn't say to her, "what about letting our Eth have a Milky Bar as a little reward for clearing up the mess?", could I?'

Miles was nearly deafened by Rodney's 'ME TOO' shouted straight into his left ear.

By the time Alice bustled back into the room, the table had

been cleared and re-set with a clean cloth, the broken china removed and the floor mopped.

'Well, what a nice surprise,' said Alice, acting enormous surprise.

'We done it, Mum,' the children cried, skipping about dangerously near the table.

'Careful,' Alice said, 'we don't want no more accidents.'

'We was wondering,' said George with a wink, 'whether a Milky Bar might be in order as a little token of appreciation, wasn't we, Mr Madgwick?'

Miles said yes and Alice said yes and George took the children into the shop. They could hear Ethel asking for two as soon as she was the other side of the door and George saying only one and Ethel saying well, one-and-a-half each and George saying yes.

Alice said she didn't know what Miles must be thinking of them and what a terrible sort of family he'd got mixed up with, and Miles felt rather guilty, because he really had been thinking something of the sort. The family he'd come to know, he'd been reflecting, was far from the idyllic little group he'd imagined. Must familiarity always take the shine off human relationships? Was the everyday intimacy he had longed for to end so quickly in disillusionment? The children were very ordinary little urchins, selfish, self-seeking and absurdly spoilt. The mother also ordinary, quite attractive in a mousy sort of way (oh dear, that word!) but knowing it and using it to play him for all she was worth.

He said, 'I wasn't thinking anything of the sort.'

'Oh, this top button,' she said, fiddling with it ostentatiously between her breasts, 'it won't stay done up.'

He had just decided not to fall for that one, when George and the children came through.

'We've had quite enough of you for one afternoon,' said Alice. 'Straight through to the kitchen.'

But Rodney approached Miles, his most charming smile decorated with Milky Bar, a dirty and chocolate-smeared hand stretched out to him and said, 'Here you are. You can have a bite if you like.'

Miles said, 'No thank you. But thank you for asking me.'

'That's all right.' Rodney didn't conceal his relief at the refusal and followed Ethel into the kitchen.

All Miles' love and trust came welling back. The child had this lovely, generous side to him, it was worthwhile all he had gone through to have achieved his affection. He looked over at Alice with renewed interest and pleasure.

So then, over fresh cups of tea, they discussed in the friendliest way how best to bring up a brilliantly clever child and Miles sketched all sorts of possibilities as he saw them, dependent on what its particular interests were going to be, the great thing being to let his own mind guide him, to learn as soon as possible to think and act for himself. Alice and George listened spellbound. They'd never heard anyone, let alone Miles, talk like that and the time slipped by till George looked at his watch and said, 'Got to open up for the evening papers.'

When he had gone through to the shop, Alice said, 'I could have listened to you for ever.'

He smiled self-consciously. He'd been quite carried away and had enjoyed it. 'At least I know some of the pitfalls. When you've fallen into most of them yourself you may be able to help someone else avoid them.'

'You can kiss me if you like.' Her face was flushed, her lips half open.

He bent over and, as they kissed, she took his right hand and put it where the top button had come open again, so that it could hardly help sliding inside and cupping her breast, the breast Rodney had sucked, the breast that he had sucked. And, once again, he felt desire for her. But the turning of the door handle made him start away from her.

Ethel looked in. 'Mum, the baby's been sick again.'

'Have you mopped him up?'

'Yes, and he needs changing.'

'All right. I'll come.'

When the children were in bed and George had shut up shop again, they talked some more before Miles left. This time it was Alice and George who did the talking. George said he hated to bring it up, but didn't they think they ought to take some sort of precaution against trouble from that cab driver. Everybody was convinced he was a dangerous customer and he certainly had it in for Miles. Alice said simple, warn the police. Just their presence would soon take the wind out of his sails. George wasn't so sure.

'They'd laugh at us, Alice. I mean, what evidence is there? Just because we heard him say he'd stop Mr Madgwick being godfather if it was the last thing he did, they're not going to fill the church with detectives and constables, just in case, like. They might consider other things a bit more important.'

Miles, who had his own reasons for wanting to keep the police out of it, came out with what George thought a brilliant idea, worthy of Joe himself. He needn't actually be there in person. He could be godfather by proxy.

Alice looked desperately disappointed. She said just because Miles wasn't there, it wouldn't stop the driver from objecting when his name was called out and, anyway, what about a bit of courage and guts? They'd nothing to fear. He wouldn't dare start anything serious up in church. She didn't mention the most important reason why she wanted him there, which was to parade him proudly before the envious eyes of their relatives and friends. She wasn't going to forego that.

George shook his head dubiously. 'I'm still worried,' he said.

But Alice laughed and said he was an old worry-guts. She knew that kind and he wouldn't have the nerve. Her laughter and optimism were so infectious that George gave up arguing and expected Alice knew best. Even Miles began to be persuaded that, unscrupulous and vicious and determined as he knew the driver to be, he would draw the line at interrupting a church service.

Before leaving, he reminded Alice to keep a close watch on Rodney in view of what the driver had said about bringing him the book, and Alice laughed again and said she was more than equal to that mister-me-gentleman and just let him try anything with her, that was all! She saw him out through the shop, squeezing his arm as they went, and, just before opening the door, she whispered, 'Here's a butterfly kiss,' and fluttered her eyelashes against his cheek and then she kissed him full on the lips and pressed herself against him, which excited him and she whispered again, 'It's going to be a busy week, but once the christening's over . . .'

Her unfinished sentence meant wonders for the future. He

was humming snatches of the Siefried Idyll on the way to Frame Street. As he passed a cab rank, one of the drivers called out, 'Glad someone's happy.'

Hc smiled back but he didn't hum any more.

26

Unlike Ethel's and Rodney's, Alice was determined this christening was going to be a slap-up affair and when she whispered to Miles there was a busy week ahead, she didn't exaggerate. The preparations were many and diverse. There were the invitations to relatives and friends and some, though not all, of the customers. Mrs Treasure for instance; in the end it was decided she should be invited to the church but not to the tea after. As Alice pointed out, anyone had a right to go into a church so they might as well give her the pleasure of an invitation, since she would be there whether she had one or not. Some of the more distant relatives, too, had caused some heart-searching. George remembered a second cousin Alice swore he'd never mentioned to her during the whole of their life together. She said if he'd agree to forget this second cousin, she'd agree to forget her mother's best friend's niece who used to be a terrible mischief-maker and, as far as Alice knew, still was.

Aunt Annie, of course, was consulted about Alice's and Ethel's clothes. There wasn't all that much time, but she had the idea to dress Ethel the same as Alice so they'd be alike as two peas.

'Picture hats, gauzy summer frocks worn with feather boas,' she decreed. 'It won't cost you more than a few shillings, Alice, just some extra trimmings for the hats, I've got most of them. And I've got a couple of hats won't recognise themselves when I've finished with them. You and our Eth's going to send them swooning in the aisles.'

Aunt Annie had come round to tea and the more she talked about the clothes, the more excited Alice and Ethel became.

Ethel was prompted by Aunt Annie to give yet another rendering of *When you give that sideways look* so as to let off a bit of steam. When it was over and she was acknowledging the applause, Rodney said, 'What can I wear?'

'Somebody's feeling left out in the cold,' said Aunt Annie. 'Don't you worry, Rod. Your old Auntie hasn't forgotten you. You remember them white ladies' tennis knickers? They'll alter down nicely. We'll put three brass buttons each side just above the knee, white socks and a very pretty jabot blouse—very petite size it is—come in the post this morning. Won't matter if it's a bit full on you. Maybe buckle shoes.'

George, who'd been reading the evening paper, looked round it and said, 'What you going to dress me in, Auntie?'

And Aunt Annie said, 'We're not dressing you in a jabot blouse and white tennis knickers, George. Sorry to disappoint you.' And they all laughed at the picture this conjured up.

Then there was the question of the christening tea and, in this too, Alice took Aunt Annie's advice. She quoted some interesting suggestions she'd been reading in the *Lady* and how it was better not to have a sit-down meal round the table if you were expecting a lot of people. Have a buffet. Little piles of plates and cutlery and everyone help themselves.

Alice liked the idea. She had a picture of Miles hob-nobbing with the vicar (goodness, most important to invite him), cups of tea in one hand, plates of cold ham and tongue and salad in the other, their conversation way above everyone else's heads and using long words as if they owned them.

Ethel sang 'little Miss Muffet sat on a buffet, eating her bread and jam' and Aunt Annie said she was a clever little puss and everyone laughed except Rodney.

There was, of course, the christening cake to be ordered. Here again, Aunt Annie was invaluable, because she'd had dealings with the wife of a baker just off the Hampstead Road.

As Aunt Annie put it, 'I've supplied almost everything she's had on her back for the last four years and she was saying only the other day how satisfied she was and if there was anything she could do for me by way of a little return, I'd only got to say the word and, hey presto! So hey presto, her old man can make a three-tier cake for the price of one. How about that?'

Alice said it was wonderful, but was she sure he was good at icing and, anyway, was he open to persuasion from his wife sufficiently to throw in a couple of tiers for free?

Aunt Annie was immediately on her dignity. 'Only the other day, when I was fitting her for an alteration to a lovely gown, worn only once by a member of the aristocracy who must be nameless, she was holding forth about her husband. "His reputation, Miss Burton," she said, "has spread right up to the big houses. His artistry in icing has drawn compliments from the highest in the land." Of course, if you care to go to some little man round the corner, that's up to you, Alice. As for influencing her husband, well . . .' and here Aunt Annie allowed herself a suggestion of a wink and a shrug of the shoulders, '. . . any woman worth her salt can get what she wants out of a man, and if you don't know that, Alice, you're a sight more innocent than your old Aunt knows you to be.'

So it was settled; Aunt Annie should call round to see the lady on her way back to Frame Street that very evening, and Alice and the children were to go round to tea and have preliminary fittings the following afternoon, when Aunt Annie would also have news about the cake. By this time they were all in a high state of anticipation and excitement and Aunt Annie said it was quite like a party and what about Ethel giving them a recitation like *If* by Rudyard Kipling and Ethel pouted and said no, she'd much rather do *That sideways look* again and, without waiting for anyone else's opinion, she went into it and had just got to the little reprise between the first and second verses when there was a ring at the side door. She stopped and made a bolt for the door, but just failed to beat Rodney to it.

'Ten to one it's a runaway,' said Aunt Annie, 'kids nowadays are a bloody torment.'

Rodney ran excitedly into the room, followed closely by Ethel.

'Well?' said Alice.

'It's that cab driver,' said Ethel.

'He's wearing dark glasses,' said Rodney.

'He's nice.'

'He's got the book. He might give it to me.'

'If he tells the truth about what happened.'

'He'll give me another ride in his cab.'

'He says I can go too.'

George had risen uncertainly and looked anxiously at Alice. She and Aunt Annie also rose and Aunt Annie said, 'What a nerve,' and started towards the door but, before she reached it, the driver walked into the room. He carried a book under his arm and he was smiling ingratiatingly. Before Aunt Annie could come out with her rapidly prepared speech of non-welcome, he said, 'Sorry if I interrupt. No offence intended, none. Neither past nor present. I got a strong sense of duty—public duty you understand—and if I see something wrong or some bastard getting away with what he shouldn't . . . well, I got a conscience and my conscience won't let me rest until I do something about it.' He paused for a moment to lick his lips and Aunt Annie took her opportunity.

'It wouldn't be the first time,' she said, 'that conscience has been a convenient excuse for nose-poking.'

The driver looked pained behind his smile. 'Now that's not nice to question somebody's motives, especially when they're honest. I come in a friendly spirit and I ask you to reciprocate.'

He sounded so reasonable, in contrast to his two previous visits, even Aunt Annie was disarmed and said, 'Well, I don't know, I'm sure.'

Alice said, 'If, when you talk of some bastard, you're referring to Mr Madgwick, let me tell you you're talking of a friend of ours and a gentleman who we know and trust. What's more, if we choose him for godfather to our new baby, it's our affair and I'm asking you now once and for all to keep out of it.'

The driver looked as if he was going to get angry but then, with a visible effort, managed to maintain his friendly manner and even his smile. 'Now look. What you think and what I think isn't important. What's important is proof. If it was proved to your satisfaction this bastard had assaulted your little boy—and when I say assaulted I mean something real nasty, something might affect the kid for the rest of his poor, sodding little life, I won't go into details there being ladies present—the question I ask is would you or would you not take such a prick into the bosom of your family and, what's more, ask him to be godfather to the baby brother of the very kid he's done dirt to?' He looked aggressively at the three grown-ups in turn. Nobody spoke. Then he remembered to smile again. 'Well would you?' he asked.

George said, 'Of course not. Not if there was proof. Only there isn't.'

'That,' said the driver, 'is where we differ.'

'Don't argue with him, George,' said Alice, 'you'd better go for the police.'

Aunt Annie took over. 'I always understood barging unasked into other people's houses was an offence.'

'The kids invited me in.'

'Well, we're ordering you out. You and your suspicions can get back into that cab of yours and drive to Kingdom Come as far as we're concerned.'

'If the old lady will allow me to get a word in edgeways, I haven't been to the police because I didn't think a nice, respectable little family like yours would want to be involved in some sordid case in the courts.'

'You're right there,' said George.

Alice was blazing. 'Don't have no truck with him.'

But the driver was quick to sense that George was weakening. 'As I said, it's proof that matters and I got enough proof to send him down for quite a while. Imagine my feelings when I hear how he's led you up the fucking garden. Bloody imagine! That bastard and me . . .'

Alice tried to interrupt, but the driver raised his voice and over-rode her.

'. . . that sod and me have had words. Quite a few. He knows I got my eye on him sufficient to make him watch his step. We got that understanding. But if you go and put temptation in his way . . . well, I'll have to think twice about going to police and telling them what I know.' He had stopped smiling and was looking at George. 'You wouldn't want that I suppose?'

George shifted uncomfortably and wished the driver had asked Alice. 'Well, of course we wouldn't want that,' he said, 'Alice, don't you think perhaps we ought to . . .'

'Listen.' Alice's voice was small and cold and angry. 'As far as I'm concerned, Mr Madgwick is going to be my baby's godfather even if he turns out to be the greatest criminal there's ever been. Now, are you getting out or are we going for the police?'

The driver turned back to George. 'Get the police by all means. And while they're coming, we'll ask your little boy to tell you what he told me in my cab when I gave him a ride the other day.'

Rodney and Ethel had been listening spellbound, though only half understanding. Now that everyone was looking at him, Rodney felt important but frightened. His eyes looked large, the rest of him very small.

Alice said, 'Rod, you're not to open your mouth.'

And Aunt Annie said, 'You're right Alice. He wants that book. He'd say anything to get it.'

But George, to everyone's surprise including his own, said, 'You'd better tell us, son, what you told this man.'

Alice was outraged. 'George,' she cried, 'who's side are you supposed to be on, for Christ's sake?'

'Traitor,' said Aunt Annie.

'Shut up, Alice. Go on, Rod.'

Rodney looked anxiously round from face to face, his eyes coming to rest on the driver. 'You said I could have that book if I tell the truth.'

'That's right. What you said to me in the cab.'

'Yes.' Rodney looked longingly at the book under the driver's arm. 'He come out on the pavement and takes me into his room.'

The driver smiled. 'That's a good boy. Go on.'

But Alice went up to him, took him by the shoulders and, looking straight into his eyes, said, 'That's not what you told us.'

'No.'

'All right then, which is the truth?'

Rodney started to cry. He knew his mother wanted him to stick to his original story. His chances of getting the book were fading. 'I don't know.'

'You must know.'

'I don't.'

Ethel said, 'He's a big baby. He cries for nothing at all.' And then started to cry too.

The driver said, 'Look, you want this book, don't you?'

'Yes,' sobbed Rodney.

'All you got to do is tell the truth and you can have it.'

'That's bribery,' said Aunt Annie. 'You ought to be ashamed. A little boy and all.'

The driver was getting angry. 'You told me he got into bed with you,' he shouted.

Rodney's sobs developed into a bawl and he clung to Alice's skirts. 'I don't know.'

Ethel joined in. 'Tell him to go away,' she cried, 'I hate him.' And she, too, clung to her mother.

'See what you've done. Upset a couple of innocent little children and . . .'

The driver ignored Aunt Annie and spoke directly to Alice. 'I'll say no more for the moment, since you're scared to let the truth be told and . . .'

'If you mean by truth, putting filth into a kid's mind and then bribing him to say it really happened, I'm not scared of it because it's as far from being the truth as you are from being welcome in my house.'

'Right, Alice,' said Aunt Annie with the emphasis of finality, 'and that's John o' Groats to Land's End and then some.'

The driver very deliberately spat on the floor. Then he walked out, taking the book with him. The children were so astonished by this behaviour that they stopped crying and gazed in wonder at the gob of spit on the polished linoleum.

After an outraged pause, Aunt Annie was the first to recover. 'Ethel, go and get your Auntie four pieces of toilet paper. A rag's too good.'

Ethel was pleased to go. When she came back Rodney, snivelling again, was being harangued by Alice. 'How could you tell such stories, when Uncle Miles has been so good to us all and specially to you? Just because you cast your greedy little optics on that book . . . you'd say anything to get it, true or not, wouldn't you?'

'I don't know,' wailed Rodney.

'What don't you know?'

'I don't know what's true.'

'Then it's time you learned. Off to bed with you this instant.'

'I haven't had my supper.'

Aunt Annie had taken the pieces of toilet paper from Ethel and made a pad of them. With a preliminary grunt of distaste she got on her knees in front of the driver's spit and scooped it up, closely watched by Ethel. Then she laboriously got to her feet and carried it daintily and at arm's length out to the lav. Even Rodney was silent while they waited to hear her pull the chain. Pulling the chain on the driver's spit somehow signified a great victory.

When she came back into the room, Alice said, 'Thank you, Auntie, you done the right thing by that.' Suddenly she felt sorry for Rodney and put her arms round him and hugged him. 'Poor little sod. No wonder you got confused. Anybody'd say anything with that great bully glaring at them.'

That night, while George was sleepily looking at the evening paper and Alice was brushing her hair in front of the mirror, she said, 'We called his bluff all right. No question about that.'

'Whose bluff?' said George vaguely. He had just seen a news item headed *Scoutmaster on Serious Charge*.

'That cab driver of course.'

'What about him?'

'We called his bluff all right.'

'Ah. Yes.' He read on. The scoutmaster was in his thirties. Respectable family background. And married. Trusted and respected by the parents as well as the boys. And yet . . .

When she got into bed, he took off his spectacles, put the light out and said, 'I'm not so sure.'

She snuggled down under the bedclothes. 'You're hopeless, George,' she whispered. The next minute she was asleep.

27

Saturday nights Daisy always spent with Minnie and Reg, either supping with them at home or, if Reg was wrestling in London, they'd eat at the nearest café to the hall or stadium and then go on to watch him. During the week she had kept a wary eye on Bert, anxious to note any significant shifts or changes that might be a clue to what was in his unpleasant mind. But, as always, he gave nothing away. He kept to his routine and, with the exception of Tuesday morning when he came in for his supper very bad tempered, he had been unusually affable as the week went on.

'It makes a change,' Daisy reported to Minnie, 'though on the rare occasions when he tries to be nice I find him just that little bit more repulsive. What's more, it makes me suspicious.'

'On account it's not natural?'

'Right. On account it's not natural.'

By Saturday, the day before the christening, Daisy's suspicions sharpened when, over his supper at seven-thirty a.m., he announced he wasn't going to work that night. And when she asked him why, was he ill or tired or what, he took no notice but asked her what her plans were for the evening.

'I'm going over to Hounslow with Minnie to watch Reg Combermere fight.'

'How'd you like me to come too?'

She was so surprised, she couldn't answer for a moment. Never once, in all their married life, had he suggested going out with her for the evening.

She said, 'I'll have to ask Min.'

'I've only met her once. At the wedding. Fat old trout.'

'She didn't exactly take to you.'

'I improve on acquaintance. You should know.'

How she loathed those glittering little eyes. How she loathed him! 'Not half you do.'

'I'll take you all in the cab.'

'We'll see. I'm not promising.'

He got up, sucking his teeth after finishing his tea and made an attempt to pinch her cheek. She moved quickly away from him and he laughed.

'I am,' he said. 'Promising.'

When he'd gone to bed, she went over to Minnie's place and reported this new development. At first Minnie said she wouldn't have him near her, but Reg pointed out that if there was something funny going on, like trouble at the christening, they'd stand a better chance of finding out by going along with him. And Minnie reluctantly agreed.

Daisy said they'd have to be careful. Bert must have a reason for wanting to go out with them and it could only be he suspected they'd rumbled what he was up to and wanted to find out for sure.

'All that good humour,' she said, 'it's put on. You can tell that. We got to be careful.'

Bert woke up about four p.m. She was already back and preparing his breakfast. She heard him go into the bathroom. After a minute, he appeared round the kitchen door, lathering his chin. His puffy face, which she'd been accustomed to think of as white, looked quite dark against the surrounding soap suds. His eyes were bleary with sleep. He was wearing trousers and a vest and his huge arm wobbled flabbily as he worked the brush round his chin.

'What time are we off?'

What a nerve he had, calmly assuming, as he always did, everything was going to be the way he wanted it. At that moment she would have liked to tell him he wasn't wanted and the reason he wasn't wanted was because he was such a dislikeable bastard. Minnie had once mooted the idea there must be some reason for his being the way he was; lonely perhaps, sex starved, maybe something happened to him when he was a kid, or like he's ashamed of something; and Daisy nearly told her what it was he was ashamed of. But something stopped her, she couldn't think what; she usually told Minnie everything. But the thought of Bert's genitals so disgusted her she couldn't bring herself to talk about them, not even to Minnie. Whatever the reason, she had said, didn't matter to her. She was no psychiatrist. She just had the job of day to day coping with him.

She said, 'You really mean you want to come?'

'I said so, didn't I?'

'Reg got to be at the hall at eight. There's a café nearby.'

He went back to the bathroom, shouting over his shoulder, 'I know it. Don't drive a cab for nothing. We start at six-thirty.'

She felt quite nervous getting into the cab and wondering if he'd behave himself with Minnie and Reg. She slid open the glass partition and called through, 'Don't forget, Minnie's respectable. She don't like swear words.'

He laughed shortly and suddenly swerved to avoid a car which pulled out sharply from the kerb.

'Cunt!' he called out. 'If you want a road to yourself go and fucking buy one.' Then he said over his shoulder to Daisy, 'If anyone's going to worry about me, it's me. What I say and how I say it is my affair.'

She watched his broad back, slightly swaying from side to side as he turned the wheel, threading his way through the Saturday evening traffic and marvelled at how expert he was at his job. He never took risks, nor did he drive very fast, but somehow always seemed to find his way to the front when nearing lights and was on the move away from them before anyone else. He had that sixth sense which anticipated what other people were going to do or not do. And if an opportunity came to get the better of another vehicle he deftly took it. She really began to feel a little more tolerant towards him as they drew up in front of the house where Minnie and Reg had the ground floor.

She got out and rang the bell. Bert let the engine idle and sat waiting in the cab.

Minnie came to the door. 'Goodness, you're early,' she said, 'Reg is still asleep. He always has a ziz before he fights. Why don't you ask Bert to come in?'

Daisy called, 'Bert, why don't you come in for a moment? They won't be long.'

He switched off the engine. 'I'll stay here. Quite used to waiting for fares that aren't ready.'

While Reg got dressed and collected his wrestling gear in a bag, Minnie and Daisy were peering at Bert out of the window behind the lace curtains.

'He's even bulkier than I remember,' said Minnie in an awed whisper.

'He's flabby.'

'Oh, I'm not saying Reg couldn't take care of him if it came to it.'

'In a straight fight, yes. But Bert's cunning and mean. I wouldn't put it past him to spring some nasty surprise.'

'How d'you mean?' Minnie looked alarmed.

'Well, like a knife or something. He's mean, I tell you.'

Reg filled the doorway. He looked enormous and very fit. He was grinning. 'Sizing up the opposition?'

'Well,' said Minnie nervously, 'we hope it won't come to that.'

'Minnie's right. We're not looking for trouble, Reg. Prevention's better than cure.'

Reg looked knowing. 'You mean warn him?'

'Yes, but, Reg,' Minnie winked at Daisy behind his back, 'any warning, we do it. We keep you in the background like.'

'In case of emergencies?'

'That's right, Reg.'

Daisy looked anxiously out of the window again. 'Better not keep him waiting too long.'

They went out to the cab, laughing and talking and acting as if everything was ordinary.

Bert didn't even look at them. Just said, 'Climb in.'

'Well,' said Minnie, 'fancy seeing you, Bert, after all this time.'

'I don't know how I've lived without you.' He was smiling and Minnie didn't know whether to laugh or be indignant, he said it so impudently. Reg helped her heave herself into the cab and politely handed Daisy in after her. She sat beside Minnie in the back. Reg overflowed on one of the little tip-ups.

Bert said, 'It's the hall at Hounslow then and Sandy's café first?'

'That's right,' said Minnie.

'I just like to know. It helps.'

'Cheeky,' she whispered to Daisy as they drove off.

They didn't talk much on the way because they were listening to Bert's remarks to, and comments about, other drivers, which were so studiously polite as to be quite frightening. Every so often, when stopped at a light, he'd turn and wink at Daisy and ask, 'How am I doing?'

'Fine.' She whispered to the others, 'It's all on account I told him not to swear in front of you.'

'Listen to that,' said Minnie, as they came alongside a Rover driven by an elderly man with a grizzled moustache.

Bert was saying, 'Pardon my saying so, but the road is marked out in two lanes. The idea is you and your shiny new motor-car should keep to one or the other but not both.'

The grizzled moustache lowered his window and said, 'Don't you try and tell me what to do. I've been driving for forty-five years.'

Bert put his fingers to his lips. 'Shshshsh . . . I'd keep that dark if I were you,' and drove on.

Even Daisy had to laugh and Minnie rolled about and said she'd no idea he could be so amusing.

'When it's other people,' Daisy said. 'Always at, never with.'

He pulled up outside Sandy's café and they all went in. They had some difficulty in finding seats. Sandy, a wizened little man with a drooping Chinese moustache, was busy behind a large, steaming urn dishing out cups of tea and passing them along the counter to a young man with a cow-lick forelock and an expression of suppressed fury which 'belied his charming nature' as Minnie whispered to Daisy. He was cooking on a grill, slapped the various results on a tray, added the cups of tea and passed on the trays to two girls in short skirts and aprons who took them to the tables. Sandy also presided over the till which was beside the urn. The place was stifling hot and thick with tobacco smoke and steam from the urn, which condensed and ran down the walls in greasy streaks.

Sandy called across to them, 'Who's going to win, Reg?'

Reg smiled, put his finger to his nose and said, 'Ah!' Everybody stopped talking and stared at them. They sat down and, in the silence, Bert said loudly: 'What are you going to have? I wouldn't recommend the bangers on account they're always gristly here but the grilled ham, bacon, tomatoes and chips with a bit of hot toast and butter is passable.'

Reg looked him straight in the eye and said equally loud, so that Sandy could hear behind the counter, 'The bangers at Sandy's are as good bangers as any I came across. I've had 'em in the past. I'll be having 'em in the future. And I'm having 'em in the present, which means right now.'

Bert opened his mouth to say something which Daisy guessed, from his expression, was going to be unpleasant. She put her hand on his sleeve, but he threw it off impatiently. Most of the room was still quiet and listening.

'Some people got odd tastes. Me, for instance, I like brains. Then again, I've gone off brawn.'

No question he was needling Reg and Minnie flicked a quick look of alarm at Daisy but—thank God for his thickness!—he'd missed the point.

Bert's tone had been civil enough.

'They don't have brains here.'

'You're too right, Reg.'

Reg looked at him quite sharply, but Bert was all smiles and affability. He called over one of the girls, who looked sultry and bored when he lifted her skirt an inch and pretended to look up it while he said, 'What have you got on tonight, sweetheart?'

She slapped his hand and spoke in a high, nasal cockney. 'Ham and eggs and chips, bacon and eggs and chips, sausage and mash, fish and chips, tea, coffee, toast.'

'You must be joking.'

'I haven't got all night.'

'The day's all right with me.'

One or two men at adjoining tables laughed. He looked round and noticed Reg didn't. He was looking straight ahead and frowning.

Daisy cut in quickly. 'Oh, do order, Bert, We're all starving. If you don't I will.'

When the girl went off with the order, Bert got up. 'I'm off to the gents.' Then, in a 'posh' voice, 'I do beg your pardon. I really must go and wash my hands, don't yer know.'

Two men at the next table laughed again as he minced past them.

Daisy leaned over to Minnie. 'I don't like the way he's playing up,' she whispered.

Reg was glowering. 'He rubs me up the wrong way, Min.'

'Don't start anything with him. You got enough on your hands tonight with Fowler Jack. You said yourself he's bursting for revenge for last time. He'll have it in for you, Reg, and for that ankle of yours.'

'I thought the ankle was okay again,' said Daisy.

'Well, officially it is, but if you ask me he's no business to be fighting tonight. He gets twinges in it, don't you, Reg?'

'My ankle's all right.'

Minnie shrugged her shoulders. 'Obstinate! But don't blame me if you have to submit again. Jack's going straight for that ankle to test it out like. He may not have much up there, but he's got a memory and you can bet your ankle's figuring quite large in it tonight.'

'I got my bread and butter to earn.'

'I give up.'

'And I got a little plan.' Reg looked round the room and then lowered his voice. 'Innocent enough; it's an old trick. But you're right, Min, Jack's not got much up there. If I put a bit of strapping on the other ankle, that's going to get him worried his memory's played him false.'

Daisy was impressed. 'Foxy,' she said admiringly. And Reg beamed at her.

But Minnie said Jack didn't come down in the last shower, not when it was wrestling, and he wouldn't fall for that one and well Reg knew it.

But he only grinned and said, 'We'll see, won't we?'

'And what will we see?' They hadn't noticed Bert had come back and was standing behind them. 'And what does Reg well know?'

'Don't tell him,' said Daisy, a bit sharper than she meant to. She mistrusted him at all times.

'The plot thickens,' he said, taking his seat. 'What have you three been cooking up while I was paying my respects to Mother Nature?' He was still putting on a posh accent and talking loud enough for most of the café to hear. He seemed to Daisy to be unnaturally excited. She could tell by his eyes, the way they glittered between the creases of fat. And she smelt the whisky on his breath. Going to pee, her foot! He'd slipped out to the pub and had a quick one. Always a bad sign when he started on the whisky. Oh yes, up to something he was and no mistake.

The girl came with the food and there was much noise and clatter while she slapped the plates and cutlery on the table and Bert was sending her up rotten for the benefit of the men at the neighbouring tables. Reg was glowering disapproval and Min and Daisy weren't enjoying it one little bit, though Min couldn't help an occasional giggle because some of it would have been amusing if it hadn't been so embarrassing. The girl went on doing her job with a haughty insolence which only increased Bert's determination to make a fool of her and finally, as she was leaving, he said: 'Do tell us, my darling, what it is you've got between those scrumptious thighs.'

This got a roar of laughter from the surrounding tables, which stopped abruptly when Reg stood up and said, 'Turn it up.'

Bert acted all innocence. 'What have I said wrong?'

Reg was deadly quiet and was standing very straight and square. His huge fists were hanging by his sides and clenched tight.

'You said something disgusting.'

Bert stood up, too. They faced each other over the table. The café was silent and Sandy was looking anxious behind the till. The girl was hovering. Her expression hadn't changed throughout.

'I asked the young lady an innocent question.'

'Innocent it was not.'

Bert turned an injured expression to the rest of the room. 'I asked her what was between her thighs, didn't I? And if any of you can bear to look, you'll see there's a little book dangling on a string from her waist. Now that little book might be a pocket diary, it might be a book of pay checks or her favourite poetry. It might be one of a dozen things. All I wanted to know was which. What's wrong with that?'

There was a stir in the café. A smothered laugh here and there and a shuffling of feet as all eyes turned to Reg.

He wasn't falling for that clever stuff. 'Disgusting. From start to finish. That's what you've been. So turn it up.'

There was tense silence as they glared at each other and Min and Daisy were quite sure there was going to be a fight and were preparing to play the woman's part and step in between. But the squeaky voice of the girl cut through the silence.

'Talk about boring. We had all that crap at kid's school when we were just out of our nappies. Same old questions, "What you got? What you got?" ' She turned her world weary eyes full on Bert. 'I tell you what I got. I got a cunt. And as for you, fatty, you bore me right up to the top of it.'

She teetered back to the counter on her high heels and still her expression hadn't altered one iota.

'She can't be more than fifteen,' Minnie whispered to Daisy.

'That's put you in your place, Bert,' said Daisy, thankful for the interruption, and Minnie told both men they ought to be ashamed of themselves and to sit down and eat their food before it got cold. The bacon was congealing already.

During the meal, the two women kept the conversation going. Bert and Reg hardly said a word and, when they did, it was never to each other.

Once again, Bert got up and said he was going to the gents and when he came back, Daisy was quite sure it was an excuse to have another quick one. Anyway, it put him in a better humour and, in no time, he was pumping Minnie and Daisy about what they'd been saying when he came back the first time. Daisy wasn't for telling but Minnie, who was all for peace and quiet and for keeping Bert sweet, thought there'd be no harm in it. But first she thought she'd better ask Reg. He replied with a grunt that might have meant anything. So she went ahead and told him, in a hushed whisper, about the plaster on the good ankle and Bert laughed and said he'd never have credited Reg with such cunning.

'Mind you,' said Minnie, pleased with herself for having restored a bit of good humour to the party, 'you got to keep it to yourself, Bert'.

Bert looked injured. 'As if I wouldn't, Min.'

And Daisy thought, 'As if he would, the sly bastard.'

When they'd finished the meal the girl brought the check and the two men payed half each in silence. She fetched their change and they both gave her half a crown for herself, which she accepted without comment and as haughtily and insolently as ever.

At the hall Reg went off to the dressing rooms after kissing Minnie and Minnie saying, 'Good luck, and watch that ankle,' and Reg saying, 'Smile at me,' and Minnie smiling at him and

Reg smiling too for the first time that evening and saying, 'That's how I like to see you, Min, and have you got them chocs?' and Min nodding, not trusting herself to speak because she loved him and felt rather weepy. She always did when Reg was going to fight.

After he'd gone, they went in and found their seats which were at the ringside and Minnie waved to one or two acquaintances like the timekeeper and wives of other wrestlers. The hall was filling rapidly and there was the usual buzz of expectancy from the strangely assorted spectators. There were quite a lot of white-haired women, whose mild, granny exteriors belied their thirst for savage spectacle, family parties with even quite young children who'd been brought because they couldn't be left behind, young couples holding hands, some of the girls looking apprehensive, and men of all sorts, lone bachelors, older drinking companions and groups of adolescents who were noisier than all the rest put together.

Bert said he'd got to go to the gents again and Minnie laughed and said, 'What again?'

And Bert said, 'It's all that tea.'

After he'd gone Daisy said, 'It's all that whisky. And I wish you hadn't told him about Reg's ankle.'

'What's the harm? He couldn't do anything about it, could he?'

Daisy looked serious. 'I don't know. But I wish you hadn't.'

Bert came back to his seat just as the first two wrestlers were climbing into the ring. Daisy stole a quick look at him but his face was expressionless. It was a dull fight and before long the spectators were roaring their disapproval. In the last round they went through a routine which looked suspiciously as if it had been fixed and ended in a folding press. The ensuing announcement over the microphone and subsequent departure from the ring were greeted with boos and catcalls.

And then, in came Reg and Fowler Jack to prolonged cheers. Jack wore a glittering silk robe embroidered with gold thread, and was preceded, as always, by a blonde dolly in a bra and the briefest of tight shorts and the highest of high-heeled shoes. She carried a large banner, which proclaimed that Jack was the all-time greatest, and paraded it round the ring. Reg, in contrast, was modestly attired in his old dressing gown and looked rather drab until he took it off and displayed his magnificent physique. Somebody called out, 'Follow that, Jack!' and Jack turned and put two fingers up, which might have been interpreted as the victory sign but was more likely to have meant stuff it up.

Soon the dolly was hustled out of the ring. The referee inspected boots and hands and took a special look at the strapping on Reg's ankle and had a quick word with him about it. He seemed satisfied and beckoned them both to the centre of the ring where he lectured them for a few seconds. Reg offered to shake hands, but Jack wasn't having any of that gentlemanly stuff and the fight began.

From the start there was no doubt that Jack's principal target was going to be Reg's ankle. He made several grabs for it, but Reg was wary and managed to keep him off it while producing some good moves of his own. The first round, as nearly always, was a limbering up and try out for more exciting things to come. The spectators sensed this and there was polite applause when they went to their corners.

'Jack's behaving quite the gentleman,' said Daisy.

But Minnie warned, 'He always starts off okay. The dirty stuff comes later.'

It did, very quickly after the second round had started. Reg had got him in a useful wrist lock and Jack danced round for a bit and then tried a grapevine and a cross-buttock, but had to follow on to the mat, still in the wrist lock. He swung his legs from side to side and, with the impetus this gave him, managed to get to his feet with Reg in close attendance. For a moment, they were on the blind side of the ref and Jack landed a nasty punch in the guts. Reg gasped and jack-knifed and the crowd roared their ritual disapproval, though most of them were delighted the fouling had started. While Reg was writhing on the mat, Fowler gave him a hefty kick on the ankle and the crowd roared again.

Minnie looked at Daisy. 'What did I tell you? He's gone for the bad one. That strapping hasn't fooled him one little bit.'

The ref cautioned Jack—too soon, it seemed, for a public warning—and stood between them, with no count, while Reg got to his feet and retreated round the ring to give himself a breather. At the next grapple, Reg managed to get another wrist lock on and, for a short while, had the Fowler gasping with the pain of it. But he made for the ropes, to the jeers of the crowd, and the ref said break and as Reg, always the gentleman, did, he got another savage punch in the midriff but, as he was backing away, he didn't get the full force of it. The ref gave another caution and Jack made a great show of innocence and 'what have I done?', and turned to the crowd who yelled at him all the more.

Then Reg made his first mistake. He made a great leap to put on a flying body scissors, but didn't get his feet properly locked and Jack managed to undress it and hang on to one of his legs and, in no time, was applying a really savage toe and ankle and it wasn't the one with the strapping.

Minnie gripped Daisy's hand. 'Oh, my God,' she said, 'here we go!'

Reg was on his back, his face contorted with pain and the sweat pouring off him. He kept slapping the mat with the palms of his hands. Jack was laying it on all the time and Minnie could see the ankle wasn't liking it one little bit. Then Reg made several attempts to sit up and reach one of Jack's legs, but each time got pushed back with a thump on the mat. Finally he was able to turn over on his stomach and Minnie yelled, 'Go for the ropes, Reg!' but she knew he wouldn't, being such a bloody gentleman. Jack hung on to that ankle and crossed it over the strapped one and bent both feet back against the buttocks, still twisting the bad ankle. The ref kept on asking Reg whether he wanted to submit, but he shook his head. And then the bell saved him, though the ref had to make Jack release him by getting hold of his ears and twisting them hard.

Reg's second rushed into the ring, helped him up and supported him as he limped to his corner. The ref spoke to him, asking him no doubt whether he was fit enough to continue.

'He ought to say no, but you know Reg as well as I do. He'd rather die than quit.' Minnie was popping the chocs into her mouth one after the other and her jaws were in perpetual motion as if she was chewing gum.

The bell went all too quickly and Jack made a rush at him before Reg had time to come out from his corner, but he managed to hop aside at the last moment and Jack hit the post with such a bang, it knocked him down. The crowd laughed its delight. The ref started counting, but Jack was up at four and making rude signals to all parts of the hall which was now an uproar. He suddenly tried a flying drop-kick, but again Reg hopped out of the way and Jack went through the ropes and fell on the floor below at Minnie's feet. For a moment he seemed stunned, but he'd fallen well and no damage done.

As he got up, his whisper cut through the crowd's derision. 'I hate to do it, Min. I really do.' He was grinning all over his ugly face as he climbed back into the ring.

Min called after him, 'You dirty fouling bastard.' She was grinning too, though she felt like crying, and Daisy was surprised till she explained, 'You got to keep your end up, haven't you?'

Things were happening so fast in the ring now, it needed concentration to follow them all and the crowd had gone very silent and still. Reg was cleverly keeping his ankle out of trouble and moving much easier on it. There were successions of head throws, full and half Nelsons, postings and shoulder wrenches, whips, wrist locks, grabbits, Japanese strangleholds and, all the time, Reg was avoiding those dives at his ankle and looking for a chance to put on his famous head chancery and, at last, he got it. And how he laid it on! Jack kept trying to get to the blind side of the ref, who knew a thing or two and followed round each time. Then he tried to get to the ropes, but the head chancery was too much for him. As Reg swung him round, he got another savage punch and doubled up in agony. 'Punch! Punch!' yelled the crowd.

Jack turned to them. 'It was a straight finger-jab' and held his fingers up to show. As the ref hadn't seen it, he signalled wrestle on. Reg hadn't fallen but was still jack-knifed and it was then the Fowler made a dive for his ankle again. He went over on his back and the crowd groaned.

Jack was grinning. 'What's the matter with you?' he shouted and he pointed to the strapping. 'D'you want me to work on his bad one?'

One of the mildest and whitest-haired of the elderly ladies called out 'yes' in an excited, thin squawk and this was taken up by some of the youths, but they were soon drowned by the 'noes'.

Jack shouted, 'And why not? I'll tell you. Because, as well as being the greatest, I'm too much of a sportsman and a gentleman.'

At this, there were renewed whistles and catcalls from the rowdies, but also some hand clapping. He then proceeded to rough up the ankle all over again with considerable skill and venom.

Minnie couldn't look. She covered her eyes with one hand and put another chocolate in her mouth with the other. Daisy patted her knee and then glanced at Bert. He seemed to be enjoying it.

When Jack turned Reg over, still holding the ankle, and laid on a half Boston crab, Reg had to submit. There were cheers and some boos when the announcement was made over the microphone. Reg had to hop back to his corner and Minnie could see the ankle had swollen up badly. The ref went over to him and said what about retiring, but he shook his head violently.

Minnie said, 'He's mad. He'll be out of the ring for months if Jack does any more to that ankle.'

The fourth round was over almost before it had begun. Reg was half walking and half hopping round the ring and Jack was following him, waiting his opportunity for the *coup de grâce* and looking round to the crowd as if to say, 'Watch this, fellers' and it was during one of these lapses of concentration that Reg jumped in and got a wrist lever which developed into the perfect preparation for a straight arm lift and everyone knew that was about the one thing Jack couldn't take and he was shouting 'no, no' and the crowd was shouting 'yes, yes' and Reg was looking desperate and triumphant all in one moment and, with a great heave, hoisted Jack up in the air on the straight arm and he submitted at once with a 'yes, yes, yes' at the top of his voice and the crowd went mad and roared its approval for Reg's brave and unexpected come-back.

Before the bell for the fifth round Jack acted he was furious at having to submit and strutted round the ring, arguing with the crowd. Suddenly he made a dash at Reg, who was sitting in his corner quite unprepared, and seized his ankle again. But the ref wouldn't have that and said, 'Break!' and, when Jack persisted, pulled him away by the ears again and immediately gave him another public warning.

When the round started, Reg couldn't put the damaged foot to the ground and it was obvious the end was only a matter of time. Jack began with a series of head throws across the ring. Reg couldn't get away from him and was weakening so much he seemed to walk into them each time. Finally, with a mighty heave, Jack threw him out of the ring between the ropes and his bad ankle somehow got caught between the two lower ones, which twisted round it, and there he was hanging from it, groaning with the pain. There was no question of his being able to continue. Releasing him was a further agony and he had to be carried to the dressing room with Minnie in close attendance. Daisy said she and Bert would wait in the cab till needed.

The doctor was called and, after as gentle an examination as possible which nevertheless drew groans from poor Reg, pronounced no bones broken, but severe spraining and torn ligaments. Minnie was waiting outside the door and heard the news with relief.

Jack passed by in his glittering dressing gown, his arm round the blonde dolly. He was grinning maliciously.

'How's the ankle?'

'Not broken, no thanks to you.'

'It was a good fight.'

'What about them punches?'

'Straight fingers.'

'Don't give me that crap.'

'That's not nice, Minnie. Anyway, it wasn't all that bloody honest to try and fool me with that strapping. I could have fallen for it if it hadn't been for . . .'

While he hesitated, a terrible suspicion struck Minnie like a sudden slap. 'If it hadn't been for what?' she asked sharply.

'If it hadn't been I got a good memory.

'That you haven't. Someone let on, didn't they?'

'I got friends same as anyone else.'

'I knew it.'

'It was overheard at Sandy's.'

'Couldn't have been. We were talking in whispers.'

'All right then, put it down to my good memory.'

Minnie was quivering with rage. She gulped once or twice as if trying to say something, but she couldn't get it out. The blonde dolly, who had been hovering on the edge of this confrontation, said, 'Come on, Jacky boy, she's going to have a fit or explode or something.'

Ordinarily, Minnie would have been more than capable of annihilating a chit like that, but she was wholly occupied with the enormity of Bert's duplicity. Though she knew he was a mean, rotten bastard, she couldn't believe he would have betrayed her like that. Suddenly, and with astonishing rapidity for one so bulky, she darted up the corridor and out through the stage door. Her shoes, which were really quite large, looked doll-like under her massive calves. The cab was waiting outside. Se ignored Daisy's anxious face at the window and went straight to the driver's side and flung open the door.

'Bert Shoesmith,' she said, breathless and choking with rage, so that the words came out like bursts from a machine-gun, 'you're a low down, double-crossing bastard and . . . and when Reg is fit again I'll see to it he . . . gives you the biggest bloody hiding of your . . . life. You've been asking for it this many a day, the way you've treated . . . Daisy. But this has put the lid on it and I hope Reg's ankle will lie heavy on your . . . conscience.'

Bert remained impassive. 'I don't know what you're talking about.'

Daisy had joined Minnie at the side of the cab. 'You don't mean to say he . . . ?' She was so appalled and ashamed, she couldn't put it into words.

'He's betrayed a confidence and done my Reg dirt and I'll never forgive him as long as I live.'

Bert said, 'She's imagining things.'

Tears of rage and distress were finding their way with difficulty in and out of the creases between Minnie's eyes and her chins, as if running an obstacle race, and, having completed the course, dropped with a final spurt to her breasts below and disappeared between them. She fished out a handkerchief from her bag and dabbed at her eyes and her cleavage.

'Some people,' she sobbed, 'couldn't tell the truth, no, not even if it was the Last Judgement.'

'You're jumping to conclusions.'

'You bet I am.' She turned to Daisy. 'And I'm not demeaning myself bandying words with such as him. He can take himself orf and his cab with him and he hasn't heard the last of this that I can promise.'

Bert started the engine and said, 'Get in Dais.'

'I'm stopping with Min.'

'I said get in.'

Daisy took Minnie's arm, turned her round and led her back through the stage door. They heard the cab accelerate and move off.

28

Whatever your religious or non-religious convictions, you would have to admit that evensong at St Mary's had a simple dignity. The Sarum or English 'use' which claims to be a faithful reproduction of the ritual indigenous to the Church of England before, during and for some time after the Reformation is less elaborate, less fussy than the Roman version to be seen in the so-called Anglo-Catholic churches. Yet it manages to be as theatrically stunning at the climactic moments of the various Offices. Evensong doesn't offer the spectacular opportunities for theatrically as the High Mass of the morning.

'Theologically less meaningful and therefore not a must like the morning service, though one should not only support the Church of one's faith, but be *seen* to support it both morning *and* evening on the Lord's Day unless one is prevented by sickness or business that won't wait.' Miles remembered his godmother's words as he got off the 31 bus at the corner of Primrose Hill Road and walked down to the church. He thought that sickness and business that wouldn't wait must be fairly prevalent in the parish, for few of the faithful were entering the door on the north side when he reached it. The interior, in contrast to the grubby red brick outside, was white and light, the furnishings simple and stylish. Opposite, near the south door and against the west wall, was the font, mounted on a hexagonal stone slab.

Rush chairs, divided by a central and two side aisles made up all the seating except for the back row, which consisted of plain, high-backed wooden benches. He saw the Remnants had already filled the one nearest the font. He was glad he had put on a suit, for they were resplendent. It was Aunt Annie's hat which first drew his attention to them. No doubt, like a brilliant butterfly, it had had its two or three hours of glory at last year's Ascot. Once and once only are such hats for such owners. So it had come to Aunt Annie on appro and was having a second glory, all the more startling because of the less glamorous surroundings and the lack of any worthwhile competition. True, Alice and Ethel had attractive and identical picture hats, beige with pink trimmings tied in a bow at the back and pink roses at the side. They had feather boas over gauzy pink summer dresses and long pink gloves to the elbow and would have been sufficiently eye-catching in most circumstances. But not set against the supreme glory of Aunt Annie's hat. It was a tall toque trimmed all over with scarlet and yellow flowers, and on top was a plaited straw nest and in the nest a stuffed bird of paradise, balefully looking straight ahead with boot button eyes.

Alice was holding the sleeping baby, which was in a long lace christening robe. She nudged Aunt Annie to draw her attention to Miles and as she turned, so did the bird of paradise and he was quite startled at being surveyed by two pairs of eyes instead of the expected one. Alice waved and beckoned him over but, before he moved, he took a quick look round the church. To his great relief there was no sign of the cab driver. They had kept a seat for him in one of the rush chairs just in front of Alice and he sidled into it, stepping over the calves and feet of a kneeling elderly man in black and a thin, little lady with her hair done in a bun under a flowered, close-fitting hat.

He shook hands with Alice and George behind him and Alice whispered, 'You made it all right then?'

'Yes.'

She was sitting between Aunt Annie and George. Ethel was on Aunt Annie's left and Rodney, self-conscious in his white jabot blouse and tennis knickers and looking pale and solemn, on George's right. Aunt Annie thought it her right to do the honours. There was something macabre about the lifeless magnificence of her hat brooding over her fluttering excitement.

'On your left, Mr Madgwick, and still engaged in their devotions, is George's cousin, Mr Jobson, and with him is Mrs Jobson, who is, of course, his wife.' She spoke in a piercing whisper. 'He is the well known undertaker and funeral furnisher. Two beautiful little chapels of rest, Mr Madgwick, for those who prefer not to have the corpse in their homes.'

Mrs Jobson stirred uneasily on her knees and then looked round and said, 'Hush!' before returning to her prayers. Mr Jobson, whose calling required him to be the master of any occasion, however painful or difficult, turned a devout face, smiled and nodded at Miles, switched off the smile, looked devout again, bowed his head his lips moving, whispered, 'Amen,' and then sat back in his rush chair. Mrs Jobson apparently had quite a lot more to say to her Maker and remained where she was. Mr Jobson leaned across and gravely shook Miles' hand, giving it a slight but reassuring pressure as if to condole with him on the fate that must come, sooner or later, to us all.

'Sunday,' Aunt Annie went on in the same piercing whisper, 'is a day of rest for him, barring exceptional cases where the corpse won't wait, if you understand my meaning. So, as he said in his letter to Alice, "a christening makes a nice change".'

'In the midst of death we are in life,' Miles murmured.

Alice tittered and George said, 'Shush.' She stopped and pretended to turn it into a cough.

'On your right,' Aunt Annie whispered on inexorably, 'is the godmother, Nurse Clarke from the hospital.'

'So it is,' said Miles, now recognising the red-haired nurse, who looked a different person in civvies—and very natty ones at that.

'We meet again.' She was smiling and friendly. They shook hands.

'And on her right is the other godfather, Mr Rumbold.'

Joe leaned across the nurse and offered a horny hand which Miles shook. 'Me and George,' he said, 'are friends since we were at school together at the bottom of Haverstock Hill. Lifelong as you might say.'

'Lifelong is right.' Aunt Annie had paused between each introduction just sufficiently for it to be acknowledged, but wasn't going to let subsidiary conversations develop. ' "Loyal" is the word that comes to mind. You think of Mr Rumbold and you think of loyal. Stop fiddling, Eth, and remember you're in church. Mrs Jobson wishes to shake hands.'

Miles turned. Mrs Jobson was now sitting in her rush chair

and looking at him unsmilingly. She had a pinched, long-suffering expression and he wondered what it was she was suffering from; her personal relationship with Mr Jobson? a conscience about his financial interest in other people's deaths? or just a secret sorrow? They shook hands and Mrs Jobson said, 'A happy occasion,' and managed to make it sound as if it were something not to be pleased about.

'Sitting in the two rows in front of you are relatives and friends of the family, twenty in all,' said Aunt Annie proudly. 'You'll meet them at the tea afterwards, but that needn't stop me telling you who they are now.'

It didn't. While she was starting on twenty thumb-nail sketches, the church was filling and there were signs that evensong was about to begin. A server, in decorated alb and amice, appeared with a taper and lit the candles on the altar. The organist was playing a simple voluntary, based on one of the old modal scales. The curtains across the entrance to the choir vestry were drawn and ten little boys in blue cassocks and white surplices preceded four men and three women in surplices and black cassocks. The vicar, who brought up the rear, had a black stole over his surplice and was wearing an academic hood. They processed round to the chancel steps, mounted them and the choir filed into the double rows of facing stalls. The vicar sat alone, with his back to the congregation, on one of the two benches set at right angles to the stalls on either side of the chancel steps. The organ stopped and the silence was broken when the vicar knelt and the congregation followed suit.

Aunt Annie had reluctantly broken off in the middle of the thirteenth thumb-nail sketch when the service began. But Miles heard her whispering again, 'On your knees, Eth.'

'Mum isn't.'

'She's holding the baby, isn't she?'

'You aren't either.'

'I've got a bone in my leg.'

'I want to be like mum.'

'You'll do as you're told.'

The vicar rose and so did the congregation. He said in a loud voice, 'When the wicked man turneth away from his wickedness that he hath committed, and doeth that which is lawful and right, he shall save his soul and live.' He turned and faced the congregation and began, 'Dearly beloved brethren, the scripture moveth us in sundry places to . . .'

But Miles was listening to Aunt Annie and Ethel.

'There you are, Eth, you heard what the parson said.'

'He was talking about some wicked man.'

'That means you.'

'I'm not a man. I'm a little girl.'

'You got to turn away from your wickedness same as all of us.'

'I'm not wicked.' Ethel said this quite loud and began to snivel. Mrs Jobson turned a shocked face and said, 'Hush!' again.

The vicar was saying, 'Wherefore I pray and beseech you, as many of you as are here present, to accompany me with a pure heart and humble voice unto the throne of the heavenly grace, saying after me. . . .'

The congregation repeated the General Confession in a rhythmical jumble of monotones. Through it the whispering continued.

'Kneel down like the good little girl you are and tell God you're sorry you've been so wicked.'

'But I haven't done anything, Auntie.'

'What about all them fibs?'

'Your hat's on crooked.'

There was a pause, during which Miles heard heavy breathing and assumed the hat was being rearranged. The vicar was on his feet again and, while he was delivering the absolution, Aunt Annie asked Alice if that was better and Alice said a little more to the right and Aunt Annie said the only thing against it was that it was a bit top heavy—there was always something, wasn't there?—and Alice said never mind it was worth a little inconvenience because what a hat, you couldn't help noticing it, which Miles thought an understatement though it seemed to restore Aunt Annie's self-confidence and there was another spate of whispering.

But now he was only half aware of it. The vicar spoke the lucid prose of the liturgy directly and without affectation and those words remembered so well from his childhood took him easily back to it. He turned to glance at Rodney. George had stood him on the bench to get a better view. His eyes were shining and he kept whispering, 'Cor,' to himself at the strange goings on in the chancel. That glimpse of him made Miles want to cry. The nostalgia was poignant and disturbing. That familiar prose was as unintelligible and every bit as spell-binding to Rodney as it had been to him all those years ago; the pass-words to a world where everyone differed from their everyday selves and became solemn and knelt down and stood up and sang and said 'our men' or 'a men', and there was this Jesus Christ and things had to be for His sake and He loved just everyone, especially little boys and girls though He 'suffered' little children to come unto Him, which didn't sound as if He enjoyed it very much, still there were things about it even grown-ups didn't understand and anyway, it was safe to be doing what everyone else was doing.

Safe, yes. Miles sought and found safety in the predatory act of penetrating Rodney's mind through the shared experience and finding there the assurance and acceptance of his own childhood. He turned again, caught Rodney's eye and saw his mouth turn up at the corners in a smile of pleasure and affection, then hastily correct itself for having done something out of keeping with the occasion and settle back into a proper composure.

The Lord's prayer was over and after the responses, which the vicar and the congregation chanted to each other in high monotones, the choir sang two psalms to plainsong chants while everyone sat and listened, presumably in contemplation.

During the first lesson, which the vicar read over the outstretched wings and furious head of the obligatory brass eagle, there was a commotion at the north door and most people in the back seats turned round to look and some of them said, 'Hush.' Miles was alarmed to see one of the swing doors being held open by the cab driver's wife and a very fat lady struggling to push a wheel-chair through. It was occupied by Reg, who had one foot swathed in bandages, and was trying to keep the other door open with a walking stick. It wasn't difficult to recognise him and Miles momentarily felt again that painful head chancery. He was instantly alert. This meant trouble: it meant they expected the driver. He looked round the church again. That back was unmistakable; he was sure he would have spotted him if he'd been there. The fat lady, Reg's wife no doubt, had now successfully negotiated the doors. A churchwarden approached and, after some whispering, ushered them to seats across the church half-way up the north side-aisle. They disappeared from Miles' view behind a pillar.

Now everything was different. No safety any more. He tried to damp down a suffocating apprehension. Their presence was an insurance. They were there to see nothing outrageous occurred. He couldn't imagine what had happened to Reg's foot, but even in a wheel-chair he looked a formidable deterrent. All the same, he was scared now. He would have given anything to get out of it all. An apologetic whisper to Alice behind him. Not feeling well. A sudden nausea, yes that was it, and then once outside he would run, never mind where, but run as far as his strength would take him away from the unspeakable horror of . . . what? He didn't know. Could only guess. That was what was so frightening.

They were singing the Magnificat. A priest in a decorated cope, attended by a thurifer and two servers carrying lighted candles, had entered and was standing in front of the altar. He turned and the thurifer handed him the boat-shaped incense casket. He raised the lid of the thurible, while the priest spooned incense on to the burning charcoal. The sweet scented smoke rose and hung in the air. The thurifer lowered the lid and the priest took the thurible, turned and swung it reverently three times towards the altar, producing three little puffs of blue smoke. After returning it, he faced the altar, while the thurifer swung it in rhythmical arcs behind him. The music soared and floated with the incense. It was Tallis' setting, Miles recognised it at once. But now the peace, the assurance, the faith it affirmed only seemed to mock him as it came to an end with the triumphant Gloria. The priest and the two servers retired to seats at the side of the altar while the vicar read the second lesson.

In his agitation, Miles was still standing up, trying once again to recognise among all those backs the familiar one he feared. He felt a polite little tug at his sleeve and jumped almost out of his skin. It was Mrs Jobson.

'Pardon me,' she whispered.

'Yes?'

'It's the second lesson.'

'Oh! So it is.'

Mr Jobson was looking at him with a grave smile, which managed to express friendliness, concern and surprise all at the same time, Miles could take his choice. 'We're all sitting down,' he whispered.

'So you are. Stupid of me.'

He sat down and turned to Alice. He started to say, 'I'm so sorry, but I'm feeling . . .' and then he couldn't go on. She was smiling radiantly. He had never seen her look so attractive. All the same, he couldn't stay. He really was feeling sick. The fear seemed contracted into a hard knot in his stomach and it was beginning to make him retch.

At last the vicar finished reading and said, 'Here endeth the second lesson,' and, as the choir launched into the Nunc Dimittis, everyone stood up except Miles, who took the first words as a call from the God he would have so liked, at that moment, to believe in, that he should follow his instincts and go.

'Pardon me.' It was Mrs Jobson whispering again.

And then Mr Jobson and his smile. 'We're all standing up.'

He got to his feet and turned. He couldn't look at Alice. He was looking at Rodney's big, surprised eyes and solemn face.

'Now lettest thou thy servant depart in peace,' he murmured.

'What's he talking about, dad?'

'Shh.'

He heard Alice's questioning exclamation as he whispered 'Excuse me,' to the Jobsons and pushed in front of them. Then Mrs Jobson's, 'Is anything the matter?' and Mr Jobson's, 'Sorry old man, so sorry.' He tiptoed rapidly round the back of the bench and was aware of turned faces and questioning eyes. For a moment he hesitated. Then opened the door and almost fell down the three steps into the arms of the cab driver.

'And where are we off to in such a tearing hurry?'

He wasn't even surprised. It was inevitable. Too late now for escape. Why, oh why, hadn't he gone before? Why had he ever persuaded himself to come at all?

'I'm not feeling well.'

'You surprise me.'

The driver was now supporting him with one arm, tilting his face up with the other hand and speaking directly into it. The stench of stale whisky and sweat made him retch again.

'I'm going to be sick.'

'Not over me, you fucking aren't.'

He was shoved roughly away, stumbled, and then fell on to his hands and knees. If only he could be sick, get rid of that burning knot of fear. He was coughing and retching, but it was no good. The fear was going to stay with him.

'Are you all right?'

He looked up. It was the red-haired nurse. He even remembered her name.

'I felt sick, Miss Clarke.'

'It's awfully hot in there. And all that incense.'

The driver was grinning. 'Can't have a christening without the godfather. Bit of a waste being on his knees here with the church so handy. Feeling better now, mate, aren't you? Ready to pull yourself together and go back to face the music?'

It sounded friendly and plausible enough and the nurse smiled at him and then helped Miles stand up.

'Better now?'

He nodded. 'A bit swimmy still. But I'll be all right.' He didn't know how he manged to say it. He felt awful. He made for the steps.

She said, 'I shouldn't go back yet. Give yourself a breather.'

But he wasn't going to stay out there with the driver The church was safer. For the time being. He made himself say, 'I'll be all right. Really.'

As she was following him she turned to the driver. 'Aren't you coming in?'

'I'm waiting for the christening. Couldn't miss that, could I?' He cleared his throat and spat juicily. 'Till then I'll just watch the proceedings through this door. Just in case he feels ill again and tries to go out through the other. Because I'd take a poor view—a very poor view I might say—if there wasn't a full quota of godfathers.'

She looked at him uncertainly. Miles heard her say, 'That would never do.'

She took his arm and helped him back to his seat. They had to brave all the turned faces and questioning eyes again. The priest was intoning prayers in front of the altar and everyone was kneeling. As they stepped over the Jobsons, Mr Jobson whispered, 'Too bad, old man,' in tones of deep sympathy and

Mrs Jobson clicked her tongue and murmured, 'Unfortunate,' and made it sound as if Miles had done something sacrilegious.

As he was about to kneel, Alice leaned forward from behind and pulled at his sleeve. 'Are you all right?'

He whispered, 'I'd better tell you. He's outside.'

He couldn't look at her. He was looking at Rodney again. His head was on a level with the chair-back in front of him, his eyes peering through his fingers which were shielding his face. Love and infinite pity, that's what Miles felt. And there was nothing wrong about it. Surely it was good. What Christianity was all about. For that matter what humanism was all about. But Christianity taught that you had to achieve love through suffering and, by Christ! he was suffering now. Like an endless tunnel. No light anywhere. On and on.

He was on his knees now. Against the interminable droning of the priest, he heard whispering behind him. Alice and George and Aunt Annie. Another tug at his sleeve. He turned. Alice again.

'So what?'

'What did you say?'

'I said "so what?" He can't do a thing. He wouldn't have the nerve.' She didn't sound very confident.

'I hope not,' he whispered. But she didn't know the driver as he did.

At last the priest had reached the prayer of St Chrysostom. 'The grace of our Lord, Jesus Christ,' he intoned, 'and the love of God and the fellowship of the Holy Ghost be with you all this night and evermore.'

'Amen!' The congregation joined in with a mixture of heartfelt devotion and relief. After a pause, everyone got to their feet and the vicar announced a hymn and soon they were singing *To be a pilgrim.* Mrs Jobson had a piercing contralto, which was surprising from such a skinny little woman. She was evidently proud of her voice, but was at odds with the organist's tempo and, soon after the start, was several beats behind, so that while everyone else was singing 'Amen' she was singing 'his first avowed intent, To be a pilgrim' with enormous enthusiasm and deep feeling. In the silence that followed her solo 'Amen' throbbed through the church and came as a big surprise to everyone in front.

'You'd think they'd be ashamed to stare,' she whispered to Mr Jobson. 'So rude.'

He pressed her hand. A world of meaning in that pressure. But she wasn't comforted and continued to look cross.

The verger appeared, bowed to the vicar and led him to the pulpit.

'As if he didn't know the way.' It was the nurse, smiling at Miles. 'Did you know that funny man outside?' she asked.

'I'm afraid so.'

'I didn't take to him exactly.'

'I'm afraid he's going to make trouble.'

'Good lord, why?'

Mrs Jobson was looking even crosser. 'Shhh,' she hissed.

'I can't explain now.'

The vicar read out a few notices and then delivered a brief and not particularly intellectual sermon, though judging by the shuffling feet and restlessness, it was way above most of the congregation's heads. It was about courage.

'Courage,' said the vicar, 'must be thought of as one of the great christian virtues. The most courageous man who ever lived was the son of God, our Lord Jesus Christ himself. And He knew, as we know, that it is a virtue in its own right. It isn't just the converse of being afraid. God knows, we are all afraid and with justification. It's a frightening and wicked world and only through our faith in Him can we find the splendid courage that will carry us through and beyond our fears to the peace which passeth understanding.'

'All very well,' thought Miles. 'It may be true what you say, but without faith, how on this earth can you conquer fear? How can I conquer it?'

The vicar was recalling the courage of the Christian martyrs —superhuman he called it—superhuman must mean God-like, for we know of no earth creature that is above man and, since we are not in God, then He at such times must be in us. Only that way can we be superhuman.

He instanced a man he knew during the war who would like to have been a conscientious objector but hadn't got quite that sort of conscience, though he knew he would be incapable of killing. So, being a brilliant engineer, he got himself into bomb disposal, one of the most dangerous and frightening jobs going, but at least he was trying to stop other people's attempts to kill. He was a nervous, sensitive man and every time he had to defuse a bomb he was most desperately afraid. And he was frightened of being afraid because his hands might become unsteady. The mechanisms he had to deal with were so fine and delicately adjusted, the smallest clumsiness would be disastrous. So he must somehow not be frightened. Or rather, not show that he was by any outward sign. How did he do it?

The vicar paused for a moment to blow his nose and made a loud trumpeting noise which woke up Joe who had been peacefully dozing and said, 'Good God!' quite loudly. The congregation was still now. Bomb disposal was something exciting.

'No sir,' said the vicar, peering through his glasses in Joe's direction, 'not the good God as you suggest. Christ's teaching, yes, he believed in that. But not His divinity and not the miracles. He told me he did it by thinking of the bomb as a symbol of the world's evil, and his hands and brain as representing the good. He firmly believed that good must overcome evil, so that defusing a bomb became a great spiritual exercise, in which he was fortified by what he described as an inner strength, which, in spite of his fear, exalted his spirit to a sort of controlled ecstasy. He didn't conquer fear. He found superhumanity. For I believe most devoutly God was in that man when he died. The bomb exploded before he'd even had time to examine it. It was a true selflessness. He really did die that others might live.'

Miles wasn't listening any more. 'Inner strength.' 'Controlled ecstasy.' It wasn't like that with him. He did, in a sense, subscribe to the concept of God in man, the spark of divinity which must account for so much in our thoughts and behaviour we can't explain and which makes every man, woman and child a potential genius. But it was a philosophical concept. There was no actuality, no real presence. And though it was perfectly possible to experience controlled ecstasy inspired by a philosophical concept, it had never happened to him.

For his money, the old locksmith's 'brotherhood of fear', depressing as it was, still held a grain of comfort. But it was doing absolutely nothing for him at the moment. That terrible driver outside—Shoesmith—Bert Shoesmith—was he frightened? Miles doubted it. Was God within him? If not, what was driving him with such compulsion? The same motives as the bomb disposal man perhaps, a genuine belief that it was his mission to destroy evil. Miles stirred in his seat. Strange to think of that loathsome driver as St George and himself as the dragon. He glanced back at the south door, it was open just a crack. The driver was a man of his word. He was there all right.

The sermon was over. 'And now to God the Father, God the Son and God the Holy Ghost be all might, majesty, power and dominion, henceforth and for evermore. Amen,' said the vicar and the verger led him back to his place. Miles glanced at the nurse. She was smiling.

'He still doesn't know the way.'

He smiled too. Surprising he could bring himself to share a joke. Like laughing on the scaffold.

There was another hymn, during which the collection was taken and, once again, Mrs Jobson was a line behind at the end. This time her solo 'amen' had a ring of defiance, inferring her tempo was right and everyone else's was wrong. Ethel got the giggles and Aunt Annie expostulated.

'No giggling in church.'

'I can't help it.'

'Oh yes you can.'

'It's her.'

'Don't point. It's rude.'

Mrs Jobson turned and shushed loudly, but this made Ethel giggle all the more.

'What are you laughing at, child?' Mr Jobson asked in a sepulchral whisper.

Ethel was a quick thinker. 'My Aunt Annie's hat!' she said and went into paroxysms of giggling, she was so pleased with herself.

'Don't be personal.' Aunt Annie admired such adroitness, but of course she couldn't show it.

'That bird,' spluttered Ethel, pointing at Mrs Jobson's back, 'she's so funny.'

The priest was in front of the altar again, intoning more prayers. Everyone had knelt.

Rodney was giggling too. He didn't know what it was all about, but giggling was infectious. He and Ethel were sitting back on their heels so they could see each other behind the intervening backs.

'One more peep out of you two and you'll go home. No christening, no tea. Straight to bed.' Alice's whisper meant business and the children knew it and were silent, though Ethel couldn't resist putting her tongue out at her mother as she turned away.

The priest gave the blessing. 'The Lord lift up the light of His countenance upon you and give you peace and the blessing of God Almighty, the Father, the Son and the Holy Ghost be amongst you and remain with you this night and for evermore. Amen.' The organist played Purcell's joyous march from *Diocletian* and the verger led the choir and the vicar down the chancel steps and through the curtains leading to the choir vestry. The priest had departed and most of the congregation were leaving. One of the servers reappeared with a snuffer on a pole and put out the candles one by one.

'Now,' said Aunt Annie, straightening her hat again and relieved not to be whispering, 'now at last we come to it.'

The nurse took the baby from Alice and the christening party stood up to stretch their legs and talk in suitably reverential undertones, gradually making their way out of their seats and towards the font. Miles was trying to take in what Joe was saying. The nurse had gone ahead, dandling the baby who was beginning to whimper, and they were left temporarily sitting in their rush chairs with the nurse's empty one between them. Joe sidled into it.

'Mr Madgwick?'

'Yes?'

'Will I have to say anything?'

'What d'you mean?'

'Will I have to say anything? Being godfather, like?'

But Miles was looking across the church to where the wheel-chair was emerging from behind the pillar and joining the file of departing worshippers.

'I mean, you're godfather too. Aren't you? Two godfathers, one godmother for a boy. That's right, isn't it?'

'Yes.'

The wheel-chair hadn't followed the main stream out of the north door. It turned left at the end of the aisle and was making its way towards the font, along with several people who were interested enough to stay, against a departing stream from the centre aisle. Mrs Shoesmith and the fat lady were whispering together excitedly. Reg was looking about him, very stern and determined.

'Well, do I have to say anything? I thought you might know?'

Miles turned back with an effort to Joe's anxious face. 'Only a few words, I think. It's in the prayer book.'

'Ah! In the prayer book. It would be.' Joe looked relieved. 'Between you and me, Mr Madgwick, I'm not partial to being in the public eye. Behind the scenes is where I like to be. The onlooker sees most of the game, as they say. I think things up, Mr Madgwick, but I've never been one for taking part . . . '

By now, there was quite a knot of people round the font. Miles couldn't see through to the south door any longer.

He interrupted. 'Perhaps we ought to join them.' As they moved out of their row, they met the nurse taking the baby for a little walk up the side aisle. He was grizzling; miniature, preparatory coughs and then a drawn-out wail. She was dandling and soothing him.

'Pity about him,' she said. 'So good at being a spectator, but now it's his big moment I'm afraid he's going to bawl.'

'He'll have to do better than that,' said Joe, lightly podging the baby's cheek with his forefinger.

It stopped crying and looked him straight in the eye.

'There you are. Recognises the voice of authority.' Joe was delighted.

The baby did its little half-moon smile.

'Sense of humour, too,' said Joe.

Miles could see the south door now. It was shut. He could see no sign of the driver.

'Come along now. We don't want to be here all night.' It was the vicar, making his way to the font.

They moved aside to let him through and followed him. He mounted the step behind the font and stood, a tall, commanding figure, facing the semi-circle of upturned faces. The nurse was below him on his right, Joe and Miles behind her, their backs to the south door. Miles looked quickly round. It was still shut. Alice, George, Aunt Annie and the children were on the vicar's left. Beyond them, discreetly in the background, he caught a glimpse of Reg in his wheel-chair. The fat lady was leaning over the back of it, whispering to him. Mrs Shoesmith was standing a little apart. She kept looking anxiously round the church.

The vicar, in a conversational tone of voice, said, 'Hath this child been already baptised or no?'

There was an awkward pause. As no one else seemed prepared to volunteer the information and she was its mother, Alice decided it was up to her and said 'no'.

While the vicar launched into 'Dearly beloved, forasmuch as all men are conceived and born in sin, and that our Saviour Jesus Christ saith . . . ' Aunt Annie was whispering to George, 'Why did he ask that? What does he think we've gone to all this trouble for?'

'It's in the prayer book. He's got to say it.'

'It's daft. Never ought to have been put in. A christening's a christening. We don't make a habit of it.'

The vicar looked at her severely, but it took more than a vicar to put her out of countenance and she and the bird of paradise stared unashamedly back at him. He was finishing the opening exhortation and said, as if it was a reproach, 'Let us pray.'

Nobody knew whether to remain standing or to kneel on the stone floor, and some did and some didn't. Then came the prayer about saving Noah and his family in the ark from perishing by water and leading the children of Israel safely through the Red Sea. During it, Rodney was pulling at Alice's sleeve.

'Mum.'

'What is it?'

'I want to go somewhere.'

Alice was exasperated. She looked at Aunt Annie. 'He would, wouldn't he?'

Aunt Annie was quite equal to the situation. 'It's all that talk about water. You can go outside, Rod. There's a bit of grass and some trees. Don't forget you've no flies. You'll have to lift the knicker leg.'

Rodney was off at once, pushing his way through the kneeling and standing worshippers and creating a good deal of disturbance. Mrs Jobson was outraged. She had been the first to kneel and was now bitterly regretting it. Nothing would induce her to admit she'd made a mistake, though her knees were causing her agony. 'No control,' she hissed, as Rodney fell over her feet and steadied himself with his hands on her thin shoulders, knocking her hat sideways. 'Hold up, little man,' said Mr Jobson, lifting him off and depositing him at a safe distance further on his way.

Miles watched him go through the door, which was now ajar again. Of course that man was still there. During the last minutes, he had tried to pretend everything was going to be all right, that he'd thought better of it and gone. Now it was just a question of when. God knows what he was saying to Rodney and, more alarming, what Rodney was saying to him. His heart was beating so fast and loud, he thought Joe and the nurse must hear it. Touch and go whether he would be sick. He began to shake. He could hardly hold the prayer book and the words were running together. He took off his glasses and wiped them. The nurse had noticed.

'Sure you're all right?' she whispered.

He could only nod. Of course he wasn't all right. He'd had some bad moments in his life, but nothing to touch this.

The vicar read the short gospel and, during the following exposition and prayer, Miles knew the door behind him had opened wide. He felt the sudden draught on his back. He couldn't bring himself to look round. He saw Alice's start of recognition and heard her smothered exclamation. She whispered something to George. He looked towards the door and was visibly alarmed. The baby started to cry again. The nurse jogged it up and down soothingly, but it didn't stop.

The vicar turned and whispered, 'Are you the godparents?' The nurse and Joe nodded.

Miles thought, 'If I say no, it won't happen. All I've got to do is say no.' He opened his mouth to say it, but the question had been a formality. The vicar had already begun, 'Dearly beloved, ye have brought this child here to be baptised . . .' and the moment had gone. Whatever was going to happen would happen soon now. It couldn't be worse than the waiting.

'. . . wherefore, after this promise made by Christ, this infant must also faithfully, for his part, promise by you that are his sureties (until he come of age to take it upon himself) that he will renounce the devil and all his works and constantly believe God's holy word and obediently keep his commandments.'

Miles heard footsteps approaching from the door. The driver

was close behind him. He could feel his breath on the back of his neck. He could smell it.

The vicar, patiently smiling, raised his voice above the baby's cries. 'I demand therefore—Dost thou, in the name of this child, renounce the devil and all his works, the vain pomp and glory of the world, with all covetous desires of the same, and the carnal desires of the flesh, so that thou wilt not follow or be led by them. . . .'

'I don't think!'

The driver shouted it right into Miles' ear and, at the same time, gripped his shoulders. Shocked faces turned towards them. There was a chorus of 'shushes'. The coarseness, the unseemliness was a blasphemy. The vicar turned again to the godparents questioningly.

'I said I don't think!'

There was an uncomfortable stir round the font. Everyone knew something ought to be done and hoped someone else was going to do it.

Above the ensuing whispering, Mrs Jobson's voice was the first to be clearly audible. 'He's drunk. Do something,' she said to her husband.

'Leave it to me.' He threaded his way towards the offender.

The vicar said, 'You are interrupting the service of God. I must ask you to leave the church.'

'I'm *doing* the service of God.'

'You're drunk.' It was Mrs Jobson, her voice trembling with indignation.

'Thank you for those kind words, lady. I may have had a few, but I'm here for God's purpose as much as all you lot. I'm here because God cares that kids shouldn't be taken advantage of.'

Mr Jobson laid a hand on his shoulder. 'Now look here, my man . . .'

Joe said, 'Come on, mate. Wrap it up, there's a good chap.'

They were both brushed aside.

'Anybody who tries to stop me is asking for trouble.'

Mr Jobson and Joe retreated.

'This man . . .' —he lifted Miles off his feet and presented him, as it were, for inspection—'. . . this man is a bloody menace to kids. He loves them all right. But he loves them unnatural.' He lowered Miles and picked up Rodney. 'He had this poor little sod in his bed half one night and, if you're thinking the worst, you'd be right.'

Rodney was holding the Hieronymus Bosch. He was smiling happily. The vicar whispered to the verger, who hastily left the church to 'phone for the police.

Alice's frustration and anger were turned on George. 'Get rid of him. Go on, do something. Kick him out.'

'They're sending for the police. What more can we do?'

'If you were half a man, you'd tackle him yourself.'

'That's not fair, Alice.'

'No, it's not fair, Alice. George take on a hulking brute like that. You're up the pole.'

George was grateful. It wasn't often Aunt Annie took his side. The driver laughed scornfully.

'Don't worry, Alice,' she went on, 'we'll stand our ground and wait for the authorities. He'll be laughing the other side of his face when they arrive.'

'I'd be laughing both sides of my face, the spectacle you make Auntie, if it wasn't I'd made up my mind to stop this godfather business if it was the last thing I done. Him godfather! God help his sodding little godson!'

He had Miles by the collar and shook him violently so that his head jerked backwards and forwards. He gasped out, 'It's not true what he says. You must believe me. It's not true.'

The vicar said, 'I warn you. I have sent for the police. Leave that man alone. Whatever complaint you have against him, this is neither the time nor the place to make it.'

There was silence as everyone turned their eyes back to the driver.

'And I warn you. If you go on with this, I'll smash your bloody . . .'

'Don't worry, sir. Leave him to me.'

It was Reg. He was out of his chair, supported on either side by Min and Daisy.

Bert stopped shouting. For the first time he seemed unsure of himself. Then he recovered.

'If you lay a finger on me, I'll fucking well put paid to that ankle for good.'

Reg didn't say anything. He hopped forward on his good leg,

still supported by Min and Daisy, as the knot of people parted and drew back apprehensively.

The vicar shouted, 'There must be no fighting in church. Wait for the police.'

Bert and Reg were face to face.

Reg said, 'I'll give you five seconds to get out.'

Bert suddenly dived for the bandaged ankle and brought him down heavily with a roar of pain. Some of the women screamed. The men stood by, helpless. As they struggled, rolling over and over, the nurse hastily moved up beside the vicar as the best hope for the baby's safety. He stood in front of her with his arms outstretched.

Bert freed himself, stood up and kicked savagely at the ankle. Miles in desperation, tried to stop him and got a fierce punch full in the face. Blood came trickling from his nose and a cut lip.

This diversion gave Reg his chance. He got hold of Bert's foot and pulled him off balance. As he fell, he knocked against Rodney who went spinning backwards. In two seconds Reg had a merciless toe and ankle on.

Bert's cry of pain was drowned by a woman's scream, so blood-chilling that, for a moment, there was silence except for the baby's crying. Alice had mounted the step behind the font to be near her baby. She was pointing downwards. She was pointing at Rodney. He had fallen, his head against the pointed angle of the stone step. Blood was oozing from under it. His eyes were wide open. He was still clutching the Hieronymus Bosch. Mr Jobson moved quickly to him and raised him up. His head lolled back unnaturally. He was dead.

Mr Jobson stood up, holding him in his arms. He looked towards Alice and slowly shook his head. She was staring at him incredulously. 'Oh God,' she said, 'Oh my God.' She pushed past the nurse and the vicar and took him from Mr Jobson, holding him like a baby and rocking him to and fro. The blood dripped from the gash in his head on to the white jabot blouse and the tennis knickers and her pink dress. One of his buckled shoes had fallen off.

The nurse handed the baby to the vicar and said, 'Give him to me, dear. It's no good. You must give him to me.'

But Alice clung to him. 'No. It isn't true. I won't let it be true. Oh God, don't let it be true.'

Miles stumbled towards the door. Mr Jobson tried to stop him. 'I think you ought to stay, old man. The police . . .'

'George knows my address.'

Then he ran. He was at the top of Primrose Hill before he realised what direction he had taken. He plunged down the other side, tripped and fell. He rolled down several yards and, for a brief moment, lay panting and winded. Then he picked himself up and ran on past the zoo. There wasn't much traffic about. A lion was roaring. He didn't hear it. He heard Alice's voice. 'Oh God, don't let it be true. Don't let it be true.'

The rhythm of it had been regulating his stride. It got slower and slower as his exhaustion increased until he could only walk. Somewhere near Clarence Gate in the Regent's Park circle he had to stop. He leaned against the railings. He started to retch again. This time he really was sick.

He was conscious two little boys were watching him, fascinated. He couldn't look at them. He started to cry. He couldn't remember how he got to Frame Street and his room.

He must have fallen asleep, because the next thing he knew it was dark and he was holding the miniature teddy bear. His brain was clear again. The police would be coming. There would be some sort of charge against Bert for assault. There would be an inquest. There would be awkward questions.

That didn't matter any more. Nothing mattered any more. He was quite innocent. That didn't matter either. Because, with Rodney, something else had died too. Something in him.

Two knocks. That meant him. He walked slowly and calmly to open the front door.